The Good Thief

Also by Hannah Tinti and available from Headline Review

Animal Crackers

The Good Thief
Hannah Tinti

headline
review

First published in Great Britain in 2008 by
HEADLINE REVIEW
An imprint of HEADLINE PUBLISHING GROUP

1

Cataloguing in Publication Data is available from the British Library

Hardback ISBN 978 0 7553 0746 3
Trade paperback ISBN 978 0 7553 2949 6

Typeset in Bembo Light by Avon DataSet Ltd,
Bidford-on-Avon, Warwickshire

Printed and bound in the UK by
CPI Mackays, Chatham ME5 8TD

Headline's policy is to use papers that are natural, renewable and recyclable
products and made from wood grown in sustainable forests. The logging and
manufacturing processes are expected to conform to the environmental
regulations of the country of origin.

HEADLINE PUBLISHING GROUP
An Hachette Livre UK Company
338 Euston Road
London NW1 3BH

www.headline.co.uk
www.hachettelivre.co.uk

For my sisters, Hester and Honorah

If a man can write a better book, preach a better sermon, or make a better mousetrap than his neighbor, though he build his house in the woods, the world will make a beaten path to his door.

Ralph Waldo Emerson

ACKNOWLEDGEMENTS

Writing a novel takes all kinds of support. My agent, Nicole Aragi, has proven her stripes, again and again, as the hands-down best agent in publishing. Her co-agents, Arabella Stein, Kate Walker, Paul Marsh, Camilla Ferrier and Caroline Hardman opened the doors to new countries. My editors, Susan Kamil, Charlotte Mendelson and Geraldine Cooke inspired me with their enthusiasm and gave edits that helped transform this novel from rough pages into a completely imagined world. My readers, Helen Ellis and Ann Napolitano, tirelessly went through early drafts, carried me when things were most difficult, and helped me figure out the structure I needed to make my story succeed. Alice Shepherd, Emily Furniss, Becky Fincham, Noah Eaker, Theresa Zoro, Susan Corcoran, Elizabeth Hulsebosch, as well as Lily Oei and Jim Hanks took care of all the details and brought *The Good Thief* properly into the world. Blue Mountain Center and UCross offered me beautiful spaces and days of quiet to get the hard work done. Maribeth Batcha, Marie-Helene Bertino and the staff of *One Story* picked up the slack whenever I needed to pull another all-nighter. The one hundred (and counting) authors I have had the privilege to edit for *One Story* taught me how to be a better writer. Dani Shapiro offered sage advice, and then, along with Michael Maren, Antonio and Carla Sersale, brought me to Italy. My friends Yuka & Kareem Lawrence, Karin Schulze, Cynthia Medalie and Francesco Vitelli fed me, bought me drinks, and listened. My dog Canada took me for long walks that refreshed my senses. But I owe the biggest debt to my family. My sisters, Hester Tinti-Kane and Honorah Tinti, kept me laughing even when I wanted to cry; my father, William Tinti, gave me the courage to continue on; and my mother, Hester Tinti, lifted me with her faith and love. She also came up with the title for this book. Thanks, Mom.

PART 1

CHAPTER ONE

THE MAN ARRIVED after morning prayers. Word spread quickly that someone had come, and the boys of Saint Anthony's Orphanage elbowed each other and strained to catch a glimpse as he unhitched his horse and led it to the trough for drinking. The man's face was hard to make out, his hat pulled so far down that the brim nearly touched his nose. He tied the reins to a post and then stood there, patting the horse's neck as it drank. The man waited, and the boys watched, and when the mare finally lifted her head, they saw the man lean forward, stroke the animal's nose, and kiss her. Then he wiped his lips with the back of his hand, removed his hat, and made his way across the yard to the monastery.

Men often came for children. Sometimes it was for cheap labor, sometimes for a sense of doing good. The brothers of Saint Anthony's would stand the orphans in a line, and the men would walk back and forth, inspecting. It was easy to tell what they were looking for by where their eyes went. Usually it was to boys almost fourteen, the taller ones, the loudest, the strongest. Then their eyes went down to the barely crawling, the stumbling two year olds – still untainted and fresh. This left the in-betweens – those who had lost their baby fat and curls but were not yet old enough to be helpful. These children were usually ill-tempered, and had little to offer but empty stomachs and a bad case of lice. Ren was one of them.

He had no memory of a beginning – of a mother or father, sister or brother. His life was simply there, at Saint Anthony's, and what he remembered began in the middle of things – the smell of boiled sheets and lye; the taste of watery oatmeal; the feel of dropping a brick onto a piece of stone, watching the red pieces split off, then using those broken shards to write on the wall of the monastery, and being slapped for this, and being forced to wash the dust away with a cold, wet rag.

Ren's name had been sewn into the collar of his nightshirt: three letters embroidered in dark blue thread. The cloth was made of good linen, and he had worn it until he was nearly two. After that it was taken away and given to a smaller child to wear. Ren learned to keep an eye on Edward, then James, then Nicholas – and corner them in the yard. He would pin the squirming child to the ground and examine the fading letters closely, wondering what kind of hand had worked them. The R and E were sewn boldly in a cross-stitch, but the N was thinner, slanting to the right, as if the person working the thread had rushed to complete the job. When the shirt wore thin, it was cut into bandages. Brother Joseph gave Ren the piece of collar with the letters, and the boy kept it underneath his pillow at night.

Ren watched now as the visitor waited on the steps of the priory. The man passed his hat back and forth in his hands, leaving damp marks along the felt. The door opened and he stepped inside. A few minutes later Brother Joseph came to gather the children, and said, 'Get to the statue.'

The statue of Saint Anthony sat in the center of the yard. It was carved from marble, dressed in the robes of the Franciscan friars. The dome of Saint Anthony's head was bald, with a halo circling his brow. In one hand he held a lily and in the other a small child wearing a crown. The child was holding out one palm in supplication and using the other to touch the saint's cheek. There were times, when the sun receded in the afternoon and shadows played across the stone, that the touch looked more like a slap. This child was Jesus Christ, and the pairing was proof of Saint Anthony's ability to carry messages to God. When a loaf of bread went missing from the kitchen, or Father John couldn't find the keys to the chapel, the children were sent to the statue. *Saint Anthony, Saint Anthony, come bring what I've lost back to me.*

Catholics were rare in this part of New England. A local Irishman who'd made a fortune pressing cheap grapes into strong port had left his vineyard to the church in a desperate bid for heaven before he died. The brothers of Saint Anthony were sent to claim the land and build the monastery. They found themselves surrounded by Protestants, who, in the first month of their arrival, burned down the barn, fouled the well, and caught two brothers after dark on the road and sent them home tarred and feathered.

After praying for guidance, the brothers turned to the Irishman's wine press, which was still intact and on the grounds. Plants were sent from Italy, and after some trial and error the brothers matched the right vine with their stony New England soil. Before long Saint Anthony's became well-known for their particular vintage, which they aged in old wooden casks and used for their morning and evening masses. The unconsecrated wine was sold to the local taverns and also to individual land owners, who sent their servants to collect the bottles in the night so that their neighbors would not see them doing business with Catholics.

Soon after this the first child was left. Brother Joseph heard cries one morning before sunrise and opened the door to find a baby wrapped in a soiled dress. The second child was left in a bucket near the well. The third in a basket by the outhouse. Girls were collected every few months by the Sisters of Charity, who worked in a hospital some distance away. What happened to them, no one knew, but the boys were left at Saint Anthony's, and before long the monastery had turned into a de facto orphanage for the bastard children of the local townspeople, who still occasionally tried to burn the place to the ground.

To control these attempts at arson, the brothers built a high brick wall around the property, which sloped and towered like a fortress along the road. At the bottom of the wooden gate that served as the entrance they cut a small swinging door, and it was through this tiny opening that the babies were pushed. Ren was told that he, too, had been pushed through this gate and found the following morning, covered in mud in the prior's garden. It had rained the night before, and although Ren had no memory of the storm, he often wondered why he had been left in bad weather. It always led to the same conclusion: that whoever had brought him there could not wait to be rid of him.

The gate was hinged to open one way – in. When Ren pushed at the tiny door with his finger, he could feel the strength of the wooden frame behind it. There was no handle on the children's side, no groove to lift from underneath. The wood was heavy, thick, and old – a fine piece of oak planed years before from the woods beyond the orphanage. Ren liked to imagine he felt a pressure in return, a mother reaching back through, changing her mind, groping wildly, a thin white arm.

Underneath Saint Anthony's statue the younger boys fidgeted and pushed, the older ones cleared their throats nervously. Brother Joseph walked down the line and straightened their clothes, or spit on his hand and scrubbed their faces, bumping his large stomach into the children who had fallen out of place. He pushed it now toward a six-year-old who had suddenly sprung a bloody nose from the excitement.

'Hide it quick,' he said, shielding the boy with his body. Across the yard Father John was solemnly approaching, and behind him was the man who had kissed the horse.

He was a farmer. Perhaps forty years old. His shoulders were strong, his fingers thick with calluses, his skin the color of rawhide from the sun. There was a rash of brown spots across his forehead and the backs of his hands. His face was not unkind, and his coat was clean, his shirt pressed white, his collar tight against his neck. A woman had dressed him. So there would be a wife. A mother.

The man began to make his way down the line. He paused before two blond boys, Brom and Ichy. They were also in-betweens, twins left five winters after Ren. Brom's neck was thicker, by about two inches, and Ichy's feet were longer, by about two inches, but beyond those distinguishing characteristics it was hard to tell the boys apart when they were standing still. It was only when they were out in the fields working, or throwing stones at a pine tree, or washing their faces in the morning that the differences became clear. Brom would splash a handful of water over his head and be done with it. Ichy would fold a handkerchief into fourths, dab it into the basin, then set to work carefully and slowly behind his ears.

It was said that no one would adopt Brom and Ichy because they were twins. One was sure to be unlucky. Second-borns were usually considered changelings and drowned right after birth. But no one knew who came first, Brom or Ichy, so there was no way to tell where the bad luck was coming from. What the brothers needed to do was separate, make themselves look as different as possible. Ren kept this information to himself. They were his only friends, and he did not want to lose them.

Standing together now the twins grinned at the farmer, and then, suddenly, Brom threw his arms around his brother and attempted to lift him off the ground. He had done this once before, as a show of strength in front of two elderly gentlemen, and it had ended badly. Ren watched from the other end of the line as Ichy, taken by surprise, began to recite his multiplication tables, all the while struggling violently against his brother, to the point that one of his boots flew into the air and sailed past the farmer's ear.

Father John kept a small switch up the sleeve of his robe, and he put it to work now on the twins, while Brother Joseph fetched Ichy's boot and the farmer continued down the line. Ren put his arms behind his back and stood at attention. He held his breath as the man stopped in front of him.

'How old are you?'

Ren opened his mouth to answer, but the man spoke for him.

'You look about twelve.'

Ren wanted to say that he could be any age, that he could make himself into anything the man wanted, but instead he followed what he had been taught by the brothers, and said nothing.

'I want a boy,' said the farmer. 'Old enough to help me work and young enough for my wife to feel she has a child. Someone who's honest and willing to learn. Someone who can be a son to us.' He leaned forward and lowered his voice so that only Ren could hear him. 'Do you think you could do that?'

Father John came up behind them. 'You don't want that one.'

The farmer stepped back. He looked confused, then angry at being interrupted. 'Why not?'

Father John pointed to Ren's arm. 'Show him.'

Now the other children leaned forward. The priest and the farmer stood waiting. Ren did not move, as if somehow he could wait this moment out until it transformed into something else. He stared past the farmer at a maple tree just beyond the stone wall, its fall leaves beginning to turn. Soon those leaves would be a different color, and then the wind would come, and the tree would look like something else completely. Father John's hand disappeared into the sleeve of his robe, and then the switch came down, leaving a thin red line that smarted enough to make the boy give up his secret.

He was missing a hand. Ren's left arm simply ended, a piece of skin pulled neatly over the bone and sewn crookedly in the shape of a V – the scar tissue raised but healed. The skin was white in places, the stitching like the legs of a centipede, fanned out, frozen and fossilized.

Somewhere between his entry into the world and his delivery through the door of Saint Anthony's, Ren had lost it. He wondered where the hand was now. He closed his eyes and saw it clearly, palm open, the fingers slightly curled. He imagined it behind a dustbin, inside a wooden box, hidden in the grasses of a field. He did not consider size. He did not think that it would no longer fit him. Ren simply looked at his right hand and thought about its match waiting patiently somewhere in the world for him to retrieve it.

The farmer tried not to react, but Ren could see the disgust hidden in his face as he turned away and moved down the line. When he chose a boy from the other end, named William, with red hair and a bad habit of chewing his fingers, the man acted as though it was the only decision he'd made.

Ren watched as the farmer lifted his new son into the wagon. The man patted William on the head, then turned and counted out some money and handed it to Father John, who quickly slipped it into the sleeve of his robe. The farmer climbed up onto the driver's seat and made ready to leave, but at the last moment lowered the reins and glanced back at the statue of Saint Anthony.

'What happens to the ones no one takes?'

'They are conscripted,' said Father John, 'into the army.'

'Not an easy life.'

'It's the will of God,' said Father John. 'We do not question His ways.'

The farmer looked down at the priest, then at his new son, nervously biting the skin on his thumb. He released the brake on the wagon. 'I do,' he said, and then called to his horse and started off down the road.

CHAPTER TWO

IN THE BARN Brother Joseph poured himself a mug of wine and settled into his seat. Underneath his robe was a foot warmer – a small tin box full of coals from the kitchen fireplace. He put one sandal on it and then the other as he supervised the children working. Occasionally he would fall asleep and his robe would catch on fire. Somehow he always woke in time to douse the flames with his sampling cup.

Around him the boys de-stemmed, pressed and strained the grapes. It was fall, and the harvest was nearly over. Brother Joseph supervised as they added the sugar and yeast to the collected juice, covered the pails with cheesecloth and set them aside. Later they would skim off the sediment, pour the liquid into the wooden casks, add a bit of finished wine and leave the batch to ferment. The final step was to siphon the wine into bottles and cork them. Three months later it would be ready to drink.

Brother Joseph did not excuse Ren from any of this work, but he did find ways to help him. He tied a basket to Ren's waist when the boy was picking in the fields; he showed Ren how to steady the skimmer using the crook of his arm; he placed the funnel between Ren's fingers and the empty stub of the boy's wrist. Sometimes it took Ren twice as long as the other boys to accomplish the tasks, but Brother Joseph offered small words to encourage him, and this usually gave Ren the heart to finish.

Now the monk peered into his mug and inspected the dark residue collecting at the bottom. Then he looked at the children, going about in the silent way they always did after one of their group had been chosen, their faces somber and resentful. Brother Joseph set his cup on the floor and pushed the foot warmer aside. 'I think we should all say a prayer for William,' he said.

'He doesn't need one,' said Ichy.

'We all need prayers,' said Brother Joseph. 'Especially when something good happens to us.' He sighed. 'Bad luck follows anything that's good. And bad things always happen in threes.'

The boys contemplated this as they continued with their work. And more than a few were secretly glad.

'What kind of bad luck do you think William will get?' Ichy asked.

'That's hard to say,' said Brother Joseph. 'It could be anything.'

'I'll bet they get robbed on the way home,' said Ichy.

'And when they get there,' said Brom, 'their house is on fire.'

The other boys joined in, each with his own vision of bad luck for William and his new father. They were caught in swarms of bees and chased by packs of wolves. They were given the gout, the chickenpox, the plague.

'That's enough!' said Brother Joseph. 'It's only supposed to happen three times.' But the boys kept at it, imagining worse things, giddy with their own meanness.

Ren tried to think of his own bad fate for William, but he

could not get past the image of the farmer lifting the boy into the cart. He wondered if William would write, once he was settled. Some of the boys who were adopted sent letters, detailing their new lives, the warm beds and clean clothes and special meals their mothers prepared for them. These letters were cherished and passed from boy to boy until the pages were torn and the ink had faded.

Ren pictured the supper waiting for William at home. The farmer's wife would have taken out the good plates, if they had good plates. Yes, Ren decided, they would have good plates. Plates of white porcelain. And there would be a small bowl of wildflowers, picked from behind the kitchen door, pink and blue with tiny yellow buttercups. There would be bread, still warm, sliced and covered with a napkin in a basket. There would be stew of some kind, hot and full of meat that had been rubbed with herbs, tender and soft to chew. And a mountain of potatoes. And corn scraped from the cob. And glasses of fresh milk. And cooling on a windowsill, just behind the farmer's wife, who was standing in the door frame now looking for her husband's wagon, would be a blackberry pie. Just for the three of them.

She would not have minded his hand. She would not have minded at all.

Ren sat on the floor of the distillery and sorted grapes, pulling leaves and bits of vine from the flesh, tossing the damaged and unripe fruit to the side. There were always spiders in the baskets from the fields, and clouds of gnats, and sometimes thin black snakes. Ren's fingers were stained with red. It would be days before the color faded from his skin.

When he was through, he dumped the grapes over the top

of the wine press, an enormous contraption that held court in the center of the barn. The children huddled by the chutes at the bottom, holding buckets, collecting the juice, while others pushed the crank, which was set in the middle of the press like a windmill on its side. It was heavy work. The oldest boys were assigned to the crank, one on each arm, walking in circles. In another year, Ren would be one of them.

Only a few boys had grown old enough and been passed over enough at Saint Anthony's to be sent into the army. One was named Frederick, a stout child who had trouble breathing and would often faint, crumpling to the floor with barely a sound. The soldiers came in the night and took him. From the window of the small boys' room, Ren had seen the men drag Frederick across the yard and through the wooden gate, his body limp, his feet bouncing off the cobblestones. He was not heard from again.

Another was named Sebastian, a boy remarkably pale and thin. Six months after he'd left with the soldiers he appeared at the gate of the orphanage, and he was so changed that the children did not recognize him. His face was haggard, and both eyes had been blackened. His lip was split in two and his leg appeared to be broken. Sebastian pushed open the little wooden door in the gate, the same one he had been passed through as a child, and begged the brothers to take him back. Father John approached, murmured a prayer, and threw the extra bolt. The boy stayed out there for three days, crying first, then pleading, then shouting, then praying, then cursing, until he fell silent, and a wagon came, driven by three soldiers, and they put Sebastian in the back of it and carried him away.

It was rumored that Father John accepted payment from the soldiers, and also signed a contract of some kind, giving over ownership of the boys. A day did not go by that Ren did not think of this, and whenever he did, the scar on his arm began to itch. Every time he was passed over in the line of children, every time he watched another boy taken, and every year he grew older, it itched more.

To make up for this, Ren stole things. It began with small items of food. He'd stand in front of the cook after cleaning out the fireplace, and the man would glance at the boy's scar, and then turn and study a pile of cabbages while shouting for someone to wash the beans, and it was just enough time for Ren to slip one of the pieces of bread left out on the counter into his pocket.

He never took anything that couldn't be easily hidden away. He stole socks and shoelaces, combs and prayer cards, buttons, keys, and crucifixes. Whatever crossed his path. Sometimes he would keep the items, sometimes he would return them, sometimes he would toss them down the well. In this way Ren was responsible for most of the lost things being prayed for at the statue of Saint Anthony.

The items he kept were stashed inside a small crack about a foot from the edge of the well. Leaning over the stone wall, Ren could fit his hand inside the hiding place, his breath echoing back to him from the water far below. There was a broken piece of blue and white pottery, a snake skin he'd found in the woods, a set of rosary beads he'd stolen from Father John, made from real roses, and, most important of all, his rocks.

Every boy at Saint Anthony's collected rocks. They hoarded stones as if they were precious objects, as if the accumulation of feldspar and shale would pave their way to a new life. If they dug in the right places, they found rarer things – pieces of quartz, or mica, or arrowheads. These stones were kept and traded and loved, and sometimes, when the children were adopted, they were left behind.

That afternoon, when Brother Joseph had fallen asleep, William's rocks were spread out across the floor of the barn, and the boys began to argue over how to divide them. There were perhaps thirty or forty pieces. Rocks that gleamed like metal, or had brown and black stripes, or reds and oranges the color of the sunset. But the best of the collection was a wishing stone, a soft gray rock with an unbroken circling band of white. Good for one wish to come true.

Ren had seen only one before – it had belonged to Sebastian. He'd shown it to Ren once, but he wouldn't let anyone hold it. He was afraid of losing the wish. He was saving it, he said, for a time when he was in trouble, and he'd taken it with him when he left for the army. Later, outside the brick wall that surrounded the orphanage, his lips cracked from the sun, Sebastian told Ren through the swinging door in the gate that someone had stolen the wishing stone while he slept. 'I shouldn't have held on to it,' he wept. 'I should have used it as soon as it came into my hands.'

The rafters of the barn caught the boys' voices and sent them back, louder and more forceful as they bargained over William's collection. A few had already noticed the wishing stone. Once the rocks were divided, Ren was sure to lose his chance. He edged closer to where it lay on the ground, rolling up his sleeve as he went. Then he pretended that someone had shoved him from behind, and threw his body into the center of the group, scrambling on the floor, the stub of his left arm covering his right. The group elbowed him to the side.

'Shove off.'

'Leper.'

'Get out of the way.'

Ren moved to the back of the room as the boys continued to argue, the stone safe in his fingers. He opened his palm and glanced down. The wishing stone was the color of rain. The edges smooth. He felt the indentation where the ring of white began and thought of all the things he was going to ask for.

Brom and Ichy whispered to each other, then left the group and followed Ren. They knew he had taken something. They were his friends but they wanted their share.

'What's that in your hand?'

'Nothing.'

'Give it here.'

The rest of the children began to notice. First Edward, with his runny nose, then Luke and Marcus. Ren knew he had only a moment before they would all be upon him. He punched Brom, the weight of his friend's chin hard against his knuckles. Then he ducked under Ichy's arm and burst out of the barn, running as fast as he could to the well, hoping he could reach it in time to hide the stone, praying all the while that the boys wouldn't come after him. But they did – they were close behind, Brom in the lead and nearly grabbing Ren's shoulder, and then he did, and they both fell to the ground.

Ichy sat on Ren's chest and Brom twisted his arm until his fingers opened. Ren tried to kick them off, biting and scratching, but he knew in his heart that he was going to lose, and he felt the stone slip out of his hand. The boys left him panting in the dirt and clustered around what they had taken.

'I want to wish for an arrowhead,' said Ichy.

'That's not good enough,' said Brom.

'For candy then.'

'For Father John to break his neck.'

'For toys!'

'To get picked from the line.'

'For a hundred wishes instead of one.'

Ren listened to his friends. He had never hated anyone more. He thrust himself forward and snatched the stone back. If he couldn't use the wish, then no one would. The twins grabbed hold of his shirt and he pulled desperately away, the hate inside giving him strength, more than he'd ever had before, and he leaned over and threw the rock down into the well. There was no sound as it descended, just the echo of Ren's own breathing in the dark, and then the smallest splash that told him it had hit water.

CHAPTER THREE

FATHER JOHN'S STUDY was on the second floor of the monastery. From this small room came dictations and benedictions, portion sizes and bedtime procedures, prayer schedules, catalogs of sins, a rotation of privy duty, and the sounds of these rules and regulations being enforced. Ren had been caned there three times for hoarding food, six times for leaving his bed at night, fifteen times for being on the roof without permission, and twenty-seven times for cursing. He knew the room well and was sure that the priest whipped him less harshly – he'd seen welts inches deep on others.

Father John chose a volume from a shelf on the wall: *The Lives of the Saints*. He walked over to his desk and began to read while Ren stood in the corner, watching and waiting. Thirty minutes passed. Father John sometimes kept the children for hours this way. The waiting was always worse than the punishment.

In his own way Ren was a believer. It came as easily as breathing. There was a stream in the woods behind the orphanage. Ren liked to put his hand in and feel the water rush through his fingers. He watched leaves and twigs floating downstream and felt the tug of the current on his wrist. It was the same pull that came sometimes when he prayed – the sense of being carried on to a deeper place. But he never had the courage to follow it through. As soon as he felt the urge to let go, he'd take his hand out of the water.

The priest turned a page in his book. He ran his finger along the center of the spine and began to read aloud: '"In Padua a young man named Leonardo kicked his mother in a fit of anger. He was then so remorseful that he confessed to Saint Anthony. The saint told the young man that he needed to remove the part of himself that had committed the sin. Leonardo went home and cut off his foot. Saint Anthony, upon hearing this, went to visit the injured man. And with one touch he reattached the foot."' Father John closed the book but kept his finger in the page. 'I thought you might be interested in that story.'

Ren knew not to answer, not to say a word. His left eye was swollen, his face smeared with mud where Brom had pressed it into the ground. The twins had pulled his hair until he told them where his collection was hidden, then made off with all that he had saved, slipping back into the barn before Brother Joseph had stirred. Father John had heard the fight from his study and discovered Ren alone by the well, bruised and bloody and weeping at what he had lost.

'Sin does not only reside in the flesh.' Father John stood and walked across the room. 'It is an indelible part of your soul. Each transgression a black mark that cannot be removed, except by holy confession and the sacred fire of God's judgment.' He closed the book and slid it back into its place on the shelf. 'The saints are examples for the rest of us. You should think of them the next time you are tempted.' The priest pulled the switch from his sleeve and inspected it, pulling a small hair from the bark. 'It is what I always do.' He pointed to the whipping stool, and the boy walked over and lowered his trousers.

The whipping stool had held Ren's weight and the weight of many other boys over the years. Ren remembered the first time he had taken his place across it, after he was caught in a lie by Brother Peter. Now there were even more scratches in the wood, places where the joints were failing. It seemed close to falling apart.

'Who hit you?'

The first strike was always a shock. The boy tried not to move as it seared into his skin. Sweat gathered on his lower back. Between his legs.

'Who hit you?'

Ren tried to think of other things. He could feel the edges of the cuts begin to separate, the sting working its way across his body. Saliva dripped from his mouth and pooled on the floor.

'Food will be rationed until you reveal their names. The shoes and blankets for the winter returned.'

Ren gripped the stool. He waited for it to break. Every year there was talk of new shoes and blankets. And every year they never arrived.

The small boys' room was a long, narrow attic space lined with cots and bits of bedding, with slanted walls and a ceiling that ran like a stripe down the length of it. There were two latched windows, one by the door and one at the far dark end and it was by this particular window that Ren was trying to sleep, the backs of his legs still burning.

The room smelled like boiled fish. It was the same oily smell that covered the rest of the orphanage. This oil came from the bodies of the children and seeped into the tables and chairs, into the stone walls of the building. The boys were washed twice a month, along with their linens, by a group of charitable grandmothers. On those days the brothers would prop open the doors and windows, trying to air the place, but it did little good. By the end of the first night the smell would return − a combination of bedwets, worry, and sickness.

Brom and Ichy were in the next bed, as they had been ever since they were first brought to Saint Anthony's. Ren still remembered the night when Brother Joseph had shuffled into the room, the twins bundled in his arms. The little boys were soaking wet, their bodies shaking. Ren had watched as Brother Joseph set them on the bed and began to unwrap the blankets.

'The mother drowned herself.' Brother Joseph threw the wet clothes onto the floor, muttering into the dark. 'Nothing but bad luck. No one's going to want these two.' He rubbed the boys' arms and legs. 'They need to get warm.' And with that he slipped first one, then the other into Ren's bed, then hurried down the hall to look for something dry to put them in.

The boys squirmed against Ren under the blanket. They were perhaps a year younger, but took up twice the room, and he considered kicking them out onto the floor. Ichy grabbed hold of Ren's nightshirt, as if sensing this, and promptly stuffed the piece of fabric into his mouth. Brom sobbed with rage. Ren thought of their mother, floating in the river. He wondered what color her hair was. He decided that it was blond. He decided the color of her eyes (blue) and her skin (pale) and the print of her dress (pink), until he could see her standing before him, dripping with water. Her shoes were caked with sludge, her hair tangled with branches. She crossed her arms, as if she were chilled, and it took a few moments before Ren understood that she was waiting for him to do something.

'What do you want?' he asked. But she would not answer. So he began to whistle, just to hear the sound of something in the room. Beside him, the twins stopped their crying and went still. They went so still that Ren worried they might be dead. He sat up and watched their sleeping faces until he was sure that they were breathing. When he turned around their mother had disappeared.

Now Ren shifted his stinging legs and tried to ignore the pain. Father John was right-handed, and because of this he favored the left when leaving his marks. Ren turned to one side and then the other. The skin around his eye throbbed and his arm was sore where Brom had twisted it. He picked at a scab starting to form on his knee and sucked his breath between his teeth as it came loose.

'Does it hurt?' Ichy whispered from the next bed.

Ren did not want to seem a coward. 'No.'

'You shouldn't have punched me,' said Brom.

Ren turned and looked out the window. He was not ready to be friends again.

'Do you think William's home by now?' Ichy asked.

'He must be,' said Brom.

'Unless he was captured by pirates,' said Ichy.

The twins were silent then, and eventually their breathing became shallow. Ren rested on his side and thought about Saint Anthony reattaching Leonardo's foot. He wondered if the skin was left scarred, or if the saint had been able to make the ankle completely smooth again. He slid his hand underneath the covers and took out *The Lives of the Saints*.

After Father John had finished the beating and turned to put the switch back into his sleeve, the boy had reached out and lifted the volume from the bookcase. He'd hidden it underneath his shirt, curling around the book on the whipping stool until he was dismissed. He'd kept the leather binding next to his skin and now it was warm, as if it were a living thing.

Ren propped the volume with his elbow so that he could get enough light from the moon to read. He turned to Saint Anthony's feast day, June thirteenth, and learned that Leonardo's foot was not his only miracle. Anthony also lived in a walnut tree and magically transported himself from country to country. He preached sermons to fishes, sent angels after thieves, and made mules reject hay for consecrated hosts. He saved fishermen from storms, converted thousands of heretics, guided nuns through Morocco and, perhaps most impressively, brought a boy back from the dead.

The boy had been found buried in the garden of Saint Anthony's father. The saint's father was arrested and charged with murder. But then Saint Anthony came, and touched the dead boy, and brought him back to life. The child opened his eyes and named the real killer. The book didn't say what happened next, and Ren was left wondering if the boy had gone back to his grave. It didn't seem fair. *If you had to die*, Ren thought, *you should only have to die once.*

There was weeping at the other end of the small boys' room. Ren listened for a few moments, and then slid his book carefully underneath the blanket. The other boys began to stir; he could hear one or two mumbling, half-asleep. Brom sat up and shouted for quiet. Another boy cursed. Then someone got out from under their covers. Ren could hear the footsteps crossing the floor. There was a moment when all the children held their breath, and then a loud, hard smack. The crying stopped, and the footsteps returned to bed.

They were all awake now, staring up into the darkness of the rafters, listening. The children took turns crying at night. It was only a matter of time before another boy began. And when those small sounds started, Ren knew that it would be hours before he could read again.

He shut the book and closed his eyes. He imagined the wishing stone resting at the bottom of the well. He had held it, even if it was for only a moment. Ren pulled his hand into a fist, trying to remember the shape. He could feel the blood pulsing there, underneath the skin, and for a moment the heat of the stone was against his fingertips again, all of his possible wishes spread out before him. Ren moved his hand into the moonlight and slowly opened it, half-expecting the stone to reappear. But there was no magic in the small boys' room that night. Only Ren's open palm, empty and cooling in the dark. A few rows over, another boy began to cry, and Ren pressed his face into his pillow. He was glad he'd thrown the stone away. Now no one would ever be able to wish on it again.

CHAPTER FOUR

BROTHER PETER'S CLASSES took place each day in the front room of the monastery. What these classes were meant to teach the boys varied on the occasion and, it seemed, the weather. On rainy days he pulled out maps and talked about where things were in the world. When the sun was out, he recited poetry. In the snow he removed an abacus from his desk and discussed numbers. And when the wind was strong he did nothing at all, but simply stared out the windows at the trees blowing back and forth.

It had been decided that the brothers must give the children some knowledge; at the very least enough language to read the Bible, and enough arithmetic so that the Protestants could not cheat them. Why this task of education was given to Brother Peter, the boys did not know, for more often than not he would simply rest his forehead on the table before him and ignore the children completely. Much of what the boys had learned had been transferred from child to child like a disease, and mostly concerned bits of New England history: minutemen and the North Bridge, Giles Corey and Crispus Attucks.

Today the boys practiced writing and rewriting psalms on

tiny bits of slate, which they passed around and shared. The psalm was 118, verse 8: 'It is better to take refuge in the Lord than to trust in man.' Brother Peter had just put his head on the table when the boys began to whisper and point out the window. Ren looked up from the words spelled out before him. There was a stranger crossing the yard.

The man wore glasses. He had straw-colored hair tied with a ribbon that made him look like a student. He had no hat, but he was wearing boots and a long dark coat with a turned-up collar, like a coachman's. Brother Joseph was leading the man toward the priory, and the children watched as the stranger paused in his step for a moment and leaned to one side, as if his leg pained him. He had a slight build, and before he slipped into the building, Ren could see that his hands were pale and thin. He was no farmer.

Fifteen minutes later Brother Joseph burst into the classroom, out of breath, his robe stained down the front with wine. He scanned the room of boys and said the words they were all waiting for: 'Get to the statue.'

Ren scrambled out of the room and dashed toward Saint Anthony, feeling somehow that his luck was running out ahead of him. He took his place in line along with the other boys. Brother Joseph passed in front, tucking in shirts and fixing collars, while across the yard the door to the priory opened.

Father John approached the children with the same uncomfortable posture he took before beating them. In one hand he held some papers. The other was tucked into his sleeve, which meant he was carrying his switch. The stranger followed at a short distance, his long coat trailing in the dirt.

He was a young man, his face rugged and handsome, his ears

27

a bit too large for his head. When he came to the statue of Saint Anthony, he folded his arms and leaned against it. He looked at the boys over the top of his glasses. His eyes were blue, summer-sky blue, the bluest eyes that Ren had ever seen.

'This is Mister Nab,' said Father John. He glanced at the paper in his hand, then turned to stare at the stranger, who was now standing on one foot and twirling his ankle in the air.

'Old war wound,' the man said. 'When the weather turns cold, it aches a bit.' He put his foot back on the ground, stomped it once, then once again, and opened his mouth into a broad, bright, beaming smile. It was winning, and he turned it with force, first on the priest, then on the line of boys.

Father John collected himself and turned back to the paper. 'Mister Nab is looking for his brother, who was sent this way as an infant. He says that he is approximately eleven years of age – is that correct?'

'I believe so. Although it's been so long now it's hard to remember.'

'Well,' said Father John, pausing for a moment. Ren could see that he was losing his patience. 'Do any of these boys look familiar?'

Benjamin Nab stepped forward and gave each of the children a thorough going-over. He seemed to be looking for something, but it was hard to say what it was, for with each boy he searched in a different place. He took hold of their chins and tilted their faces into the light. He felt their necks, measured the length of their brows with his finger, and twice lifted a patch of brown hair to his nose.

'Too short,' he said to one boy.

'Too tall,' he said to another.

'Show me your tongue.' Marcus stretched it out into the sunlight, and the man considered it, then shook his head again.

Ren could sense the twins fidgeting next to him. Brom's hands were clenched into fists. Ichy lined up his feet perfectly. But Benjamin Nab did not even take the time to examine them. He moved further around, as if he knew their bad luck and was afraid of catching it. Then he came to Ren.

Benjamin Nab poked the boy once in the shoulder. It was a hard poke, as if he'd caught Ren sleeping.

'You look like a little man.'

It was said like a compliment, but Ren was worried it might mean something else. He knew that he was smaller than the other boys. Benjamin Nab stepped forward, his blue eyes passing over every inch of Ren's face, neck, and shoulders. Ren waited, his heart hammering in his chest. He stood as straight as a board. He tried to flex as the man reached down and squeezed his arm. Then there was a sudden stillness, and Ren knew that Benjamin Nab had noticed the missing hand.

The man closed his eyes, as if he were trying hard to remember something. And then he was on his knees, his arms thrown around the boy, and Ren's face was pressed into the coachman's collar, which smelled of sweat and dirt from the road, and he could hear Benjamin Nab's voice crying out: 'This is him. This is the one.'

Ren barely knew what had happened. One moment he had been a part of the line and the next he was caught up in the stranger's embrace, shouts and exclamations ringing in his ears and kisses being planted on his forehead. The rest of the boys exchanged glances. Ren could feel ripples going out from his place in the line, spreading across the courtyard. When it became clear that he'd been chosen, that he had a family now and would be leaving the orphanage forever, he felt a surge of joy through his body, flushing his cheeks, until, just as suddenly, it turned into an overwhelming dizziness, and he vomited onto the ground.

Benjamin Nab shoved the boy away from him, then pulled a handkerchief from his pocket and used it to wipe at his coat for a few moments, a look of revulsion on his face, before glancing at the priest, and smiling again, and passing the handkerchief to Ren. He gave the boy a tap on the head.

'Didn't mean to get you so excited.'

Father John stood by, watching this unfold, and then did something unusual. He invited Benjamin Nab in for a cup of tea. Through his nausea, Ren felt a tug of fear that Father John was planning on talking the stranger out of taking him. He held the man's handkerchief but was too ashamed to use it, and so wiped his mouth as he usually did, with the back of his sleeve. He prayed that his sickness had not changed things, and when he looked up, God seemed to have answered, for Benjamin Nab had not moved down the line. He was still wearing the same strange smile as he reached over and plucked his handkerchief back.

In his study Father John settled behind the desk and gestured for Benjamin Nab to take the only other chair – the whipping stool. The man drew it to the center of the room, positioned himself, and leaned back, so much that Ren feared it would collapse. The boy took his regular spot in the corner, but Father John gave him a stern look, and he realized he had a new place now, next to Benjamin Nab.

Once the tea was brought, the priest sipped quietly, as though he did not expect any conversation. Father John used this kind of silence to draw confessions from the boys, but it did not intimidate Benjamin Nab. The man seemed perfectly at ease as he slurped the tea that had spilled into his saucer. He smacked his lips, put down the teacup and then told them how Ren had lost his hand.

'It all started when our father took us out West on the wagons. We cleared a field near one of the outposts – Fort Wagaponick – do you know it?' Father John said he did not. Benjamin Nab looked to Ren, and the boy realized he was waiting for his answer before continuing the story. Ren shook his head.

'Well,' said Benjamin Nab. 'You used to know it. But you were too little to remember, I guess. There were trees there that were as big as houses, so wide it took twenty men to circle them with their arms. The birds that lived in those branches were as large as donkeys and would take away dogs and children to feed their young a mile high in the sky. The mountains touched the clouds and created their own kind of weather – snow in the summer and desert heat in the middle of January. That's where you were born, in the valley just below, between the woods and a river full of danger.

'Our father was all dreams. Always trying to get to the edge of nowhere. Well, that was it. Nothing but wildness and things you don't know the names for – strange little scuttlings that moved through the leaves in the woods and big gallumps that went past in the night. I was a lot bigger than you,' he said, nodding at Ren, 'but I was scared to go looking for water.

'We bargained with trappers and local soldiers for labor and raised our first cabin. It was dark. There was no glass for windows, and the logs were smeared with pitch to keep the wind out. We made a fireplace from piled stones, with a pipe to take the smoke that never worked. All the same, we'd sleep around it at night, on mattresses stuffed with corn husks, our eyes burning. You got sick from it. Terrible sick and coughing. Mother was so worried she moved with you to the fort for a week to try and clear your lungs.'

Ren took a deep breath, in and out. He could feel the smoke lingering in the corners. Spots of soot in the back of his throat. He imagined his mother's long walk through the forest, his body tightly bundled in her arms, the sensation of her hurried gait beneath the blanket.

'When spring came, we were able to keep the fire outside. The few seeds we'd planted before the frost began to show themselves, and the river that had frozen over began to break loose and run again, pieces of ice collecting along the waterbank. The days got longer, and with all that light we turned over five acres, axing trees, clearing rocks and roots, chasing out woodchucks and rabbits, foxes and field mice, deer, bears, elks, and weasels.

'Our father was happy. He dreamed of building us a castle, of digging a moat and filling it with alligators. He said there'd be giant beds and rugs on the walls and chandeliers full of candles and thousands of rooms; we could live in one for a day and just leave it behind. There'd be servants, of course, and dozens of cooks ready to make us whatever we wanted. There'd be peasants to tend the fields. There'd be new clothes for the winter. There'd be cows and chickens and pigs and horses and wizards to weave spells so we'd never get old.

'You learned how to walk that summer,' said Benjamin Nab. 'Mother kept you tied so you wouldn't wander off. She was afraid a wolf would get you when her back was turned. But it wasn't a wolf that came. It was an Indian.'

The air in the room went still. Ren had never seen an Indian before, but he could almost feel one now, hidden in the shadows of the bookcase, the native's body strong and marked with paint, his stale breath close enough to smell.

'I'd been off to fetch some water,' said Benjamin Nab. 'Two buckets on my shoulder, and when I got to the cabin I heard this strange sound, sort of like bed moans. So I rested my buckets and stayed in the trees and when I got closer I saw a group of Indians. They were small brown men, and they were wearing women's nightgowns — white with ruffles, like our mother's. Only one had it on properly. The others wore theirs around their shoulders, and one had tied the arms around his waist like an apron. They were standing over something in the vegetable garden and hacking at it with their clubs. It was Father. I could tell when one of them picked up his leg to remove the shoes.

'The moans were coming from Mother. There was blood on her face and she was stretched out on the ground, holding on to your ankles. An Indian had you by the hands, pulling you away, dragging Mother behind in the dirt. They went right past the woodpile, and I saw Mother grope for the ax, and before I knew it she had swung it down over her head and cut your arm in two.' Benjamin Nab looked Ren in the eye. 'I believe she was aiming for the Indian.

'She took down three men before the others reached her. It gave me time to snatch you up and get away. You were screaming when we reached the woods. I had to stuff my shirt in your mouth. I took us into the river and I swam for it. Kept your head up and let the current take me when it could. Cold water's the only reason you didn't die.'

Ren put his arms behind his back and cupped his right hand

around the stump. It was tingling, as if it were touching ice. Father John was leaning forward. The heavy wooden beads he kept on his belt swung with a light clack against the side of the desk, in and out with his breath.

'I gave you to a wagon full of people returning East, cutting their losses. I asked them to put you in a good home. Somewhere civilized, where you could get an education.' Benjamin Nab's face turned serious. 'Then I went after those Indians.

'I learned how to shoot. Learned how to drink and how to gamble. I joined up with Indians – good ones – and spent a few years hunting buffalo and living in tents, all the while searching for the ones who'd done it. I learned how to find water where there wasn't water, learned how to find a trail where there wasn't a trail, learned how to find hiding places when there was no place to hide.'

At this point Benjamin Nab paused and squinted. 'It took me ten years. But I tracked those Indians down, and I found our mother and father.' He pulled a leather pouch from the pocket of his long coat and loosened the strings. He placed two strips of hair on the desk. One square cut of brownish fuzz and the other a jagged scrap of faded yellow curls.

'That's all that was left.'

Benjamin Nab, Father John, and Ren looked down at the scalps. The priest cleared his throat. Ren felt the urge to reach forward and touch the hair. He could see where two blond curls were knotted together.

'Please,' Father John finally said, 'put those away.'

Benjamin Nab tucked the scalps back inside his coat. 'He's my brother. He's mine and no one else's.'

'Well,' said Father John. 'Of course.' And suddenly Ren knew that the priest was going to give him up. He'd spent his life here; he'd learned to speak and read within these walls, but Father John was not asking any more questions. He laid his hand on the boy's head and gave him a blessing. Then he told him to gather his things.

Brother Joseph was waiting outside in the hallway. When he saw Ren's face he let out a puff of air and said, 'Well, that's it then.' He led Ren to the small boys' room, straining heavily up the stairs. He said, 'I thought we had a few more years.' Then he opened the door, walked down the aisle, and stood by while the boy collected what was underneath his pillow. There was not much. The scrap of cloth with blue letters, a pair of socks, and *The Lives of the Saints*.

Brother Joseph picked up the volume and flipped through the pages. 'Where'd you get this?'

Ren looked at the monk's stained and dirty robe, the belly hanging over the cord that served as a belt. He would never see this man again. And yet he could not bring himself to lie. 'I stole it.'

'That's a commandment broken.'

Ren shrugged his shoulders.

The monk closed the book. 'Why did you take it?'

Ren didn't know how to answer. He had reached for the volume because he wanted to hear the rest of Saint Anthony's story. But then he'd read about Saint Veronica curing Tiberius with her veil; Saint Benedict flowing water from a rock; Saint Elizabeth, with her apron full of roses. Possessing the book had made what happened inside the pages somehow belong to him. During the day he looked forward to the sun setting, to the time when everyone else would go to bed and he could read the stories again. He cared for this more than eating. More than sleeping. He finally said, 'I wanted the miracles.'

Brother Joseph glanced from the book to the boy and back again. He ran his finger down the cover. 'We better make your penance quick.'

The boy got on his knees by the side of the bed. Brother Joseph sat on the cot, his weight making the small wooden frame groan, as Ren whispered the prayers. When he finished, the monk handed him *The Lives of the Saints*.

'Shouldn't I return it?'

Brother Joseph made the sign of the cross on the boy's forehead. 'Take it with you,' he said. 'It's not stolen anymore.'

On his way back down the stairs Ren ran his hand along the old wooden banister. *This is the last time I will touch this*, he thought, and just as he did a splinter jammed its way into his palm. Ren went outside and crossed the yard, sucking at his skin, trying to pull the piece of wood out with his teeth, feeling the edge of it with his tongue. In the sunlight he examined the sliver nestled under the surface, a tiny piece of Saint Anthony's determined to come with him.

He turned around and looked at the winery, then the chapel, then the orphanage. It was hard to believe that he was no longer going to work or pray or sleep on these grounds. All he'd ever wanted was to leave, but now as he was about to, he felt uneasy. He walked over to the high brick wall surrounding the buildings and pressed his wet palm against it. The masonry felt as thick and substantial as ever.

'Good-bye,' he said. But it didn't seem like enough. So he kicked the wall, as hard as he could. The impact made the bones in his leg shake. He stood there panting for a moment, then limped away, his toe throbbing inside his boot.

At the well Brom and Ichy were waiting for him.

'Are you really leaving?'

Ren nodded. The twins stuffed their hands into their pockets. Ren knew they were trying to be glad for him. Brom frowned, and Ichy dug his shoe into the dirt. Everything the boys had shared seemed captured in the line Ichy made on the ground between them. The twins had eaten every meal with Ren, played with him at every first snow, watched with him from the window every time the soldiers came and took another boy away. Since their arrival, they had stretched beside him every night of his life and opened their eyes next to him every morning.

The three boys stood together awkwardly in silence, until Ichy reached down and pulled a stone from the mark he'd made at their feet. He cleaned it with the tail of his shirt, then handed it to Ren. The rock was warm from the sun, its surface black and craggy, with bits of red garnet that sparkled. Ren admired the stone for a moment, then closed his fingers around it, feeling the splinter still in his palm.

'Where's he taking you?' Brom asked.

'I don't know,' said Ren. And he was filled with a kind of regret – a nostalgia for everything he was about to lose – the smell of fish, the oatmeal for breakfast, the thin blankets, the cold stone walls that echoed. But he knew what it felt like to be left behind, and for the first time in his life he wasn't the one watching with an aching stomach from the gate as someone else was taken home. He knew then to say what they all said – 'I'll come back to visit' – and, like them, he knew he never would.

CHAPTER FIVE

I T WASN'T UNTIL the latch was closed on the gate that Ren thought to be afraid. Afternoon prayers were about to begin. Father John would be leading the first decade of the rosary, and Ren would not be there. Instead he was outside, following a stranger down the road. The sun and the grass and the trees seemed to know this; even the air felt charged as they walked through it. He wasn't sure what to say, so he tried to match Benjamin Nab's stride.

They'd walked for only half a mile when they reached the end of the blueberry bushes. This was the farthest Ren had ever been from the orphanage. The boys were sent to pick the blueberries in the middle of the summer. It was always a thrill to be outside the brick wall, and Ren connected the feeling with the taste of the berries, the stain of the juice, the thin blue skin so easily damaged. Now it was fall, and the bushes looked completely different, the leaves turned orange and red.

Ren and Benjamin Nab continued along the road. They passed several fields and came over a hill, breathing heavily as they reached the top. Ren could see a far distance, out to the edges of the mountains and down into the valley. The trees covered every inch, the fall foliage in full color, catching the light of the afternoon sun – yellow, red, and orange, but also ocher, vermillion, magenta, and gold – a brilliant, shimmering view.

Benjamin Nab put his hands on his hips and surveyed the land as if it all belonged to him. Then he turned back to the boy. 'Let's have another look at you.'

Ren stood perfectly still as the man walked around him. Benjamin Nab crouched down, then lifted the boy's arm and examined the end of the wrist where the skin was sewn over. Ren watched for the usual signs of discomfort or shock. But Benjamin Nab's face held none of these things. He raised his eyebrows.

'Well,' he said, 'you have another one, don't you?'

There were marks beneath his cheekbones, signs of worried skin. His eyebrows were fair, but the outline of the glasses made up for this, bringing a sturdy look. 'You'll do just fine,' Benjamin said. Then he stood up, and they continued down the road and into the valley. The sun set behind them, and Saint Anthony's went with it.

Benjamin Nab was a fast walker, easily avoiding ruts in the earth and piles of manure with a quick turn of his boot – the war wound that he had complained of at Saint Anthony's seemed to have disappeared. Ren struggled to keep pace. He hoped that Benjamin Nab would tell another story about their parents, but the man remained silent as the trees turned into shadows, then dark silhouettes against the sky.

'Where are we going?' Ren finally asked.

'You'll find out soon enough.'

'I have to use the privy.'

Benjamin Nab stopped. He pulled his hair back and retied it, then gestured to the woods. 'There's your privy.'

Ren stepped tentatively into the underbrush just beyond the road.

'Not too far,' said Benjamin. 'There's things in the forest that might carry you off.'

Ren listened to the sound of the trees as he unbuttoned his trousers. The breeze was stirring, the stars just starting to show themselves. The boy could hear the scraping of the branches overhead, the groan of a trunk as it swayed. Something scattered on his left, and he jumped to his feet, crashing into thorns that grabbed at his hair as he rushed back to the road.

When he pushed through the leaves, Benjamin was waiting, his hands clasped behind him and his long coat swinging in the wind. He was looking at the tops of the trees. Ren followed his gaze and saw a farmhouse on a hill above, and a trail leading to a barn some distance from the road. No light came from the windows, but there was still a bit of smoke drifting from the chimney. A fire nearly out.

Benjamin straightened Ren's jacket. He looked the boy up and down.

'Fix your trousers.'

Ren buttoned up the fly and tied the bit of rope that held his pants together.

'No talking,' said Benjamin. 'You just keep quiet. And watch me. And learn.' With that he took hold of Ren's hand and marched up the path to the farmhouse.

It was a small building, with a vegetable garden and five or six acres behind it. The roof was made of slate and the chimney was set in the middle of the house. There was a rosebush by the door, a few tight buds still holding on in the chill. Benjamin knocked, and after a few minutes a candle appeared at one of the windows, and then the sash was up, and the barrel of a shotgun slid out and pointed at them.

Benjamin nodded at the gun as if it were a person. 'We're traveling to Wenham, and we seem to have lost our way on the road. I was hoping that you'd let us spend the night in your barn.'

'I don't let strangers on to my property, day or night,' said a man's voice. 'Be off.'

'I'd be glad to pay you for your trouble,' said Benjamin, and he made a show of searching his pockets. 'It's the boy I'm worried about. I'm afraid to take him any farther this way in the dark. We've been going all day, and he's awful tired.'

As he said this, Benjamin kicked Ren behind the knees. The boy stumbled to the ground in front of the window, the shotgun inches from his head.

'Jim.' There was a woman's voice. Ren looked up and saw her face in the candlelight. She had brown hair, plaited in braids, and a shawl pulled over her nightgown. Her forehead touched the glass as she peered at them. She whispered something into the darkness of the house. There was a low murmur in return. The shotgun slid back inside the window.

The door opened.

'Please come in,' said the woman.

Benjamin picked Ren up off the ground, dusted him off, took him by the elbow, and led him across the threshold. 'We can't thank you enough.'

'Any Christian would do the same,' she said.

The light from the candle was barely enough for them to see

their way. Ren knocked into something that felt like a stool, and then something else that felt like the edge of a table. The woman put the candle down and lit another with the flame of the first. She lifted the second candle into a fixture that hung from the ceiling and covered it with a hurricane glass, sending a glow across the room, and it was then that Ren saw the farmer who had passed him over at Saint Anthony's, standing by the fireplace in a nightshirt, the shotgun steady in his hand.

When the farmer recognized the boy a look came over him, almost as if he was ashamed, and he lowered the shotgun, peering for a moment down the front of his nightshirt. When he raised his face again he said, 'Seems you found someone to take you after all.'

Ren didn't know what to say. Then he remembered that he wasn't supposed to say anything, and felt relieved.

'William's asleep,' said the farmer. 'But I'm sure he'll be pleased to see you in the morning.' He turned to Benjamin and extended his hand. 'We've also got a boy from Saint Anthony's.'

'Ah,' Benjamin replied, as if he didn't quite understand. Then he said it again – 'Ah!' – and began to pump the farmer's hand enthusiastically.

They took their seats around the table and the farmer's wife quickly got the fire going, made some coffee and served out the remains of a cold meat pie. Ren shoveled the food in his mouth. It was just as he'd imagined. The beef was soft and flavorful, the vegetables slippery with gravy, the crust crimped in a perfect pattern that left the taste of fresh butter on his lips. The men watched Ren eat and discussed the best roads to Wenham. When they had cleaned their plates, the farmer offered Benjamin some tobacco and the men pulled their chairs to the hearth.

The farmer's wife took down a jar from a high shelf and opened it. She removed something twisted and black. She handed it to Ren and the boy stared at it, unsure of what to do.

'It's licorice,' she said. And when he continued to stare she said, 'You eat it.'

Ren held the piece of candy to his nose. The scent was strange but not entirely unappealing. The farmer's wife stood by, her face amused. The boy carefully put the licorice inside his mouth. The consistency was soft, the flavor more of a scent than a taste. There was something in it that turned his stomach. He looked up at the woman and tried to smile.

'We're going to my uncle's farm,' said Benjamin. 'I haven't been there in years.'

'You've been traveling,' said the farmer.

Benjamin nodded. 'I served as a cook on a merchant ship. We put into Boston three weeks ago.'

Ren stopped chewing his licorice.

The farmer lowered his pipe. 'And what countries have you seen?'

'I've been to China. And to India, once.'

'What's it like?'

'Hot.' Benjamin pulled on his pipe, released a stream of smoke, and leaned forward. 'Like summer all year round. The food is too spicy to eat, and the jungles are full of giant snakes that can swallow men whole.'

'It sounds frightening,' said the farmer's wife.

'It made me appreciate New England,' said Benjamin. 'I longed for snow.'

'See if you can find some extra blankets, Mary,' said the farmer.

The woman drew away from the table. She climbed a ladder that leaned against the chimney and disappeared into a crawl space over their heads. The men continued smoking and watching the fire.

'You have a wife?'

Benjamin hesitated for only a moment. 'Not yet.'

'So the boy goes to your relatives?'

'To my aunt and uncle. They've no children of their own.'

The farmer glanced at Ren, then turned back to the fire and lowered his voice. 'Did you not notice?'

'What do you mean?'

'He's damaged.'

'That's why I chose him.'

'But you said that they were farmers. He'll be no use to them.'

'They wanted a companion, not a laborer,' said Benjamin, 'and the boy has other qualities.'

The farmer and Benjamin Nab turned in their seats together and looked at Ren, who was in the process of spitting what was left of the licorice into his hand.

'Tell the man what you can do,' Benjamin said.

They all waited, the fire popping.

'I can whistle,' Ren ventured.

'Well, that's something at least,' said the farmer. 'Can you give us a song, boy?'

Ren slipped the remains of the licorice into his pocket. The inside of his mouth felt like paste. He wet his lips. He thought of the chants the brothers sang in chapel and he gave one now, his breath following the notes. When he was nearly finished, he noticed the farmer's wife, standing on the ladder halfway down, listening, a bundle of blankets under her arm.

She was how he'd dreamed his own mother would be. Beautiful, and half-lit by shadows. He did not want to stop, but the hymn was over, and she turned her face away, and put her hands back on to the ladder and climbed down.

The farmer stood and clapped Ren on the back. 'Come,' he said, taking the blankets from his wife. 'I'll show you the way to the barn.'

They stepped out into the night, the farmer leading with a lantern. The trees were swaying and clacking against one another in the wind. A swarm of leaves blew across the field. The farmer unlatched the door to the barn and held it open as Benjamin and Ren walked in.

It was a small building with a hayloft overhead, which filled the air with a sweet smell and nearly covered the scent of manure. Ren could hear animals moving in their stalls, stirred by the light of the lantern. To the side was the cart the farmer had brought to Saint Anthony's.

'Just some chickens and a cow,' said the farmer, 'and the horse. There's bats, too, in the rafters, but they shouldn't bother you any.' He handed Benjamin the blankets.

'We can't thank you enough.'

'My wife will be in early for the milking.' The farmer hesitated. He looked at Ren as if he wanted to say something, but instead he walked over to his horse. The brown mare lifted her head and nuzzled the side of the farmer's neck. He stroked the animal's forehead and gave her another kiss on the nose. 'I'll leave you the light.' It could have been directed to them or the horse. But with those words he put the lantern on the ground and closed the door.

Benjamin threw the blankets on some straw in the corner,

then sat and removed his boots. He turned them upside down, knocking out a number of pebbles, then put them back on. Ren rubbed his arms against the cold and thought of all the places his brother had traveled to and seen, all the adventures he'd experienced. The boy had so many questions to ask he didn't know where to begin.

'Have you ever seen an elephant?'

'A what?'

'An elephant. In India. I saw a picture of one once, in a book.'

'Don't be a fool,' said Benjamin. 'I've never been to India.' He bunched one of the blankets behind his head. 'You better get some rest. We've got to be up in an hour or two.'

The boy took a step back. 'But you said—' he began.

'I know what I said. Didn't you listen? What did I tell you before we went inside?'

'You told me not to say anything.'

'And what else?'

'To learn.'

'We needed a place to sleep. And now we have it. I told them what they wanted to hear so they'd give it to us. It's as simple as that.'

Ren watched Benjamin Nab settle in for the night with a growing sense of alarm. The man gathered a bunch of dry straw with one arm and covered it with a blanket. He took some more straw and stuffed it inside of his coat and down into his boots. Then he took the collar of his coachman's coat and turned it up around his face, wrapped another blanket around his shoulders, and curled into a ball on the bed he'd made. It was as if he slept outside every day of his life.

'I'd like to see them again,' said Ren.

'Who?'

'Our parents.'

Benjamin reached into his coat pocket. 'Here,' he said, 'you can have them.' He threw the leather pouch onto the ground.

Ren opened the drawstring. He pulled both scalps out and examined them by the lantern light. The brown piece was small and stiff. It looked like boar's hair, the follicles thick and shiny and flat against the skin. The blond piece was softer, but the strands were dry as flax. Ren could see where the curls had been glued to the leather.

'They're not bad if you don't look at them closely. I think we had that Father fooled at least. He gave you up quickly enough, didn't he?'

Ren put the scalps back into the pouch and settled onto a pile of straw. He could hear the chickens rustling in the coop, their tiny claws scratching. A breeze threaded through the slats of the barn. 'What really happened to our parents?'

Benjamin rolled over onto his back and stared up into the rafters. A long time passed, so long Ren believed he was not going to answer. But just then Benjamin said, 'They were murdered. They were killed by a terrible man.'

A moth fluttered against the lamp, its shadow spread across the wall. Ren pulled the collar of his jacket close. 'Why did you lie to me?'

'Because you wouldn't want to hear what really happened.' Benjamin sat up, looking irritated and angry. He pushed the blankets off, marched toward the barn door and opened it. For a moment he stood there on the threshold as if he was going to leave, his shoulders hunched against the cold night air. Then he closed the door and sat down next to Ren.

'Our father was a soldier. Our mother a woman of station and wealth. They met one day in the woods. She was out picking mushrooms, and he – I'm not sure what he was doing. Maybe he'd spent so much time fighting that he'd lost what it was like to be quiet, and surrounded by trees, without worrying that someone was about to come from behind one and try to kill him. Maybe he was just standing there, looking up at the way the branches swayed against the sky, when she came and stood beside him, in a dress as green as the moss under their feet, and said nothing, and looked up as well.

'Our mother had a brother. Some people called him terrible. Others were so afraid of him they didn't call him anything at all. But he loved his sister. Loved her so much that he wouldn't let anyone else love her. And it was because of him that our parents kept their meetings secret, until our father was pressed again into the service and sent west. They wrote letters. Wonderful letters that sustained them both as much as food and water, but the mail was slow in coming and often misdirected, and so when our father heard that she was going to have his child it was half a year too late.

'In the end he deserted. He left his station and his horse and traveled the miles back, through forests and over rivers, lakes, and mountains. All the while she tried to hide that a child was on the way. Then her time came and her brother discovered her secret, and he cut off her hands, and her feet, and her nose; every part of her that our father had loved. She was taken away, piece by piece, until there was nothing left of her.'

Benjamin reached out for the lantern and drew it close.

'Give me your arm.'

Ren gave it.

Benjamin held the wrist to the light and ran a finger along the scar, outlining where the skin had been folded over and stitched. Where he touched felt numb in some places and sensitive in others, tiny bumps on the surface tickling. Ren tried to take his arm away, but Benjamin held it tightly.

'I don't want to know anymore.'

'All right.' Benjamin let go. 'Is that what you wanted to hear?'

'No.'

The man reached over, took hold of the lantern, and blew it out. Night enveloped the barn. 'Well,' he said at last to the darkness between them, 'that's when you know it's the truth.'

CHAPTER SIX

R EN WOKE TO the sound of chains rattling in the early morning. The barn was still dark, but the boy could make out the shape of the farmer's wagon. Scurrying back and forth, attaching the horse to the braces, was Benjamin Nab.

'What are you doing?'

'Quiet!' The man crawled underneath the cart. 'Get over here and help me.'

Ren stood and moved closer. The straw was damp and stuck to his clothes, a thick cloying smell that filled his nostrils and made it clear that he was not dreaming: Benjamin was taking the horse. Ren felt the same quickening of blood that happened whenever he stole at Saint Anthony's. The cow in the back of the barn let out a snort and shifted her weight. She was ready to be milked.

Benjamin finished attaching the buckles and threaded the reins through to the driver's seat. The brown mare was shaking her head back and forth, muscles twitching across her back. Ren took hold of the bridle and tried to stroke the animal's nose.

'They'll be up soon. Hurry!' Benjamin rushed over to the hay where they'd been sleeping, gathered the blankets in his arms and threw the pile at the boy. Ren deposited them into the back of the wagon and stood beside the wheels, wondering if there was any possible way that he could stay behind. If he could somehow convince the farmer and his wife that he'd had no part in this. If they would adopt him, too. But then Benjamin climbed into the driver's seat and told him to open the barn doors, and as he trembled in the cold and the wagon passed through, he knew there wasn't a chance. He jumped up onto the seat next to Benjamin, who cracked the whip over the head of the brown mare, and the wagon thundered down the hill.

Ren clung to the wooden seat and turned to look at the house as they sped away. There was a light in one of the windows. He held his breath, waiting for the farmer to come rushing after them, waiting to hear the shotgun blast. The front door opened just as they reached the road. The wheels of the cart lifted as they took the turn. Ren held on to the side of the wagon, certain that someone was following, but when he glanced behind again at the house all he saw was the farmer's wife, silhouetted in the frame, a pail in each of her hands.

It was another hour before the sun began to rise. Ren kept one of the blankets around his shoulders and watched the sky slowly turning pale. The air was crisp, the color of the leaves a dull bronze. They came out of the valley and the land around them began to flatten, the oaks and maples and elms towering overhead.

Benjamin was in much better spirits and began to point out things along the road, as if they were on some sort of holiday instead of running off with stolen goods. He told a story about the marks on birch trees, and another about a stone wall that went all the way to Maine.

As he listened, Ren tried to imagine the proper penance for their crime. The longest he'd ever received was ten Our Fathers and fifteen Hail Marys. Running away with another man's horse and carriage was an entirely different category, and probably deserved twice, if not three times as many.

'What are you doing?' Benjamin asked.

'Praying.'

'So we won't be followed?'

'No,' Ren said. 'For stealing.'

'This isn't stealing,' said Benjamin. 'It's borrowing, with good intent.'

Ren pulled the blanket closer. He'd told himself similar things when he'd stolen at Saint Anthony's, but in his heart he knew God would find a way to punish him. Ren often thought of the old man as a benignly neglectful gardener, carefully snipping His roses but leaving other areas to go wild, until something caught His notice, a tendril poking its way beyond the fence, and then His full wrath would come thundering down and the entire bed would be ripped out. Ren knew this sin was too big to hide. It would take some work to garner God's patience.

Benjamin Nab spit off the side of the wagon. He slowed the horse. 'Listen,' he said. 'I've seen a lot, and praying never made any difference for anything. Now, I understand you've been raised with a different set of rules, but if you want to stay alive out here you're going to be forced to break them. Know what you need, and if it crosses your path, take it.'

The boy watched the back of the mare bobbing up and down. She was a powerful animal and could easily outmaster them if she wanted, but she kept the bit in her mouth and continued moving down the road.

'How'd you end up at Saint Anthony's in the first place?' Benjamin asked.

'I don't remember.'

'You must remember something.'

'I was put through the door. Just like everyone else.'

'You're not like everyone else.' Benjamin said it with approval, and Ren felt a blush spread across his cheek. Just to hear the words was thrilling.

'I have a good eye,' said Benjamin. 'Most of the time I can look at a person and see their whole life. Small things give them away. That farmer, for instance. I could tell by the way he tied his shoes that he'd never traveled more than twenty miles from his home, and it was unlikely that he'd follow us for long. And that Father John of yours. I knew he had something hidden in that sleeve. And I knew he'd used it on you. The only thing I didn't know was if you deserved it.'

The birds were awake. It was not possible to see them yet, but as the wagon passed the trees there was a cacophony of chirps and songs going back and forth, repeating on one side of the road and then the other, so loud it was as if all the winged creatures in the world had surrounded them.

'I'm not your brother,' said Benjamin.

'I know,' said Ren, although he had not given up hope until that very moment.

Benjamin pulled his coat back and revealed a pistol stuffed into the belt of his trousers. 'Showing this doesn't mean I'm going to hurt you,' he said. 'I just want you to know you're dealing with a man who knows his business.'

Ren tried to keep his face passive, but the moment Benjamin said he wouldn't harm him, the boy was somehow convinced that he would. He looked into the woods. He wondered if he should jump off the wagon.

'That hand of yours is going to open wallets faster than any gun.' Benjamin pulled his jacket closed. He brought the horse to a stop. 'Now I've told you where I'm coming from. And even though you're signed over to me and legally bound to do as I say, and I'm armed and could shoot you if it pleased me, on my word I'll let you out here and you can find your way back.' He smiled. 'Or you can stay with me and take your chances.'

Around the wagon the birds continued their calls. They were softer now as the sun was rising, but to Ren they still seemed frantic.

Benjamin leaned in close. 'What's the thing you want most in the world?'

Ren had never been asked this before. As he considered the question, he realized that he was more certain about what he *didn't* want. He didn't want to be shot by the gun he'd just seen. He didn't want to be left alone on the road. He looked up at the early-morning sky and thought of the farmer's wife.

'A family,' he said at last.

'Don't be simpleminded,' said Benjamin. 'I mean anything. Anything in the world.'

The boy tried to think of something else, something beyond the limits. 'An orange,' he said. 'I want an orange.'

'I can get you that.' Benjamin held out his hand. 'What do you say, little man?'

His fingers were long and thin. But there were no calluses, nor any sign that he had ever worked hard labor. His wrists were

54

delicate, his nails remarkably clean. Ren noticed a freckle, nestled in his palm like a coin – a mark of good fortune – and it was this, more than anything, that made him reach forward and take it.

CHAPTER SEVEN

T HEY ARRIVED AT Granston in the late afternoon, hungry and thirsty, the horse covered in sweat. It was a harbor town; the shops and houses hugged the circle of the shore, and a small jetty served as the mouth to the ocean, with a lighthouse at the very tip. The roads all led to the water, and before long the wagon was in the chaos of the docks. Fishermen unloaded nets of salted fish and stacks of crates full of crabs and lobsters, still alive, their pincers snapping against the bars. There were casks of oil being lifted from the whaling ships, the men tattooed and hard-muscled. From the merchant vessels came barrels of spices and bolts of fabric and boxes of dishes.

Vendors were selling their goods right on the street, barking and haggling as money was exchanged and the buyers sorted through the wares. A fisherman took hold of a wriggling octopus and ripped off a leg before adding it to a scale set up on the dock. A sailor lifted a monkey over his head. A group of women dressed as if they were going to a party, in satin gowns and lace shawls, broke open a crate of glasses and began inspecting them, right there on the ground. A soldier opened an umbrella and held it against the sun. The painted green paper

changed the color of the light. Above the crowd the masts of the
tall ships shot straight to the clear blue sky. A group of dirty
children were climbing from one mast to the other, and
shouting, and balancing on the ropes and swinging off them into
the harbor. Hovering over it all was the stench of fish.

Ren had smelled the fish from miles away, before they even
reached the town itself. The horse and cart had rounded a
corner and they were suddenly surrounded by the rotten scent,
as if they had stepped into a fog. The odor pushed away the
image of the farmer's wife, which had been haunting Ren since
they'd left the farmhouse, and by the time they reached the
wharf he could no longer distinguish the smell from anything
else.

The sun reflected off the water, and Ren lifted his hand to
shield his eyes. He had never seen the ocean before, and now it
laid itself out before him, the waves rippling together in patterns
of light, spreading out toward the horizon, a giant roiling
creature of openness and space. It was as if Ren's forehead had
unlocked, and the breeze coming off the waves was channeling
through him, pushing all the cluttered thoughts in his mind
aside, clearing room for something new and exciting to move
in.

He peered over the edge of the dock. Clumps of brown
seaweed swayed back and forth in the tide, like fields in a storm.
Mussels and periwinkles covered the rotting wood, along with
bands of sharp white barnacles. Seagulls rested on the tips of
pilings or dove overhead, screeching and fearless.

Benjamin led the horse away from the water, and they
crossed three streets, cobblestones making way to dirt and sand
alleys. Wooden row houses lined up on either side, the homes of

sailors in port for a few weeks only, or fishermen waiting for the next trip to the Grand Banks. The road squeezed close as it wove between the buildings, until there was barely space enough for the cart to fit through.

Ahead two women were talking to a soldier. They were dressed in colorful layers, with low-cut bodices and painted cheeks. One of the women was lifting her skirt, and the other had her hands around the soldier's waist. Benjamin had to slow the wagon to fit by the group. He kept his face hidden as they passed, but Ren was curious. He had never seen women like this before. He turned around so that he could keep watching, and the soldier grinned at him, then winked.

They stopped the cart two streets down, in front of an abandoned building. The windows were boarded up and the brick blackened, as if it had been through a fire. Benjamin handed Ren the reins and opened a broken wooden gate into a small yard. He tied the horse and led Ren to the back, where they stood before a rusted door that didn't quite fit on its hinges. He knocked. They waited. He knocked again. There was a sound of shuffling inside.

'Who's there?' A low voice came through the cracks.

'It's only me,' Benjamin said. 'Let us in.'

Ren heard a fumbling of metal locks. A heavyset man with a full, red beard opened the door as carefully as a prison cell, then stood in the entrance, blinking at them. His shirt looked like it had been slept in, and there was a stain down one side of his pants.

'You're looking good,' said Benjamin.

'Liar,' said the man. 'Who's this? Another victim?'

'My son,' Benjamin said.

'Ha!' said the man.

'Are you letting us in or not, Tom?'

The man muttered something to himself, then stood aside and let them pass.

There was a small flight of stairs down into a cellar room. The floor was hard-packed dirt, the walls whitewash over stone. There was a shoddy sunken bed and a table with two chairs. On the table was a candle and several pipes knocked out onto a plate. Next to the bed was a row of bottles.

'Entertaining?' Benjamin asked.

'Not lately,' said Tom. He eyed Ren warily.

Benjamin picked up a pipe and cleaned out the bowl with his finger. It came out black with soot and he used it to write on the table – A, B, C. He turned to Ren. 'This man used to be a teacher.'

Ren was afraid, suddenly, that Benjamin would leave him here. 'I already know how to spell.'

'See how smart he is?' Benjamin took one of the bottles and poured out a drink. 'I thought we could use some help.'

'With what?' said Tom. 'We need to move on. We can't be dragging a child along.'

'This isn't a child.' Benjamin took hold of Ren's sleeve and pushed it up, revealing his scar. 'This is a gold mine.'

Tom squinted, then shook his head. 'For God's sake, Benji,' he said.

'This boy's been mine for twenty-four hours, and I've been given a good meal, a smoke, a place to sleep, and come into possession of a horse and wagon.'

'You're going to use him, then, for what – bait?'

'He's going to open doors. Enough for us to get in.'

Benjamin reached over and took the whiskey away, just as Tom was about to pour a glass.

'You don't know anything about children,' Tom said. 'They're nothing but trouble. Little monsters.'

'He'll be *our* little monster,' said Benjamin.

Tom slumped in his seat. He offered no more arguments. Benjamin waited another minute, then returned the whiskey to the table. The schoolteacher snatched it and poured a drink for himself.

'It's decided, then.' Benjamin gave a nod, and Ren could see that his staying had never truly been in question. Tom sulked and sipped at his drink, and Benjamin cleaned his glasses before folding them carefully and slipping them into his pocket. 'Now I have to unhitch the horse before somebody else steals it,' he said, and he turned and walked back up the stairs.

As soon as they were alone, Tom emptied out Ren's pockets. There wasn't much to be found. The three stitched letters of Ren's name were tossed on the table, along with the rock that Ichy had given him. Then *The Lives of the Saints* came out from his sleeve. Tom took the volume over to the candle and studied it. By the light Ren could see that the man was younger than he'd thought. His lips were chapped, his beard stuck out in tangles, and his eyes were a deep sea-green, like the water they'd passed along the harbor. Tom checked the spine, ran his fingers along the leather, then opened the cover and began to read. He frowned as he turned the pages. Ren wished that Benjamin would return.

'Do you actually believe this?' Tom said at last.

'No,' Ren said, although he did.

Tom turned the book over and ran his palm across it. 'Could be worth something.'

'I don't want to sell it.'

'That's not for you to decide.' Tom reached underneath his beard and began to pick at the skin there.

Ren looked around the room at the painted stone walls, the empty bottles, and the caved-in bed. 'Do you really live here?'

'For the past month I have.' Tom put the book on the table and now thrust his other hand underneath his beard and continued scratching, his fingers lost in the mass of red hair. 'We go from place to place. Wherever the job takes us.'

'What job?'

'Hard to say,' said Tom. 'It's always changing. As Ophelia said, "We know what we are, but know not what we may be".' He pulled something from his beard and rolled it between his fingertips before flicking it onto the floor. 'Mostly we sell things.'

'What kind of things?'

Tom leaned over so that his face was level with the boy's, his green eyes searching, as if he were deciding whether or not to trust him. When Ren did not look away, Tom pointed to a suitcase in the corner. 'Go on,' he said. 'Open it.'

The case was made of wood, with leather straps to hold it together. Ren brushed a bit of dust from the top, then pushed the strap through the buckle and undid the pin. The case fell open with a crash. It was full of small glass bottles, about two dozen, each stopped with a cork and each with the same handwritten label: Doctor Faust's Medical Salts for Pleasant Dreams.

'Is that all that's left?' Benjamin stood in the doorway.

'All I could save,' said Tom. 'The rest are the property of the state of New Hampshire.'

Benjamin picked up one of the bottles, uncorked it and

sniffed the top. 'I think we may have used too much opium.'

'I don't think that's even a question.' Tom nudged Ren with his elbow. 'He turned the last mayor's wife into a hop fiend.'

'Not on purpose,' said Benjamin.

'All the same,' said Tom. 'I don't think we should sell any more.'

'We'll dilute it.' Benjamin turned the bottle over in his hand, then held it to the light. 'We'll call it something else. Rewrite the labels.'

'I'd rather rob a bank,' said Tom.

It was clear that the men had known each other for years, maybe longer. They spoke easily and cursed without losing their tempers. Tom was full of bluster, but Ren could see that he constantly wavered, and it took only a breath from Benjamin to decide the place he was going to fall.

'We'll wait until the spring,' said Benjamin. 'When we're ready to move on. Then we'll start selling again.'

Tom wiped his face. 'Fine.'

'Is there any money left?'

There was an awkward silence and then Tom began to laugh. Benjamin smiled too, as if he had been expecting this. He reached for one of the pipes on the table. He took a bit of tobacco from the pouch in his coat and pressed it into the head of the pipe with his thumb. 'Then we should go fishing. Before the ground freezes.'

'We'll need another shovel.'

'What happened to the one I bought?'

Tom lifted the bottle.

Benjamin shook his head. 'One day you're going to sell your soul.'

Tom poured out another drink. 'Yours, too,' he said.

'Why do you need a shovel to go fishing?' Ren asked.

The men looked uncomfortable for a moment. Then Tom pointed a finger at Benjamin. 'I told you,' he said. 'Little monsters.'

Benjamin lit the pipe in his hand with the candle. He drew on the mouthpiece, and a thin stream of smoke passed through his lips. 'We need a shovel to find the worms.'

Ren leaned against the table. The smell of the tobacco made him feel faint. He hadn't eaten anything since their meal at the farmer's. He'd been hoping for some supper, and now he realized that he probably wouldn't get any that day, or maybe the next, if Benjamin didn't catch any fish. His stomach growled at the thought and the men stopped talking.

'It's hungry,' Tom said.

'There's got to be something here.' Benjamin searched through the empty cupboards, pulling out drawers.

Tom tried to pour another glass, but the bottle was done. He scowled. 'So big when you were setting off. I knew you'd come back empty-handed.'

'I'm not empty-handed,' Benjamin said. 'I have a boy.'

CHAPTER EIGHT

THE SIGN OUTSIDE the shop read: MR JEFFERSON'S NEW, USED & RARE. It was a dusty storefront, the paint worn thin from the salt air. Ren tried to peer in the window but it was blocked with books, the pages rumpled, the spines faded and torn.

A small bell rang as they opened the door. The room was dark enough that there were candles lit, even though it was the middle of the day. There seemed to be no shelves in the shop. Just piles of books of various heights, all the way up to the ceiling, leaning against the wall, scattered across a table or underfoot.

'Buying or selling?' The voice came from somewhere on their right, behind a mound of anatomical sketchbooks.

'Selling,' said Benjamin.

'Well,' said a stout black man, now climbing over the pile. 'I hope it's interesting.' He was of average height and perhaps sixty years old, with long white sideburns and a well-made but worn charcoal gray suit. There were several pins affixed to his jacket, a starched collar around his neck, and, tucked into his vest, a bright green handkerchief.

'Is Mister Jefferson in?' Benjamin asked.

'I'm Mister Jefferson,' said the man.

Benjamin paused for only a moment. Then he reached into his coat pocket and handed over *The Lives of the Saints*.

Jefferson moved a pile of biographies and a set of dictionaries from the table and put them on the floor. Then he brought several of the candles and arranged them around Ren's book. He did this all very carefully and surely, and once everything was settled he took a pair of glasses from his coat pocket and began to inspect the volume, checking the seams of the leather, turning the pages, slipping the tip of his smallest finger into the spine and wiggling it back and forth.

Ren felt cheated as he watched Mister Jefferson determine the price. *The Lives of the Saints* belonged to him, and he did not want to part with it, even though it was all they had to bargain with. He strayed to a table nearby, piled high with small leather-bound volumes. One of them had an etching of an Indian on the cover, with a necklace of bear claws and two feathers dangling from his ear. Ren turned his head and read the title – *The Deerslayer*.

Jefferson took off his glasses. 'I'll give you five cents.'

'It's got to be worth more than that,' said Benjamin, snatching the book back.

'It's a fair price,' said Jefferson.

'We'll take it somewhere else.'

'There is nowhere else. Not in this town, at least. You could take it to Rockport, but I doubt they'd offer more. No one around here is interested in saints.'

'Fine.' Benjamin dropped the book onto the table and picked up a large dictionary, weighing it in his hands. 'Five. Hand it over, then.'

Jefferson crawled behind his desk and counted out the pennies. There was a moment, when his back was turned, that Ren was certain Benjamin was going to smash the dictionary over his head. But instead Benjamin opened the volume, licked his finger, and turned a page. ' "Parsimonious," ' he read. ' "Exhibiting or marked by parsimony, excessively frugal, penurious, niggardly, poor in quality or meager in quantity. See stingy." '

The Lives of the Saints rested on the desk. Ren thought of Brother Joseph giving the book to him, the weight of it in his hand. He walked over to Jefferson and tugged on the man's sleeve.

'It's mine,' Ren said.

Jefferson stopped counting the coins. 'Pardon me?'

'I want to keep it.'

Benjamin closed the dictionary. 'Don't bother with the boy. My sister dropped him on his head when he was a baby, and he's never been right since. Always walking into things and kneeling down in the middle of the street.' Benjamin leaned in and whispered, 'He thinks he's a *Catholic*.'

Jefferson raised his eyebrows.

'It's true,' said Benjamin. 'He's collected all kinds of popery. If you don't take the book, I'll have to burn it.'

Ren could see that the thought of burning any book, even a Catholic one, was distasteful to Mister Jefferson. The man bent over his purse again.

Benjamin gave Ren a savage look and pointed at the door. Ren let go of Jefferson's sleeve. He pressed his fingernails into his palm. There was no way to get *The Lives of the Saints* back, but he decided right then that he was not going to leave Mister Jefferson's New, Used & Rare empty-handed.

If he was going to steal a book, he would need a distraction. Ren closed his eyes, and instead of going to the door as he was instructed, he walked deliberately straight into the nearest pile. It toppled over. Volumes went crashing into the next stack, and the next, histories and biographies and collections of maps, science textbooks and series of lithographs, slave narratives and song books, were all mixed together, a huge mess across the floor.

Benjamin crawled out from under a mound of pamphlets. He shook his head, then got unsteadily to his feet. Jefferson stood in the back, his store ruined. With a grim face he handed Benjamin the money. Then he plucked his green handkerchief from his pocket, reached down, took up a collection of poetry, and began to dust the jacket.

'You better leave now,' Jefferson said to the book in his hands.

Benjamin nodded. And with that he pushed Ren out the door, slammed it behind them, and started off down the street.

Ren lagged behind. 'It was an accident,' he said feebly.

'No it wasn't,' said Benjamin. He turned to look at the store, and when it was clear that Jefferson had not chased after them, he started to laugh. 'He deserved it, though. Five cents!' He slipped his fist into his pocket and rattled the coins, then slapped the boy once on the back of the neck. 'That's for not telling me first.'

Ren nearly lost his grip on *The Deerslayer*, now tucked underneath his coat. It was smaller than *The Lives of the Saints* and fit between his shirt and where the sleeve began. Ren slipped his arm inside his jacket and took hold of the leather binding. It had been easier to take than he'd thought.

They went past candlemakers and blacksmiths, fishmongers and cloth merchants. Before long Ren realized that they were walking in circles. Down to the wharf and back again, in and out of side streets, and then returning to the main square, where the people bargained over prices and smoked in circles and gathered in a crowd around a small puppet show. All the while Benjamin was scanning the street, looking into people's faces.

They came to the butcher shop. Carcasses hung in the window, white and red hollow casings. There was a row of tiny rabbit skulls, the flesh still hanging from the bone. Benjamin stopped and Ren stopped beside him. Somewhere close by, a bell began to ring. Ren turned and saw a square stone church with an iron steeple set back from the road and he remembered that it was Sunday. He had never missed a mass before. And he realized, in the confusion and transition of the days past, he also had not gone to confession. He could see the doors of the church beginning to open, and he almost expected Brother Joseph and Father John to emerge and point him out.

Parishioners were coming down the stairs. There were families. Lots of families. Mothers and fathers and grandmothers in their best clothes, children in starched white linen. They were laughing and talking and wishing each other good morning, the boys and girls screaming and chasing one another up and down the street. The pastor stood at the gate in his robes, a short, wiry man with a large mole on his chin, trying to look dignified as the people walked by, but instead seeming rather afraid of them.

Ren felt a familiar shove from behind. He tumbled off the sidewalk and into a mountain of horse manure, right in front of the church. The families stepped back. The pastor lifted his robe.

And they all looked at the boy in the gutter, streaked brown from head to toe.

'Hey there!' A voice came from the crowd. People were moving aside; someone was pushing through. Ren saw that it was Benjamin. He had his spectacles on and his hair neatly pulled back. 'Are you all right?' He lifted Ren from the gutter, shook the dirty lumps from his shoulders and looked through the pieces of glass on his nose directly into Ren's eyes, as if he were searching for a piece of manure there, too.

'I'm fine,' the boy said quietly. He tried not to look at the pastor or the women gathered round.

'What's this?' Benjamin said loudly. He took hold of Ren's left arm and pushed back the sleeve. The boy's wrist was revealed before all of them, a cold and lonely nub. Ren tried to pull away, believing this was payback for what he'd done in Jefferson's store. But Benjamin held on tight and turned to the families on the sidewalk, his face a combination of horror and pity. 'Here, take something that will help your poor, miserable life. Here, here,' said Benjamin, and he dug into his pocket and held out Jefferson's five cents. 'It's not much, but I hope that it will bring you comfort.' He blinked rapidly, as if he were trying to hold back tears. Then he took his pocket handkerchief and began fiercely rubbing manure from the boy's cheeks.

The parishioners gaped at Ren's arm. Some whispered among themselves and moved off. A few of the children looked frightened. Ren tried to yank free, but Benjamin refused to let go until an old, bent lady came forward.

'Poor thing,' she said. 'Here, boy, here you are.' And she reached into the inner folds of her bosom and produced a large coin. She touched it to his nose and it was warm.

'Thank you,' said Ren. His cheeks burned. The woman slipped the coin into the pocket of his coat. Benjamin paused for a moment, then continued to vigorously rub away the manure.

'*I* want to give money to the cripple.' A small girl stamped her foot on the sidewalk. Her mother tried to pull her away, but the child fussed, shaking her dark, shiny ringlets until the woman gave in and handed her a penny from her purse. The girl approached, holding her coin out far away from her, as if she were feeding a wild animal. Ren stared. He had never seen hair this perfect. It was the color of a crow's wings – so black and so rich.

'Go on,' she said, 'take it.' She held the coin up to his face.

Ren's left arm was useless. His right was tucked inside of his jacket, holding on to the book he had stolen. He did not want to let it go, and so instead of reaching for the money the boy opened his mouth and stuck out his tongue, and the girl, understanding, placed the coin upon it like a communion wafer. Ren stood there for a moment, feeling the weight of the metal, the tang of the copper. The crowd lightly applauded. More people came forward, coins in their fists, and began stuffing them into Ren's pockets.

'Hank hoo,' said Ren. 'Hank hoo, hank hoo.' The coin dropped from his lips, and Benjamin caught it.

CHAPTER NINE

THE MEN WENT out that night. They left Ren behind in the crumbling basement, with a few candles and a promise that he would not open the door, not to anyone, no matter what was said or who came knocking. Tom took the lantern and Benjamin grabbed the wooden shovel he'd bought earlier that afternoon. It had cost five cents, the same amount they'd received for *The Lives of the Saints*.

When they were gone and the locks were fastened, Ren made his way down the dark staircase and settled himself at the table. There were still a few chunks of bread and sausages and pieces of salted cod, purchased with the money from the parishioners. The boy chose a piece of bread and gnawed at it, even though he was no longer hungry. The bread was fresh, the inside soft and chewy.

The men had left one candle going, and the dim light made shadows on the walls. It felt strange to be there alone. Ren had hardly ever been by himself at Saint Anthony's. The last time was two years before, when the twins had come down with the measles, and then one by one all the small boys were sick – all but Ren. By the time it was over, three children had died. The

71

brothers had made Ren sleep out in the barn so he would not catch the disease. It had been lonely, and Ren was glad when it was over.

There was whiskey on the table that the men had shared before they left. Tom's mood had changed with each sip, from an initial jovial gladness at the meal before them, to a numbed silence and then finally back to his regular irritated state, as if he had not been drinking at all. Ren lifted the bottle and sniffed. It made the hair inside his nose tingle, but when he tried a sip the whiskey scalded his throat, and he spit what was left in his mouth onto the floor. He had never tasted anything so terrible, except perhaps the wine they made at Saint Anthony's. He'd stolen a bottle once and shared it with the twins. Hidden in the field, the boys had passed the wine among them until they felt dizzy. Then Brom had twisted his ankle doing cartwheels, and Ichy had thrown up, and Ren had caught the hiccups so badly that it was two whole days before he was right again.

Looking back, Ren realized how much he missed his friends, and decided right then to write Brom and Ichy a letter. He searched the small apartment and found a pen and a bottle of ink but no paper. He looked through the rest of the room, until at last he discovered a stack of printed advertisements for Doctor Faust's Medical Salts for Pleasant Dreams. He turned over the bill and began to write. He had never written a letter before, but he had some idea that they should carry good news.

Dear Brom and Ichy,

First, I should tell you that I'm drunk. I've had a whole bottle of whiskey. I will probably throw up before I finish this.

Benjamin bought a horse and carriage and we rode to a town full of ships and sailors from far away places. Benjamin said we're going to take one to India to see the elephants.

I have my own room and he doesn't make me go to church. I hope that you both get a family soon and don't have to go into the army.

Your friend,
Ren

It needed an envelope. And a stamp. And those would cost money, he supposed. He folded the letter in half, and then in half again. With each fold he became less enthusiastic about sending it. He felt somehow they would know that he was lying. Then he realized that all the letters sent from the children who had been adopted had probably also been lies.

Ren heard something outside the door. He crept carefully up the stairs and listened, wishing all the while that he was not alone. He checked the locks again, put his eye to a crack in the wood and peered out. He could see a bit of the yard, but nothing was there. He waited, and waited some more, then went back down the stairs and took out *The Deerslayer*.

The Indian gazed at him from the cover, cool and exotic. Ren ran his fingers over the picture, moved closer to the light, opened the book, and began to read. As he entered the story, hemlocks and pine trees soared overhead, a lake spread out before him like a mirror reflecting the sky, and the sound of a rifle shot boomed in his ears. Ren made his way through the dense forest with Deerslayer, chopping down trees and turning them into canoes, hunting and fishing and saving Indian maidens. Then there was an ambush, and Deerslayer shot a native down and was given a new name for doing so – Hawkeye – from the very man he'd killed.

This was better than histories or psalms, better even than *The Lives of the Saints*. At times Ren felt like he was reading fragments of his own dreams, reassembled into words that pulled at his heart, as if there were a string tied somewhere inside his chest that ran down into the book and attached itself to the characters, drawing him through the pages. The boy read and read and read and read, until his eyes burned and the candle went out, and even then, in the darkness, he could still see Deerslayer, pushing his way through the thick leaves, sighting his mark, raising his long thin rifle to his shoulder and firing.

The men returned just before dawn. Ren lifted his head from the table as they came down the stairs, the glow from Tom's lantern lighting the way. They were filthy, their pants and shoes covered with muck. Ren expected to smell fish, but the only scent in the room was that of damp earth. Tom set the lamp down, and Benjamin began emptying his pockets onto the table.

He took out a necklace made of seed pearls. And then one made of coral, turquoise, and colored glass. He removed a pocket watch, listening to it for a moment before setting it down. Then he took out three pairs of earrings, a belt buckle, several thin gold chains, a bracelet covered with tiny charms, a set of cameo pins, two pairs of leather gloves and half a dozen rings.

Tom opened the bottle on the table. 'It's been a good night, boy!' He took a drink, swirling the whiskey in his mouth before swallowing it down. 'We deserve our own Pontic triumph. "Veni, vidi, vici." '

The jewelry was covered with dust and dirt, bits of earth caked in where the beads were attached and along the creases of the buckle. The cameos were smudged, the pocket watch lined with black. Only the rings seemed fairly clean. They were, for the most part, simple gold bands. Wedding rings. A few had engravings on the inside. Initials. Or maybe something else. A poem. A promise.

'It looks like you dug them up from the ground,' said Ren.

'We did,' said Tom. He began rummaging around in his pockets, set the bottle down, rummaged some more, and finally pulled out a handkerchief tied in knots. He shook the handkerchief back and forth in the air until it rattled, then threw it on the table toward the boy. 'Take a look,' Tom said.

The handkerchief was full of teeth. Ren poured them out on the table beside the necklaces and rings. There must have been several dozen in various stages of decay, some the size of peas and others fully formed, nearly as large as acorns, with pointed roots twisted together. The teeth looked like tiny headless porcelain dolls, with bits of pink still clinging to the sides, as if they had been feasting on human flesh.

Ren yanked his fingers away and understood.

The wedding rings, the limp sets of gloves, the teeth laid out across the table: Everything had been taken from the dead. Ren felt as if the floor itself were moving, and a jolt of fear shot through him as he imagined what kind of punishment God would send down for this sin. In his mind he pictured his companions digging in a cemetery, lifting the lids of coffins. Their hands rifling through the pockets of corpses, their faces greedy and hideous. And then Benjamin yawned. And Tom scratched his beard, and they seemed just the same as before.

'It's too much work taking them out,' said Benjamin.

'Not when you see how much I can sell them for,' said Tom. 'I know a man who said a good set will go for ten dollars.' He opened the drawer underneath the table and began to go through it. He took out a small brush. 'Move aside,' he said to Ren, and settled himself into a chair, pouring a tiny amount of whiskey into a glass. He dipped the brush into it, then set to work on the teeth, scrubbing away at the soft parts.

'I studied Latin with a man who had no teeth at all,' said Tom. 'He always smelled like lavender soap, but he was a smart old codger.'

'How'd you pay for that?' Benjamin asked.

'My mother cleaned his house,' said Tom. 'She paid for all my lessons that way.'

'Too bad she isn't here,' said Benjamin.

Tom stopped scrubbing. His mouth set in a line. Then he put the tooth down and reached for the bottle.

Benjamin called Ren over. He held up a bracelet and a watch.

'Which do you think is worth more?'

The watch was gold, with a tree carved into the face. The bracelet was made of silver and consisted of tiny charms in the shape of musical instruments. Ren fingered a tiny piano. He thought of the lifeless arm that it had adorned.

'Don't get distracted,' Benjamin said. He pulled a knife from his boot, slipped it into the back of the watch and popped it open. There were hundreds of gears inside, all turning together. 'You should look at every part of something before you choose.' He fit the piece back into place and snapped it shut. 'Then, always take the watch.'

The rings and necklaces were spread out and inspected. The cameos were polished, the pictures delicately wrought, with images of fairies and profiles of beautiful young women. A set of earrings sparkled as Benjamin rubbed away the grime, and the pearls shone like new skin in the lamplight.

'This will keep us until spring,' said Tom.

Benjamin nodded. 'We'll have to sell them a few towns over so they won't be recognized.' He finished cleaning the earrings and set them aside. Then he began to arrange the rest of the jewelry into piles, estimating the worth of each and calculating the numbers on his fingers. He moved a pair of gloves and noticed the copy of *The Deerslayer* on the table.

Tom stopped his scrubbing. 'Did you get that tonight?'

The Indian on the cover looked out impassively as the spine of the book was read and turned over. Benjamin ran his finger across the necklace of bear claws, tracing each point.

'I believe this was borrowed from Mister Jefferson.' Benjamin narrowed his eyes at Ren, and the boy felt his stomach drop. He'd stolen many things at Saint Anthony's over the years, but this was the first time he'd ever been caught.

Tom glanced back and forth between them, then turned to Ren with a grin. 'And to think I wanted to send you back.'

'I can't believe I didn't notice.' Benjamin was smiling now. 'Show me how you did it. Take something else.'

Ren paused for a moment, tensed and ready; then he brought his fist from behind his back, opened his fingers, and showed the ring he had already stolen from the table. It was etched in gold with a fine pattern of leaves. There was a date carved inside, *1831*, and the words *Forget Me Not*. Tom and Benjamin moved forward to see, then leaned back and roared with laughter.

Benjamin pulled his collar up and began fussing over the book with a rag, in a surprisingly accurate imitation of Mister Jefferson. Then he chased Ren around the table, shouting, 'STOP THIEF!,' the boy scrambling under the chairs, darting this way and that, until Tom was wiping tears and Ren was laughing too, and it was as if something had been released inside the basement room, their voices flying high into the corners and each of them gasping for breath.

Benjamin collapsed in a chair and threw his legs out before him. He rubbed his nose and kept his blue eyes set on Ren, as if the boy were capable of taking the world.

'This one doesn't need any training at all,' said Tom.

'No,' Benjamin said. 'He's already one of us.'

CHAPTER TEN

IN THE BOATYARD all kinds of ships were hauled out from the water. Carpenters scuttled underneath the braces, wool scarves tied around their necks and fingerless gloves over their hands. The men scraped the hulls from a season's worth of voyages, cleaning away the seaweed and replacing the wood that was rotten, tapping in caulk between the boards. Ren saw one boat being built, the empty ribs stretching up to the sky like an open mouth, at least seventy feet long. On another schooner the builders were in the middle of setting the mast, a giant tree trunk planed of branches and covered with grease, slowly hauled into place with ropes, and sliding down through the heart of the ship.

Next to the boatyard was a line of shops selling tackle and nets and ropes, brass fittings and sails and anchors, salt and ice and oars and oil and buckets and harpoons. The place smelled of commerce – wood shavings and polish. Tom led them around the corner to a rickety staircase. A faded sign was nailed to the side of the building, with the words MISTER BOWERS, DENTISTRY AND TOOTH WORK written in red paint. Underneath, a hand was etched into the wood, pointing up the steep spiral stairs.

Tom and Benjamin looked at each other, then gave Ren a small shove, and the boy started up the stairs, with the men behind him. The railing shook and the steps seemed ready to fall apart underneath his feet. Before Ren reached the top, a man's head popped over the edge and looked down at them.

He had hollow cheeks, covered in a gray stubble, and an ancient white wig of tight curls that covered only half of his balding head. There was a napkin tucked into his collar. As they climbed higher, Ren saw that he also had a painful-looking black eye. Swollen, purple, and nearly closed shut.

'Mister Bowers?' Tom asked.

'Who wants to know?'

'Our boy has a toothache,' said Benjamin, gesturing to Ren.

'I don't usually get customers so early,' said Bowers. He seemed uncertain, but once they reached the top of the stairs he was quite anxious that they shouldn't leave. His breath smelled of coffee with too much sugar. His hands were damp as he shook theirs. 'Come in, come in.'

The shop was nothing more than a room, with a faded rug over a stained wood floor and newspaper advertisements for wallpaper. A padded chair stood in the center, along with a footstool, a table, and a tall cabinet with glass doors. On top of the table was a washbasin, full of pink water, as well as an open box containing instruments – small hammers, pliers, drills, and files. Ren looked at the tools with horror and hoped they would not get anywhere near his mouth.

Beside the box rested the remains of Mister Bowers's breakfast: a piece of dark bread with jam and a mug of coffee. Bowers pulled the napkin from his collar and began to cover the plate with it. Then he paused.

'Do you like jam?' he asked Ren.

'Yes,' said Ren, hoping the man would offer some.

Bowers stuck out his lower lip and looked at Ren as if he were across a great distance. Then he reached inside his mouth and pulled out his teeth, top and bottom. They were connected with wire – a complete set of dentures. He held them, wet and glistening, in the palm of his hand. His mouth was shrunken without them, the skin around his chin loose.

'This is what happens to people who eat jam.' Bowers gave a grin, or as much of one as he could manage with his empty mouth. Then he pushed his teeth back inside of his head. When he finished adjusting his dentures, he tugged on the front of his coat, straightened his wig, and said, 'Have a seat.'

Ren was still staring at Bowers's teeth. Benjamin had to give the boy a nudge before he climbed up onto the padded chair.

'Let's take a gander,' said Bowers. Ren opened his mouth and the man leaned close and peered inside. 'What seems to be the trouble?'

'My teeth are loose,' said Ren.

'Is that so?' said Bowers. He prodded Ren's gums, first the bottom, then the top, running a fingernail along the tongue, wiggling a tooth here and there. He stopped where Ren had knocked out a molar years before and fondled the hole. His fingers were salty.

'We've been collecting them,' said Tom. And he put the handkerchief full of teeth on the table, near the dentist's elbow.

'Ah,' said Bowers, glancing at the handkerchief. 'That changes things.' He took his hands from Ren's mouth and immersed them in the basin of pink water, then dried them on his coat. Ren scrambled down from the chair, relieved that his part in the performance was over, the taste of the dentist's fingers lingering in his mouth.

Bowers walked over to the window, drew the curtains, then closed the shop door, his hand against the wood, before turning the lock. He untied the knot in the handkerchief and spread the teeth out along the table. From the instrument box he took out a small pair of tongs and a magnifying glass. 'These are fresh.' Bowers inspected a molar. 'From a young woman. Twenty-three or twenty-four. Cause of death,' he said, leveling the magnifying glass over the tooth, 'probably childbirth. A little grinding here – you can see the scratches.'

'How much are they worth?' Tom asked.

'It's hard to say.' Bowers turned his back to the group and held an incisor up to the light coming through the window. 'You see there? That crack? That means it's decayed inside.' He picked up another from the table. 'This one too. Gum disease. Rots from the root.'

Tom took up one of the discarded teeth and examined it, rolling it back and forth in his palm. 'You're just trying to bring down the price.'

'I know what I'm talking about,' said Bowers. 'I have a degree. A diploma from the American Society of Dental Surgeons.'

'I don't give a damn about your degree,' said Tom.

Bowers swept one tooth into his hand, selected a hammer from his instrument box, and cracked it open with one tap, revealing the black inside.

Tom looked it over carefully, then snatched the rest of the teeth from the counter, cursing, and threw the whole lot into the corner of the room. 'All that work for nothing.'

'I told you,' said Benjamin.

'If you please,' said Bowers, going after the teeth. He scrambled about on the floor, reaching underneath the cabinet and plucking the tiny white pieces from the rug. Benjamin and Tom began to walk out and the dentist followed them, crawling on his knees. He took hold of Ren's arm and tried to force the rotten teeth on him. The teeth clattered across the floor and Bowers looked surprised, and then amused, as he saw that Ren had no hand for them to fall into.

'My God.' He took hold of Ren's sleeve and peered down into it. 'Don't you need a hook?'

Benjamin stopped, his hand on the door. A small vein pulsed just beneath the skin of his temple. Ren thought for a moment that he might lose his temper, but instead a cool smile slid across his face. 'You're a comedian.'

'It's interesting you should say that,' said Bowers. 'I am known for my sense of humor, particularly among members of the American Society of Dental Surgeons.'

'Is that how you got that shiner?' Tom asked.

Bowers's hand reached up and touched the swollen edge of his black eye. He seemed surprised that it was still there. 'Oh, no,' he said. 'That was simply a misunderstanding.'

'A misunderstanding of what?'

'Of a bicuspid and an incisor,' said Bowers. He waited for the men to laugh. Benjamin shot Tom a look, and they did their best. Ren tried to laugh too, but it came out sounding more like a cough. All the same, the dentist seemed to appreciate the effort and looked at them with a much more generous countenance than before.

'In this case, however, I'm being quite serious,' said Bowers.

'The sailors here, they fashion all kinds of tools for their missing limbs. There's a place on the wharf that makes wooden hands, quite lifelike. Wooden legs, too. I know the man that carves them – he's done some teeth for me.'

Bowers walked over to the glass cabinet and opened it. Inside were rows and rows of dentures – some ivory, some porcelain, some made from animal bones, some carved and painted wood. Each pair was held together with wire, bonded to a piece of thin metal, with a set of springs on the end to allow them to open and close. Bowers took out a set that looked like a small wooden trap. Ren could see where the paint had dried across the perfectly straight and flattened teeth. They seemed much too large to fit inside anyone's mouth.

'That's nice work,' said Benjamin.

Bowers nodded, then reached inside the cabinet again and took out another set of dentures. It was clear, in an instant, that this set was made from real teeth. The color and shape were uneven, but the effect was much more natural-looking. 'Beautiful, aren't they? I have an arrangement with a man at a teaching hospital near North Umbrage.'

'North Umbrage.' Benjamin said the name as if he had been kicked in the chest. Ren knew at once that something was wrong. Bowers continued to chatter even as Benjamin stepped away, his face dimming.

'He sends me what's left when they're through with the dissections. Of course, these are much more expensive.'

Tom gave Benjamin a glance. 'Why is that?'

'The doctor has to pay the resurrection men. I believe the going rate is a hundred dollars a corpse.'

'A hundred dollars!' cried Tom.

'It's risky work.' Bowers put the dentures back in the case and shut the door. 'But you look like the kind that wouldn't mind a little danger.'

'For the right price,' said Tom.

Benjamin shook his head. 'That kind of job's not worth the trouble.'

'It's a lot of money, Benji,' said Tom.

'Not enough.'

Tom seemed bewildered. 'What are you afraid of?'

Benjamin glanced at Ren. He pressed his fingers against the tip of his nose, as if he were holding in a sneeze.

'The doctor needs someone reliable,' said Bowers. 'Someone who will make good choices and check the teeth first. A good body is always reflected in the teeth.'

Tom pulled Benjamin aside and began whispering furiously in his ear, but Benjamin paid no attention. He turned to the window and the sky outside – steel gray, threatening rain. He scratched the side of his face and Ren could read the hidden emotion there, something unfixed and undone.

Bowers was busy collecting the teeth again. He tied them up in the handkerchief and held them out in the air. Ren waited, and when no one else came forward, he snatched them from the dentist's hand.

'I can put you in touch with the doctor,' said Bowers, 'if you're interested.'

Benjamin turned away from the window. He stuffed his hands in his pockets and kept an eye on Ren, as if the boy would somehow decide things. 'We'll think about it.'

'Don't think too long.' The dentist took his place in the examination chair, pulled the table close, and removed the napkin from the remains of his breakfast. He lifted the bread and made a gesture, offering Ren a bite.

The purple jam shone on top. It smelled like berries and sugar, wonderful and sticky, but Ren shook his head and shrank back. Bowers seemed pleased and looked at Ren keenly with his blackened eye, as if he were making great plans for him. Then he tore the piece of toast in half, stuffed it into his mouth, and began to chew it apart. His dentures mashed together, as if they had their own mind.

'Teeth want to be lost,' he said. 'Don't give them an excuse to leave you.'

CHAPTER ELEVEN

A NOR'EASTER CAME through Granston a few weeks later. The harbor froze several feet deep, hard enough to walk across. The fishermen came out each morning and broke their boats free with pickaxes, then raised their sails in the snow and cast their nets and pulled their lobster traps from the water.

Ren spent most of his time in the basement, rereading *The Deerslayer*. Tom and Benjamin played cards or went out to the local saloon. In the middle of January Tom came down with the chickenpox. Ren had caught it years before at Saint Anthony's, and Benjamin said he had had it as a child, so Tom spent a month alone in bed, itching and moaning. Ren was glad of this, for Benjamin took him to the saloon instead, and taught him how to smoke a pipe, and gave him ale to drink, and together they would have a comfortable supper, and afterward Benjamin would tell stories.

Benjamin liked to talk about his supposed life as a sailor and all the places he'd traveled to over the years. He said that he'd crossed mighty rivers and deserts, volcanoes and mountains. And in these places he'd seen lizards and monkeys, cows with hairy udders and fish with three eyes. He spoke of the time he'd been sold as a slave in Morocco, and nearly eaten by cannibals in the South Seas, and how once he'd visited the harem of a Turkish prince and seen a thousand women dressed in solid gold.

Ren watched the other men in the bar, their mouths open, shifting their chairs closer to hear. They were mostly local fishermen and had tales of their own, about strange creatures they'd seen out on the water, and men cut in half by their own rigging. They displayed scars where hooks had gone through their bodies. And it was always at that point when Benjamin would call Ren forward and ask him to show the missing hand.

Sometimes Benjamin repeated the story of their mother and the Indian. Other times it was a lion who'd eaten Ren's hand, or a snapping turtle as he dangled his fingers in a stream. The fishermen did not seem to care which story was being told. They only laughed and passed Ren around the room so they could see. A few had their own missing parts – an ear gone from frostbite, a leg lost to a shark. An old weathered captain had a wooden hand, just as Mister Bowers had described, and he let Ren try it on, tying the straps across his shoulder. It was three times too big and hung heavy and strange at the end of Ren's arm, the fingers open and curved, ready to receive a shake.

When the stories were finished, the bartender would buy a round of drinks. Toasts were made. Ren's scar was celebrated. He held it up and the fishermen cheered. Across the room Benjamin raised his glass and smiled. The smile was different from the one he'd used on Father John and the farmer. His mouth was more relaxed, his eyes merry behind the grin. If Ren did not know any better, he would have believed that Benjamin had meant it.

★

By the time the winter was over and the snow had melted, Granston was soggy and damp, the streets full of mud. The snowdrops pushed their tiny white flowers from the ground and then the cherry trees blossomed in all their glory. The money from the stolen jewelry had been exhausted, and Benjamin said it was time to move on.

They followed the river out of town the following day. It was hard work for the mare. They'd found a stable close by to keep her for the winter, but she had not been exercised much. Ren had visited her every week, making sure she was fed properly and when he felt brave enough resting his head against her flank, listening to her giant heart. Now she toiled in front of the wagon on the warm spring day, carrying three people uphill. They rode all afternoon, stopping to eat in a field, then napping in the shade of the trees. It would be another day before they reached North Umbrage.

It had taken some time for Benjamin to change his mind about Mister Bowers's offer. Ren had heard the men whispering at night, Tom pressing for them to take the job, but Benjamin only said that North Umbrage was a place he would never go back to again. And then one afternoon in the basement, when Tom was nearly finished with his chickenpox, the last scabs peeling off his skin, the schoolteacher had opened a flask of whiskey to celebrate and asked Ren what he wanted to be when he grew up.

'I don't know,' said Ren, looking over from his book.

'You've never thought about it? Not once?' Tom asked. 'What about a fisherman, like those fellows you met at the bar?'

Benjamin was cleaning his boots at the table. He smeared a streak of black polish across a toe, then rubbed it in. 'Leave him alone.'

'Don't you think the little monster needs a profession?' Tom took another sip of whiskey. 'Maybe he doesn't want to spend the rest of his life living in a basement.'

'We won't be pulling these kinds of jobs forever.'

'You keep saying that,' said Tom, flicking away a bit of scab. 'But what we need is something to tide us over for a few years instead of a couple of months.'

This conversation was one they'd had before. But this time Benjamin stopped what he was doing and gazed at his half-polished shoes. They were old boots, the heels cracked and in need of repair. He looked at Ren. He looked at his shoes again. Then he walked across the floor in his socks and spent the afternoon sharing Tom's whiskey. Every once in a while he would turn to Ren in the corner, and each time the boy glanced back, Benjamin's face was more troubled.

When Ren woke the next day Benjamin was gone. He returned later that evening, smelling of tobacco, and said that he'd changed his mind about North Umbrage. The men began to make their plans, and Benjamin stopped going to the tavern. Instead he spent most of his time counting out figures, and visiting graveyards, and taking notes in a small black book he kept in his pocket. He disappeared for days from the basement, and when asked of his whereabouts answered simply, 'Research.' Ren had followed him once, crossing street after street through the marketplace before he saw him slip into a lawyer's office. When Benjamin came out, he was biting his nails, and then he stopped in the middle of the sidewalk and laughed, as if he'd just been told something he couldn't believe.

Ren watched him now, holding the reins tight, steering their cart around the ruts ahead. He kept his eyes forward and his pipe set firmly between his lips, puffs of smoke trailing behind them on the road.

Soon they came upon a valley between two hills, the pastures surrounding it covered with sheep. White and brown and black-faced animals stretched across the landscape. The wagon passed a group of farmers, washing their herds in the river to prepare them for shearing. The men gave directions to a nearby town. There the group found an inn, where they paid for a room with the last of their money. Inside, the floors were covered with dust, the beds stained with tobacco burns. Tom settled himself at the table and Benjamin began unpacking the trunk.

Ren sat quietly in a corner, rereading the last pages of his book. Deerslayer was refusing Judith Hutter's proposal of marriage. She had done all she could to make him love her, but it hadn't been enough. Ren had read the ending many times, and he still felt terrible about it. Hawkeye spent the entire novel fighting Indians and righting wrongs, but when he left Judith to her lonely fate, he always seemed less of a hero.

'There'll be a crowd tomorrow at the shearing.' Benjamin opened the wooden case and took out one of the brown bottles of Doctor Faust's Medical Salts for Pleasant Dreams.

'Someone might recognize us,' said Tom.

'Recognize me, you mean.'

'Does it matter?' Tom took off his coat and flung it onto the bed.

'We're out of money. And I've got an idea for using the boy.'

'You should leave him out of it.'

'He wants to do it. Don't you, Ren?'

Ren looked up from his book. He could see that Benjamin was itching for something new. Over the winter he'd told Ren about the jobs he'd pulled: impersonating sea captains, doctors, and men of the cloth; selling items from a catalog that would never arrive; forging wills and false deeds. They all followed a similar pattern: winning over the mark, a fast exchange of property, and then leaving town as quickly as possible. When they needed to stay in one place for a while, Benjamin and Tom turned to the graveyards, where the marks were more agreeable and did not take pains to pursue them.

Ren closed his book. 'I want to do it.'

Tom looked worried. 'I don't think he's ready for this.'

'Nonsense,' said Benjamin.

'He's only a child. He's going to get us caught.'

Benjamin sat down on the mattress, leaned back, and pulled the blankets over him. He closed his eyes and let out a puff of air. 'Not yet.'

That afternoon Benjamin went to find some supper and Tom and Ren set to changing the labels, from Doctor Faust's Medical Salts for Pleasant Dreams to Mother Jones's Elixir for Misbehaving Children. Ren soaked the old bottles and scraped the paper away with a knife while Tom set himself up at the table with pen and ink and wrote the new words out, taking a sip of whiskey between each finished piece.

Before they left Granston, Tom had trimmed his beard and purchased a new shirt. Now he tucked a napkin into the collar to keep it from getting stained and carefully pushed up his sleeves. The light from the candle flickered across his face. He appeared calm and nearly sober.

Ren could see that his penmanship was distinguished. The ends of the letters curled into patterns; his dashes and crosses fell in waves of varying thickness. When the labels were glued into place, they looked quite professional. Tom poured himself another drink and stretched his ink-stained fingers.

Ren leaned over the table, admiring the words. 'Why'd you stop teaching?'

Tom frowned. He ran a hand over his face, leaving streaks of black ink on his forehead. 'Do you have any fellows?'

'I used to,' Ren said. 'They were twins. Brom and Ichy.'

'And do you miss them?'

'Yes,' said Ren. As he said it, he knew it was true. He missed everything about the twins, from the way they made him laugh in chapel to their secret codes over dinner. He even missed the parts he'd always hated, like the way Brom would continue to punch him, even after he'd given up, and the way that Ichy liked to confess to things he hadn't done.

'It's a damned shame to lose your fellows.' Tom took another drink. There were tiny red scars on his arm, left over from the chickenpox. He pulled his sleeve down over them, then wiped his nose against the cuff. 'I had a fellow, once. We grew up together, and it was just as Aristotle said: "One soul, two bodies". A true friendship. You don't get many of those in this life, I can tell you now.

'We loved the same girl and asked her to choose between us. I was a teacher and didn't have much money; Christian had some land and an inheritance. So she got engaged to him. But she continued to meet me in the woods at night. And God help me, I would have done anything she asked.'

Tom lifted the whiskey to his lips and finished it, keeping the glass there for a moment, his teeth biting down on the edge.

'He shook my hand in church, smiling with her arm through his. And right under his nose, she still reeked of it, like a buttered bun. I had too much to drink one night and told him everything. I said, "Do you know what her skin tastes like?" I said, "Can you smell me on her fingers?" He took a pistol out of a drawer. He told me to stop talking. I said, "Don't you think we laughed at you?" He pointed the pistol at his own head then and screamed at me to stop, and I said, "Pull the trigger," and he did.'

Ren gripped the empty bottle of Doctor Faust's Medical Salts for Pleasant Dreams. He stared at the label so that he would not have to look at Tom. He knew from Brother Joseph that suicides were not laid to rest in the churchyard. They were buried at the crossroads, in unconsecrated ground, like Brom's and Ichy's mother. Their souls were sent to hell, and their ghosts turned into white rabbits that haunted the unmarked grave, startling horses and fooling travelers into taking the wrong path.

Tom's eyes were shut tight. He wiped his palm back and forth across his forehead, smearing the ink deeper into his skin.

'After that I stopped being a teacher.'

For a few moments they sat in silence. Ren watched Tom for a sign of what might happen next, a curse or a sob, but the schoolteacher simply rubbed his fingertips together, then began making marks across the table, a line of thumbprints, all in a row.

The boy went back to scraping the labels off, and Tom sighed and began to mix together Mother Jones's Elixir for Misbehaving Children. He used a funnel to fill the bottles with maple syrup, diluted opium, castor oil, and a bit of soured milk, until the consistency was light and sticky, with a tinge of brownness. He poured a tiny bit into a glass and handed it to Ren.

'Bottoms up.'

The boy sniffed the liquid, then stuck his tongue in. It tasted sweet and bitter at once.

'You'll have to be more convincing than that.'

Ren lifted the glass. The medicine took its time, sliding slowly along the edge of the cup like molasses. Only a drop fell into his mouth. It tasted terrible, but he swallowed it down. 'Now what?'

'Now,' said Tom, 'you have to be good.'

The next morning when Tom and Ren arrived at the shearing, it was well under way, the fields still damp with dew. Nearly one hundred men, women, and children were talking and milling about and inspecting each other's herds. Tables with food and drink were set up on the grass. Ribbons of different colors were tied to the trees and fence railings.

Ren looked over the people gathered and searched for Benjamin. He'd left before dawn, taking the wooden case with him.

'Remember,' Benjamin had said just before he closed the door, 'you aren't supposed to know who I am.'

Ren's boots were soaked through from crossing the field. The wet leather rubbed against his bare ankles. Tom stopped just outside the crowd, reached down, and took Ren's hand. It was strange, pretending to be father and son. They were both ill-suited for their roles. Ren's hair stuck out in all directions and the schoolteacher reeked of whiskey. Tom tightened his grip, and Ren looked up at him.

'No heroics,' he said. 'If something goes wrong, I want you to run.'

Ren nodded, and the man and the boy stepped into the

crowd. They passed the tables piled high with scones and muffins, a side of ham, a barrel of cider, and a smattering of cakes covered in sugar. As they moved closer to the shearing the smell changed to that of fresh manure and the heavy scent of wool.

The farmers took the sheep one at a time and tossed them onto their backs, then went to work with the hand clippers, starting at the head and making their way across the spine and down the sides, until the animal's coat came off in a single matted piece. The coat was then set apart, weighed, and examined, until its price was decided.

Bits of white filament floated in the air. The fingers of the shearers shone with lanolin, their leather aprons stained with it. As the day wore on and the sun grew high, a few took off their shirts and worked bare-chested, suspenders at their waists and kerchiefs tied around their necks.

The sheep waited behind a fence, watched their herd being shorn, and bleated. One by one the sheep were taken, thrown on their sides, and expertly cut. Afterward they looked naked and stunned. When they were released, the animals shook their heads and stumbled against each other in the grass, their steps wobbling, as if they had been reborn.

A contest began. A man in a vest and high boots and another with a scar along his cheek were timed against each other, their clippers flying, the sheep struggling in protest, the crowd cheering them on. When the men were finished they were covered in sweat and wool shavings. The judges inspected the fleeces, and declared the man with the scar the winner. Everyone cheered, and the next two competitors stepped forward. Nearby, a group of children climbed a tree to get a better view.

'Go on,' said Tom.

Ren left his side reluctantly and joined the other boys and girls. The children scrambled in the branches and chased each other round the trunk. Curious, a few eyed Ren as he walked over and stood next to the tree. On the other side of the field, Tom pointed at him and made slashing motions in the air. Ren wet his lips. He pulled his hand into a fist. Then he held his breath, walked up to a towheaded boy and punched him as hard as he could in the neck.

The boy fell to the ground, gasping and wheezing. The other children dropped from the tree and formed a circle around him. Ren's hand throbbed. He felt surprisingly good.

A boy in overalls stepped forward. 'What'd you do that for?'

'I don't know,' said Ren. 'Because I felt like it.'

They watched the boy struggling for air. A few of the children backed away, and a few came closer.

'Is he going to die?' one of the girls asked.

'No,' said another. 'But if he does, we know who did it.'

The boy in the overalls shoved Ren to the ground. 'How's this feel?' he said, then he started kicking. Ren tried to fight back, but the other children joined in, even the girls, so finally he just went limp, waiting for it to be over, feeling a sense of injustice all the while. He could make out the boy he'd punched, only a few feet away on the grass. The boy had recovered his strength and was now crawling over to spit on him.

'Get off,' said one of the farmers. 'I mean it, Charlie.'

'He started it,' the boy in the overalls said.

'I don't give a damn who did.' The children backed away, and the man took Ren by the coat and pulled him to his feet. He brushed some dirt from the boy's jacket, then hesitated. 'Jesus Christ.'

Ren pulled his scarred wrist back inside his sleeve. The other children hushed. He glared at them all, his face red.

'He lost his hand in a thresher,' Tom said, stepping forward. 'Ever since, he's always starting fights.'

'Well, he got this one finished for him, all right,' said the farmer.

'I'm sorry for the trouble.' Tom took Ren roughly by the arm. 'I just can't make him behave.'

'All that boy needs is some tonic.' Benjamin appeared, slipping out of the crowd, swinging the wooden case, and smiling. He set the case down, unbuckled the straps and pulled out a bottle. 'And I just happen to have some with me today. Mother Jones's Elixir for Misbehaving Children.'

'If it'll stop my boy from getting into trouble, I'll pay you five dollars for it,' said Tom.

'That's kind of you, friend,' said Benjamin. 'But it's only a dollar a bottle.'

'One dollar,' said Tom. 'That's a bargain.'

'It is,' said Benjamin.

Tom handed him a wrinkled dollar bill, and the tonic was passed over.

Ren's lip was split and his ribs ached. 'I'm not going to drink it.'

'If you don't, I'll tan your hide.'

The bottle was opened and put in his mouth, and Ren drank all of it, the thick liquid sliding down and nearly gagging him, sweet and sour. When he couldn't take any more, he wiped his mouth with the back of his sleeve, walked over to the boy he had punched in the neck, fell to his knees, and asked forgiveness.

'It's a miracle!' said Tom.

The farmers were not convinced. It was only when Ren started praying with a face of genuine gratitude, because the opium had lifted the pain from his ribs, that a few of the farmers' wives approached.

'Satisfaction guaranteed,' said Benjamin. Those seemed to be the magic words, for as soon as they came out of his mouth the first bottle sold, to the mother of the towheaded boy.

Once the medicine was administered, the children stopped fighting and chasing each other and climbing trees. They stopped roughhousing and spitting and stealing bits of food from the table. In fact, they stopped doing much of anything at all. They sat down in the grass, and stared off into space, and were silent.

'It's amazing,' said one of the mothers. She sniffed the bottle.

'Natural ingredients,' said Benjamin. He'd sold almost the entire case. The crowd had left the shearers and surrounded him instead.

Ren felt his eyes opening and closing against his will. His mouth was full of saliva, and it ran down the corners of his lips. He turned his head. Over to the side, near the edge of the field, there was a man. For a moment Ren thought it was Father John, and then he was sure of it, and then he thought he must be dreaming, because the man was smoking and Father John had never smoked. The man was watching Benjamin closely, and before he had finished his cigar he put it out on his boot and cut purposefully through the crowd.

'What do they call you?'

'Johnson,' said Benjamin. He held out his hand, but the man didn't take it.

'I've seen you before, but that wasn't the name.'

'It must have been someone else.'

The man spit on the ground. 'You calling me a liar?'

'Not at all.' Benjamin turned to the people gathered, to show his good intentions, but it was clear that this fellow was known to them and Benjamin was not.

'Where'd you see him, Jasper?' someone asked.

'On a poster in Galesburg,' said the man. 'He's wanted for armed robbery. I'm sure of it.'

One of the mothers screamed. The women elbowed past and rushed to their children, shaking and slapping the girls and boys and crying their names. Several men lunged forward. Benjamin threw the wooden case, knocking them down, then hopped the fence, fell to his hands and knees, and disappeared among the herd. The farmers called the rest of the men away from the shearing, and they started off in different directions with their shotguns, the sheep bleating in fear as they rushed past.

Tom took hold of Ren's hand and led him off at a strong pace, back to the wagon. 'Don't stop,' he said. 'Keep moving.'

Ren held on to his stomach. He pretended to be sick from the tonic. But in fact he was feeling wonderful. Better than he'd ever felt before. The grass was so green underneath their feet, it was as if he could fall into it and keep on falling forever.

'I told him,' said Tom. 'Didn't I tell him?'

Ren nodded, though he had no idea what Tom was saying. The wagon was right where they'd left it, between two trees. When the mare raised her head from grazing, Ren was certain he saw a look of disappointment in her eyes.

He was sorry for taking her away from the farmer, who had loved her so well and who had kissed her nose. And suddenly the boy thought, *I will kiss her nose*, and he tried to take hold of her bridle. Tom cursed him and told him to get in the cart. But Ren was determined to kiss the horse, just as she was determined not to be kissed by him. She swung her head from side to side and pointed her nose out of his reach. Ren got hold of the harness and pulled hard, leaning his weight, trying to bring the animal down to him. Tom was out of the wagon now, he was hitting the boy about the legs with the whip, but still Ren wouldn't let go, and the horse bucked, her hooves beating against the wood, until a shape rose from inside the wagon.

'Are you trying to get us killed?' Benjamin whispered. He was crouched behind the driver's seat, a fleece pulled over his head and shoulders. He looked so strange that Ren let go of the horse. Tom dragged the boy across the grass and threw him into the back of the cart.

'I have to kiss her,' Ren explained.

'Don't worry,' said Benjamin. 'You can kiss me instead.'

Tom pulled the wagon onto the road. He kept the horse going at a slow trot. The voices of the mothers began to fall away behind them. Occasionally there was a gunshot across the fields. When they were half a mile away, Tom made the horse pick up the pace. Ren watched the clouds pass over their heads, the shapes drifting in and out. As soon as he thought he'd recognized one, it changed.

'I think we're clear,' Tom said.

Benjamin crawled out from under the blankets. 'Thank God that's over.'

'Thank God they didn't catch us,' said Tom.

Benjamin took the fleece from his shoulders and threw it

aside. He gave a worried glance at Ren, who was flat on his back, seeing all kinds of things in the sky.

Tom shook his head. 'He's high as a kite.'

Benjamin began to search the pockets of his coachman's coat. He took the money and shook it under Tom's nose. Then he pulled out three oranges. The fruit was slightly bruised, the peel thick and heavy, but the color was perfect – cheerful and bright as the sun. Benjamin passed one over to Tom. 'You were right. But it was worth it.'

'I'm always right,' said Tom.

'Here.' Benjamin tossed an orange into the back of the wagon. It hit the boy in the head.

'Ouch,' said Ren. But he didn't move.

'Come on,' said Benjamin. 'Open your eyes.'

Ren thought they were open. He ran his fingers across his eyelids.

'Open your mouth.'

He did, and Benjamin fed him a slice of orange. The smell of citrus bloomed like a flower underneath Ren's nose. His tongue swelled as he brought his teeth together and the juice slid down his throat. He felt something hard, and bit down. *A seed*, Ren thought. *It must have been a seed.* Benjamin continued feeding him, separating the pieces, until the sky turned the same glorious color as the fruit and Ren's jaw ached with happiness.

PART 2

CHAPTER TWELVE

B Y THE TIME they crossed the bridge into North Umbrage it was dark. The houses rose up from behind a hill, the road narrowing between them. There was nothing of the chaos of the docks here. The streets were nearly deserted, and those people out were gathered on the corners, smoking and eyeing the wagon as they passed. Ren saw a pack of thin dogs fighting, and a man and a woman pushing against each other in an alley. The gutters smelled of rotting garbage. Tom took out a pistol and set it on the seat beside him.

It was the same gun that Benjamin had showed Ren on their way to Granston. Benjamin had seemed happy and relaxed in those days, but now he was pressed to the edge of his seat. He pulled the buttons on his collar and kept turning his head when they passed a window, as if he expected to find someone he knew behind the curtains.

The wagon jostled back and forth along the cobblestones. Up ahead, a large shadow covered the road. It went along the length of the street and shed a wall of blackness across the roofs and homes of North Umbrage. As the horse entered the air around them turned cold, and Ren lifted his head, expecting to see a giant towering over them. But instead he saw a factory, a building built like a fortress, straight up into the sky.

It was four stories, with a large, thick chimney spewing black smoke. The brick walls gave way on the second floor to enormous windows with bars across them. Carved over the main entrance, into the keystone of the arch, was a sign: MCGINTY MOUSETRAP FACTORY AND DISTRIBUTION CO.

'This is a cheery place,' said Tom.

'It used to be a mining town,' said Benjamin.

'I've never heard of it.'

'You wouldn't,' said Benjamin. 'There was an accident, and it nearly closed the place. A container of charges went off near the entrance, and all the men were buried. They never found the bodies, and the company sealed the tunnels and left. When I passed through here a while back, there were still women on their knees in the middle of the marketplace, with their ears to the ground, listening for their husbands.'

The wagon bumped the edge of the sidewalk and Ren thought of the men trapped in the earth along with all the other things people had thrown away over the years – rusted pots and pans and old boots and horseshoes and bits of broken china. The cart passed an ancient chestnut tree, and Ren imagined its roots reaching underneath the ground, sifting through everything there, just like the fingers of the miners' widows, going at the soil that held their men, with shovels and pickaxes, with others' wives and children, and with the farmers from the hills. The scene began to form in Ren's mind, the details coming one after another, until he could see the whole town digging, afraid of losing time – and then a whistle going out, and everyone stopping, listening. And after a few minutes one of the women crying: 'What are you waiting for?' And another saying: 'No! Just there now – there – did you hear that? There – there!'

Tom drove the cart down a street of boarded-up and abandoned houses. On the next street the buildings were raucous, with lights blazing, and the sound of smashing glass, and music pouring from the open windows. The wagon turned another corner, where everything was silent and dark, and then another, and then another and another. None of these homes had lights on. Then one of them did. There was a small wooden sign affixed to the gate out front, painted by hand: ROOMS TO LET.

'This is it,' said Benjamin. 'Stop here.'

'You sure?' Tom asked.

'Stay with the horse.' Benjamin climbed out of the back and Ren followed.

They knocked for some time before a woman came to answer. She was taller than Benjamin by at least a head and had broad shoulders, thick arms, and a very long, thin neck. Her face was middle-aged, with bright, quick eyes and a nose with one nostril larger than the other. Her hair was tucked away into a cap and she wore a coarse apron covering a brown dress. A ring of keys was tied to a thick leather belt around her waist.

'WHAT ARE YOU KNOCKING FOR?' she shouted.

'We're looking for a room,' said Benjamin.

'I DON'T OPEN THE PLACE TO STRANGERS.'

'My name is Benjamin Nab.' He held out his hand, using his smile. 'There, you see, I'm no longer a stranger.'

'MISTER NAB, I'M A HARDWORKING WOMAN WITH A HARD LIFE, AND I DON'T NEED THINGS ANY HARDER.' She showed the shotgun at her side. 'NOW, MOVE ALONG.'

Ren knew this was his cue to look pitiful, and he did, to the best of his ability, crouching a bit so he'd look smaller and rapidly blinking his eyes.

'I would,' said Benjamin, 'if it wasn't for my poor crippled nephew, who's just lost both his parents and traveled for miles to get here.'

Ren lifted his arm and waved the scar before the landlady's face, as if he were saying hello.

'His mother was tending a sick neighbor,' said Benjamin. 'Then she fell ill herself. Her husband watched over her night and day. He left his fields to rot. He sold everything they had for doctors. People said my sister's skin turned yellow – and her teeth went green. Then the boy's father became sick with it too, ranting and raving and licking the walls. I got word and hired my friend Tom here to drive me to their village, but they were already put in the earth when I arrived, leaving this poor orphan boy behind.' Benjamin removed his hat as he said this and held it over his heart.

Out of nowhere the landlady's teeth appeared. A long, thin set, with significant gaps, as crooked as any farmer's. 'AH,' she said, and sucked her lower lip, considering what she'd heard. Then she set aside the gun, scooped Ren into her arms, and shook him from side to side, as if she were attempting to finish him off. She was a tough creature, with a few proportionate soft spots, into which she now pushed Ren's face. She smelled like the yeast of rising bread – earthy and sour – and Ren was so confused that his body went limp. He gave himself over until he began to feel suffocated, and the landlady placed him on his feet again.

Benjamin signaled to Tom, who stepped down from the

wagon and led the horse to a small stable behind the house. 'We're so grateful to you. I don't know how much farther we could have gone along this road. And I'm just a young man on his own, and don't know much about taking care of children.'

'SURE YOU DON'T!' said the landlady. And she let them into the house. 'IT'S THREE DOLLARS A NIGHT FOR THE ROOM. A DOLLAR EACH FOR FOOD.'

'Very reasonable,' Benjamin said. But he made no move to pay.

The landlady took his coat and hung it in the closet. Benjamin thanked her and asked her name which she gave as Mrs Sands.

'And your husband, does he run this establishment?'

'MY HUSBAND'S DEAD AND BURIED IN THE MINE.'

'My dear, dear Mrs Sands.' Benjamin dropped to one knee, took the landlady's hand and held it between both of his. Mrs Sands stood perfectly still as he did this. Then Tom came through the door, his beard in tangles. As he shut the latch he dropped the revolver, then quickly snatched it up and shoved it down the front of his pants. The woman gave a snort and pulled away.

'SOME FRIENDS YOU'VE GOT, MISTER NAB.'

It was not long before they realized that Mrs Sands always shouted. There'd been an accident with a gun when she was girl, and afterward she could read what people were saying from their lips, but she couldn't hear herself talking back. She sent Benjamin and Tom to the washbasin upstairs. 'THERE'S A ROOM THERE YOU CAN USE FOR THE NIGHT. GO INTO THE CLOSET. THERE'LL BE SOME CLOTHES THAT SHOULD FIT THE BOY WELL. I'VE GOT A

FRIEND WHO USED TO HAVE A SON THIS AGE. SHE THOUGHT I MIGHT HAVE A CHILD SOMEDAY, SO SHE SENT ME ALL HIS THINGS AFTER HE DROWNED IN THE RIVER. A DROWNED BOY! AND THIS ONE SEEMS DROWNED TOO, DON'T YOU?' She held on to the tail of Ren's coat and pulled it up and down, then moved into the next room, dragging him behind.

As he walked into the kitchen Ren could smell something delicious – a large roast, smothered in gravy. It must have been cooked recently, although there was no sign of it on the table or counter, which were scrubbed clean, the pots shining, the plates all put away in the glass cupboard in the corner.

The room was mostly a fireplace – the largest Ren had ever seen. It went one length of the wall, and then, as if for good measure, rounded the corner and continued halfway down the next, an overlaying of bricks and shelves. Over the hearth hung a framed needlepoint of the Lord's Prayer, and underneath was a complex network of fire irons running back and forth with such a number of arms and kettles and pans that it seemed capable of stretching its claws, stepping out of the masonry, and taking a walk. At the center was a roaring fire made of half a dozen well-split logs.

From this mass of ironwork Mrs Sands dragged out a cauldron that was the size and shape of a fattened pig. 'I WAS HEATING THIS WATER FOR MYSELF,' she said, 'BUT IT WILL DO FOR YOU.'

Ren had never seen a pot so large, and before he knew it he was sitting inside, Mrs Sands having stripped him down, smacking his bottom when he hesitated stepping in. Now she pulled up a bench, settled herself, and took a knife to an enormous basket of potatoes. Ren could still smell the roast in the air and his stomach growled.

She said, 'WE NEED TO FATTEN YOU.'

Ren kept his stump tucked underneath his armpit, his legs crossed, and his knees pulled in tight. He knocked his elbow and the pot echoed with a bong. The inside of the cauldron was rough, the water only slightly warm.

Mrs Sands squinted at Ren, then reached into the pot and took hold of his left arm and examined the scar again. 'WHAT'S YOUR MUM'S NAME?'

Ren looked down into the water and pretended not to hear her.

'WHO'S YOUR FATHER?'

Ren shrugged his shoulders.

'DON'T ROLL YOUR ELBOWS AT ME.' Mrs Sands slapped at the water. 'AND DON'T PRETEND NOT TO KNOW THE THINGS THAT YOU DO.'

Ren sank halfway down into the pot.

'NOW,' she said, putting down her slick, half-peeled potato and leaning over until Ren could feel her breath on his cheek. 'IS THIS MISTER NAB YOUR UNCLE FOR SURE?'

Ren dug his nails into his stump and nodded his head.

'AND YOUR FOLKS ARE TRULY DEAD?'

Ren nodded at this more forcefully.

Mrs Sands squeezed the potato in her lap. The boy felt that he was done for. But just then Benjamin and Tom returned, with a set of the drowned boy's clothes.

Mrs Sands gave the men a suspicious look, then snatched the trousers from Tom's hand, inspected them for moth holes, and declared, 'THESE WILL DO FOR NOW.' She gestured to the fire, and Ren saw that his own clothes were on the logs. They were smoking and coming apart in the flames – orange strands sparkling in the dark. The boy watched the pieces unraveling and thought of when he'd first put them on – it was at least two years before – a gift from one of the grandmothers who scrubbed the orphans twice a month. Ren had been proud of the clothes, the stitches new in some places and the legs long. He had not realized they were bad enough to be burned. But there they were, smoking on the logs, and here he was, in a pot before the fire, watching them go, as naked as he could ever be.

Benjamin took a seat beside Mrs Sands on the bench. He asked her permission to remove his boots and when she nodded he put them next to the fire. He had thick woolen socks on with holes in the heels and toes, and they were sour with sweat. Ren could smell them from the pot. Tom stood by uncomfortably until Mrs Sands shouted for him to sit for God's sake, and she would find them something to eat.

From the kitchen she produced a loaf of brown bread, some sliced ham, a pitcher of milk and coffee. She set it on the table, handed a piece of bread and ham to the boy in the tub, and went back to peeling her potatoes. It had been nearly a day since they'd eaten, and the group tore into the food with a fury.

'WHERE'S YOUR HOME, MISTER NAB?'

'I've spent most of my life as a sailor. First on a merchant ship, sailing the East Indies, and then later I did some whaling. I'd still be out on the water if I hadn't heard about my sister's illness.'

'THAT'S DANGEROUS WORK.'

Benjamin slurped his coffee. 'And lonely.'

112

Tom rolled his eyes.

'AND YOUR FRIEND?'

'Unemployed,' said Tom.

'He's a schoolteacher,' said Benjamin.

'SOME TEACHER.'

Tom got to his feet. 'What do you mean?'

But Mrs Sands had her back to him, and so continued on, not hearing. 'A TEACHER SHOULD KNOW IT'S TOO LATE FOR A CHILD TO BE OUT. A TEACHER SHOULD KNOW NOT TO LET A BOY RUN ABOUT IN RAGS.'

'I'll tell you what,' said Tom, but he didn't finish the sentence. He just stared at the landlady, and then at his half-finished dinner, until finally he said, 'I'm going to bed.' He snatched his plate, put two more pieces of ham and bread upon it, and stomped away up the stairs.

'You'll have to forgive him,' said Benjamin. 'He used to be in love with my sister.'

'SHE WAS SMART NOT TO MARRY HIM.'

'I suppose she was,' said Benjamin, looking thoughtful and a little sad. He fished into his pocket for his pipe, and removed a stick from the fire to light it. Then he picked up a potato and took out his knife. He started peeling, and together with Mrs Sands went forth with the work, not speaking.

Ren was chilled and wanted another piece of bread, but he was afraid to break the silence or attempt to leave the cauldron without the approval of Mrs Sands. His toes were shriveling. One side of the pot was warmer, facing the fire, and he leaned his body against it.

Mrs Sands was watching Benjamin's face. In the firelight, with his shirt collar unbuttoned and hair pushed back, he looked younger than he was. When he finished the potato he was working on, Benjamin leaned forward and took a long pull from his pipe. The smoke smelled like sugar. Ren inhaled deeply. Then he watched as Benjamin lifted a fold of Mrs Sands's brown dress and slipped his fingers onto her knee. With his other hand Benjamin continued smoking his pipe, and Mrs Sands turned back to her potato, diligently removing the skin. A light pattern of red spread its way across her cheeks.

Ren rested his chin against the lip of the cauldron. The fire was beginning to die. The logs had caved in from the middle, blackened with ash. The boy's clothes were finished. There were only a few small scraps smoldering beneath the grate. He watched them until he couldn't bear it any longer, then held his breath and ducked under the water. He was submerged for only a moment before he heard a knock on the side of the cauldron. He raised his head, blinking against the bathwater. Benjamin still had a hand in Mrs Sands's skirts, but he was winking at Ren and motioning with his head toward the door.

'I need to get out,' Ren said. Mrs Sands looked up at him strangely. She closed her eyes, and then suddenly Benjamin had two hands again, and he was using them to pick up his boots.

Mrs Sands put her work aside and stood. She lifted Ren in one swift movement onto the hearth and began to rub the back of his neck with a small hand towel, as if she were angry with him. He was not prepared for the cold air. His skin rippled in goose bumps and his teeth chattered until Mrs Sands said, 'KEEP STILL!'

'You should be kind to him,' Benjamin said, 'or my sister will haunt us.'

Mrs Sands smacked Ren once with the towel, to make it clear that she was not afraid of ghosts. Then she pulled a wool undershirt over his head and forced his body into the clothes the men had brought.

He was smaller than the drowned boy. The trousers went past his feet and his arms were lost in the sleeves. Mrs Sands rolled up the cuffs, measured the collar with her finger, then yanked the clothes off. She jammed a nightdress over his head that was more like a blanket – fabric that itched and buttons to the neck and a hem that trailed behind him. She gathered the boy in her arms as if he were an infant and carried him up the stairs.

'HERE NOW,' said Mrs Sands, kicking open a door. It was a small space, with two beds pushed into the corners. Tom was snoring away in one, and Mrs Sands dumped Ren into the other. At Saint Anthony's Ren had often thought of a mother putting him to bed at night. But it was not anything like this. In his dream the mother was quiet and beautiful. She smoothed his hair and gently kissed his cheek. Mrs Sands pounded the pillows as if they had wronged her, and tucked Ren in so tightly he could barely breathe.

'WELL, DO YOU KNOW PRAYERS OR NOT?' Mrs Sands shouted at him.

This he could do. Ren pushed his way quickly through a decade of the rosary and a benediction for Mrs Sands for giving them shelter and for good measure his parents supposedly dead from the fever and his newfound 'uncle' Benjamin. This seemed to please Mrs Sands, although Ren noticed that she did not say the words along with him.

'Do you have any children?' Ren asked.

'GOOD GOD, NO. WHAT DO I NEED A CHILD FOR?'

'But your friend sent you the drowned boy's clothes.'

'SHE DID.' Mrs Sands gazed out the window, her face suddenly drained.

Ren huddled under the blankets. He felt that he had said something wrong. 'You would have been a good mother,' he offered.

'I'M NOT CERTAIN ABOUT THAT.' Her hands floated to her hair. She tucked a few stray curls back into her cap, then pinched him on the arm. 'BUT I FOUND A USE FOR THOSE OLD CLOTHES, DIDN'T I?'

'I guess so,' said Ren, rubbing the place where she'd pinched him.

'I hope you said my prayers too,' said Benjamin. He was standing in the door frame, his boots in his hand. He put the shoes in the closet, then started to remove his shirt.

All at once Mrs Sands seemed in a hurry. She put the key on top of the dresser and stepped out of the room. Then she burst back through the doorway with a pile of towels and left them on the bureau. A few moments later she returned with three extra pillows and threw them into the rocking chair in the corner. Then she came in once more with a mountain of blankets – crocheted and knitted and patchworks of quilts – all of which she dumped on top of Ren's head.

'GOOD NIGHT,' she shouted.

'Good night,' said Benjamin, and turned the lock when she was gone.

'How long do we have to stay here?' Ren asked, pushing aside the blankets.

Benjamin slipped off his suspenders. 'For now.'

'I don't like her.'

'Really?' Benjamin said. 'I thought you were in love with her.'

'I thought *you* were.'

'I was just making her happy a little.'

Ren imagined night after night of tub washings. He kicked the base of the bed and something heavy fell onto the floor. Benjamin leaned over and lifted it with his hand. It was a hot water bottle, made of thick brown pottery and stopped with a cork.

Ren had always dreamed of having one.

'Can I fill it?' he asked.

'Suit yourself,' said Benjamin. 'But don't wake Mrs Sands.'

Ren slipped out of bed and, after unlocking the door, made his way cautiously down the stairs, the hot water bottle under his arm and the long hem of the nightgown clutched in his fingers. In the kitchen the fire was finished, nothing but small bits of cinder in the dark. Ren quickly filled the hot water bottle from the cauldron, then pushed it into the embers. The stones of the hearth were still warm, and the boy rubbed his feet against them. He looked over the tidy kitchen, the shiny copper pots hanging from the wall, the painted pineapples along the edge of the molding, the wood stacked neatly in a basket. It felt like a real home, the kind he'd always imagined.

On a table beside the fireplace was a tray covered with a napkin. Ren peeked under a corner and discovered a complete meal – not the simple bread and ham served earlier, but sliced beef with potatoes and carrots and gravy. The same roast Ren had smelled cooking when he'd first walked into the kitchen. There was a fork and knife beside it, and a mug filled with beer. And an apple. And also a small piece of cake.

The boy's mouth watered. The cake, the perfect slice of it,

was lying on its side, just waiting for him to reach forward and stuff it into his mouth. He could not get his teeth to work fast enough to get it down, the taste of lemon and sugar and poppy seeds melting on his tongue. He brushed the crumbs from the plate and covered the tray again with the napkin.

As soon as he had done this, Ren began to worry. Mrs Sands would certainly know that he had eaten the cake. He held his breath, expecting the landlady to come around the corner. But a moment went by, and then another, and Mrs Sands did not appear.

A bit of soot began to sprinkle down from the chimney into the fireplace. Ren could hear a scraping noise. Something was caught inside the flue – a bird, or perhaps a squirrel. At Saint Anthony's when it was cold birds would fall down the chimney, drawn in by the heat. Then they would dart around the kitchen, and usually spent the rest of the day throwing themselves against the windows. Whatever creature was traveling through Mrs Sands's chimney was taking its time, and the boy realized after a few minutes that it must be climbing down. His heart beat quickly, and the scratching stopped, as if the creature inside the chimney had heard it.

Ren crouched down and looked. About halfway up the flue there was a man, propping himself with his legs and shoulders. He slid his heels against the brick, first one, and then the other, sending a cloud of black dust onto Ren's face. The boy stepped away and tried not to sneeze. He covered his nose with the edge of the nightgown and held it tight. He looked about frantically for a place to hide and slipped into the potato basket. A few small roots had been left in the bottom, and the boy could feel them pressing into his knees.

A leg dangled from the chimney. Then another. The feet

kicked aside the logs and ashes and the final remnants of Ren's clothes. The man untied a rope that was fastened to his belt and bent over, his hands on the floor as he crawled out of the fireplace. Then he stood, brushing off his coat and shaking his legs. He was no more than four feet tall.

It was as if he had been made from other people, none of whom were originally the same size. His head was too large for his body. His feet too small. His arms were long and powerful, but his legs were short. His eyes were dark and sloped down at the corners, while his brows went in the opposite direction, giving him a clever look. His hair was black and shiny, along with his beard, which was neatly trimmed around his jaw.

The small man walked over to the table, lifted the napkin off the tray, and began eating what was left of the meal. When he was through, a jackknife appeared from under his sleeve and he cut the apple into pieces. He smacked his lips and ground his teeth, using all the effort of his tongue and jaw. Ren imagined it was the same way the man would eat a person, if given the chance.

The dwarf set the apple core next to the fireplace. Then he took off his boots and removed his socks. They were made of soft checkered wool and full of ashes. He shook them and Ren saw clouds appear – tiny, dark explosions of soot. The socks were placed next to the apple core. Then his coat came off. Then his shirt. Then his trousers. Ren saw his humped, misshapen body for an instant before he climbed into the pot. The water splashed and echoed in the empty room as the man washed, rinsed himself, and came out. Ren saw him plainly now – strong arms over a curved spine and a tiny dangling penis no bigger than his own. The dwarf took the same towel Mrs Sands had used on

Ren and rubbed it quickly over his back and down each of his legs before slipping back into his clothes.

On a table beside the fireplace was a pair of clean, mended socks. Ren caught a glance of the dwarf's knobby feet before they disappeared into the new socks and then into boots. When the small man was finished tying the laces, he crawled back into the fireplace, wrapped the rope around his waist again and began to climb. His rumbling echoed in the hollow of the chimney as he rose, then grew quieter halfway up the flue. Ren peeked over the edge of the basket. The dwarf had left his dirty socks. He had left his apple core. He had also left a small wooden horse.

The boy pushed the potatoes aside and climbed out. The horse fit in the palm of his hand. It had been cut from a wood knot – he could see where the branch had started to grow – the burr was twisted where the saddle should have been. There were delicate cuts on the legs for hooves. There were tiny holes for the nostrils and careful lines carved to show the movement of the tail.

Ren took up the hot water bottle, brushed the ashes off with his nightgown, and tucked it into the crook of his elbow. It was warm and heavy, and the boy wrapped his body instinctively around it. Overhead, the scratching in the chimney was muffled. There was the sound of a kick. Ren got to his knees in the fireplace and peered up into the darkness. He couldn't see anything. And then he saw the night and the stars.

CHAPTER THIRTEEN

IT WAS BARELY dawn, the sky outside still dark. Ren's shoulder itched. He could feel the woolen nightgown tangled about his legs. He was half-asleep, and just beginning to realize that he was in a real bed, not wrapped in a blanket on the cellar floor, when he heard a banging right outside the window. Ren bolted out of the sheets and rushed over to look. Mrs Sands was down below on the sidewalk, clutching a bin and a tiny metal broom, dumping ashes from the fireplace into the street. She hit the back of the bin with another bang, and one last final cloud of gray smoke filtered out and into the air around her.

She was wearing an apron and a deep purple shift with the sleeves rolled to her elbows. On her head was the same cap she'd worn the night before. It was clear that Mrs Sands had been up for hours, scrubbing her house. Ren looked at her face as she tucked the bin and broom beneath her arm and glared at the clouds. The expression was hard, as if she expected someone to start throwing things at her.

Across the room Tom let out a snort. Benjamin rolled to the side and pulled the quilt over his head. The room had seemed cold and friendless to Ren the night before, but now, in the morning light, he could tell that it was well-kept. The floor was oiled; the rugs faded in places from the sun, but clean. The bureaus were covered with crocheted doilies, and the mirrors were polished and free of dust. On one wall there was a quilt sampler. On the other hung a bouquet of wildflowers, pressed under glass and framed. And on the far wall was a shelf, with only one book on it – a King James Bible.

Ren heard a pair of footsteps go by the door. He ran over and pressed his eye against the keyhole, but all he caught was a blur and a thundering of boots on the stairs. A stream of air blew in, making him blink, and as he drew away he could smell the greasy scent of bacon.

Ren tried the lock. There was a click, and then he was through. Outside he found the drowned boy's clothes, folded and waiting in a basket. They had been mended – the trousers turned and hemmed, the waist taken in, the sleeves shortened. Ren pulled the nightgown over his head and tried them on. The clothes were now exactly his size. The inside of the jacket was lined, the buttons polished. The cuffs of the shirt were finished, and the trousers had pockets without any holes. Ren slipped his hand inside and pulled out a handkerchief, ironed into a perfect square.

These were not the short pants and tattered coat of an orphan. They were the clothes of a man. Ren spread his arms out, his fingers stretching at the end of one sleeve, his stump peeking out of the other. The fabric fell straight and true, a clean line right past his shoulders. Mrs Sands must have been up most of the night tailoring the fit. Ren turned the cuff and looked at her stitches – they were perfectly proportioned, even, and true. He felt a rush of delight. No one had ever done anything like this for him before.

There were voices coming from the kitchen. Ren made his way to the staircase, his hand pressed against the wall. On the last step he paused and listened.

'GET YOUR FINGERS OUT OF THERE.'

A highly pitched set of giggles burst forth from inside the kitchen, making it clear that Mrs Sands and her shouting were of no consequence to the gigglers. Ren turned the corner, and that's when he saw them – four girls lined up on the bench – plain, plain, plain, plain. They all wore heavy boots and the same coarse dress of navy blue. One of them had a harelip.

'I didn't touch anything,' said the girl with the harelip. Behind her back she was holding a piece of bacon. The grease was staining her dress, a small circle of widening darkness.

'YOU'RE THE WORST OF THEM ALL,' said Mrs Sands, and clapped the girl once on the ear. The girl went down, her hands coming out to stop the fall. She landed on the floor and the bacon broke in two and Mrs Sands snatched the pieces up like a bird. The landlady grimaced, showing her crooked teeth, and cleaned the meat with the skirt of her apron.

The girl touched her head where it had hit the edge of the bench. The corners of her mouth turned around her harelip. She held her fingertips up. 'No blood this morning,' the girl said. 'You're slipping, Mrs Sands.'

Everything stilled for a moment. Then Mrs Sands began to cough – *hengh, hengh, hengh* – and the rest of the girls on the bench burst into laughter, as if they had been holding it in for years. The girls banged their heels into the floor and howled as the girl with the harelip rose to her feet. Mrs Sands turned and laid the bacon carefully on a plate. It wasn't until she wiped her eyes that Ren realized she was laughing too.

'HUSH!' she said. 'YOU'LL WAKE EVERYONE!'

'They should be awake already,' said the Harelip. 'Honest people don't sleep in the morning.'

One of the girls on the bench, with long brown hair and a gap between her front teeth, saw Ren hiding behind the door. 'Who's that?'

'THAT'S OUR NEW DROWNED BOY!' said Mrs Sands. She walked over and took hold of Ren's collar and dragged him into the room.

'Why didn't you tell us about him?' asked the Harelip.

'IT'S NOT MY BUSINESS TO TELL ANYONE ANYTHING!' Mrs Sands said, and she suddenly picked up Ren as before and held him to her, squeezing hard. Then she dropped him to the floor, twisted his ear between her fingers, and used it to lead him into a chair.

'YOU SLEEP WELL IN THAT OLD BED?' she asked.

'Yes,' said Ren. 'But there was something in the chimney.'

Mrs Sands paused, as if she was giving this information time enough to leave the room. Then she shouted, 'YOU HUNGRY THEN, BOY?' Ren said yes he was, and it was only a moment before Mrs Sands pushed a plate in front of him, full of eggs and butter and bacon and bread.

Ren forgot all about the dwarf. He tucked a napkin into his collar and ate everything in front of him. He finished the bacon and Mrs Sands added more. He ate all of the bread and she followed it with muffins. He licked the last piece of yellow from his spoon and she had another soft-boiled egg cracked, the shell peeling off from the pure white jelly with the fresh smell of vinegar and salt.

The girls watched this happen silently from the bench, swinging their boots. The one with the gap in her teeth rolled her eyes, and the Harelip caught Ren looking and stuck out her tongue. It was bright red-pink, mirroring the turn of skin above it. Ren could not look away, and when he didn't, she blew him a kiss.

'Is there any water?' Benjamin stood in the doorway, half-dressed. His hair was loose, his eyes shot with red.

Mrs Sands's cheeks colored. She quickly drew a basin from underneath the counter and began to fill it from a pail. Benjamin walked over to the table and put his face in the bucket instead. He rested there for a moment, bubbles coming up beside his ears, and then he threw his head back and shook it like a dog. Mrs Sands began to cough.

The girl with the gap in her teeth elbowed the girl with the harelip, who stared at Benjamin as the water soaked his shirt, running down his chest and shoulders.

'Who do you think you are?' said the Harelip.

Benjamin walked over to the bench and stood before the girls. He buttoned his shirt, then slipped his suspenders on. 'I believe,' he said, 'I'm your neighbor.'

Mrs Sands began rolling dough on the counter, sprinkling flour and pressing her weight rhythmically into the wooden pin. Ren leaned his head against the back of the chair and watched her, as if he had done this a hundred mornings. At the other end of the room the girls let out another torrent of giggles while Benjamin introduced himself. Mrs Sands slapped the dough harder against the counter.

A loud clanging of a bell sounded – followed by another, of higher pitch. The girls tore up from the bench, reaching for their shawls, holding them above their heads like sails before bringing them down and tying the corners around their necks.

'We'll see you at supper,' the Harelip said, looking back over her shoulder at Benjamin. A moment later they were all gone, the kitchen door banged shut.

'Who are they?' Ren asked.

'MOUSETRAPPERS,' said Mrs Sands, and threw another mound of dough on top of the first. She motioned with her head to the corner of the room. On the floor was a small wooden container. When Ren crouched down he could smell the freshly cut wood. In the side there was a circular opening, covered with a piece of tin. It was hinged one way, like the door in the gate at Saint Anthony's. Ren reached out with his finger and pushed it open. The box shuddered, suddenly coming to life, and the boy drew his finger back quickly. He could hear the mouse scratching on the other side of the door.

'THEY WORK FOR MCGINTY,' said Mrs Sands. 'HE BOUGHT UP THE LAND AFTER THE MINE CLOSED AND BUILT THE MOUSETRAP FACTORY.'

Benjamin took a toothpick from the table, slipped the wooden point in his mouth and bit down. 'I've heard about him.'

'THEN YOU KNOW WHAT HE'S DONE TO THE PLACE.' Mrs Sands rubbed the flour from her hands. 'WE WERE GLAD AT FIRST. WE NEEDED THE WORK AND THE MONEY. BUT HE BROUGHT THOSE GIRLS WITH HIM. UGLY GIRLS WITH NO HUSBANDS AND NO HOMES. HE PAYS THEM CHEAP AND KEEPS THEM WORKING AT THE FACTORY ALL DAY AND ALL NIGHT. MOST EVERYONE DECENT IN THIS TOWN HAS LEFT. BUT I WAS BORN HERE, AND MY

HUSBAND'S BURIED HERE, AND I'VE NOWHERE ELSE TO GO.'

Mrs Sands coughed into her apron. Then she set her mouth and returned to her pies, lifting a sheet of dough and stretching it gently across a plate. The air smelled like flour and water and salt. Ren watched as the landlady used her hands to press the dough into place, a knife to cut it to size, and a fork to poke holes across the bottom. She filled the shell with some kind of meat and covered it all with another sheet of dough and sealed the two crusts together, tucking around the edge with a twist, making a pattern. There was no hesitation in her fingers.

Ren left his chair and walked over to the table where she was working. He reached out and touched her flour-covered hand. 'Thank you for fixing these clothes for me,' he said.

Mrs Sands looked at the place where Ren's hand covered hers. She pressed her lips together and raised her head. Her face seemed on the verge of breaking, and then, just as suddenly, it cleared. 'I WAS GLAD TO DO IT FOR YOU.' She reached over and straightened the jacket on his shoulders, admiring her work, then sighed and took a rag to wipe away the flour left behind.

'I SUPPOSE SOME PEOPLE ARE MEANT TO BE DROWNED.'

'Maybe the boy deserved it,' Ren offered.

'WHAT ARE YOU SAYING?'

'That God was punishing him.'

'GOD'S TOO BUSY TO GO AROUND PUNISHING LITTLE BOYS.' She tapped Ren on the shoulder as if he should have known this already, and with that she went back to her pie-making.

All this time Benjamin sat at the kitchen table and watched them, rolling the toothpick back and forth with his tongue. He bit down on the sliver of wood and said, 'This McGinty, does he have any family?'

Mrs Sands lifted more dough and slapped it down on the counter. 'NONE THAT I KNOW OF. HE USED TO HAVE A SISTER.'

Ren saw Benjamin's interest rise. This always happened, before they started a job, and Ren wondered if McGinty's sister would be their next target. He got the feeling that Benjamin knew more than he was showing. 'What happened to her?'

'HE SENT HER AWAY SOMEWHERE. THEY SAID SHE'D LOST HER MIND. I WOULD TOO, WITH A BROTHER LIKE THAT.'

Benjamin ran his fingers through his hair and stared thoughtfully into his mug of coffee. Footsteps sounded on the stairs and Tom appeared, his shirt undone. Mrs Sands took one look in his direction and pointed at the bucket on the table. Tom splashed his face and ended up spilling most of the water on the floor. Mrs Sands took a mop from a closet nearby and handed it to him.

'I'M A LANDLADY, NOT A MAID.'

When she turned her back Tom let out a string of curses but remained in place, wiping the floor until the food was served. Mrs Sands put a plate of eggs and bacon in front of each of the men. She toasted some bread on the stove and piled it into a basket. Once Benjamin and Tom were taken care of, Mrs Sands took her pies over to the oven and slid them onto a rack. Ren could see the white pastry, shining for a moment as she shut the door.

He realized then that Mrs Sands already knew about the

dwarf in the chimney. She had put out the meal for him. She had mended his socks. The toy horse must have been left for her. Ren slid his hand into his coat and touched the horse with the tip of his finger. The wood was polished and smooth.

The only toy he'd ever owned was a broken tin soldier, swiped from one of the charitable grandmothers when he was not much older than five or six. He'd shared the toy with Brom and Ichy for nearly a year. Its face had been chewed away and it was missing a leg and its rifle, but the boys had spent countless hours re-creating its battles and fashioning substitute appendages. Then Ichy lost it down the well. The boys had mourned the soldier for months, even marking his years into the base of the well as a record of their time with him.

Ren felt guilty for stealing from Mrs Sands, but he did not want to part with the horse.

'Are you ready?' Benjamin was putting on his coat.

Ren was not sure what he was supposed to be ready for, but he nodded and stood up from his chair as Tom snatched an extra piece of bread from the table.

'YOU OWE ME SIX DOLLARS.'

'And we're certainly going to pay you,' Benjamin said. He put a hand on her shoulder, then slid it down to her waist.

She stepped back. 'IT HAS TO BE TODAY.' Mrs Sands held on to the basin Benjamin hadn't used, as if she were about to knock him senseless with it. Tom moved over to the door, one hand holding the bread, the other on the gun stuffed into his belt.

Benjamin took the bowl away from her. He set it on the counter. 'Today.'

'SHOULD I SEE YOU FOR SUPPER?'

'Yes,' said Benjamin. 'You'll see all of us.' He took hold of Ren by his sleeve, and before she could say anything else, they were gone.

CHAPTER FOURTEEN

NORTH UMBRAGE LOOKED different in the daylight. The empty buildings they'd passed the night before had been transformed into shops. Blacksmiths and potters, fruit stands and handkerchief stalls. All of them were run by women. There was a woman baker with loaves of bread on the shelves, the scent of rising dough spilling out the window. There was a woman blacksmith, a horse's foot between her knees, children working the bellows behind her. There was a woman butcher, her sleeves rolled up past her elbows and her apron covered with blood. There was even a woman garbage collector, her donkey cart full of rotting vegetables and torn rags and broken crockery, followed by a small herd of pigs.

Benjamin took the wagon past the mousetrap factory. Now that it was morning, Ren could see the intricate red brickwork, the smoke churning black against the sky. The place made Ren feel strange, and a little queasy, and he was glad when Benjamin turned the horse toward the bridge leading out of town.

The overpass was well-used, lined with sand and stone and marked with two gulleys from a century of crossings over. Gathered on either side were a few groups of old men. Some with rods, on their way to fish. Some smoking. Others leaning back and appraising the horse's worth.

It was another mile before they entered the woods, the grass and bushes slowly building up on either side. In the distance Ren could make out the corner of the hospital. It looked just as the dentist had described it, with thick stone walls and one lonely turret, like a castle out on its own. The men were in high spirits as they drew closer. Benjamin hummed a tune as the cart bumped along, and Tom chewed a bit of tobacco. Ren tried to join in the good feeling, but he grew nervous as they approached the gate. 'What am I supposed to do when we get there?'

'Just ask for Doctor Milton,' said Benjamin. 'You're supposed to be his patient.'

'Why do *I* have to go?'

'He thinks you'll make it safe. He's had trouble before.' Benjamin took hold of the boy's shoulder. 'This could be our ticket. Don't disappoint me.'

Ren forced himself to climb down from the cart. He wanted to please Benjamin, but he had never done a job by himself before. He stayed by the front wheel, holding on to the spokes, hoping one of the men would change his mind and trade places with him.

'We'll wait for you down the road,' said Tom, and the wheels began to turn, pulling the spoke from Ren's hand. He watched the wagon make its way under the trees and disappear. Then he turned to face the hospital.

The foundation of the building was made of granite. There were three sets of gates – entry to the yard, entry to the inner yard, and entry to the hospital itself. The boy was not sure where to begin. He touched the wall of the building. It was cold. He circled twice before finding the bell. When he rang, it was heavy and reverberating, as if the noise was not meant to announce visitors but to frighten the ringer off. Soon after a nun appeared. Ren could see her beyond the first two gates, weaving her way through the ironwork with a bedpan, going about her task with a grim look.

'Sister!' Ren shouted.

The nun banged her bedpan against the inner wall. 'Who's there?' she asked with impatience, then walked up closer to the fence and stopped. She was about fifty years old, her nose and chin pointed, her eyes so dark and heavy that her iris and pupil seemed one.

Ren pushed back his sleeve and lifted his scar. 'Doctor Milton said he could help me.'

The nun stared at Ren's arm, then at his face, then at his arm again. 'God be praised,' she said quietly. Something passed over her features for a moment, then her expression slid back to the same uninviting look. She tucked the bedpan under her arm and unlocked the gate.

'You're very early,' she said. 'He's still in surgery.'

She showed him inside the building and past a series of large rooms. The beds were pushed in side by side, and in some places there were mattresses right on the ground, spilling into the hallway. Ren tried to hold his breath. The building smelled like stale smoke and boiled meat. In the corners there were bedpans overflowing.

The patients wore nightgowns. Thick heavy woolens not unlike what Mrs Sands had dressed Ren in after his bath. A few glanced up as he passed, but most were asleep, their arms or legs wrapped in layers of bandages. One man reached for the boy and caught hold of his trousers.

'I need water,' the man said. His head was shaved, and there were scabs on his arms.

'I'll see that you get some,' said the nun. 'Now, let him go.'

The man obeyed and sank back into the blankets. The nun took Ren by the shoulder and moved him toward the stairs.

She was a Sister of Mercy. Ren knew from the gray color of her dress. Brother Joseph's cousin, also a Sister of Mercy, had visited them once at Saint Anthony's. Her name was Sister Sarah, and she had stayed with them only five days, but within that time she had rid the small boys' room of its fishy smell. All of the children's bedding was taken outside and beaten in the sunlight. The floors were scrubbed with carbolic acid. She set the boys sewing each child a new pair of underwear, and provided the linen and needles herself. When she left, many of the children had cried. It took a full week for the oiliness to return, and Ren remembered going to bed those nights before it came and inhaling deeply into his pillow.

'How did you lose your hand?' the nun asked.

'I don't remember.'

The nun frowned, as if the answer did not satisfy her, and pointed to a bench in the corner. Ren took a seat and watched as she hurried behind a door at the end of the hall, the edges of her habit lightly bouncing with each step.

Ren swung his feet back and forth and looked up and down the hallway. The walls were decorated with portraits of aristocrats, men and women posing with their hunting dogs or standing beside windows that looked out on their country estates. Only one portrait was markedly different. It showed a man in a well-made but slightly rumpled jacket, seated at a desk piled with books. Behind him on a shelf was a frog in a glass jar, a stuffed bird of some kind, and the unmistakable shape of a human skull. The man in the portrait was touching his chin, posed in the middle of some illuminating thought.

Ren tried to imagine what this thought could be. He guessed that it was scientific in nature, but the more Ren studied the portrait, the more he realized that the man didn't look intelligent at all. He looked hungry. He was probably thinking of sausages, and Ren was nearly decided on this when a scream came from down the hall. The boy jumped out of his seat. Another scream came. And then another.

At first the screams were pleading. Ren could make out words. '*Stop! Leave it on! Please!*' the voice begged. It called someone a murderer, and then it gave up and simply shrieked, over and over, until Ren couldn't take it anymore – he put his hand over one ear and pressed his stump against the other and hummed and hummed until his lips felt numb. The voice in the other room grew hoarse and then it simply moaned and then it stopped completely.

Ren lowered his arms. He considered trying to find a way out of the building. But before he could make up his mind, the doors opened and a large basket came down the corridor. Four men were carrying it, their jackets off and their sleeves rolled up. Inside was a pale man, the lower half of him covered with bandages, blood soaking through and onto the basket, staining the pattern of the reeds. Ren leaned slightly forward to get a look at the patient's face. It was caved-in, as if all the screaming had pulled the flesh from his bones.

The nun came behind, holding the man's leg. It was wrapped

in a sheet and she was cradling it in her two arms like a baby. Blood was dripping from the cloth in a steady stream, making thin lines across her apron as she walked past.

Ren dropped back onto the bench.

'I told him you were here.' The nun said this without stopping or turning her head or losing her grip on the leg. Then she followed the basket down the stairs.

A crowd of young doctors now burst forth, carrying books and papers. They wore suits with vests and matching topcoats, cuff links and pocket watches and shiny shoes. One opened a small silver case and pinched a bit of snuff. Another removed his gold-rimmed glasses and rubbed them with a piece of chamois. A few glanced at Ren as they passed, and the boy felt suddenly awkward in his drowned-boy clothes. Some disappeared along the corridor, and others went downstairs. Then the hall was empty and it was quiet again.

'Boy!' A voice came from the room.

Ren stood. He put his hand on the banister. He wanted to run down the stairs, but the thought of failing Benjamin stopped him. Ren took a few steps toward the voice, then followed the narrow trail of blood to the room that everyone had left.

As he turned the corner, he was surprised by the amount of light. There were windows in the ceiling – the roof above had been dismantled and replaced with thick panes of glass. It was designed for an assembly. Benches surrounded a central raised platform, and on that platform, wiping down a bone saw with an oiled cloth, was the man from the portrait in the hall.

He was a bit different from the painting. Ren could see that he was older. His eyebrows were bushy, his hair thick and gray. But Doctor Milton's forehead was unmistakable, bulbous and oddly formed, and his expression held the same hunger for sausages as the man on the canvas, even as he spit into the cloth and scrubbed away at a spot of dried blood.

'From now on you come at ten. Once a week. A regular appointment.' The doctor's suit was impeccably tidy. There was only one stain, in the shape of a butterfly, on one of the sleeves. Doctor Milton finished cleaning the saw, then set it carefully on the table. 'Come here.'

Ren walked down the row of benches and climbed onto the stage. Doctor Milton looked the boy over, then lifted Ren onto the edge of the operating table. It gave Ren a strange sense of vertigo; as if he were balanced on the edge of a cliff. He gripped the corner. There was sawdust there and it stuck to his fingers.

The doctor bent close. His beard smelled of tobacco. 'Your job is going to be doing what you're told. Exactly. Do you think you can do that?'

Ren nodded.

'Good boy.' Doctor Milton picked up a knife. 'See the way the end is hooked? That's to make it easier to cut around the veins.' He wiped the blade with the cloth, then handed it to Ren. 'Now,' he said. 'Put it back.'

The knife had a smooth and solid weight. Across the table was an open wooden case, a multitude of shining silver instruments inside. Two interior tool trays had been removed and set to the left. Each apparatus had a designated spot. There were indentations in green velveteen, dozens of empty places. The boy could feel his palm start to sweat, the handle sliding against his fingers. At last he saw where it should go – in one of the trays, beneath the bone saw. The velvet had been worn away by the hook.

He set it down and Doctor Milton looked pleased. His eyes traveled over the boy, and when they rested on the scar, he gave a small grunt of surprise. Doctor Milton studied the arm, turning it this way and that. 'The cut is crude, but the arteries were clamped off early. Whoever did this knew what they were doing. You're a lucky boy. Say it.'

'I'm lucky.'

Doctor Milton pinched a bit of skin. 'I got my first training doing amputations. I'm always curious to see how the skin regenerates in these situations.' He removed a small scalpel from the instrument case. 'Would you mind if I take a sample?'

Before Ren could answer, the doctor was dabbing a bit of cloth in water and cleaning the tip of the boy's arm. 'You'll only feel a pinch.' As he said this, he cut. The knife went right through the scar and sliced a thin sliver of tissue from the top. It happened so quickly that the boy didn't realize what had happened until the skin was already lifted away.

Ren clapped his hand over the cut. It wasn't deep, but it hurt. Doctor Milton took the skin with a pair of tweezers and set it in a small glass dish, then carried the sample over to a microscope, as if he had just peeled a piece of bark from a tree. He put his eye to the microscope and began adjusting the knobs.

'Normal skin looks like scales,' Doctor Milton said. 'Precise, interlocking pieces. But scar tissue is different. There are no hair follicles or sweat glands.' He motioned for Ren to come closer, and then stepped aside so that the boy could look.

Ren leaned forward, still holding his arm. He couldn't see anything at first. Just a bit of light. The magnification made him lightheaded. Then the picture came into focus. The piece of scar was smooth on one side, but Ren could see that underneath it fanned into a pattern of thin lines, like frost on a windowpane.

'I've observed the same kind of markings on internal organs. Buried in hearts, and livers, and threaded through the musculature. A scar can take over, given the right conditions.' Doctor Milton took hold of Ren's arm again and dabbed a bit of liquid from a brown bottle onto the cut he had made. 'Have you ever seen inside a body?'

'No.'

'It's beautiful.' Doctor Milton pressed two fingers above the boy's elbow. 'Particularly the muscles closest the bone. *Flexor pollicis longus*' – he pinched the right side – '*flexor digitorum profundus*' – he ran his fingers down the front of the arm – 'and *flexor carpi ulnaris*, which, normally, would be somewhere around here' – he tapped the left side of Ren's stub. 'Never knew you had that much inside you, now did you, boy?' Doctor Milton took the piece of scar from the microscope and dropped it into a glass jar. He secured the lid. He asked Ren's name and wrote it on a label glued to the back.

'What did this look like to you, under the microscope?'

Ren thought for a moment. 'Old cobwebs.'

The doctor set down the jar. He considered Ren with new interest. A notebook was produced and Doctor Milton scribbled down what the boy had said. Then he folded the book neatly back into his pocket. 'My friend Mister Bowers says that you and your friends can be trusted. Do you think I should believe him?'

Mister Bowers had been paid to say so. Still, Ren tried his best to be convincing. 'Yes.'

Doctor Milton grunted again, and the expression in his eyes went from sausages to Christmas goose and custard pie. From a side pocket in his instrument box he took out a set of keys and pressed them into Ren's hand. 'Do you know your numbers?'

The boy nodded.

'Tell your man I need four. They must be fresh, no more than a day or two gone. He should bring them at night, to the door that leads to the basement. No one must see him. Will you remember?'

'Yes.'

'How many?'

'Four.'

'I'll need them by next Thursday.' He pointed at the set of keys, and Ren understood they were for the gates outside. 'You will keep those safe. And you will return them to me.' The doctor tapped the place where he'd cut the boy's skin. 'Now remember – you're my patient and this is infected and I'm trying to save you from losing it up to here.' Doctor Milton opened two fingers like scissors and cut across to the top of Ren's arm. 'That's why you're coming to see me. Tell Sister Agnes when you leave.'

'I will,' said Ren, and he did. Sister Agnes was waiting for him on the bench outside, and he explained his situation as she led him through the hospital doors. Ren kept his arm cradled. Next visit, he decided, he would wear a sling.

It was a relief to be outside again. Ren took a deep breath, trying to rid his lungs of the hospital smell. The weight of the keys felt important in his pocket. He'd done the job. And he'd done it right.

Sister Agnes opened the gates and let him out. 'Where do you live?' she asked.

'North Umbrage.'

'It's a long way to walk.'

'Someone's coming for me.'

The nun glanced down the road. It was shaded by trees, the leaves connecting overhead. Benjamin and Tom passed underneath this canopy, driving the horse before them, their faces expectant but wary. Sister Agnes frowned, as if the men were approaching with a mountain of bedpans.

'Are you a Christian?' she asked quickly.

'Yes.'

'God be praised.' She said this as if a disaster had been averted, then crossed herself, twice. 'Would you like me to pray for you?'

Ren's fingers instinctively went to his forehead. He could still feel where Brother Joseph had drawn the cross with his thumb before he gave over *The Lives of the Saints*. The boy dropped his hand and wrapped it over his scar. He told Sister Agnes that he would.

The nun rested her palm on the top of his head. Her hand was warm and soft but also strong, and Ren could imagine all the good work it had done. Benjamin brought the cart up next to them on the road. He pulled the brake and rapped his fingers against the side of the wagon, as if he was knocking at a door. Ren could hear the horse grating its teeth, and Tom cough to get his attention, but he waited until the prayer was finished. Sister Agnes was standing over him, and he did not want to move until she took her hand away.

CHAPTER FIFTEEN

T HE FENCE SURROUNDING the graveyard was at least thirteen feet high, with a tight curling black pattern of iron too close to pass through. The corners were set with granite pillars. The top was lined with spikes that curled over, like the heads of flowers, dipping toward the ground. Details of ivy and leaves were wrought into the main gate, along with a cross, hinged at the center with an enormous padlock.

As they pulled in front, Benjamin and Tom were silent. Then they stepped from the wagon and walked the perimeter, testing the bars here and there, checking a shed nearby to make sure that it was empty. Ren kept his eyes on the church, waiting for a light to go on, but the stained-glass windows remained quiet and dark.

When Benjamin had dragged Ren from his bed earlier that evening and told him to get dressed, the boy had pulled on his clothes straight from the floor, not awake enough yet to be afraid. Now his body was full of nausea and dread. In the distance he could hear music playing from one of the brothels. The graveyard was on the outskirts of town, near a public common, but there was still the chance that they could be caught.

'Anything?' Benjamin asked when he returned.

'No,' said Ren. 'No one's here.'

Benjamin clapped the boy on the shoulder, as if he'd accomplished some great task. Then he removed a needle from his boot. He bent over the cemetery gate and picked the lock, his face set in concentration, listening for the turn. Tom stood closely behind, biting his lip as the door swung open.

Together the men carried the shovels through the gate. Ren stayed behind with the horse, holding on to the reins, watching the entrance and worrying. There was too much moon. It was nearly full and seemed to fill the sky. He held his hand up to the light and left a shadow across the road. Beyond the iron fence he could hear shovels in dirt, the huff of a boot kicking in. Every sound seemed louder in the dark. The boy crouched in the driver's seat, his heart beating against his chest, his breath sending small clouds into the cold night air.

He'd never seen a churchyard surrounded by its own fence. At Saint Anthony's there was only a small field next to the chapel where some of the monks were buried and a few of the children. It was a simple place, the graves set with wooden markers. There was often talk among the boys of ghosts weaving around this field at night, and Ichy swore that he'd seen the spirit of little Michael, who'd died of a fever the summer before, hovering outside the privy. Ren looked at the black ironwork surrounding the cemetery now, and hoped that it was high enough to keep the ghosts from getting out.

It seemed like forever before Tom and Benjamin emerged from the gate. They were dragging a burlap sack between them, so large that they had to pull at one end, then go around and pull from the other to make any progress. Tom stopped to rest.

Benjamin sneezed and wiped his nose. Then they started up again, rolling the bag across the grass. Together they were barely able to heave the body into the wagon. It hit with a low thud and sent a small cloud of dust from the wooden boards.

'That's one, anyway,' Benjamin said.

'They should pay us double for him,' said Tom. He used a shovel to push the bag to the rear of the wagon. The horse shifted – backed up, then forward – 'Hey there!' – Tom hit the side of the cart with his fist, and the wood shook all the way to the driver's seat. 'Watch it,' he said.

Ren pulled hard on the brake until the horse stopped shifting. The mare chomped on the bit in her mouth. Green saliva gathered around her lips. The horse turned her head, trying to see around her blinders. Benjamin and Tom went back into the graveyard, and all Ren could think about was the bag in the wagon.

It smelled of molted leaves and rotting bark and old pine needles, all the decaying bits of forest that rested under the trees. Ren twisted the reins in his hand, the leather cutting into his fingers. Everything around him was silent except for the buzzing of insects, and the boy imagined that he could hear them eating through the bag, trying to get at whatever was inside.

Ren blew on his fingers. He glanced into the back of the wagon. He could not look at the bag for long. Each time he did, it seemed more human and his conscience grew more troubled. He could feel God's eye upon him, like a pointed stick at the back of his neck. Ren tried to whistle, but his lips were dry.

Benjamin and Tom carried the rest of the bodies in their arms like firewood. The men moved easily but kept their faces turned to the side. After crossing the lawn they dropped the sacks behind the wagon. Each bag smelled worse than the last.

'This better be worth it,' said Tom, sliding the last one off his back.

The men raised the bodies one by one into the wagon. When they were finished, Tom paused for only a moment to sip from his flask, then went to fill in the graves. Benjamin took a deep breath, cleared his throat, and spit. His coat was covered with filth, his fingernails crusted. He brushed some dirt from his hair, then turned and arranged the blankets in the back. As he did, he held his hand over his nose.

'They smell awful,' said Ren.

'They won't be with us long.'

'What if their families come looking for them?'

'They won't.'

'But what if they do?'

'By the time they come after us, there'll be nothing left.'

Ren thought of Doctor Milton's box of surgical instruments. The pliers. The needles. The selection of knives. The curve of the blades. The bone saw.

'Aren't you tough, little man?'

'I'm tough,' said Ren.

'Then show it.' Benjamin took up the end of a bag that had come loose. He finished retying the knot and went back through the gate.

The horse snorted as he left. The muscles in her body shivered and twitched, as if she was trying to shake something off. Ren got down from the seat onto the road and began to pat the mare quietly with his hand, just above the leg. It had been a long journey from the barn to this graveyard. The animal was no longer in top form, but she still had the same thick coat and sharp eyes. Ren wondered if the farmer had found a replacement yet. If he kissed the second horse too.

As he watched the mare's nostrils flaring open and closed Ren heard something shift behind him. He held still. He held his good hand against the horse. A few moments passed before he found enough courage to look. When he did, he found nothing but the empty road. To his right the cemetery gate stood open. To his left was the town common, the grass bending in the wind. *I'm not afraid*, Ren thought. Then he glanced into the back of the wagon. One of the bags was sitting up.

It was the largest sack, the one that Tom and Benjamin had brought out first. The burlap was pulled close, and Ren could see the outline of a head and shoulders. The boy dropped the reins and the bag turned toward him, its neck slightly tilted, as if it were listening for something, as if it were waiting to hear him speak.

Ren tried to call out for Benjamin, but his voice was gone. He opened his mouth, his throat tightening. He took a few slow steps toward the gate. The head of the bag turned, watching him. The boy froze. He began to shuffle in the other direction, and the head of the bag followed this, too.

Benjamin came out of the graveyard with a bounce in his step. Then he saw it all. The spade on his shoulder fell to the road. The bag turned sharply toward this sound and leaned in Benjamin's direction. More than anything Ren wanted to run, but Benjamin motioned with his hand for the boy to stay put. With the other hand he pulled his knife slowly from his boot, as if he were trying not to startle the bag in the wagon. As if his life and Ren's life and everything around them – the moon and the horse and the wagon and the dead – all of it depended on how carefully he did this. Then, in a moment, he was up beside the body, cutting at the burlap.

The horse began to shuffle. She gave a small kick with her legs that banged against the wood, and Ren suddenly found his voice again. Tom stumbled out of the churchyard and clapped his hand over the boy's mouth, but Ren continued screaming straight through Tom's fingers.

'It's all right,' said Benjamin. 'Don't move,' he said.

In the wagon was a dead man, sitting up with his eyes open. The burlap hung like a hood around his shoulders. His head was square and short and dirty. He was bald.

'I'm hungry,' the dead man said. There was mud on his lips.

'Yes,' said Benjamin. He looked nervous, but he continued to use his knife to cut the bag off the body. He made small slashes and ripped the rest apart with his hands. He pulled the remains away and revealed a purple velvet suit.

'Cripes,' said Tom. The grit from his fingers spread across Ren's teeth. Ren had stopped screaming, but he could still feel the schoolteacher's hands trembling on either side of his throat.

The man in the purple suit sat in the wagon and blinked against the moonlight. There were rings under his eyes, as if he had been sleeping for weeks. His features were large and brutish – a jaw that flared out below his ears, a nose that looked like it had been broken more than once. Now that he was sitting up, he seemed to fill the entire back of the wagon. His shoulders stretched from either side of his neck like a wall. Even sitting down he was taller than Benjamin.

Ren stepped forward to get a closer look. Just as he did, the man closed his eyes and slumped against the side of the wagon.

'Is he dead now?' Tom asked.

Benjamin felt the man's neck hopefully. 'No.'

'Let's get out of here.'

'We can't leave him,' said Benjamin. 'Someone will find out.'

'Then we'll bury him again. He'll never know the difference.'

Benjamin stood for a moment, weighing this possibility. He rocked back and forth, his shadow swaying over the man at his feet. 'We don't have time,' Benjamin decided. He jumped down. He shoved Ren toward the horse. 'Fetch me some rope. He's coming with us.'

Ren found some cord underneath the driver's seat and Benjamin began tying up the dead man. The tools and bodies were covered with blankets. Tom fumbled in his pocket for the flask, but when he tried to drink it was empty. He slipped next to Ren and took the reins.

'Get back,' he growled.

Ren climbed over the driving board. He held on to the side of the cart as they jostled down the street. Underneath the blankets the bodies were stiff but yielding, like pieces of wood just beginning to rot. It was hard for Ren to distinguish where one body ended and another began. He scrambled over them as quickly as he could, trying not to imagine their faces as he made his way to the back of the wagon.

The dead man was not wearing a shirt. His purple suit had holes in it – tiny ones that showed bits of skin and hair. His feet were bare as well, and somehow this made his hands seem naked, resting open in his lap, the fingers thick and dry. Above the collar of the suit his neck laid itself out in folds. The skin was circled with dark bruises.

Ren kept as close to Benjamin as he could. He crouched

down and grasped the edge of the wagon. He counted everything inside. There were three bodies, two thieves, one dead man, and him. The horse continued to pull them all, its hooves echoing against the stones in the street.

Benjamin sat on the edge of the cart, his fingers in his hair. Every so often he would reach out and slap the dead man hard in the face.

'Hey there,' he said. 'Still with us, now?' There was a low gurgling noise from the suit in return. 'I guess you are,' said Benjamin. 'I guess you're with us for good.'

CHAPTER SIXTEEN

TOM AND BENJAMIN struggled as they carried the man up the stairs. Ren moved ahead, holding the lamp, opening doors, turning keys, telling them to shush for a moment until he was sure that Mrs Sands was not in the kitchen. It was close to four, the final chilled breaths of night before morning. The dead man was still snoring lightly when they rolled him on top of the bed.

'What'll we do with him?' Tom asked. 'Can't leave him here.'

'For now we will,' Benjamin said. 'There's no choice but that.' He reached into the back of his pants, pulled out the revolver, and handed it to Ren.

'Watch him,' he said. Then he blew out the light.

It took a few minutes for Ren's eyes to adjust. He listened to the men go down the stairs, then pushed the curtain aside to watch them leave. He could make out Tom in the back of the wagon. Benjamin was at the reins now, and Ren could tell by the way he leaned forward in his seat that he was worried. If they didn't get the bodies to the hospital before daylight, they would be left with a wagon full of corpses.

Ren stood alone in the dark, thinking of the mourners

coming to pray over the empty coffins they had left. Behind him, the purple suit snored. The sound was heavy and wet, increasing with each exhale, until the dead man seemed to be filling not only the bed but half the room, all the way to the ceiling.

Ren climbed onto Tom's mattress and rested the gun on his knee. He ran his finger over the back hammer. The metal was cold. If he pulled the trigger, the bullet would go right through the man's heart. That would stop him for sure. But Ren hoped it would not come to that. What would he tell Mrs Sands if she came and saw that he'd killed someone? She thought he was a good boy, and he did not want her to know the truth.

Ren went over to the door and listened. The house was silent. Mrs Sands was still asleep, unaware of the stranger they'd brought underneath her roof. Ren moved back to his spot, relieved. A small spider was crawling across the dead man's stomach, pausing for a moment before scurrying on. There were probably lots of bugs, Ren decided, and now they were all in his bed.

The man's mouth was open, his teeth glistening in the moonlight. Ren wondered how he had been buried alive – if a doctor had missed his heartbeat, or if the man had found some way to pull his spirit back from heaven. This wasn't like Saint Anthony in *The Lives of the Saints*, raising a child to clear his father's name. It didn't feel even remotely holy. Ren reached over the blanket and flicked the spider with his thumb and forefinger. It landed on the floor and Ren quickly stood upon it, grinding the spider into the boards. When he was finished he saw that the dead man was awake.

Ren lifted the gun. It was heavy held out in the air and his hand shook a little.

The man blinked his eyes. His belly spilled over the edge of the bed. He had his hands tucked together underneath the side of his face, as if he was used to not having a pillow. He seemed even larger now, and looked as though he could bring his foot down on a boy just as easily as a spider. Ren's arm was already feeling tired. He used his left to prop up the right, the nub just beneath his wrist.

'It looks like you're dancing,' said the man. He reached up and brushed something off his face. Ren saw a small insect hit the floor. It had many legs, and it used them now to run toward the boy's foot. Ren lifted his shoe and brought it down again, twisting at the ankle from side to side.

'There you go again,' said the man. 'Where's the music?' His voice was deep and ragged, as if he had not spoken in years. A creeping sensation began up the back of Ren's legs, as if the man before him had been buried not for just a day but for a century. The room was dark, but an even greater darkness seemed to seep directly from him, like a thick and evil fog. The man closed his eyes for a moment. 'I'm cold.'

Ren tucked the gun under his arm and yanked one of Mrs Sands's quilts across the bed, his hand shaking.

'Well, that's a treat,' said the man. Then he was quiet for a while, and Ren thought he might have fallen asleep again. Ren lowered the revolver and kept a lookout for bugs. Then he realized that the man was crying.

Ren had always believed that crying went away when you got older. Now, as he watched the man sob, he felt it must be a thing that never stopped. The bed was shuddering, the purple suit rocking back and forth. There was a deep sound coming from the man's chest, the heavy kind of moan that bends people over. Ren had heard this sort of crying before in the small boys' room. It came on bad nights, when the children remembered their mothers.

Ren sat down on the edge of the bed. The smell of the fog was all over now, so ripe and so foul he could nearly taste it. He touched the man's ankle through the quilt and felt it flex beneath his hand. Ren patted the foot. He sat there gently and continued to pat the foot, and eventually the man quieted.

The silence that came after was unnerving. The man did not wipe his eyes or his nose. He let them both run, until they dried into tiny rivers on his face. It was as if he had never cried before in his life. The man inhaled deeply, his nostrils letting out a tiny squeak as he released the air. He coughed.

'I'm thirsty.'

In the hallway Ren found a bowl and filled it at the washstand, then tucked the revolver in his pocket and carried the bowl back to the room. When he opened the door, the man was sitting up. He had taken off his jacket. His shoulders were lumpy and his body wide, his stomach hanging below his thick, hairy chest. His forehead was wrinkled, as if he was trying hard to remember something.

'What happened to the others?'

'They'll be back soon,' said Ren. He held out the bowl of water and the man reached for it.

His hands were enormous – three times the size of Ren's – the palms hard and muscled, the fingers stubby and wide. He drank in gulps, his bruised neck silently throbbing. When he finished, he set the bowl on the floor. 'Who're you?' he asked.

'I'm Ren.'

'I'm Dolly.' He eyed the gun, and Ren could see that he was

considering whether or not to take it from him. 'Are you going
to shoot me?'

'I don't think so,' Ren admitted.

'Good,' said Dolly. 'Because I don't think I can sit up
anymore.'

Ren helped him lie down, lifting the quilt, and saw a dozen
crawling things set out across the mattress.

Dolly sighed. 'Thank you,' he said. He turned his face to the
ceiling and scratched at the hair on his chest. He did not seem
concerned about his circumstances, or the fact that he'd been
buried. There were tattoo marks across the man's sternum – an
anchor, and a chain that wrapped around his thick waist twice.
The links were shaded in black and about the length of Ren's
finger. He half expected them to rattle as Dolly breathed, but
they only stretched the skin, silently coiling in and out.

'Where'd you get that?'

'New York.' Dolly passed a massive hand across his chest, then
traced each circle at the end of the chain. 'Philadelphia. Boston.'
He looked up at Ren and his face hardened. 'It's how I keep
track of things.'

Something in the way he spoke made Ren tighten his grip
on the gun. The fog was crossing the room now and the boy felt
desperate, wishing for Benjamin to return. Even so he could not
stop the question from coming out. 'What are you doing here?'

'I came to murder someone.'

Ren had seen it coming, and now he could barely whisper.
'Did you do it?'

'No. I didn't have the chance.' Dolly patted his stomach
where the chain ended. 'But I'll get another job. New England's
full of grudges, and there's lots of people that need to be

murdered, and people looking for someone to murder them. I've been doing it for years. I was made for it.' Dolly pointed to the row of links. 'There's a mark here for every man I've killed.'

He was boasting. Even as the stench of the grave clung to him; even as he brushed insects off his face. It was clear to Ren that he felt no sympathy for his victims, no regret for what he'd done in his life. Something about the man was off; as if he were not of this world, or the next. It was chilling to be standing this close to a murderer, but Ren also considered for a moment what it might be like – to have no feelings, no guilt. To never say penance again. 'Is that how you hurt your neck?' he asked.

'No,' said Dolly. 'I was strangled.'

Ren looked at Dolly's throat again, the purple bruises patterned like fingerprints. 'Why?'

'I'm not sure.'

'People don't get strangled for nothing.'

'Well,' said Dolly, 'I suppose it was for *something*.'

'Did it hurt?'

Dolly looked thoughtful. 'They came after me with a rope,' he said. 'Two men with old hats. Surprised me in the stairwell of a tavern. Got the cord around my neck and started pulling. I broke off a piece of railing, then used it to beat one of them in the nose until he let go. I knocked the other down the stairs, but not before he got his teeth into me.' He lifted his arm and showed a pattern of half-moons. Scars of bites up and down his skin.

'Then what?'

'I kicked their faces in. Those two won't come back.'

'But you did.'

'Yes,' said Dolly. And he did something with his face that

might have been a smile. 'When I woke up it was morning and I was at the bottom of the stairs. I kept thinking, *Why hasn't anyone come?* And then the landlady walked in and she screamed and she cried a little and closed the lids of my eyes with her fingers. She thought I'd saved her from being robbed. She sent for the undertakers to remove the other bodies and paid for a coffin for me.

'The undertakers covered my face with a sheet. They stole my shoes and my shirt but left my suit. They said it was too ruined to sell. I heard them complaining about how heavy I was. I tried to stop them, but I couldn't lift my arms. And then I was in the coffin. And then the lid was on. And then the nails came. One went straight through my ear.' Dolly lifted his hand and pointed. On the lobe there was a caking of red scab. Behind it the upper throat had been pierced, just above the line of purple bruises.

'Everything split once that nail went in. I was lifted and I was lowered. I could feel the weight of the dirt as they shoveled it in. It was like a blanket pulled over my head.' Dolly said, 'I'm just supposing now.' As he spoke he drooled; there were two small stains of saliva gathering on the pillow, white foam in the corners of his mouth.

Ren took up the side of the quilt and wiped the foam away. Then he folded the area of wetness over and tucked it underneath the mattress. Dolly could not have been under-ground long, Ren decided. It might have been hours, it might have been a day, but it was a miracle that he was alive at all.

'Am I awake?' Dolly groaned.

'I think so,' said Ren.

There was a light banging coming from somewhere in the

156

house, and Ren knew that it was Mrs Sands, cleaning out the ashes from the fireplace in the kitchen. Dolly began to cry again, and Ren went back to patting his foot. The man's sobs were softer now. He cupped his giant hands over his mouth, as if he were trying to catch the words he was saying.

'I'm sorry.'

Ren didn't know what Dolly was sorry for, but he knew what it felt like to want to take something back.

'I know,' he said.

Dolly began to rub his eyes. There were streaks across his cheeks and chin from the tears, and it made him look pitiful, as if someone had just thrown dirt in his face. His jaw clenched, and suddenly his massive arms grabbed for the boy. Ren panicked, thinking he was going for the gun, but instead Dolly seized Ren by the stump and squeezed it hard, as if it were a hand.

Ren was sure that he could hear Benjamin on the stairs. He tried to twist his arm away but Dolly was holding fast.

'We're friends now.'

It was not a question. Still, Ren answered it. 'Yes.'

CHAPTER SEVENTEEN

Benjamin slipped into their room after dawn. His clothes smelled strange, sharp and sweet, as if they had been soaked in spirits.

'Where's the purple suit?'

'Under the bed. I think his eyes hurt.'

Benjamin lifted one of the blankets. When he was satisfied that Dolly was asleep, he opened his coat. 'Look at this.' Inside his pockets were mounds of bills and coins. It was more money than they'd made from the church, or the stolen jewelry, or from Mother Jones's Elixir for Misbehaving Children. It was more money than Ren had ever seen.

'You should have seen us outside the hospital gates,' said Benjamin. 'Tom had the shakes, and I thought we'd never get in. But the doctor was waiting for us, just like you said. He had the money all out and ready.' Benjamin picked up a handful of coins. 'You're lucky to me, did you know?'

The boy shook his head. He felt a small flush of pride.

'I should have picked you up sooner.'

The bills were spread across the bed, and together the two of them began counting. Ren knew how to multiply using his fingers, his thumb working back and forth across the tips. *Fifteen. Thirty-six. Forty-two. Sixty-seven. Seventy-five.* He piled the numbers on top of each other, and Benjamin seemed impressed when he counted the bills for a second time and came to the same amounts. When they were finished, he gave a few dollars to Ren. Then he unscrewed a knob from one of the bedposts, rolled the rest of the money inside, and put the knob back in place.

'I'm going to buy a new pair of boots.' Benjamin sat down on the bed. 'How about you. Another orange?'

Ren lifted the bills to his nose and inhaled. The money smelled of dirty fingers. His mind swam with all the objects that had been bought and sold with it – new clothes and peaches and horseshoes and lumber and books and ribbons and frying pans. He closed his eyes. He was too tired to think.

Benjamin took his knife from his boot. He opened it and cleaned the blade with the edge of his shirt. 'Here,' he said. 'Why don't you take this until you think of something.'

Ren had seen the knife before but never up close. A bear was carved into the handle, its paws reaching around the center as if it were climbing a tree. The animal's head rested on the end with a sleepy expression, the eyes twice as large as the nose. Ren touched the tip of the knife with his finger. It was sharp and gleaming and threw a small bright spot of light onto his face.

'That's the first time I've seen you smile,' Benjamin said.

Ren *was* smiling. He could not stop. He felt his teeth against the cool morning air, his cheeks tightening until they began to hurt. The knife rested in his open palm, shiny and dangerous. It was more than a gift – he had earned it. Benjamin had trusted him to see the night through, and he had come out the other side.

A factory whistle sounded, followed by another. Ren could hear the boots of the mousetrap girls leaving. One pair paused for a moment outside their door, then continued down the stairs. Ren glanced out the window and saw dozens of girls dressed in blue running in the street, their shawls over their heads. It was raining.

There was a moan from Dolly underneath the mattress. Suddenly the bed lifted off its feet, levitating for a moment before settling back to the floor. Benjamin and Ren stepped against the wall and waited until they heard the man begin to snore again.

'What are we going to do with him?' Ren whispered.

'Tom took his share straight to the bar. He'll be on a bender for the next few weeks.' Benjamin sat down on the other bed and began to unbutton his coat. 'We'll need an extra set of hands.'

'Then we're keeping him?'

'If we can.'

'I think he's a killer,' said Ren.

'That could be helpful.' Benjamin leaned back into the pillows. 'As long as he doesn't kill us.'

When Ren woke again, the sun was bright through the curtains. He could not be sure if it had been days or hours that had passed. Beside him on the bed he could feel the heat of Benjamin's body. In his hand was the revolver. Benjamin had told him to keep an eye on Dolly, but Ren had fallen asleep. Now his neck felt stiff from leaning against the headboard and his fingers were full of pins and needles.

The boy rolled over. Across the room the other mattress was still empty, and probably still full of bugs. Underneath it, on the floor, was a pile of blankets. Dolly was gone.

Ren shoved the covers off. He checked the closet and looked out the window, throwing up the sash in a panic and leaning out over the street. He pulled open the door and hurried down the stairs. He stopped when he heard a small scraping sound coming from the kitchen. There was also a rumbling. A series of muffled knocks.

The boy slowly peered around the corner. Dolly was sitting on a chest near the fireplace, his jacket on, buttoned at the top, his stomach hanging out below. He was eating a bowl of porridge, the spoon a tiny instrument in his hand.

'Are you looking for the woman?'

Ren nodded.

Dolly thumped the side of the chest.

'Let her out!' Ren cried. He snatched the bowl away and pushed at Dolly to get him off the chest. 'Mrs Sands!' He pressed his mouth against the keyhole.

Dolly stood and Ren lifted the lid. Mrs Sands was inside with her shoes off, her knees bent. A sock stuffed in her mouth. Her skin looked pale but her eyes flashed, blinking against the sudden light as Ren pulled the damp wool free of her teeth.

'**WHO IS THIS?!**' she shouted, her throat covered in blotches of red. Ren had never heard her so loud. Mrs Sands pushed herself up in the box and crawled onto the floor. Then she began to cough. Deep, shaking coughs turning over something wet and heavy inside of her chest. On her hands and knees she reached for the fireplace poker and began beating Dolly in the leg.

The dead man blinked at her but did not move.

'Don't hit him like that!' Ren took hold of the iron and tried to pull it away, but Mrs Sands kept on coughing and striking out at him. Dolly easily pinned her arms and covered her mouth, his hand reaching across her face from ear to ear.

'That's why I put her in the box.'

Mrs Sands swung her feet.

'Let her go!'

The boy tried to pry Dolly's fingers off her mouth, but just as he got a thumb loose, Benjamin came rushing into the room, holding the King James Bible from their room. He thrust the book at Dolly, who dropped Mrs Sands in surprise.

'That's our landlady,' said Benjamin. 'You don't touch the landlady.' Then he began to scold the dead man as if he were a child.

Dolly backed up against the fireplace. 'I was just trying to eat,' he said.

Ren helped Mrs Sands onto the bench, her body thin in his arms. When she finally caught her breath she broke into another series of coughs. Benjamin went to fetch some water, then stood by with a look of concern.

'THAT MURDERER PUT ME IN THE BOX!'

'My dear Mrs Sands,' said Benjamin. 'There's a perfectly good reason why he put you in there.'

They all turned to hear this explanation. Dolly clutched the book. Ren bit his lip, and the landlady stared as if Benjamin had lost his mind.

'This man's our cousin and a traveling preacher,' said Benjamin. 'He heard about my sister's death and came looking for us.'

162

Mrs Sands sniffed once at the purple suit, then waved her hand in front of her face. 'HE SMELLS LIKE MANURE.'

'It's interesting that you should say that,' said Benjamin. 'Because he has passed through every kind of manure, animal and human, carrying this Bible across the country while converting the heathens of the forest. And it was in that very forest that he met an Indian princess, named Happy Feather, who became his Christian wife. But Happy Feather didn't take to Jesus, and while our cousin was preaching God's word, she ran away with a witch doctor from another tribe.'

Dolly studied the book Benjamin had given him, turning it this way and that. Ren watched Mrs Sands, wondering when she'd realize that Dolly had her own King James Bible, and was reading it upside down. The landlady was rummaging about on the floor for her shoes, but her head was tilted toward Benjamin's face, watching the words, her face a mixture of anger and impatience.

'Since then our cousin's been searching for her, half-crazy, living hand to mouth and mouth to hand. And then this morning he saw you, and you looked so beautiful, just like Happy Feather, and he lost his mind for a moment. He was afraid that his wife would run away again. So he locked you in the chest. He did it out of love.' With one hand Benjamin straightened Dolly's coat, and with the other brushed some porridge from his chest. 'Have some pity, Mrs Sands.'

'GIVE ME THAT,' said the landlady. She snatched the Bible away from Dolly. She eyed the pages, which were edged with gold, worn away in the corners. The letters were tiny blocks of script and she frowned over them, then back at Dolly. She put down the Bible. Then she picked up her broom and began to beat them all. She smacked Benjamin once across the face and Dolly on his shoulders. Ren ducked and she got him in the legs with the handle. 'YOU'RE ALL THE WORST OF ANY KIND!'

The group retreated quickly, Ren scrambling ahead and a bewildered Dolly catching the rear. They made for the door and stumbled into the street, Mrs Sands lurching after them with the broom in hand. 'I WON'T BE BOXED!' she cried. With that she slammed the door so hard that the knocker knocked itself.

The three of them stood outside in the gutter. Ren rubbed his legs. Dolly flexed his giant fingers. Benjamin pulled a few straws from his hair.

'Well,' he said. 'That was quite a beginning.' He held out his hand and introduced himself to Dolly. 'Welcome back to the world.'

His hand disappeared up to the wrist. When Dolly finally let go Benjamin bent his fingers, trying to get the blood back. The late afternoon sun was bright, and Dolly squinted against it. He seemed disoriented at the people going by, the bustle of the carriages in the street. He hunched his shoulders and shuffled closer to Ren.

'He seems to like you,' Benjamin said, raising an eyebrow.

Ren was embarrassed. 'I suppose so.'

Benjamin dusted off his coat as if it were all the same to him. He picked one last piece of straw from his collar. 'It's time we fetched Tom from the bar.'

The market was about to close, the grocers rearranging their fruits and vegetables to hide the rotted parts, the baker cutting dried-out bread into toast, the butcher on the corner boiling leftover bones.

'I'm hungry,' said Dolly.

'You just ate,' said Ren.

'Yes,' said Benjamin. 'And we've had nothing.'

Dolly took a seat on the sidewalk, his head in his hands. People began to stare, and Ren suddenly saw how out of place he was. An old woman in rags held her nose as she passed. A boy leaned from a moving carriage and pointed at the purple suit. On the street corner ahead, a small group of soldiers were smoking. One of them paused as he lit his cigar. He lifted his chin toward them. Then he dropped the match.

'Let's get out of here,' said Benjamin.

'I'm not moving,' said Dolly.

'You have to,' said Benjamin. He kept his face turned from the soldiers. Ren saw that he was moving, sliding one foot and then the other along the sidewalk. In a moment he would abandon them both.

'Please,' cried Ren. 'Please, Dolly.' He took hold of the purple jacket, then threw his arms around the man's shoulder. Ren buried his face into the soggy velvet until he felt a pat on his back.

'All right now,' said Dolly. 'Don't fret.'

They cleaned Dolly off behind an abandoned church, showered him with rain buckets, and dumped his suit in the garbage. Dolly did not protest. He gave the purple velvet one sad glance, and then offered his face to be shaved. Benjamin took the bear knife from Ren and went to work, barely nicking the skin. With the whiskers gone, in his long breeches, Dolly looked much better than before – his cheeks rosy, his bald head shining. It was as if he had never been dead.

They decided that Dolly needed a disguise, at least while he was in North Umbrage. Benjamin lifted Ren through an open window of the church to look for some new clothes. Inside the pews had been removed, the stained glass pulled down, but the lectern was still there, as well as a pile of prayer books. The boy began to forage through a closet behind the altar. Inside a trunk he found the makings of a nativity scene: the dusty head of a donkey, a baby doll with a wire halo attached to its head, and a coarse brown shepherd's robe that fell across the floor.

'A preacher's collar would've been better,' said Benjamin, once they had Dolly dressed.

'He's not a preacher,' Ren said, 'he's a monk.' And somehow it seemed right. The boy remembered a group of Capuchins who had passed by and stayed until morning at Saint Anthony's. They were strange, rugged men. They did not eat. And they slept outside on the stone courtyard, without any blankets. Ren had watched them from the window of the small boys' room. Their bodies were curled, their robes spread across the ground. They had looked like fallen angels in the moonlight.

Ren tried his best to explain the difference between God and the Holy Spirit, *Our Father* and the *Glory Be*. They had no rosary to work on, but Benjamin produced a necklace made of paste, and it was on this trinket that Ren taught Dolly how to say a *Hail Mary*, how to make his way through a decade of the rosary, and how to observe the mysteries: the joyful, the sorrowful, and the glorious.

Dolly held a bead between his enormous fingers. He turned to Ren, his face blank. 'I won't remember.'

'Never mind,' said Benjamin. 'Just do this.' He motioned in

the air with two fingers, drawing an invisible cross. 'Then you don't have to say anything.'

Dolly signed the cross.

'Good,' said Benjamin.

He did it again.

'That's right!' Ren shouted.

With this encouragement, Dolly continued to sign the cross, drawing it lightly, then fiercely, over and over, until Ren was certain that he had used his fingers to express every possible emotion.

'It's a good thing we came along when we did,' said Benjamin, cleaning the bear knife with the corner of his jacket. 'Or you'd still be in underground.'

Dolly paused, his finger in the air, and appraised Benjamin coolly. His hands dropped to his sides and began to open and close, open and close. 'You want something for it?'

'Oh, no,' said Benjamin, carefully stepping out of reach. 'But I do believe you owe us a debt of some kind. Not that I'm the kind of person who collects debts.' He cleared his throat. 'All the same, I think it's time we talked business.'

'You want somebody murdered?' Dolly asked.

Benjamin seemed taken aback. 'Not at all.'

'Then I can't help you.'

The church window sent a rainbow of color across the alley. Benjamin grit his teeth and rubbed his hands together, the way he always did when he was preparing to persuade someone to go against their better instincts. 'What we need is another man,' he said. 'Someone to lend a hand with the digging.'

'I work alone.'

'There's money in it. More than you'll probably see in a year.'

Dolly considered this, rubbing the sleeve of his robe back and forth underneath his chin.

Benjamin handed the knife to Ren. 'Let me buy you a drink,' he said, and his smile appeared, bright and beaming and beautiful. Ren watched as Dolly was slowly disarmed by it, until the man gave a crooked grin of his own in return. Benjamin reached forward and shook Dolly's stubby fingers. 'I know just the place.'

He escorted them through the central common, one arm pushing Ren ahead and the other hanging on Dolly's massive shoulders. They passed a bandstand that was falling apart and a pond that was overrun with weeds. Benjamin pointed across the way. On the street facing the common sat a busy tavern. But when they started for it, Dolly held back.

'Those people,' said Dolly. 'I know them.'

Standing outside the tavern, smoking their pipes, were two young men. One wore a black porkpie hat, the other a disagreeable expression and a pair of spats buttoned up to his knees.

'Who are they?' Benjamin asked.

'Hat boys,' said Dolly.

'Are they dangerous?'

'If they see me, there'll be trouble.'

Benjamin sucked his teeth. 'Then they won't.' He pulled the hood of the robe over Dolly's face and led him behind a giant oak tree. 'Stay here,' he said. 'Stay out of sight.' Then he took hold of Ren, and walked past the hat boys, straight into O'Sullivan's bar.

CHAPTER EIGHTEEN

THERE WAS NO sign to speak of, just the name – Dennis O'Sullivan – and the date carved into a ledge of granite above the entryway. Beyond the front door, lanterns hung from hooks along the walls and from two long chains above the bar. An orange glow spread across the faces of the men, leaving shadows, especially in the corners, where the lamps had long ago been blown out and never refilled. The tables were rough maple softened by beer and a century of card playing. A head resting on the wood could smell it all – thousands of dirty, greasy hands and the rank scent of hops in the fibers. Below, the uneven floor held the shaky legs of chairs. Heavy benches were crosshatched with the markings of knives. The seats permanently fashioned to the worn-down ends of men.

The pub was full. The customers barely glanced as Benjamin and Ren maneuvered through the crowd. There was little conversation in the room. These were quiet men, men who had been at O'Sullivan's since sometime the day before, and perhaps the day before that.

Benjamin and Ren found Tom in the back of the bar, surrounded by empty glasses and attempting to pour himself another. He seemed years older. The bags under his eyes were dark and there were lines on his face – ridges spreading across his cheeks. Ren slid into the other side of the booth, and Benjamin took the chair on the end.

'We've got a new man.'

Tom sat up in alarm. 'You can't keep him.'

Benjamin put his foot on the bench. 'You said yourself that we needed help.'

'Somebody murdered him,' said Tom. 'Don't you think they'll notice that he's up and about?'

'He already killed the men who killed him,' said Benjamin.

Tom turned to the boy. 'Is that right?'

Ren felt somehow guilty for answering. 'He told me that he kicked their faces in.'

Tom stared into his empty glass. 'I don't want to get mixed up with a murderer.'

'With his help we could clear twice as much.' Benjamin passed Ren a coin. 'Get me some ale and bitters.'

Ren wanted to stay, but when Benjamin shot him a second look he maneuvered out of the booth and made his way across the floor. He knew it would take some time before Tom was convinced, and it worried him to keep Dolly waiting.

He found the bartender asleep. The man's body was slumped against a stool, his face resting on the bar next to a bowl of soup. The contents had spilled across the wood and down the front of his already stained and dirty apron; his head was surrounded by an army of pint glasses. Ren looked around to get some idea of how to wake him, but no one would meet his eye.

A girl walked past, carrying a tray full of drinks. She was no

more than twelve years old, and walked carefully and deliberately among the customers. Her ears were pierced with small
hoops, and she had skin that was slightly green and sallow. She
gave the beer to a table of men playing cards, then came over to
the bar and began filling her tray with empty glasses. Ren gave
her Benjamin's order.

The girl nodded. Her hair was in a yellow braid straight
down her back, and Ren thought about the girl who'd put the
penny in his mouth, the curls on her head like crow's wings. This
girl was not nearly as pretty, but her eyes were hazel-colored, and
Ren had never seen a girl with hazel eyes before. He watched
her as she slipped through a swinging door. It was only a few
moments before she came back with the drink.

'Here,' she said, and Ren paid her. She put the beer on the
bar, then lifted her skirt and began to pick a scab off her knee.

'Thank you,' said Ren.

The girl gave him a closer look. 'What happened to your
hand?'

Ren tried to think of something interesting to say, but the
small blond hairs on the girl's thigh made his mind go
temporarily blank. 'A lion ate it,' he said at last, trying out one
of Benjamin's stories. 'He was from the circus. And his name was
Pierre.' The words sounded wrong in his mouth.

The girl stopped scratching at the scab on her leg. 'You're not
very good at lying.'

Behind her came a rush of daylight as the door to the bar
pushed open. Three men in black walked through and over to
where Ren was standing. He was sure that they had found Dolly
outside and had come to arrest them, but instead the men
stopped beside the bartender. The shortest reached across the

counter, touched the bartender's eyelid, and lifted it. The iris underneath looked hard and shiny as a marble.

'They don't last long in this place, do they?' the man said. He reached into his pocket and took out a small bag, which he quickly slipped over the bartender's head and tightened with a knot at the neck. 'Where's the boss?' he said to the girl.

She pointed to the back room, as if this kind of thing happened at the bar every day.

'I'll leave you to it,' the man said to the others, and he tipped his hat, then went through the swinging door.

The undertakers tried to straighten the body, but it was too stiff, so they simply rolled it to the floor, the bartender still holding his spoon. One of the men grabbed under the knees and the other hooked beneath the arms and across the chest. Everyone shuffled their chairs aside, and the undertakers made clumsily for the door, taking small steps. The bartender's arm swung out over heads as he passed. The patrons hid their faces, eyes keen on cards or the dissolving foam in their glasses of beer.

As the undertakers maneuvered around a table, one of them stumbled, and the bartender's soup spoon, still firmly gripped in his fingers, knocked off a hat. The brim was wide like a minister's, with a blood red band. It spun as if caught in a wind, and landed near the bar rail in the sawdust, quite knocked out of shape.

The owner of the hat stood up from his chair like a shadow stretching across a wall. His eyes were too far apart. Ren saw this first before anything else. There was so much space between them that his face looked pushed in – an open plain of blankness. His skin was pale, his hair long and plastered to the sides of his chin. His coat was made of leather and he wore red gloves – the same red that was in the band of the hat.

The undertakers stopped in their tracks. As the man in the red gloves approached, they dropped the bartender to the floor. 'It wasn't intentional,' one of them said. The other backed away. Patrons at the tables nearby picked up and moved to the other side of the room. The man in the red gloves didn't say a word. But as they all watched, he removed a large knife from his belt, put it against the bartender's wrist, and sawed off the dead man's hand.

The green girl took hold of Ren's sleeve and hid her face against it. He could feel her breath, hot and blowing through the cloth against his skin. The bartender's arm shook as the man made his way through the bone. When he finished, the man in the red gloves reached over and picked up his hat from the floor. He dusted it off, shaped it with his fingers, and placed it on his head. Then he took the hand of the bartender, still holding the spoon, and brought it back to his table. He pointed at the green girl. 'Bring me some stew.'

The girl rushed into the kitchen while the drinkers kicked sawdust over the blood and settled back in their seats. The undertakers seemed relieved. They scurried around the body, heaved it between them, and rushed out the door. The latch closed and the daylight crawled away into the corners and the hurricane lamps sent out their glow, and all of the men – all of them – suddenly began talking, as if they had been holding their breath until the body was gone.

The green girl came back holding a bowl of stew. Ren watched her maneuver her way through the crowd. He closed his eyes, but it didn't change anything. He could still see the back-and-forth motion of the knife, the fleshy end of the bartender's arm. It was as if the blade was cutting into his own body. He pressed tightly against his scar. He dug his nails in.

The room narrowed and pulled away, until Ren felt as if he were leaning over the well at Saint Anthony's and hearing the echo of the water. Somewhere in that echo was a terror Ren had felt before; he was remembering now, almost touching it, the voices of the men in the bar mumbling in his ear, until the green girl grabbed his elbow and said, 'You're going to spill it.'

The glass of ale in his hand was tipping. Ren didn't remember picking it up from the bar. He caught it now and set it straight. He thanked the girl, who gave him a halfhearted smile before going back to work. Ren made his way unsteadily back to the table. Benjamin and Tom were watching the man in the red gloves, who was now eating stew with the bartender's hand.

'We need to leave this place,' Tom said.

'You're drunk,' said Benjamin.

'Yes,' said Tom. 'But I mean it.'

'We're not going anywhere,' said Benjamin. 'Not yet.'

Tom poured himself another glass. 'I've been in this bar for two days, and I've heard more than I care to.' He looked over at the surrounding tables, then leaned forward and lowered his voice. 'The mousetrap man, McGinty, he's running a market for smuggled things here. Opium, French novels, postcards, gold teeth, whiskey, whale oil, pistols, ivory bracelets, and lip rouge. Anything and everything that anyone could want. He controls it all from his factory, taking a cut of every bit of action. And when he doesn't get his cut, his men do some cutting of their own.'

Tom nodded at the man in red gloves, then made a gesture of apology toward Ren. 'I'm attached to my hands. I don't intend to lose them.'

Benjamin didn't respond. He was too busy studying the man in the red gloves eating, as if this act was teaching him something important, something he'd been trying to learn for years. Benjamin's face changed each time the man lifted the bartender's hand, until he looked angrier than Ren had ever seen before. He shoved away from the table. He started buttoning up his coat.

'Where are you going?' Tom asked.

'We'll do one more run,' Benjamin said. 'One more, and then we'll go.' He seemed suddenly in a rush. He handed Ren the key to their room. 'Go beg your way back with Mrs Sands.'

'What about Dolly?'

Benjamin stopped for a moment. He tapped Ren on the chin. 'Just make sure he doesn't kill anyone yet.' With that he turned the collar up on his coat, and in two steps he had slipped into the crowd.

Ren fingered the key in his hand. Tom poured a sandy liquid into two glasses, and pushed one over. 'Here,' he said. 'I'm tired of drinking alone.'

'I have to take care of Dolly.'

'One drink.'

Ren lifted the glass. He took a tentative sip and swallowed. The alcohol felt like flames in his mouth.

'What were your fellows' names again?' Tom asked.

'Brom and Ichy,' said Ren.

'Mine was Christian.'

'I remember.'

Tom blew out a stream of air. 'It's a shame to lose your fellows.'

Ren stuck his tongue into the whiskey again. He waited to see how long he could hold it in his mouth before swallowing. A warm, pleasant glow started up the back of his throat. 'Isn't Benjamin your fellow?'

Tom poured another drink. His words started to slur, one sliding into the next. Ren had to lean forward and concentrate to understand him.

'When I met Benji, he was on the run for deserting. And wasn't I struck by him? And didn't I take him in and show him every kindness, a roof over his head and something to eat and how to find his way in and out of trouble? I taught him how to play cards, and how to be sure a woman wasn't making a fool out of him. And now our paths are so twisted together that they'll hang us from the same rope.'

'He was in the army?'

'He was sold into it,' said Tom. 'His uncle turned him in to cover a gambling debt. The army sent him out west, and he saw men shot to pieces, trying to put their stomachs back inside themselves.' Tom lowered his head onto the table and groaned. 'He was only a boy when it happened. Just a few years older than you.'

Ren set his glass down. Then he lifted it back up. The bottom left a damp ring on the wooden table. A thin, unbroken line. He thought of Sebastian, whispering through the gate. *I should have used it. I should have wished on it as soon as it came to me.*

The story Tom had told was breaking up, and the boy knew that if he waited long enough the words would leave the room, threading through the tables and out the door and it would be as if he had never said them. Tom seemed to be asleep now, his head in his arms. Ren slid out of his chair, but before he could leave, the schoolteacher lifted his face.

'Brom and Ichy.'

'That's right,' said Ren.

'They're nice names.' Tom lowered his head once more. 'Hold on to them.'

CHAPTER NINETEEN

DOLLY WAS ASLEEP underneath a maple tree, and Ren thought he looked almost peaceful. His head was resting against the rough bark, his hood pulled over his face. It was a warm night. The trees on the common set in a line like pawns across a board.

Ren shouted in his ear. He held his nose and slapped his cheek but Dolly did not respond. Ren sat on the grass and watched the sun go down. Every once in a while he would lift Dolly's collar to make sure that his chest was still rising and falling. Ren counted seventeen links on the tattooed chain. He tried to imagine what it might be like to have that many ghosts behind him.

It was nearly an hour before Dolly finally opened his eyes.

'How long have I been sleeping?'

'About a hundred years,' said Ren.

Dolly felt his face for whiskers. He gave his broken grin. 'Then how come I'm not old?'

'You are,' said Ren. 'It just doesn't show.'

The streets were dark as they made their way home. Dolly followed in a daze, stumbling over bricks in the sidewalk. Ren steered him down an alley and past another group of soldiers, smoking on the corner. Their uniforms were dirty, their guns hung casually from their shoulders. When Ren turned to look, one of the men nodded, showing the gaps in his brown teeth, and Dolly made the sign of the cross in return.

By the time they approached the boardinghouse it was early evening. The windows were shuttered as they came along the sidewalk. Ren tried the door and found it unlocked. The fire in the kitchen was cold. The knife and pie-makings were still on the counter, the rolling pin covered with flour, but Mrs Sands was nowhere to be found. Dolly stood by while Ren opened cupboards and closets, turned over the potato basket, pushed the cloaks hanging by the door aside, then thundered up the stairs.

'Mrs Sands?'

Ren checked their beds, then went to the landing above. He pushed his way into the mousetrap girls' room. The space was large enough to hold four single cots. Shards of mirror hung on the walls. In the closet were their Sunday clothes – their heavy boots and navy dresses missing. He knocked over a box of rouge. He stumbled up another flight of stairs to the attic.

When no one answered his banging, he went inside. The room was narrow, with a pitched ceiling and two skylights. Underneath these openings was an old rope bed, and flung across it, still in her kitchen clothes, was Mrs Sands.

Her face was flushed, the top of her collar torn loose. Her hands were pasted with flour. Ren touched her shoulder. 'Mrs Sands,' he whispered. She began to shake, lightly at first in response and then harder, so much that she nearly fell to the floor. Ren reached for the blanket, pulled it across her body, and held her down, leaning all his weight onto the mattress.

'YOU'RE MURDERING ME.'

'I'm trying to help.'

Mrs Sands focused for a moment on Ren's face. She reached out and grabbed hold of him. 'IT'S THE DROWNED BOY.' The landlady shook her head. She tore at the sheets. 'I'VE NEVER SEEN ANYONE SO HUNGRY.'

'What's the matter with you?' Ren asked.

'I WON'T TAKE THE BOWL AWAY, I PROMISE.' She clutched his arm and tried to stand up. 'I HAVE TO MAKE SUPPER.' She got out of the bed and began to cough, her body folding in half. She bent over the ground, pressed her hands to her ribs and began to sob. A small trickle of blood fell from her mouth onto the rug.

'Dolly!' Ren screamed. He bolted to the stairs. 'Dolly!'

The staircase pounded, as if each flight were collapsing beneath the man as he ascended. Dolly burst into the room, his hands groping out before him like a blind man.

'There's blood in her mouth.'

Dolly crouched on the floor in his monk's robe. He looked the landlady up and down, then touched her stomach. Mrs Sands groaned.

'Don't do that!' Ren said.

'She's sick.'

'I know,' Ren said. 'Help me.'

Together they got Mrs Sands back on the bed and rolled her into a blanket. Ren had seen other children at Saint Anthony's come down with this kind of fever before. When they coughed blood, Brother Joseph would move them into a separate room. If the brothers waited too long to send for a doctor, another plot would soon be made in the field next to the chapel.

Dolly carried Mrs Sands downstairs while Ren unscrewed the knob from Benjamin's bedpost. They would need money, he thought, and gathered it all. The horse and wagon were in the stable; it took time before they could get the animal properly rigged and settle Mrs Sands in the back. Ren listened to her coughs, clasped the reins in his one good hand, and hoped that he would be able to remember the way in the dark.

It was nearly an hour before they reached the bridge. Ren had taken three wrong turns. Dolly could not remember what direction they had started from, and Mrs Sands had fallen into a troubled and sweaty sleep. The boy could see shapes in the alleyways as they passed, moving figures around a fire, a vagrant propped against a wall, an old woman holding her skirt up to her waist, then dropping it when she saw them pass. He looked straight ahead, as if he noticed none of this, and when he caught a glimpse of the bridge he let out a sigh of relief. There was only one road to the hospital now.

The wagon shifted as it went over the river. Ren looked into the rushing water. He thought of the drowned boy and wondered if his spirit would be able to feel his old clothes passing overhead. Ren held on to the reins tightly, and began to bargain with God. If they crossed safely over the bridge, he would say ten rosaries. If they made it to the hospital, he would say twenty.

Under a streetlight ahead were two men, smoking pipes. One wore a porkpie hat pulled to the side; the other had spats buttoned up to his knees. It was the same two men that Dolly had recognized outside O'Sullivan's bar. Ren hesitated, but drove the wagon on. As they got closer, the man in the spats took a round, flat disk from underneath his arm and slapped it against his wrist. With a pop, the disk turned into a top hat. The man placed it on his head, then jumped in front of the horse and took hold of the bridle.

'Bit late for catechism, isn't it, Father?'

The man in the top hat could not have been more than twenty. His face was smooth, his confidence untried. Behind him, the man in the porkpie hat pulled a chain from his pocket and ran it through his fingers.

'I'm a monk,' said Dolly.

'That's not what I remember,' said the Top Hat. 'I remember a purple suit.'

Ren tugged at the reins. The mare shook her head back and forth. Dolly pushed the hood of his robe from his face, then stepped down from the wagon.

'Let go of the horse.'

'All we want is a blessing,' said the Top Hat. 'Then maybe we'll forget we saw you. You've got a blessing for us, don't you, monk?'

Dolly raised his two fingers to start the cross. Behind him, the man in the porkpie hat lifted the chain. It came down hard on the back of Dolly's neck. Ren cried out, but Dolly didn't react. He simply turned and took hold of the man's throat and crushed it. The chain fell. Dolly pushed the man up against the streetlamp and then bashed his skull against it, over and over, until the man's hat fell onto the sidewalk.

Ren was yanked from his seat. The man in the top hat was shouting in his ear and it was only then that the boy realized there was a knife pressed to the side of his face. Then they were both falling over, and Dolly was on top of them. Everywhere there were elbows and knees scrambling. Ren felt a sting on his cheek. A foot in his stomach. He covered his face with his arms and rolled off the sidewalk and into the gutter. Above him someone shrieked and groaned and then the shuffling stopped and it was quiet. The boy's fingers touched something soggy. It smelled like rotten fish, and it was. Ren looked around him. He was surrounded by heads and tails, all the leftovers from a day of fishing the river.

Dolly took the boy by the elbow and set him on his feet. The shepherd's robe was sprinkled with blood. The man in the top hat slumped against the sidewalk; one of his eyes had been put out, and a slick trail of red ran from his lashes to his ear.

The boy was shaking. His legs were wet. He could hear voices, a shout in the alley, coming closer. Dolly was calmly looking out into the night, and the boy knew he could kill a dozen more like this. Ren struggled not to panic. He tried to think of what Benjamin would do.

'Get them in the wagon,' Ren said. 'Now.'

Together they loaded the men into the back of the cart, one on either side of Mrs Sands. All the commotion had stirred her from her fever. She was awake, her face spotted with red, her brow damp with perspiration.

'THEY'RE ALWAYS STEALING MY BACON!' she shouted.

'We know,' said Ren. He pulled the blankets over the bodies.

Mrs Sands seemed happier with the dead men covered up. She closed her eyes again. 'SERVES THEM RIGHT.'

Ren tucked the comforter up to her chin. He took Dolly's hand. 'Let's go.'

Dolly's fingers were slimy; Ren could feel a bit of

something left – hair, or skin – in his palm. *He didn't mean it*, he thought as they climbed back into the wagon, but in his heart Ren knew that Dolly had meant it, and he would have done it again, and again. After this Ren couldn't think anymore. Instead he felt the air on his damp skin, the smell of fish in his clothes. The lamppost disappeared behind them, and the boy realized that he was sharing a seat with a murderer. There would be no more bargaining with God. He was into hell now for sure.

Ren hurried the horse along, trying to put as much distance between the wagon and the town as possible. The law would be after them soon, if they weren't after Dolly already. Ren's palm began to sweat as he thought of getting caught. Every few minutes he checked to make sure they weren't being followed. Before long they were beyond the limits, and then in the open countryside. Dolly leaned back in his seat, as if all of this was happening to someone else. The moon came out from behind a cloud, but the man's face remained dark.

'You killed them, Dolly.'

'It's their own fault.'

'That doesn't make it right.' There was a rustling in the woods at the side of the road. Ren turned his head. He felt the trees watching them. The oaks and the elms and the maples towered over the wagon, their branches swaying. Ren felt the words of contrition at the back of his throat, and then they were spilling out, 'O my God, I am heartily sorry for having offended Thee.' He glanced over at Dolly, who was looking up at the stars. 'You're going to have to confess too.'

'For what?' Dolly asked.

'For everything.'

'That would take years,' Dolly said. 'And that's with me not remembering half of what I've done.'

'If you don't you won't be saved.' Ren glanced over to see if this made an impression. To his surprise, he saw that it did not.

The boy did his best to explain the seven signs, the Second Coming, and the end of the world. He told Dolly about how the dead were going to rise and stand among the living, and how it would be a day of judgment, and Christ would decide who went to heaven and who was cast down to hell forever.

'I've already been there,' Dolly said. 'And I've already come back.'

'But it's a sin,' Ren said. 'And it's against the law. You'll go to jail. *They'll hang you.*' He could not understand Dolly's indifference. A cold breeze blew up, and Ren's nose began to run.

A cloud passed away from the moon, and Dolly's face came out of the darkness. He patted Ren on the shoulder. 'I told you before. I was made for killing.'

In the back of the wagon the men were silent, as if agreeing with this. Ren was suddenly anxious that they were still alive. He pulled the horse to a stop, then lifted the edge of one of the blankets. The brim of the porkpie hat was pulled rakishly to the side, the back of man's skull split open. The other man's face oozed with blood; they'd left his top hat in the road. Ren waited for a sign, feeling nauseated all the while. Doctor Milton was wrong. Nothing inside their bodies was beautiful.

Ren looked down the road that stretched before them in the dark. Up ahead was a clearing, and through the leaves he could see the turret of the hospital, standing in the distance, like a giant waiting to be fed. The boy took a deep breath, then covered the hat boys again, released the brake, and set the horse moving. Father John had always told him that the Day of Judgment would come in their lifetime. But when Ren glanced behind, no one was following them, and no judgment seemed at hand.

CHAPTER TWENTY

SISTER AGNES WAS waiting at the gate as if she expected them, her arms full of bedpans. She was knocking the containers one by one against the wall of the building and kicking dirt over the waste with her foot. She looked tired, as though she'd never stopped working.

The wagon drew close and Ren realized that Sister Agnes stood between them and the basement. He began to waver, then decided to do what Benjamin would have done. He smiled, and waved, then handed the reins over to Dolly. He pulled the brake. 'Our landlady is sick.'

Sister Agnes put the bedpans down and opened the gates. 'If it's contagious you'll have to leave.' She dried her hands on her gray pinafore, walked to the back of the cart before Ren could stop her, and parted the blankets.

Ren expected her to scream. Or burst into tears. But after a cursory glance at the dead men, Sister Agnes simply pushed them aside and began taking Mrs Sands's temperature.

'Fever,' said Sister Agnes. She lifted Mrs Sands's eyelids. 'Dilation.' She felt her neck. 'Swelling.' She opened Mrs Sands's mouth, peering through the lips. 'Infection.' All this time Mrs

Sands tried to swat her away, but Sister Agnes dodged her easily. Then she took Mrs Sands by the wrists, put her ear to the landlady's chest and held it there for a moment.

'Is she going to be all right?'

'Quiet!'

'MURDERERS!' Mrs Sands shouted.

Ren felt the color drain from his face. But the nun ignored Mrs Sands completely. She continued listening for another minute, then stood and began readjusting the blanket. 'Your landlady has influenza.'

'Is that bad?'

'It can be. It's brought on by damp weather. And it's contagious. She'll spread the disease to the other patients in the ward. We can't take her here.' She tucked the blanket around the body of Mrs Sands with a practiced efficiency. 'Unless you have the funds for a private room.'

Ren dug into his pockets and turned out the money from the bedpost. Sister Agnes gathered the bills from his hand, and Ren began to worry whether it would be enough. The nun counted silently, then turned her black eyes on Dolly, still sitting on the driver's seat. He was staring ahead, his shoulders hunched. He had not acknowledged her, or Ren, or anything for the last three miles on the road.

'Brother.'

Dolly looked down at Sister Agnes.

'Are you from Saint Anthony's?' she asked.

'Yes,' said Ren, 'he is.'

Dolly made the sign of the cross, and Sister Agnes observed him carefully.

'Where did these men come from?'

It was phrased as an accusation, and Dolly's face dimmed. Ren could tell that he was sizing her up, calculating the risk. The boy rushed forward.

'We found them in the road.'

Ren could see Sister Agnes's doubts rising as she got a closer look at Dolly's costume. Then her mouth closed tight as if she had confirmed her suspicions. She tucked her hands into her sleeves and nodded at the back of the wagon.

'You can put the others through the depository. The doctor is on his morning rounds, but I'm certain you'll receive the proper compensation.'

She stood by as Dolly and Ren wrapped the bodies in blankets and carried them over to the basement door. There was a swinging section in the lower half, just like the gate at Saint Anthony's. Ren lifted the handle and peered inside. A long metal chute was attached to receive the deliveries. One by one Dolly pushed the bodies through, and Ren could hear them sliding down into the darkness.

The morning was just beginning to leak its color across the sky as Sister Agnes showed them upstairs to the private ward. Dolly took each step carefully, carrying Mrs Sands in his arms. Ren followed behind. He could hear the people from the public wards, turning in their beds, their whispers echoing throughout the hall.

On the second floor Sister Agnes took a key from the ring on her waist. She unlocked a passageway that led to a long corridor lined with rooms. Stationed outside of every other doorway was a Sister of Charity. Most of the nuns were doing needlework, but Ren could see that one or two were dozing instead. Sister Agnes prodded these women as she passed, and they slipped further into their chairs before snapping awake.

'Each sister is assigned two patients to care for. They are available day and night, and are responsible for bringing meals and cleaning linens. If your landlady needs anything, she may ring the bell and Sister Josephine will answer.' An old, freckled nun leaned against the wall outside the empty room, her habit tilted precariously to one side, her mouth open.

'New patient,' Sister Agnes said.

The nun's eyes popped open. She was nearly seventy, with gray strands of hair peeking out of her habit; a solid woman, despite her age.

'Get the tub and some water,' said Sister Agnes. 'She'll have to be deloused.'

Sister Josephine shuffled off down the hallway, rolling up the sleeves on her sizeable arms. Dolly set the landlady on the bed while Ren looked around the room. It was a pleasant space, with a clean floor and flowered wallpaper and eyelet curtains trimmed with lace.

'I'M NOT A LOUSE.'

'Quiet!' Sister Agnes said. 'She'll wake the other patients.'

'She can't help it,' Ren tried to explain.

'BOY!'

'Shhhh.' He took Mrs Sands's hand and squeezed it.

'YOU MUST MAKE HIS DINNER. YOU MUST BRING HIM HIS SOCKS.'

Ren tried to cover her mouth, but Mrs Sands took hold of his fingers.

'LEAVE THEM BY THE FIREPLACE.'

And then the boy understood. It was the chimney dwarf. Mrs

Sands knew that Ren had seen him. She knew that Ren had taken the wooden horse.

Sister Agnes pulled a small brown bottle from her sleeve. She held it underneath Mrs Sands's nose, and the landlady immediately began to sneeze. 'You've upset her.'

The door swung open, and Sister Josephine carried in a basin full of water. 'Out of the way!' She said to Dolly, who backed against the wall, holding the place on his stomach where the nun had elbowed him.

'She needs to sleep,' said Sister Agnes. 'You should go. She'll get good care here. God be praised.'

Ren leaned over the bed. Mrs Sands's eyes were unfocused. Her hands limp. Ren could see inside the landlady's mouth. There was a molar on the right side, plugged with gold. Sister Josephine began to pull at the pins in Mrs Sands's hair.

'How long will it take for her to get better?'

'There's no way to tell,' said Sister Agnes.

'I'll come back soon,' Ren said to Mrs Sands. The landlady slapped at the nuns as they tried to undress her, and Sister Agnes pushed Ren and Dolly out of the room.

'I hate this place,' Dolly said as they went through the hallway doors.

'Haven't you ever been sick?' Ren asked.

Dolly sat down on the stairs and lifted his robe. He showed Ren a sealed hole, the size of a quarter, in his thigh.

'Where'd you get that?'

'Someone shot me,' said Dolly. He traced the hole with his finger.

'Why?'

'Because I was strangling him.' Dolly's tongue pushed out the

191

side of his cheek, and Ren saw that he was boasting again. He showed Ren where the bullet had come out, on the other side of his leg.

'Just missed the bone,' said Doctor Milton. He was on the landing below, watching them through the spokes of the railing, his suit spotlessly tailored, his beard trimmed, his fingernails picked clean. 'This is an unexpected visit.'

'It's our landlady,' said Ren. 'She's sick.'

'Is it a fever?' Doctor Milton asked. 'We've had several interesting cases. Someone died of it last night.' He climbed the stairs, leaned over, and touched Dolly's bullet hole. 'This must have been exceedingly painful.'

Dolly looked away, as if he were embarrassed.

Doctor Milton studied Dolly's giant hands, his chest, his square bald head. He took his finger off the bullet hole. 'You must lead a fascinating life.'

Dolly stared back.

'Yes,' said Ren. 'He does.'

The boy could sense the hospital slowly coming to life, the doctors and students and patients starting their day. A Sister of Mercy walked by with a tray of dressings. Two young students passed on the stairs and nodded at Doctor Milton. They seemed taken aback by Dolly, his bloodied robe pulled about his knees.

'I'd like to speak with you,' said Doctor Milton. 'In the observatory, please.' He led Ren and Dolly down the hall, past the rows of paintings and his own hungry-looking portrait. The operating room was empty, the stage scrubbed clean and covered with fresh sawdust. The morning sun shone through the skylights and brightened the rows of benches. Doctor Milton closed the door.

'I received your delivery. I'm afraid there's a problem.'

'What's the matter?' Ren asked.

'They were murdered.' The doctor pointed to the corner of his eye. 'Here,' he said. 'And here.' He touched the back of his skull. 'The blood's barely dry. They've only been dead for a few hours. When a body comes in like this, I'm supposed to report it.'

Ren coughed. 'It was an accident.'

'That makes no difference to me.'

The room went still. Ren looked at Dolly, who stood near the door, his hands opening and closing, his brow creased. If only Benjamin was with them, Ren thought. They needed a story to get out of this. The boy searched for a way to explain. But instead Dolly walked up to the doctor and tapped him on the shoulder.

'I killed them,' said Dolly.

'Excuse me?' said Doctor Milton.

'I killed them and I'm not sorry,' Dolly said, and then he turned to Ren, as though he'd just done something wonderful.

'Well,' said Doctor Milton, sucking in his breath. 'That's very interesting.'

The speech Ren had given on the road had brought the truth out. Dolly had confessed, but he confessed to the wrong man. Ren groaned. *That's it*, he thought. *We're finished.* He was surprised to find that he was more relieved than afraid. He sat down on the stairs, dropped his head, and waited for Doctor Milton to send for the police. But the doctor did not raise the alarm. He took a small notebook out of his pocket and began eagerly scribbling across the paper.

'I'd like to examine you,' the doctor said to Dolly. 'If you would permit me?' He gestured to the operating table in the center of the stage. Dolly glanced at Ren, and when the boy shrugged his shoulders, he followed the doctor down the stairs. Doctor Milton brushed a bit of sawdust off the table, and Dolly settled on top, stretching out as if he were preparing to take a nap.

The doctor wrote a few more notes, then leaned over Dolly's face. 'I'm going to touch your head.'

'What for?'

'To take some measurements.' Doctor Milton rested his fingertips on either side of Dolly's forehead. Then he slowly moved them across the scalp, pausing over each bump, running his thumb along the center, as if the seam there bound the man together. The morning sun shone through the skylight, and the doctor's whole face was illuminated.

'I met a giant once,' Doctor Milton said, 'with this same shape of skull. When I heard he was ill, I tried to make arrangements, but he refused to sell his body to me. He made his friends promise to seal him in a lead coffin and dump it in the ocean. But I paid off the undertaker, and they filled the coffin with stones. He's made a wonderful addition to my collection.' Doctor Milton ran his fingers over Dolly's jaw. 'I haven't acquired any murderers yet. Perhaps I could persuade you to take part, to further my study of phrenology?'

Dolly blinked at the doctor, not understanding. And then he did. The dark fog came back into his eyes, and he reached up, and in one movement seized the doctor's arm and twisted it backward. Doctor Milton cried out and tried to get away, clawing with his free hand. Dolly sat up on the operating table and took the blows as if they were nothing.

The doctor started to scream and Dolly covered his mouth, just as he had done with Mrs Sands, muffling the cries with his giant fingers. Ren watched Doctor Milton thrashing and was reminded of how terrified he'd been on his first visit, sitting on the edge of that same table. He waited a little while longer and then he said, 'That's enough.'

Dolly let go. Doctor Milton staggered off the stage, cradling his arm and cursing. 'I think he's broken it.'

'You frightened him.'

'*I* frightened *him*?'

'He's sorry. Aren't you, Dolly?'

'No.'

Doctor Milton slowly bent his arm, wincing in pain. He pushed up his sleeve and felt the bone. 'Not broken. But sprained. It will keep me from operating for at least a week. Do you want to explain this to Mrs Fitzpatrick and her goiter?'

'Not really,' said Ren.

'It helps to understand someone's history,' said Doctor Milton. 'That's all I was trying to say. If I know a man's profession or his temperament, I can see how it affected the growth of his body. If his liver is diseased or his heart too small. An anomaly opens the door.' Doctor Milton hovered over his box of medical instruments, as if they offered some kind of protection. With his fingertips he pulled out a bandage and began to wrap it around his injured arm, all the way to the wrist.

'I'm no different from anyone else,' said Dolly.

'Yes, you are,' said Doctor Milton, brandishing a pair of scissors. Ren could tell that he was still afraid. 'You're a murderer.'

The scissors flashed like a signal. 'The men we brought were murderers too,' said Ren.

Doctor Milton seemed intrigued, if not completely pacified. 'Do they have any family? Anyone who might come looking for them?'

Ren looked the doctor straight in the eye. 'No.'

'I'm not going to pay the regular price,' said Doctor Milton. 'And I want that man off the premises first.'

'I'm not leaving Ren,' said Dolly.

The boy put his hand on Dolly's arm. 'It's only for a few minutes,' he said. 'Wait for me outside.'

Dolly cracked his massive knuckles. He gave Doctor Milton a menacing look, then threw his body forward, off the examination table. Ren watched his friend leave, and when he turned around Doctor Milton had already fashioned a sling for his arm. With a bit of fumbling, the man took out his purse and pressed the money into Ren's hand. It was less than a third of what they'd received before.

'You're a smart boy,' said Doctor Milton. 'I don't know what you're doing with a man like that.'

'He's my friend,' said Ren.

'You should be going to school. You could study science. Or get a job of some kind. Something respectable.'

These possibilities fanned out before Ren like cards on a table, then closed back together, until there was only one option left. He was never going to study science; he was never going to be respectable. And he was tired of trying to be good. The best he could do was follow the path that Benjamin had showed him. He belonged to it now.

'I don't want him coming back here,' said Doctor Milton. 'Unless you bring him as a delivery. I'd pay extra for that.'

Ren imagined Dolly's bones hanging next to the giant's. 'I don't think he'd like it.'

'He doesn't have to,' said the doctor. 'He only has to die.'

CHAPTER TWENTY-ONE

Ren and Dolly were fumbling through Mrs Sands's drawers, encountering mountains of nightgowns as they searched for the small man's socks. Ren wondered at the amount of underwear, for he'd only seen the landlady in two dresses: one purple, one brown. In her closet he'd found another, made of light gray silk, covered with paper and tied with string, that he suspected was her wedding dress.

All the time they were searching, Ren thought of what he would say to Tom and Benjamin. He wanted to tell them about the murders beneath the streetlight, but he was afraid they might turn Dolly out. And then there was the money missing from the bedpost. Benjamin would need some kind of excuse, and the more Ren tried to imagine one the more his mind was empty.

Dolly opened a small box full of ribbons, curled into circles and pinned. He pulled one out after the next, until they came undone in spirals across the bureau. He glanced into the mirror hanging over the dresser. 'Ren,' he said. 'Look!'

Piled on the crossbeam over their heads was a mountain of toys, waiting in the dust to be discovered: a marionette in the shape of a monkey; a fleet of Viking ships; letter blocks; tiny pigs; a mask in the shape of the moon; a castle with a dragon; a set of fish that came apart and fit inside of each other, the shark swallowing down to the minnow. Dolly lifted Ren onto his shoulders and together they pulled them all free, sweeping the toys out onto the bed.

Ren went to retrieve the wooden horse from where he'd hidden it in his room and set it beside the other toys. Without a doubt, it was created by the same hand. From the sharp angles of the ears to the bluntness of the face, the horse resembled the surrounding creatures. The dwarf could not be so bad, Ren thought, if he had made all of these things.

They found a bag of knitting in a chest at the foot of the bed. Underneath, wrapped in a piece of stiff canvas, was a pair of worn, clean socks. The heels and toes were ragged. Ren could see where the pattern had already been fixed dozens of times. He held them up and recognized the size and style. He was not the only one wearing the drowned boy's clothes.

Dolly began to root through the knitting bag. He emerged with a ball of yarn, a set of darning needles, and a pair of tiny scissors. 'I need a bed knob.'

'For what?'

'To fix the socks.'

They went back to their room, and Dolly slipped the ragged knitting over the bed knob. Then he threaded one of the needles with the yarn, and began to make small vertical running stitches along the ragged edges. When he finished, he connected the stitches on either side with a longer piece of yarn, creating a grid. Then he tied it off and began weaving in the opposite direction, under and over and through.

'Where did you learn that?'

'My mother taught me.'

Ren watched the pattern appear beneath Dolly's hands. It was hard to believe that Dolly had ever had a mother. He darned socks the same methodical way he'd killed the men beneath the streetlamp – with skill and without emotion. He maneuvered the needle until he'd built up a delicate web across the hole in the toe. He did the same with the heel, counting rows quietly under his breath.

'Why do you think Mrs Sands takes care of him?' Ren asked.

'I don't know,' said Dolly.

'I'll bet he did something terrible.'

'He's only a dwarf,' said Dolly. 'I don't think he could have done much of anything.' Dolly set aside the first sock and slipped the second onto the bedpost. He sucked on the end of the yarn and threaded the needle with his giant fingers. He began to weave over the missing heel. The bed knob disappeared as he brought the strands together. Ren thought of all the terrible things that Dolly had done. All the terrible things he had yet to do.

'Are you still going to kill him?' Ren asked.

'Who?'

'The man you were hired for.'

'I think I better.'

'Why?'

'I've already been paid.' He pulled the finished sock from the bedpost and handed it to Ren. 'And he knows I'm coming for him. If I don't get him, he'll get me first.' Dolly crawled to his place underneath the bed. 'But I'm too tired now. Maybe I'll do it tomorrow.'

Ren leaned over the edge of the mattress. 'How?'

Dolly was squeezed tightly into the space, his forehead nearly touching the wooden slats. 'Necks. Necks are the easiest.'

'You won't use a gun?'

'Too much noise.'

Ren rolled back onto the bed. He pulled one of Mrs Sands's quilts over his shoulders and watched the late afternoon sun cross the walls. 'What if I asked you not to kill him?'

Dolly sighed.

'We're going away. You could come with us.' Ren twisted the quilt in his hand.

'I'll think about it,' said Dolly. 'But I'm not going to promise.' After a few minutes he turned over, rolling the mattress and lifting Ren along with the frame. The bed settled back on its legs, several inches to the left, and Ren could hear Dolly's breath grow even as he started to snore.

Ren stared at the ceiling and thought of the man in the top hat, the heavy weight of his body as they pushed it through the hospital basement door. He touched the scab on his cheek where the man's knife had cut through. In a week the hard crust would be gone, the skin underneath pink and new. Ren had already convinced Dolly to confess. If he could stop him from killing anyone else, and if he prayed as hard as he could, it might be like it had never happened at all.

When Benjamin didn't return before midnight, Ren went downstairs to fulfill his promise to Mrs Sands. He took down the same dinner tray he had seen her lay out and quickly put together a supper of stale bread and dried sausage along with a small bruised apple, and covered the whole thing with a napkin. He placed the tray on the table next to the socks that Dolly had fixed. Then he crawled inside the potato basket to wait.

Almost an hour passed, until Ren had pins and needles in his legs. Just when he thought the dwarf would not come he heard something in the chimney. A few moments later the small man crawled out from the fireplace. Ren watched from the potato basket as the dwarf circled the room, then lifted the napkin and snorted. He ignored the stale bread and sausage and took the apple to a stool by the fireplace, carving the fruit expertly with his knife and eating the pieces right from the blade. He was wearing the same clothes Ren had seen him in before – a short brown jacket, green trousers, and small, rough boots. When the man was finished, he gnawed on the core, spitting the seeds into the fireplace. Then he licked his fingers, unlaced his boots, took off his socks, and reached for the ones Ren had left.

The dwarf inspected the toes. He fingered the heels. Then he was up and walking between the tables, behind the counters, lifting the lid on the trunk. Ren tried to keep an eye on him from the potato basket, but the dwarf slipped out of sight, into the back of the kitchen, moving chairs and knocking pans.

Ren held his breath, listening. Then all at once his hair was nearly torn from his head. His body was yanked from the basket onto the floor and the small man's horrible wrinkled face pressed into his own.

'Where's Mary?' the dwarf barked. Bits of apple sprayed onto Ren's forehead.

'I don't know any Mary.'

'The woman who lives here. The woman who runs this house!'

Ren tried to pry the fingers from his hair. 'She's at the hospital.'

The man loosened his grip. He looked stricken. 'Is she dead?'

'She's got influenza. She asked me to take care of you.'

The dwarf let go of the boy. He picked up the knife he'd used to cut the apple. 'Do I look like I need taking care of?' The blade was nearly the same length as the handle, the point curved at the end. The dwarf backed into the fireplace, then took hold of the rope. 'When's she coming back?'

'I don't know.'

The small man seemed undecided whether or not to leave. His voice became plaintive. 'She never gets sick.' He twisted the rope in his hands, as if Mrs Sands's illness was going to follow him up the chimney and find a way to snuff him out.

It took a few moments for Ren to realize that the man was frightened. He picked up the tray of food. 'You should take something.'

The dwarf looked over the bread and sausage. Then a thought began to form on his face, and he let go of the rope and slipped the knife back into his pocket. 'Is the pantry unlocked?'

They opened the door to the back room and found the larder full. The shelves were stocked with jars of pickles and preserves – strange colors and suspicious shapes floating in glass containers. There was a piece of cured meat wrapped in cheesecloth, a small cask of beer, a string of sausages hanging from a hook, metal canisters of flour and brown sugar, and a tin that was labeled Molasses.

The small man chose a jar that was yellowish orange. Ren took it down off the shelf for him, then watched as he opened the top with his knife. Inside were half-moons of soft molten pink. The dwarf pierced one and lifted it, glistening, to his mouth. 'Peaches,' he said, and stuck his knife in for another. He did not offer any to Ren. The boy stood by, wondering at Mrs Sands's reasons for tolerating such a visitor. The dwarf finished the jar and proceeded to lick the edges, to dip his tongue inside and clear away the remains of the juice.

'Get me another. That one, over there.' The small man pointed to a green jar in the corner. It was filled with pickled onions. He poked them with his knife, peeled them layer by layer, and slid the translucent coats between his lips. It seemed as if he would eat forever. Ren passed down jar after jar, and the dwarf made short work of them, lining the empty glasses along the pantry wall. The boy wondered if he should put a stop to it, but he kept remembering Mrs Sands and what he'd promised.

The dwarf did not slow down until he reached the herring. Then, after devouring the last piece of fish from the tin, he paused, wiped his mouth with his sleeve, and slumped against the wall. 'Have you got the key?'

'No,' said Ren.

'We've got to find it. Those mousetrap girls will clean through this in an hour.' He loosened his belt and slid to the floor. 'Christ.'

'Why do you live in the chimney?' Ren asked.

'I don't live in the chimney. I live on the roof.'

'And Mrs Sands lets you do it?'

'This house is mine as much as hers. Our mother left it to the both of us.'

Ren turned to the dwarf in surprise and was met with a hard stare. It was a look that expected ridicule, a look that dared it to come. Ren thought of how, as Sister Josephine deloused her, all that Mrs Sands cared about was that this small man had his socks.

'Did she die?'

The dwarf wiped his hands on a napkin. 'Of course she did. That's what mothers do.'

Ren clung to the empty jar of preserves. He could feel a chip in the glass, beneath his finger. 'It must be cold in the winter up there.'

'It is cold. But it's safe.'

'Safe from what?'

'From the ones who hate people like me. Or you.' He nodded at Ren's scar, and the boy instinctively pulled it into his sleeve.

'At least you can hide it,' said the dwarf.

Ren rocked back and forth on his heels, feeling caught. Then he pushed his stump out of the sleeve again. It was hard and pink and crossed with scars. But he realized that compared to the dwarf, it was not bad-looking. Not really.

The man let out a soft belch and rubbed his tiny stomach. 'I have a house up there. And a stove.' He stuffed his shirt back inside his trousers, then heaved himself forward onto his feet. 'Would you like to see it?'

'I would,' said Ren, and he realized that he did. 'Very much.'

The dwarf seemed glad of this, nearly as glad as he had been when he'd discovered the pantry unlocked. He crawled into the chimney. 'You must push yourself through it,' he said, holding on to the rope. 'Get a grip with your feet – one underneath, and one across. And keep your mouth shut and your eyes closed when you can. It will keep the dust from getting in.' With that he tied the rope around his waist, stepped onto the fireplace irons, and hoisted himself into the hole.

Ren watched from below, listening to the shuffle of the dwarf's back against the bricks. It hardly seemed to take any time for him to reach the top. Then he was gone and the pale sky showed through, a tiny window in the dark.

The rope came tumbling down the empty space toward the boy. The weight of it was thin, the ends frayed and brittle. Ren tied it around his waist as he had seen the small man do. He glanced up into the tunnel. It seemed longer than before. He crouched and climbed onto the metal grating, kicked aside the few remaining dusty logs, and ducked his head inside the flue.

The space was small, not much wider than his own shoulders. The sides were smudged black and coated with a thick, gray crust. Ren touched it with his fingers. The brick was cool. He took hold of the rope with his one good hand, dug his other elbow against the stone behind, pushed one heel to the corner, and lifted himself into the chimney.

About two thirds of the way up there was a narrowing of the flue. Ren's body would only fit through diagonally, his shoulders pressing into the corners, his head forced to one side. He could no longer lift his knees to push himself forward. He clung to the rope and began to panic.

'I'm stuck!' he called.

Ren leaned one way, and then the other. He slid several feet before he was able to jam his toe into a crack and stop his descent. A cloud of ash fell from the walls, and soot got inside his nose and his mouth, between his teeth and underneath his tongue. His arms were raked and raw, his ankle twisted painfully beneath him. 'I'm falling!'

He heard the dwarf say, 'Christ.' And then Ren felt a tug at his waist. Slowly at first, and then with gathering speed, he was helped up the chimney, knocking his head and bumping his elbows. Occasionally he lost his footing and dangled on the end of the rope like a fish. A few minutes more and he was through the window of sky, into the fresh air, the small man taking hold of his jacket and hauling him out onto the roof.

He patted Ren's back. 'It's easier going down.'

Ren rubbed his face with his sleeve. He coughed and spit the ashes from his mouth. It was nearly morning, the sun brightening the horizon in the east. From the roof Ren could make out the entire town, the mousetrap factory looming over the center of the city, the river circling it all like a protective arm. To the south the marketplace rose in the square. To the west the bridge crossed over the river and marked a passageway through the woods. Just beyond those woods was a gathering of hills. Somewhere within them was the entrance to the mine that had claimed the lives of all the men of North Umbrage, and beyond that, the road to the hospital.

The air was clearer here, the taste not as rancid as on the street. Ren thought of all he had done since he had left Saint Anthony's; every step that had brought him to this place. Spread out before him, both the town and his own past seemed less frightening. Everything was better, Ren realized, when you looked down on it from above.

The dwarf motioned for Ren to follow him into his home, which was little more than a shack from the outside; an abandoned pigeon cage wrapped in rags. But inside, the room was quite cozy, the walls lined with animal hides. Bits of worn leather and what looked like pigskin, stretched and pulled taut between pieces of fur. Squirrels and raccoons and beaver pelts covered the floor and in the corner was a large deerskin. There was still a head attached to it, with glass eyes fitted into the skull. It must have been where the dwarf slept, for there was a pillow there, and over it hung several shelves of books.

In the opposite corner was a miniature potbellied stove, and it was around this stove that the dwarf now busied himself — pulling bits of wood and paper from his pockets and stuffing them in the grate, pouring water from a small earthenware jar into a dented pan and setting it on top, digging a bit of flint from under a tile in the roof and striking it against the stone, sparking a flame which he then coaxed into a fire.

The dwarf dug around in a wooden box and pulled out a small sachet of roots and leaves, which he threw into the pot of water. Two mugs were taken down from a shelf. Carefully, he portioned out the brew he'd been stirring on the stove. Ren took a cup in his hand. It smelled bitter and burned his tongue.

'Wormwood,' said the small man. 'Our mother always made us this when we were sick. I'll put some in a jar for you to take to Mary.'

'Why don't you bring it to her?'

'I don't leave the roof,' the dwarf said.

'Why not?'

The dwarf set his mug of tea on the floor. 'I go down to the kitchen. That's the only time I go down.'

'Aren't you ever lonely?'

'Never,' the dwarf coughed.

Ren did not believe him.

There were piles of books in the corner, and more on the shelves hanging from the wall. Ren moved closer to read the titles. There were several in Greek and Latin and other languages he could not understand. A complete works of Shakespeare balanced on the floor, along with books of poetry, some novels, a history of the Roman Empire, and a large, fat, illustrated volume of *Don Quixote*. Ren picked it up and opened to the first chapter, the paper soft and thick beneath his fingers.

The water was boiling again. The dwarf turned back to the stove and filled the jar he was preparing for his sister. 'Some of those were my father's. But most of them came from a woman who used to live in North Umbrage. She was always a bit off. I watched her walk past the market one day and right into the water. She let go of her basket, and it floated away on the current. She took another step, and another, until her dress changed color and sank. Some men who were fishing pulled her out. I saw them carrying her back home. Her skirt dragged behind them, and it left a long wet trail, all the way back from the river.'

'What happened to her?' Ren asked.

'She disappeared,' said the dwarf. 'They say her brother sent her away to an institution. I saw her books being sold in the market afterward, and I asked Mary to buy them for me.' He leaned forward and flipped the pages to the frontispiece. There was a drawing of Don Quixote, riding his beaten-down horse, and in the opposite corner was a name, scribbled in the corner: Margaret McGinty. The dwarf drew his finger across the paper. 'Her brother owns the mousetrap factory. He has plenty of money. But he sold all of her things in the street, like she was some kind of criminal.'

Ren closed *Don Quixote* and slid it back onto the shelf. He understood now why the dwarf had been afraid. Without Mrs Sands, he had no food, no clothes, no family. He was completely helpless.

Outside, a whistle sounded. The dwarf pushed open the door. Smoke was rising from the factory. The mousetrap girls rushed into the streets in their blue uniforms, a few clutching bits of breakfast. They came from every corner of the town and flowed in the same direction.

'We've got to lock up the pantry,' said the small man. 'They'll eat everything if we don't.'

'Don't they pay for their food?'

'They get two meals a day. But with my sister gone they'll take everything.'

Morning spread across the rooftops, the sun so pink that it made the gutters shine. The streets below were slowly coming to life, the shops opening and the brothels closing. All the mousetrap girls had disappeared into the factory, and the door closed behind them like a giant mouth.

Ren looked out at the river circling the town. He felt the hem of his coat. The stitches there were straight and evenly paced. They traveled along the seams, across the shoulders and down the sleeves. He thought of Mrs Sands pushing the needle and thread, draining the water from the drowned boy's clothes until they were a perfect fit.

The dwarf handed him the jar full of tea. 'When you see Mary,' he said, 'I want you to remind her that she said that she would always take care of me. She promised after our mother died. A promise is a promise.'

For a moment Ren wished that he could trade places with the dwarf. He would not mind staying on the roof, he thought, if Mrs Sands was always at the other end of the chimney. He put his hand on the brick and peered down into the darkness. It was as steep as the well at Saint Anthony's. Ren pulled the jar close. Mrs Sands's tea was heavy in his arms. He tied the rope around his waist, climbed onto the chimney, and hoped that it would not break.

CHAPTER TWENTY-TWO

IT *WAS EASIER* going down. Ren simply pressed his feet against the inner bricks of the chimney and lowered himself, a bit at a time, holding on to the rope. Only once did he slip a bit, nearly dropping the jar, when he felt a wave of fatigue across his shoulders. Ren's days and nights had been completely upended, their beginnings and endings blurred. He was now more than likely to be awake at four in the morning, to be curling in a dark corner for a brief nap at noon. Ren had always thought of days in a physical sense, like the clock face in Father John's study – a sun and moon divided in two, morning and night. Now he understood that there was no precise moment when evening crossed over into morning – that there was never a brand-new day.

When he reached the end of the chimney, he heard low voices in the kitchen. He dropped quietly into the fireplace and saw Benjamin and the Harelip. She was sitting on his lap and spooning preserves from a jar into his mouth.

Benjamin had his hand under her skirt. Where the side was hitched up, Ren could see one of her black stockings. The seam was coming apart, revealing the delicate skin at the back of her knee. Benjamin was whispering something into the girl's ear and she was smiling.

'I'm already late,' she said. The Harelip slid off Benjamin's lap, her cheeks flushed. When she saw Ren standing in the fireplace, it was hard to say if she was embarrassed or angry. She snatched her shawl from the peg, then stuck her tongue out at him and left.

Ren waited until the door had closed, then crawled into the kitchen and set the jar of tea on the floor. He untied the rope from his waist and shook the dust from his clothes.

'Father Christmas!' said Benjamin. He was wearing a new coat, with a blue velvet collar that matched his eyes, and brand-new boots with rounded toes. The leather was hand-tooled and the laces barely creased.

'Where've you been?' Ren asked.

'Following the bartender. He lived out in the country, but it was worth it in the end. His whole family's gone. Struck down with a fever.' Benjamin brushed soot from Ren's jacket. 'How the hell did you end up in the chimney?'

Ren didn't have any excuses ready, and so decided to tell the truth. First he explained about finding Mrs Sands, then meeting the hat boys on the road. Benjamin frowned over the murders, then touched the cut on Ren's cheek. But as soon as the money was mentioned, Benjamin grabbed the boy's coat and began going through his pockets. He pulled out the bills that were left. He threw them down on the table.

'Where's the rest?'

'I used it to pay the doctor.'

Benjamin pushed Ren away from him. He went to the fireplace and began to throw logs onto the irons.

Ren stood still, his fingers gripping the chair. 'They said she was going to die.'

'You're supposed to steal from other people,' said Benjamin. 'Not me.'

'I wasn't stealing.'

'What would you call it, then?'

Ren remembered what Benjamin had said on the road, after they'd stolen the farmer's horse. 'Borrowing, with good intent.'

Benjamin looked up and shook his head, as if he was having his own private conversation with the ceiling. Then he threw another piece of wood onto the fire. 'Look,' he said. 'You just can't go around taking care of people. They'll grow to depend on you, and then you won't be able to leave them when you have to.'

Ren watched him bend over to light the wood. The same scent of ashes had filled the farmer's kitchen when his wife stirred the fire, trying to bring it to life enough so that she could serve them dinner.

'What if I don't want to leave them,' said Ren.

'Who?' Benjamin asked. 'The dead man?'

'He's not dead. He's my friend.'

'Now who's kidding themselves.' Benjamin threw a pine branch into the flames, and the needles crackled and smoked. 'I shouldn't have left him with you.'

'But you did,' said Ren. He picked up the jar of wormwood tea from the floor and set it carefully on the kitchen table. 'I told him that he could stay with us.'

The fireplace was now blazing, the cinders sparking in the ash. Benjamin ran his fingers across his chin and sighed. He pulled a seat forward and motioned for Ren to take it.

'That man's not your friend. He's a murderer. If he gets it in his mind, he could kill any one of us.' Ren started to protest but Benjamin held up his hand. 'I've seen his kind. Men that don't feel anything anymore. One minute they buy you a drink, and the next they slit your throat, or cut open a woman beside you, or saw off a person's hand for no reason at all.' Benjamin rubbed his nose, then looked at the boy to make sure he was following. Ren thought of the man with the red gloves, eating with the bartender's spoon. 'His only value is what he can do for us. I've tried to show you what I know,' Benjamin said. 'Anytime you get attached, you're putting yourself in danger.'

Ren felt the heat on his face. It was too warm for a fire. He knew that Mrs Sands would not approve of wasting wood, and he worried that the chimney would not cool in time for the dwarf to collect his supper. Benjamin must have been hot in his new coat, but he stayed in place, his forehead growing damp, waiting for Ren to tell him what he wanted to hear.

'I'm not in danger of anything.'

'Good,' said Benjamin.

They went out searching for Tom that afternoon. Ren looked in O'Sullivan's, and Benjamin visited three brothels on Darby Street, but no one had seen him. They bought a package of walnuts on the way back to the boardinghouse, and Benjamin proceeded to eat them all, cracking one after the other at the kitchen table and pulling out the meat.

'He'll show up soon,' Benjamin said. But Ren could tell that he was worried.

Together they went upstairs to check on Dolly. They could hear his snores in the hall as they approached. Benjamin crouched on the bedroom floor, sizing up the man underneath the mattress, like a piece of property he was not sure of keeping.

'I don't know why he sleeps so much.'

'It seems like he needs to,' said Ren.

Benjamin stood up and brushed the dust from his knees. 'I don't know about you,' he said, 'but if I had a second chance at life, I'd live it.'

There was not much to eat for supper. The mousetrap girls had made short work of the preserves, just as the dwarf had predicted, but there was still some salted pork and potatoes. Benjamin chopped the pork into pieces and fried it in lard. He sliced up a few of the potatoes and threw those on top. Then he added half a dozen eggs from the chickens in the yard, and threw the whole pan into the oven. When he took it out, the mixture had hardened, and he cut it into pieces, just like a pie.

'What is it?' Ren asked.

'Something I learned in Mexico,' said Benjamin.

Ren tasted a piece. The consistency was strange, and he rolled the food around in his mouth, trying to find a way to swallow it. 'Was it very terrible there?'

Benjamin blew on his fork. 'It wasn't good. But some men took to it.'

Ren tried to imagine what those men were like. Then he realized they were probably like Dolly. He picked at a piece of potato. 'Did you know that I was going to be sent into the army?'

'Father John may have mentioned that.'

'Is that the reason you picked me?'

'One of them.'

Ren lifted his head. He felt he should thank him. And so he did.

For once Benjamin seemed at a loss for words. He cleared his throat and gathered the plates. He brought them over to the counter, looked for a place to set them down, then balanced them carefully on top of all the other dirty dishes that had accumulated since Mrs Sands had left.

There was a knock on the window. Benjamin seemed relieved. 'That'll be Tom.'

Ren went to the door, leaned his weight back on the handle, and swung it open into the morning light. He squinted, then blinked his eyes once. Twice. For there stood Brom and Ichy. Wet, shivering, and frightened nearly out of their minds.

'I've brought your fellows,' said Tom, reeling, pushing the twins roughly forward into the room. 'Now we're a family at last.'

The boys fell to the floor and immediately got to their feet again and scurried to the corner of the room, trying to put as much distance and furniture between themselves and Tom as possible. To Ren they looked like beggars, their shirts torn, their pants too small, their jackets threadbare and full of holes.

'Have you lost your senses?' Benjamin shouted. 'What do we need three boys for?'

Tom pulled off his coat, threw it onto the ground and stumbled into a chair. Ren had never seen him so far gone. He could barely walk, and it was hard to imagine how he had made it all the way to Saint Anthony's, never mind what he had said to Father John to get the boys. Then Ren remembered what Brother Joseph had said about Brom and Ichy – that no one would ever adopt them – and he knew that Saint Anthony's had handed over the twins as easily as they had given him to Benjamin.

Tom fished for a soggy bag of tobacco and threw it on the table. From his other pocket he took out a bottle. 'They're his fellows.' Tom pounded his fist on the table. 'A boy needs his fellows.'

'We're sending them back,' said Benjamin. 'Tonight.'

'I'm their father,' Tom said.

'Don't be a fool.'

'You've got Ren.'

Benjamin walked to where Brom and Ichy were huddled together. One by one he took hold of their chins and pulled the boys forward into the light. Benjamin shook his head in disbelief. He threw his arms up in the air. 'Twins! Bad luck's going to follow us now, I can feel it.'

Brom and Ichy had been crying. Their eyes were red, their faces bleary. Ren hooked his friends by the elbow and pulled them round the corner, up the stairs and into the bedroom. The twins followed him blindly, too exhausted to ask questions. They seemed somehow younger than the boys he had left, more like children, even though they were nearly his age. Ren was grateful to see them, and as soon as they were alone, he threw his arms around them both.

'He told us he was bringing us to you,' said Brom. 'But we couldn't be sure of anything.' He looked thin and pale. 'Ichy didn't want to come.'

'Yes, I did.'

'No, you didn't. He hid in the garden and he wouldn't get his things. And then he cried all the way on the road. And Papa got furious, and said he'd strangle us both if Ichy didn't stop.'

'He told us to call him Papa.'

'He said he'd strangle us if we didn't do that, too.'

Ichy took hold of Ren's jacket. 'Do you think he'll really strangle us?'

Ren knew that his friends had already been scared enough, so he decided to do what Mrs Sands would have done, if she had been there. He found some water so the twins could wash their hands and faces. From the landlady's room he took some night-gowns and some extra quilts. The boys got changed quickly, peeling off their muddy clothes and then crawling into bed together, pulling the blankets around them.

'He took our rocks.'

'He threw them away on the road.'

'He told us that Father John was a cheat.'

'And he said that God didn't exist.'

The mattress beneath them began to tremble. The twins looked at one another, uncertain. Then the bed itself suddenly shifted, lifting from the ground for a moment, floating back and forth in the air, and then settling back on its legs. Ichy screamed and Brom gripped the bedpost.

'It's only Dolly,' Ren said. 'The bed moves when he rolls over.'

The twins peered over the edge. Dolly was underneath, still in his monk's robe, his mouth open and his chest rising and falling against the mattress.

'Where did you get him?' Brom asked.

Ren hesitated. 'We found him on the road.'

Ichy reached down and nudged Dolly with his finger. 'Why does he sleep under there?'

'He just likes it, I guess.'

Tom's voice came shouting up from below. There was the sound of a dish breaking and a chair being thrown over. The twins looked anxiously at Ren.

'This isn't what we thought it would be like at all.'

'Do you think he'll bring us back if we ask him to?'

'You could come with us.'

Ren thought of his life at Saint Anthony's. Of Brother Joseph and Father John, and being scrubbed by the charitable grandmothers, and waking each morning in the small boys' room. He remembered the letter he'd written, that first night alone in the basement. He'd never mailed it. But he saw now that it was just what the boys needed – good news.

Ren showed them his new clothes, the drowned boy's jacket and trousers, how well they had been mended, the long underwear inside, the socks darned with care. He described Mrs Sands's breakfasts, full of muffins and fresh milk and eggs and bacon and sausages, with second helpings and thirds, too, if they wanted. He talked about going to bars and being given whiskey to drink, and staying up as late as he wanted. Then he remembered the toys that the dwarf had made. Ren sneaked out of the room and came back with an armful, dumping them like an avalanche of presents across the bed.

The boys were too old for playthings, but all the fear and exhaustion left the twins' faces as they looked over the intricately carved wooden pieces. They lifted toy after toy and passed them back and forth, petting the little pigs, opening and closing the mouths of the fish, dancing the marionette across the headboard. Ichy tried on the mask of the moon and stood by the window, saying, 'I'm the full moon!' Then, turning to his side: 'Now I'm the half-moon!'

Ren watched his friends play but felt no inclination to join them. He remembered the broken soldier they'd shared, still resting somewhere at the bottom of the well, underneath all that water. No one even knew he was there, except for the three boys in this room.

Ichy was standing on his toes, trying to get a look at himself in the mirror. The moon mask was too large for his face. His eye was peering out where the nose should be. On the other side of the room Brom bit his lip in concentration and rode the Viking ships across the blankets, arranging the quilts into the ripples of the ocean. There was a storm ahead, a tidal wave coming. He lifted the end of the sheet and sent all the ships rolling.

CHAPTER TWENTY-THREE

THE FROGS WERE out. Earlier it had rained, and now as the wagon passed the marshes in the dark, there was a chorus of syncopated croaking. Benjamin sat in the driver's seat, a lantern balanced on the floor. Tom was beside him and Dolly and the boys were in the back, clinging to the sides as they bounced over holes in the rocky path. The horse strained through the night against the weight of them all. Every half-mile she stopped, as if she had given up completely. Benjamin flicked the whip, and the mare trudged on.

'Where are we going?' Ichy whispered.

Ren glanced at Benjamin and Tom, their shoulders hunched together in the darkness. 'Fishing,' he said.

The wagon crossed a covered bridge that groaned and creaked and seemed to take forever to end. When they emerged on the other side they turned south. The country here was full of swamps and wetland. Ren kept an eye on Brom and Ichy, their faces half-scared and half-exhilarated, and thought of how far they'd come from Saint Anthony's. He slipped his fingers into his pocket and felt the edge of his collar. He carried it with him everywhere now, as if the three blue letters of his name could protect him from the rest of the world.

The trees by the river gave way to open, rolling fields. Split fences marked the boundaries between farms. Occasionally a light shone from a house nearby. Brom and Ichy whispered to each other and peered at Dolly, propped up beside them and sleeping. Tom was leaning near the edge of the driver's seat, his face pale and hungover. The wagon went over a bump and he moaned.

'It's your own fault,' said Benjamin.

'Don't talk to me,' said Tom.

'You're going to slow us down.'

'I'll be fine. Just stop talking.'

It had taken most of the day and night for Tom to sober up. When he did, he stumbled out into Mrs Sands's garden and spent several hours curled beside a giant rosemary bush. The twins watched him from the window, biting their lips with worry. Ren looked at their worn-out shoes, their ill-fitting coats tied together with string. They did not know where they were headed, and Ren was not going to warn them.

When they reached the churchyard, there was no watchtower, no iron gate, no lock to pick. The graves were in an open field, unprotected, surrounded only by a low stone wall and a simple wooden stile to keep out wandering cows.

Benjamin pulled the wagon to a stop.

The wind picked up, the leaves rustling overhead. Tom slipped off the side of the cart with a pained expression. He took the lantern and one of the shovels and stepped over the wall, cutting his way through the damp grass. The twins scrambled out of the back, then stood by the side of the road. They looked from Ren to the graveyard and back again.

Benjamin tied the reins of the horse to a tree and began to unload the burlap bags from the wagon. He nodded at Dolly. 'Wake him.'

Ren pinched Dolly's hand. The man opened his eyes and climbed unsteadily out of the cart. Benjamin handed him a shovel.

'Time to pay us back.'

The spade looked like a toy in Dolly's hands. He wrinkled his brow.

'Please,' said Ren. 'We need your help.'

As soon as the boy spoke Dolly's indecision cleared. He gripped the shovel as if he would break it. 'Just show me where.'

The men went over the stile, Benjamin leading the way. As soon as they were gone, Ren crouched by the wagon, pretending to fix something so he would not have to face his friends, but the twins were behind him in an instant.

'What are we doing here?'

'You lied to us.'

Brom grabbed Ren as if he could force the answers from him, but Ren pushed him off.

'Now you know,' he said.

There was a shout from the graveyard. Benjamin was calling Ren's name. The boys were startled out of their argument and hurried over the stile. They found the shovels on the ground and Dolly holding Benjamin up against a tree.

'For Christ's sake.' Benjamin was dangling from the front of his new blue coat. He swung his legs, he slapped at the air, but Dolly would not let go.

'Put him down!' Ren cried.

'I'm not digging up the dead,' said Dolly. 'Not for you. Not for anybody.'

The jacket slipped and Dolly pressed harder into the tree, his hands moving to Benjamin's throat. Ren threw himself onto Dolly's arm. He swung his weight down, but the arm held steady, as if it were the branch of a tree.

'Listen,' Benjamin's voice was a whisper. 'Listen.'

Out of the mist Tom appeared, the heavy iron spade over his shoulder. He came up silently behind Dolly, swung wide, and hit him in the head with the shovel. Dolly stood there for a moment, twitching, and then he crumpled, taking Benjamin with him, his body hitting the earth like a clap of thunder.

'Get him off.' Benjamin cursed. Tom and the boys rushed over. They rolled Dolly clear of Benjamin's legs.

Ren pinched Dolly's hand again. He called his name. When Dolly didn't respond, Ren brought his ear to his mouth and listened. After a few moments he heard a bit of air, a low sound, like the wind coming off the water.

Tom leaned in. 'His headache's going to be worse than mine.'

'You didn't have to hit him,' Ren said.

'Really,' said Tom. 'And can you think of a better way to stop him from strangling people?'

The group stood around Dolly in the darkness, listening to his labored breathing. Ren and the twins struggled to lean him up against the tree. Dolly was still unconscious, his head against the bark, his knees peeking out from beneath his robe.

'We'll never finish without him.' Benjamin crouched down in the grass. He tugged at his hair. Then he looked at the boys, and every part of his face seemed to sharpen. He took Dolly's shovel and put it in Ren's hand. The wooden handle was rough from being left in the weather.

Benjamin corralled the twins and pushed them toward the

graves. 'Look for the markers,' he said. 'We need to be gone before the sun comes up.'

The headstones in the center of the yard were made of slate, long black shards jutting from the ground. To the side there were some made of marble, with urns and angels looking down in grief at the names and weeping. Benjamin pointed to the farthest corner. 'I put white stones at the base of each one,' he said. 'You should be able to see them in the dark.'

Tom set to work digging along the row. For that's what it was, Ren could see now – a row of freshly turned graves. There were four plots. Two medium-sized crosses, and two smaller ones. The bartender and his family.

'Get the old man first.'

'That's what I'm doing.' Tom was already ankle deep. He was breathing heavily, his face slowly gaining color as he worked.

Benjamin led the boys toward a cross farther down the row. 'Don't clear the whole grave. We only need to reach the head of the box.'

Ren walked over in a daze, the spade dragging behind him. At the bottom of the cross was a piece of clear quartz. He picked it up and ran his thumb across the surface. The corners were soft, with tiny iridescent flecks that sparkled in his hand. He closed his fingers around it. He turned to the twins. 'We've got to dig.'

Brom shook his head.

'I don't want to do this,' Ichy whispered.

Ren pushed the shovel into the ground, lifted a small patch of dirt, and steadied the handle with his stump. The earth was heavy from the rain, the top crust hardened and dry. He tried not to look at the marker, or the name – Sarah, wife of Samuel – that was carved into the wood before them. He thought of what

Dolly had said: that he'd heard them digging for him. That he'd heard them coming through the earth.

Tom cursed the twins until they began to help. Brom took turns at the spade with Ichy, while Ren cleared the rocks away. It seemed the work would never end. They drove deeper and deeper, until suddenly there was a thump when their shovel hit wood. Ren crouched near the edge of the hole. He could see the pale pine coffin far below, the end peeking out from the earth like a head from a blanket.

Benjamin came forward with a long-handled spade. He pushed the boys aside, then slid the pole in. It took three tries until the blade connected and they heard the wood break. Then Benjamin pulled the spade out, and Tom brought two chains with large metal hooks attached at the ends. They were meat hooks; Ren recognized them from the butcher shop as they were lowered into the grave.

'Have you got it?' Benjamin said.

'Almost,' said Tom. 'Just there. Yes. Got it.'

They hooked the body underneath the arms and pulled it out.

Sarah, wife of Samuel, had been buried in her wedding dress. It was not silk, but a stiff, hard linen, with pink flowers embroidered around the neck and shoulders. There was a line of pearl buttons, from the collar to the waist, and a set of crocheted gloves pulled over the dead woman's hands.

Ren tried to focus on the dress and not her face, which was terrifying – her skin stiff and cold as wax, the hair like straw. Benjamin removed the meat hooks, replaced them with his hands, and dragged her to a patch of grass, her dress trailing dirt, her small, white leather boots appearing beneath the skirt like two painted branches. Her lips were deep purple, slightly open and pulled apart.

'Give me the knife,' Benjamin said.

It took a moment before Ren understood. He reached into his pocket, took out the bear knife, and passed it over, full of apprehension. Benjamin slipped the blade beneath the collar of the woman's wedding dress and cut straight through the row of buttons in one movement. The pearls sprang into the air like rice and scattered across the grass, turning to specks in the moonlight.

Benjamin handed the knife back to Ren. 'Get the rest of her clothes off. That dress is worth five dollars, at least.' He left the children and walked over to Tom, and together the men started to unearth the next grave.

Ren turned to his friends, the knife in his hand.

'What are we going to do?' Brom whispered.

'I want to go home,' Ichy cried.

Ren could have kicked him. 'We're not going anywhere.'

He tried to pull the dress down from her shoulders, but her arms would not bend. He threatened Brom and Ichy until they got on their knees and helped, the twins too panicked now to do anything but follow. In the end they rolled her onto her face, severed the back ties, and took the dress from behind, Ren cutting along the seams. Underneath she wore a simple white petticoat and corset. There was a mole on the back of her neck, two brown spots held together that looked like a tiny, tiny mouth.

The boys stood around her, trembling and guilty. Ichy began to pray under his breath and Brom soon joined him. 'Our Father, Who Art in Heaven.' Ren turned away toward the neighboring grave and saw the naked body of an old man on the ground, his penis like a soft piece of rope, his eyes open and staring.

It took hours to finish. The boys shoveled until their arms ached, and their backs were sore and blisters rose on their fingers. Benjamin walked from the graveyard to the road, watching, listening. Each time he came back to the group, he appeared more nervous and pressed everyone to work faster.

When they had loaded the last of the bags into the wagon, Tom covered the bodies with a blanket, then took the flask from his pocket and begin to drink again. The twins scrambled up in the back and collapsed, exhausted, while Benjamin took the driver's seat.

'What about Dolly?' Ren asked.

Benjamin's face was set. 'Get in.'

The horse shifted. For a few moments the only sound in the dark night was the animal breathing. Then Ren's feet began to move, one by one, and then they were running from the wagon, over the stile, toward Dolly, and then there were other feet, he could hear them, coming faster, coming after him. Benjamin scooped Ren up into his arms and held him tight.

'He's no help for us.'

Ren struggled to get away.

'You want to stay with him? You want me to leave you here?'

Ren could just make out Dolly's profile, a mountain of misplaced earth. He was still underneath the tree, his eyes closed. Ren did not want to leave his friend. But the thought of being abandoned in the churchyard was worse. He stopped fighting, his strength gone. Benjamin loosened his grip and placed him on the ground, then led Ren back to the cart.

'I warned you,' said Benjamin.

Ren watched Dolly's tree as they pulled away. He imagined his friend calling for him in the gloom, the crosses and headstones standing close and silent. The graveyard faded around the turn in the road, and Ren hid his face in his jacket.

'Come on, now,' said Tom. 'None of that. You've got your fellows!'

Brom and Ichy were as still as dolls, their eyes on the pile of bodies next to them in the cart. Tom coughed, drew the bottle from underneath his coat, and took a long, slow drink. When he was finished, he smacked his lips.

'Let's have a song.'

The orphans did not answer.

'Don't you know any? Didn't they teach you boys to sing?'

'We know some hymns,' Brom ventured.

'They're in Latin,' said Ichy.

'Well, that's not going to raise any spirits. How's about 'Hey Nonny No'? Or 'Bonnie My Bonnie'?'

'We don't know those songs.'

'Well, it's time you did.' Tom drank from the bottle. He cleared his throat and began to sing, his voice high and surprisingly pleasant.

> '*Lavender's blue, diddle diddle*
> *Lavender's green,*
> *When I am king, diddle diddle*
> *You shall be queen.*'

'You know this one,' said Tom. He tossed the bottle to Benjamin.

'A brisk young man, diddle diddle
Met with a maid,
And laid her down, diddle diddle
Under the shade.'

Benjamin took a drink, then threw the bottle back.

'Here,' said Tom, passing it to Brom. 'Sing. All you need to know is the "diddle diddle" part.'

Brom tentatively took a sip from the bottle and grimaced. Ichy followed, coughing out what he had taken in, but when the chorus came round, they joined Tom with their small voices.

'For you and I, diddle diddle
Now all are one,
And we will lie, diddle diddle
No more alone.'

Ren watched his friends. The song had made them feel better. But the words echoed over his head like a warning. There was no rustling in the leaves. No wind through the needles. It was as if all the trees had stopped to listen. Ren glanced up at Benjamin on the driver's seat. His shoulders were slouched and he was not singing. He was looking ahead, to the crossroads.

A sense of uneasiness came over the wagon as they drew closer to the signpost. Ren leaned over the side. He could see shapes farther down the road. Fellow travelers, coming their way. Benjamin cursed and sat up in his seat, and Tom threw another blanket over the bodies.

There were five men on horseback. With the moon behind

them they nearly looked like trees themselves, their shadows stretching out before them. The men had hats of different sizes and shapes. A bowler, a straw hat, a watchman's cap, a top hat, and one with a blood-red band. The figure in the center wore a long black riding coat. The horses seemed restless, as if they'd been waiting for some time, nodding back and forth, tugging at the reins.

'Mister Nab,' said the man in the riding coat.

Benjamin pulled the wagon to a stop. He looked the men over. 'I don't know you,' he said.

The rider pushed back the collar of his coat. It was the man with the red gloves, who had cut off the bartender's hand at O'Sullivan's. By his saddle he held the length of a shotgun, but he did not make a move to lift it.

Benjamin smiled. 'There must be some kind of misunderstanding here.'

'No misunderstanding.' The man with the red gloves pointed to the wagon, and the Bowler and the Straw Hat moved their horses alongside. The Straw Hat leaned over and used his shotgun to poke at the bags, then pushed a flap of burlap aside and revealed the face of Sarah, wife of Samuel.

'Wait.' Benjamin raised his hands. 'These folks, all of them, they're my kin. The only ones I've got left. And they should've been buried with my family, not plopped into some beggar's corner in the country. So I'm bringing them home to bury them proper. It's as simple as that.'

Ren watched the man in the red gloves shift in his saddle. He was chewing a piece of tobacco and twisting his finger around and around the end of his reins.

'Doesn't matter to us who they are or how you got them,'

the man said. 'But you're not taking them any farther.'

Benjamin shrugged his shoulders and kept his hands lifted. Then he leaned forward suddenly and cracked the whip in his hand, slashing hard. 'HA!' And the mare broke through the wall of riders.

'Hang on!' cried Tom.

The wagon bounced along the road, hitting a hole and nearly throwing Ren. He gripped the side as it sped on. They hit another ditch and Brom and Ichy were tossed close to the edge. Ren grabbed Brom by his shirt, his fingers wrenching, the crook of his arm straining against the weight. Tom stretched out a leg and caught Ichy with his foot, just before the boy slid out of the back.

Benjamin was standing now. He snapped the whip again and again. The riders had recovered and were coming up behind. Ren turned and saw them through the dust, spurring on their horses. A tree branch hit Ren in the side of the face, and the sound of the wagon and hoofbeats thundered in his ears. Two of the men were holding pistols. They were beside the wagon now. Pulling ahead, then slipping back when the road narrowed.

Tom reached for one of the bodies. He nodded to Ren and together they dragged it to the edge of the wagon. It was hard to keep hold of the bag. Ren could taste dust at the back of his throat. Tom pushed the body out, and Ren watched it fall in the path of the Watchman. The man's horse stumbled and the Watchman was thrown to the ground.

They grabbed another and began sliding it toward the back. A shot rang over their heads. Tom ducked and began to kick the body with his feet. It went off the end, but this time as it landed the men spurred their horses and leaped over.

The cart rounded a bend, the wheels clattering, Brom and Ichy slipping across the boards. They hit the side next to Ren and clung to him, their fingernails raking his skin.

Two riders broke from the group and dashed into the woods. In a few moments they appeared ahead on the road, then dropped behind. It was the man with the red gloves and the Straw Hat. They were right next to the driver's bench, close enough to touch Benjamin if they wanted. They lifted their guns.

'Look out!' Ren screamed.

They shot the horse. One, two holes into the animal's neck, and then a third through her leg. The mare swerved left and right, stumbled, tried to right herself, then fell. The wagon traveled right over her, the stays hitting the ground and breaking, and Ren watched Benjamin fall and then the wagon was tipping, turning, and it felt like the earth had broken through beneath them and they were dropping into a chasm, and then Ren's face hit something and there was a heavy weight across his back.

In the silence that followed, Ren felt the trees were coming for him. He could hear their language, coming from beneath the bark. Their branches reaching out and groaning. He tried to warn the others, but his throat was closed tight. Then he felt himself being carried, and every movement was another boot crushing down upon him.

'Is he dead?'

More boots. Boots with claws. Ren tried to ask for help. He felt the tiniest slip of air go down. He sucked on it, and then another small breath came, and then another.

They had landed in a bog. The wagon was completely turned

over and half submerged, the wheels broken and dripping in the muck. Brom and Ichy were standing to the side. The man with the watchman's cap was pointing a pistol at them. Tom was underneath the wagon, his cries muffled, the bottom half of his coat just visible. The Bowler and the Straw Hat were digging him out.

The man in the top hat was carrying Ren. The brim was wide, the sides made of satin, and in one corner there was a dark red stain. It was the same hat worn by the man Dolly had killed beneath the streetlight. Ren was sure of it. But the man who had it on now was older, his face grown out with a beard.

'Pilot,' the new Top Hat said. 'I've found one more.'

The man in the red gloves eyed Ren from where he was standing. 'Put him with the rest.'

The horse was still alive. Her nostrils let out sharp bursts of breath. She blinked rapidly, as if a swarm of flies were trying to get in. Ren thought of the farmer kissing her nose and felt a crush of guilt. Pilot reloaded his shotgun. When he was through he snapped it shut, set it against the horse's head, just beneath the ear, and pulled the trigger. The boom echoed across the marsh.

'Should've been you,' Pilot said, and it was only then that Ren saw Benjamin, curled up on the ground. His blue jacket was torn, there was a cut over his eye, and his right cheek seemed to be swelling.

A scream came from underneath the wagon. It was Tom. He cursed the men who were digging. Then he began to sob and shriek, his voice carrying through the night. The man in the bowler hat reappeared.

'Leg's broken.'

'Tell him to keep quiet,' said Pilot.

The Top Hat searched Ren's pockets and took away the bear knife. Then he lifted Ren again, brought him over to the twins and set him on the ground between them. The boys were dipped with mud from head to toe. Their clothes and faces were the same spattered brown. For the first time in his life Ren could not tell them apart.

'I've got water in my ear.'

'Are they going to kill us?'

Ren tried to answer but his sides ached. He watched Benjamin talking to Pilot. He knew it would have to be a magnificent story to get them out of this. He imagined Benjamin's words, coming one by one through the air, and he began to pray on them, as he would on the beads of the rosary, each repetition gaining strength and power, until the circle was closed.

Benjamin was using his hands now. He was acting out part of the tale. Pilot nodded his head, listening intently, and then he lifted the end of the shotgun and brought it down on Benjamin's face. Blood burst from his nose. Pilot took a step back, as if he didn't want to stain his coat. Then he said something to the Bowler and the Top Hat and the men stepped in and began to beat Benjamin until he fell to the ground, his hands trying to protect his head, his voice begging them to leave him alone. Ren closed his eyes. He covered his ears. The screams continued while the bodies were collected, and the horses were rearranged, and Tom was dragged out from underneath the wagon. They kept on, howling and echoing through the woods, until all of Ren's prayers had stopped.

PART 3

CHAPTER TWENTY-FOUR

AS THE RIDERS entered North Umbrage the old fishermen moved under the bridge, the vagrants retreated to the
alleyways, and the widows closed their shop windows and pulled
the shutters. The only sight greeting Pilot and his prisoners was
the smoke from the mousetrap factory, glowing in the early
morning light. Ren remembered how the building had looked
from the rooftop – the girls in their uniforms streaming through
one door, an ocean narrowing to a river.

Two of the hat boys were sent to get rid of the bodies. The
ones that were left cut the ropes and untangled Tom, who'd been
strapped to a plank from the wagon and dragged behind the
riders. He had screamed for the first quarter of a mile, and then,
to the relief of all, passed out.

Pilot slipped off his horse. Then he reached back, took hold
of Ren's arm, and yanked him to the ground. For the past hour
Ren had been riding in front, gripping the saddle, watching the
red gloves hold the reins and feeling Pilot pressed against his
back, smelling of heat and leather. Ren kept his scar tucked up
into his sleeve, his pulse pounding along with the hoofbeats
until they reached North Umbrage.

He looked for his friends. The mud that covered the twins had now dried, leaving a thick coat of brown across their faces, caked and cracking all the way to their elbows. Brom dangled his legs from the Watchman's saddle. Ichy simply fell to a heap on the sidewalk. Benjamin descended slowly, carefully. His clothing was shredded, his face so swollen and red he looked like a different person altogether.

After spitting on the sidewalk, Pilot beat twice on the entryway with his fist, and another man, with another hat, opened the door. The inside of the building smelled like a church – chilled, dank, and slightly earthy. The group made their way up the main staircase, two men following behind with Tom. All around was the rumbling, churning sound of machinery. Even the floor beneath their feet seemed to move.

At the top of the stairs another set of doors opened into the heart of the factory – rows of workbenches, equipment, materials, and girls. Boxes of mousetraps leaned against the walls. Piles of planks and sawdust gathered in the corners. The girls stacked and cut, stacked and cut, against a row of revolving blades. In the next aisle the wooden pieces were assembled; girls slapped the edges with glue brushes while others set the vises and nailed down the corners.

The center of the room held the metalworkers. Some attached hinges, some bent corners, and some worked the cranks of machines. Thin wires were fed to the gears at one end and emerged as long spirals from the other, curling like snakes toward the ground. A girl snipped the springs and delivered them to another row of workers, who fit them into place on the mousetraps. Leaning over one of these tables, her hands black from grease, was the Harelip.

She had seen them coming. Ren caught a glimpse of her when they entered the room. She had stopped working when she saw Benjamin's swollen face. But now her head was bent over the mousetrap, her hands moving fast, manipulating the wire as if it were a needle and thread.

The floor manager, a bald man in his forties, walked along the rows extinguishing the lamps used for night work. As he passed Ren, a shriek came from the back of the room. Several girls left their places and ran over. A girl was standing by one of the revolving saws with her hand in her mouth, blood running down her chin.

'Posts! Posts!' shouted the floor manager. The girls hesitated, then scurried back to their workbenches. After her first scream, the girl had not said a word. She just stood there and bled. Ren watched as the sawdust around her began to darken.

'Here,' said the floor manager, and tried to hand her a rag.

The girl stumbled to the ground. The floor manager wrapped the rag around her hand and carried her out. A few moments later he returned and strode toward the Harelip, took hold of her arm, and led her to the revolving saw.

'Promotion!' he shouted, and slipped her into place on the line. When he turned his back, the Harelip rolled her eyes, then shot another look toward Benjamin. She chewed her lip, took a handful of sawdust, and threw it onto the machine. The shavings turned red, and she brushed them onto the floor with her fingers, then pushed them to the side of the machine with her boot.

Pilot maneuvered through the workers, turning down one row and another, then up a staircase guarded by two men, who stepped carefully aside as they passed. The hall beyond was lined with a long carpet patterned with green flowers, so thick that Ren's shoes made no sound as he trod upon it. His foot sank into the pile, and he thought of the moss in the woods behind the orphanage; the deep emerald color that grew where the trees fell down.

At the end of the hall was an open door. The hat boys carried Tom through. Ren followed, into what appeared to be an office. An accounting machine took up space in the corner. A pile of ledgers sat next to an overcrowded shelf. In the center stood a giant wooden desk, its surface scarred with crosshatches and stains, the knobs brightly polished and shining. The desk took up most of the room. Ren and the twins filed around it as if it were a dining room table.

'You'll wait here,' said Pilot.

'This is all a mistake,' said Benjamin.

'We'll find out soon enough.' The hat boys put Tom on the rug and left the room grinning. Then Pilot shut the door and locked it.

Benjamin leaned against the wall, gingerly feeling his ribs. His lips were twice their size, the skin around his eyes cut and bruised.

'You're hurt,' said Ren.

Benjamin's voice was raw. 'I'll be fine.'

'What are we going to do?'

'We need to think. What he knows. What he wants.' Benjamin felt along the edge of his jaw. He reached inside of his mouth and, wincing, removed a tooth.

Ren looked around the room, wondering what McGinty could possibly want. From the look of the place he already had plenty of money. The chairs were covered in fine leather, the brass lamps glowing. On the desk was a set of gold pens, and behind it on the wall hung a series of paintings depicting fox hunts. There was the trumpeter, leading the horses. There were the first riders, leaping over the hill. There were the packs of dogs spreading out through the grass. And there was the fox, a small patch of red, sometimes streaking across the field, sometimes huddled, terrified, just moments away from being discovered.

On the other side of the office was a large window over-looking the factory floor. Benjamin shuffled close and leaned his hand against it. He seemed to be testing the corners for an opening, and when he found none, his arm came down heavy against his side.

'I have to go to the privy,' said Ichy.

Brom shoved him. 'You should have said something before.'

Ren watched the twins argue. He could not shake the feeling that their bad luck had brought this on. He wished that Tom had never adopted them. He wished that he had never been their friend.

Ichy began to whimper and Ren felt a twinge of guilt. 'There's got to be something you can use,' he said, and searched the room until he found an old jelly jar full of pencils. He dumped them out and handed the glass jar to Ichy. For a moment Ichy seemed relieved. He ran to the corner of the room and opened the front of his trousers. When he was finished, he stood there, holding the bright yellow liquid.

'What should I do with it?'

'Here.' Ren took the jar back. The glass was warm against his fingers. He screwed the cover back on. He pulled open a drawer and hid the whole thing inside the desk.

Tom began to moan.

They hurried over, and Benjamin felt the leg carefully. But as soon as he touched it, Tom began to scream. Benjamin told him to be quiet. He took off his coat, then tore a strip of cloth from his shirt. He wrapped it around the broken leg.

Tom screamed again. 'My boys!'

Brom and Ichy watched the blood streaming from his leg, their mouths open.

'He wants you to come,' Ren said.

'Do we have to?'

Tom dug his nails into Ren's arm.

'Yes.'

Brom came forward and held Tom's hand. Ichy held the other. The schoolteacher gazed somewhere over their heads, and then his eyes closed, and he fell unconscious. Benjamin took Ren's fingers. He put them where he'd tied the shirt. He said to hold the pressure. Ren pushed down, feeling the pulse in Tom's leg.

'Do you think we could ask for a doctor?' Ren asked.

Benjamin shook his head, then glanced at the door. Someone was coming.

The Top Hat and the Straw Hat stepped in with their guns drawn. They took their places on either side of the entryway. Pilot came forward next, fixing his leather gloves. Then he held the door open for a man dressed in a yellow suit.

The man walked in like he meant to prove something. His jacket was off and carried over the shoulder, suspenders tight, shirtsleeves rolled up and tied with pink ribbons. He was nearly as fat as Brother Joseph, and carried most of the weight in his stomach, which pushed out before him into a hard round ball as he crossed the room and took a seat behind the enormous desk. He seemed annoyed, as if they were all gathered there to keep him from something more important. It was clear that everything in this room – the paintings on the walls, the rug under their feet, the factory on the other side of the window – belonged to him. Silas McGinty.

He pointed a finger at Benjamin.

'Nab,' said Pilot.

'How come I don't know 'im?'

'Because he hasn't been worth it,' said Pilot.

'And now he is.' McGinty shifted his weight. His words sounded like they were passing through a grater as he spoke them, bits and pieces falling off along the way. 'And tha children?'

'Our lookouts,' said Benjamin.

'Yah needed three?'

'One for each direction.'

McGinty fingered the ribbons on the sleeves of his shirt, then finally lowered his attention to the floor, where Tom was slowly bleeding onto the rug.

Benjamin pressed his hands together, as if he were getting ready for a bargain. 'My sister and her family died last week of a fever. The town was afraid of spreading the sickness, so they put them in the ground without telling us. When I found out, I went to fetch her and the rest so that we could give them a Christian burial.' With a wince, he tried his best to smile.

McGinty pulled a handkerchief out of his pocket and blew his nose. 'That's a good story,' he said. 'Now I'll tell yah one. Once theah was a pig who liked ta eat and sleep and roll in tha shit sometimes. One day tha fahmah who owned tha pig came along and cut his throat and cleaned out his guts and ate his ass fah bacon. End a story.'

Benjamin stopped smiling.

'Yah gotcha fingahs in tha graveyahd,' said McGinty. 'Not very nice. Not at all.'

'Please,' said Benjamin, 'just listen to me for a minute.'

Ren watched McGinty's freckled face, the bump on the bridge of his nose. He could tell that the man was losing patience.

'I won't allow it. Not in my town.' McGinty turned to Pilot. 'How much is he wohth?'

'Seven hundred dollars.'

'That's quite a lotta money. Musta done something very intahresting ta be wohth that much.'

Pilot reached into his coat, took out a folded advertisement and began to read, the words falling one after another into the room: ' "Arson, train robbery, bank robbery, horse robbery and general thieving, desertion from the military, illegal gambling and games of chance, impersonation of an officer of the law, impersonation of a naval captain, impersonation of a minister, claim jumping, vagrancy, disorderly conduct, assault with a deadly weapon, littering, loitering, and the selling of false deeds." '

Ren looked at Benjamin, who had gone as white as the notice in Pilot's hand. McGinty pulled open a drawer in the desk and removed a gun. He placed it on the table. Everyone in the room watched as he poured a few bullets from a box into his hand and began to load the pistol.

'Tell me, Mistah Nab, ah yah a religious man?'

Benjamin shook his head.

McGinty snapped the gun closed, then held it out. 'Take a look at tha inscription.'

Benjamin hesitated.

'Go on,' McGinty said. 'Read what it says on tha barrel.'

Benjamin leaned over. ' "The souls of the just are in the hand of God." '

'Have yah evah felt tha hand a God?' McGinty cleaned the inscription with his handkerchief, as if Benjamin had left a smudge just by looking at it.

Everyone waited for Benjamin to answer. Ichy's stomach growled. Tom shifted and groaned by the door. There was a clock on the wall. Ren had not heard it before, but it clicked back and forth now over their heads, sounding off the seconds.

'I can shoot yah fah what yah done. Or I can turn yah in fah tha rewahd, and given that fine list, yah'll hang.' McGinty finished wiping the gun. He spun the barrel. Once. Twice. Then he nodded at Tom. 'He's going ta ruin that rug.'

The twins looked up at McGinty, terrified. They were still holding each other's hands and Tom's as well, so that they formed a closed circle. Now they dropped Tom's fingers, as if he had suddenly become contaminated.

Ren waited for Benjamin to tell a better story, a story that would get them out of this place. But Benjamin only stood there, looking defeated, his face seeming to swell more by the minute. If anything was going to be done, Ren understood that he would have to do it. He stepped forward, and in a moment he had his coat off and spread on the rug. He tried to use it to clean up the blood, scrubbing back and forth at the carpet, and then felt the silence in the room, and turned to see everyone looking at him.

McGinty was standing behind the desk, the gun loose in his hand. His eyes darted from Ren's sleeve to the boy's face and back again.

'Who's that?'

'No one,' Benjamin said.

McGinty raised his eyebrows. He motioned with the pistol and Pilot put a gun to the back of Benjamin's head. The room became even more quiet then, as if they'd all stopped breathing, all but Benjamin, who began to choke as if he were underwater. Ren felt the Top Hat grab his collar and pull him toward the desk.

Up close McGinty smelled like peppermints. Ren could see that his freckles not only covered his face but also went over his neck, even his hands. Underneath his arms two sweat stains had started, ovals radiating down the side of his starched shirt. He took hold of Ren, pushed up the boy's sleeve, and stared at the stump. Ren tried to pull away, but McGinty's grip tightened. He groped at the scar with his fingers, then cupped the whole thing with his palm and pushed against the bone until it hurt.

'Wheahya from?'

Ren was too frightened to lie. 'Saint Anthony's.'

'Yaran orphan?'

'Yes.'

'Lucky boy.' McGinty was panting now. He let go of the scar and pinched Ren's cheek.

'He's just a kid,' Benjamin said quietly, the gun still pressed to the back of his head. 'He's not worth anything.'

McGinty let go of Ren, pulled out a gold pocket watch and opened the cover. He looked at the boy and he looked at the watch. Then he crossed his arms, and fell into thought, and appeared uninterested in speaking with any of them for a time. Benjamin closed his eyes. The rest of the group waited, feeling the heat in the room.

Ren watched Benjamin, expecting some kind of sign, but Benjamin's face was tight with fear. Ren swallowed hard. He thought back to his days in Father John's study, waiting out his punishment, the silence worse than the beating. He slowly began to back away, and it seemed to break the spell. McGinty nodded at Pilot, and the man removed the gun from Benjamin's head.

Benjamin's head fell back, as if the barrel of the gun had been supporting it. He opened his eyes. 'I'll pay you more than they'll give you,'

'I don't wancha money,' said McGinty.

Benjamin glanced at the door. Pilot was there, cleaning his knife, and his eyes did not move from Benjamin, not for an instant. 'I don't understand.'

'Yoah going ta leave this town tanight,' said McGinty. 'I'm not going ta see yah again. I'm not going ta heah yoah name. I'm not going ta know anothah thing aboutcha.'

Pilot opened the door. He pointed to the rug. The Top Hat and the Straw Hat crouched down on either side of Tom and began to roll him up inside. They did this without a word, as if they'd done it many times before. Brom and Ichy moved over and they all watched Tom disappear into the folds of the carpet. Then the hat boys grabbed either end and pulled the rug out into the hall, the twins following behind.

Benjamin took Ren's hand. One of his nails had been torn away. Ren could see the bruise folded over his knuckles, a small dark spot as they turned to leave. Pilot stepped in front of the door, blocking their way. He took the notice that he'd read from his pocket. He folded the paper in half. Then he folded it in half again.

McGinty leaned back in his chair. 'Tha boy stays.'

Benjamin hesitated. His fingers let go of Ren's and floated to the place on his head where Pilot had pressed the gun. Ren watched, his heart beating so loudly it drummed in his ears.

'Say good-bye,' said McGinty.

Ren waited for Benjamin to speak. To hear some kind of explanation. Why this was a mistake. Why they couldn't possibly be parted. But Benjamin barely looked at him.

'Good-bye,' he said.

In the next moment Ren was dragged out of the room, the green carpet a blur beneath his knees. Pilot pitched him down the stairs and past the rows of mousetrap girls. The workers continued on, pretending not to notice, but Ren could see a few stopped and stared. The Harelip was still in her place, and for a moment they looked at each other before Pilot pulled him through another door, down a corridor, and finally threw him into a storage room, piled high with papers and boxes.

'You *are* lucky,' Pilot said. Then he closed the door and locked it behind him.

CHAPTER TWENTY-FIVE

THE CLOSET HAD no windows. Piled up against the walls and strewn about the floor were a number of wooden crates. Two filing cabinets sat in the corner, along with a small writing table and a stool. On the table sat an inkwell and a set of gold pens identical to the ones that were in McGinty's office. There was also a potbellied stove with a small flue attached to the wall. Ren opened the grate and saw that it was full of ashes.

He sat on the stool and put his head down on the table. He tried to feel the wood pressing into his cheek. His body was heavy, as if there were ropes from below pulling him to the ground. He had never been so miserable and alone.

There was a part of him that wanted to believe this was a plan of some kind; that in an hour or two the door would be unlocked, and outside waiting for him would be Tom and the twins and Benjamin with his smile, in a new cart with a new horse, several hundred dollars richer. But as the morning passed and his stomach ached with hunger, Ren began to sink into despair, and ruminated on all the ways that Benjamin had failed him. It was hard to believe. And then it wasn't.

The more Ren blamed Benjamin the more he realized that he had done the same to Dolly. He had left him behind. He had saved himself. Dolly was probably awake by now, wandering the road, calling his name, stumbling across the body of the mare. Ren thought of Pilot putting the shotgun to the horse's head, the same place where the farmer used to kiss her good-bye.

He wished that he was back in Mrs Sands's kitchen. He knew that she would never have given him up. Ren imagined her bursting into the mousetrap factory with her broom, beating the hat boys senseless, and then lifting Ren into her arms. It would be just like one of Benjamin's stories. He could see the glint of her crooked teeth, the sound of the broom as it broke across Pilot's shoulders, the way she wrestled McGinty to the ground. He listened for her footsteps in the hallway. He added more details, then he listened again.

As the day passed, Ren grew weary and restless, and he began to look through the boxes stacked around the room. He even prayed to Saint Anthony for help, to find him a knife or a length of rope – anything that would aid him in escaping – but the crates were only full of springs and wood shavings and paper. One held broken mousetraps, similar to the one he'd seen in Mrs Sands's kitchen. He took one and poked the tiny metal door, then felt it snap shut as he drew his finger back.

He rummaged through the desk and pulled out a stack of old notebooks. Inside the pages he found illustrations of mousetraps. Drawing after drawing of intricate, tiny killing machines. There was a rough sketch of a mouse toppling from a baited slide into water. There was another, where the ceiling of the container crushed the mouse with the turn of an enormous screw. The next was a complicated labyrinth, the passages growing smaller and thinner, until it was impossible for the mouse to turn around or turn back.

The drawings were patents, or ideas of patents. Every possible way to rid the world of something unwanted.

Ren began to pace the room. Each time he reached the wall he circled back, until he was practically spinning, and nearly missed the sound of a key fitting into the lock. The door opened and McGinty came in, holding a paper sack the size and shape of a human head. He was dressed for business, his yellow jacket buttoned, the ribbons on his sleeves tucked in and tied. He set the bag down on the table.

'Heah,' he said.

Ren stared at the bag.

'It's fah you,' said McGinty. 'Open it.'

The boy reached out and touched the crinkled paper. He slowly pulled apart the folded edges of the top, his fingers shaking. All the while he could feel McGinty standing behind him.

The bag was full of candy. Peppermint sticks and lollipops and pieces of fudge, salt water taffy, sour balls, bars of chocolate, lemon bites, peanut brittle, butterscotch, maple sugar leaves, sponge candy, caramel chews, flavored wax, and all-day suckers. Ren had heard of such things and seen them in the windows of stores, but he had never tasted them. The smell of sugar drifted across his face in a cloud, making him feel dizzy and ravenous all at once.

McGinty poured the bag out, and the sweets tumbled across the table in a swirl of color, covering the notebooks and spilling onto the floor. 'Gowan,' he said. 'Eat it.'

Ren wondered if the candy was poisoned.

'These ah my favorite,' McGinty said, and took one of the peppermint sticks. He snapped it into pieces. He spent a few minutes sucking and moving the candy around in his mouth, then crunching it apart with his teeth. He picked up another and gave it to Ren. 'Try it.'

The boy thought of Mister Bowers, slipping his dentures out like a secret. *This is what happens to boys who eat jam.* He shook his head.

'Try something, fah Gawd's sake!' McGinty roared.

Ren snatched the candy and shoved the whole thing into his mouth. The sweetness nearly blinded him; his mouth filled with saliva, and suddenly he didn't care whether it was poisoned or not.

'That's bettah,' said McGinty.

Ren unwrapped a bar of chocolate and ate it in three bites, his tongue covered with melted goodness. He crunched the rock candy until it splintered against his teeth; he pulled the taffy, stretching it inches from his face. He sucked the juice from the flavored wax, and stuffed a piece of Turkish delight into the side of his cheek, where it stuck to his teeth and slowly disintegrated.

'Didja look at those?' McGinty pointed to the book of mousetrap sketches.

Ren wiped his mouth. 'Yes.'

McGinty chose one of the notebooks and opened it. He turned a page and then another and showed Ren a drawing of a box that hid a miniature guillotine. The mouse touched a lever as it went after the cheese, and its tiny head rolled out the other side.

'I stahted as a ratcatchah,' said McGinty. 'Black rats, brown rats and red rats. Tha black ones come up through tha drains, tha brown ones live in tha walls a yar house, and tha red ones go aftah tha livestock. They'll eat a dog, or a baby, if yah give 'em tha chance.'

McGinty flipped a few more pages, then showed Ren another drawing, of a team of rats trying to fit a child through a hole in the wall. Some pushing, some pulling, some gnawing the places in between.

'Mice ahn't as smaht as rats. But they breed fastah. When I stahted making mousetraps, they sold as soon as I could put 'em togethah. But aftah a while they stopped working. Tha mice would figure 'em out. They pass tha infahmation down tha line, from one mouse ta tha next. So I designed anothah, and stahted catching 'em again. And when that stopped working I designed anothah. Tha trick is ta keep changing tha traps, so they forget what kills 'em.'

McGinty snapped the book shut. He slipped another piece of candy into his mouth. 'Yah weran ugly baby.'

Ren was still holding on to a piece of flavored wax. He could feel it begin to soften now, as his palm grew slick with alarm, the swirl of his fingerprints leaving an impression across the surface.

'Yah don't look like hah, though. Yah don't look like harat all.'

McGinty reached into his jacket and pulled out his pocket watch. He pressed the release and the top sprang open. One side held a hand-tooled watch, the other a miniature portrait of a young woman. She was beautiful, her hair the color of chestnuts, her skin so pale it glowed. Her lips pressed into a silky mouth and her eyes were dark blue, with a hint of sparkle to them, as if she were making fun of the artist as he captured her. McGinty closed the watch. He passed his thumb back and forth across the cover, then set it on the table between them.

'That's my sistah.' McGinty chose another piece of peppermint and snapped it apart with his teeth. Tiny shards of red and white sugar glistened across his tongue. 'She told me yah died afta yah lost yah hand. I shouldha known that she was lying.'

The flavored wax had melted. Ren's hand had gone right through and now his fingers were sticky, the candy in two separate pieces on the floor. He stared at the watch. He wanted to see it open again. He could hear it working on the table, like a tiny metal heart.

'You've made a mistake,' he said.

McGinty stopped crunching the peppermint. 'I don't make mistakes.'

Ren could sense all the candy stuck together at the base of his stomach, turning over, pressing its way back up his throat. He grabbed the end of the table, then turned and vomited into an open box of mousetraps. When he was finished he brushed his sleeve across his mouth. 'I want to go home,' he cried. But as soon as the words came out, he felt the hollowness in them. He didn't have a home.

McGinty leaned against the desk. He picked up one of the gold pens and used it to clean the dirt out from underneath his nails.

'Yah said yah weran orphan.'

'Yes.' Ren leaned over the box of mousetraps, frightened and bewildered. If this man believed he was his uncle, then he was also the kind of uncle who kept his nephew locked in a closet.

'Have some moah candy.'

Ren took a piece of peppermint. The smell made his stomach clench. He stuck the peppermint in his mouth and held it with his teeth, trying to keep it from touching his tongue.

McGinty nudged him with his foot. 'No one evah came ta claim yah?'

Ren shook his head.

'Yah suah?'

Ren nodded weakly.

'Have anothah piece a candy.'

'I don't have a family!' Ren cried. 'I don't have anyone!'

'Well,' said McGinty, pausing for a moment. 'Now yah got me.' He tucked another piece of candy into the corner of his cheek and left it hanging there, a long, multicolored toothpick.

Ren imagined, for a moment, what it would be like to live in the factory with McGinty. To watch the mousetrap girls come and go. To spend the rest of his days locked in this closet.

McGinty was watching his face. 'Yah don't believe me.'

'No.'

The man's lower jaw slid forward, until his expression transformed, like a shade slowly being pulled down a window. 'I'll show yah. I'll prove it.'

He grabbed the boy's arm, and before Ren knew it, they were out of the room. Hat boys lined the corridor but stood and moved aside as they passed. One ran ahead to push open a door, and then they were making their way down a staircase. All the while McGinty kept a firm grip on the boy, only pausing once to take his overcoat from Pilot before they went through a side entrance and stepped into the street.

It was late afternoon, the shops already closed, the fires lit and the windows bright. Ren craned his neck around every corner as they passed, looking for Benjamin. He had hoped his friends would be waiting for him, but there were only more hat boys, traveling ahead, to the side, and behind, pushing the people on the street out of the way. McGinty snorted as he walked, his eyes flashing, his hand clamped over the boy's arm.

They came upon the town square and crossed the common. On the other side was a church, with a tall black railing surrounding the yard. McGinty's face grew more determined as they pressed forward; his stomach pushed out before him, his yellow suit flapping in the wind. Ren glanced up at the church tower. The building seemed familiar, like something out of a dream. And then Ren realized – it was the place where Dolly had been buried. Where they'd first dug him up from the ground. McGinty was standing next to the lock that Benjamin had picked with a needle, and he was opening it with a key.

The hat boys spread across the perimeter of the church and Pilot stepped into the yard, holding the gate. McGinty pulled Ren through by the shoulder and began shuffling past the rows of graves. Family names repeated themselves on either side: Beckford, Bartlett, Hale, Wood. Ren tripped over a row of tiny markers, a family of newborns, each one year apart.

At last they turned away from the church and toward a mausoleum, set in the back of the property. The building was the size of a carriage house, with a set of stone stairs leading up to a small portico, enclosed by another gate. On either side stood marble urns filled with pink and yellow roses. Above the portico was a turret, with a bell hanging in the center. Ren watched as McGinty removed another key from his pocket and unlocked the gate. The door behind it was carved with angels, and in the arch above was a window of multicolored glass, showing a fountain sprouting from the earth.

McGinty thrust the boy in first. The floor was made of granite; the room cold and dark. Ren could see a large white table to the left, pushed against the wall. The corners were cluttered with dirt and dead leaves. The ceiling was low, the walls close. The only way out blocked by McGinty.

'Theah she is.'

McGinty pointed to the table, and Ren saw that it wasn't a table but a tomb. The boy drew near and read the words: Margaret Ann McGinty. The lettering was finely wrought, the inscription beneath carved in a firm hand: The Souls of the Just Are in the Hand of God. Ren reached down and touched the letters. The marble was polished smooth. He felt no scratches, only the sharp edges where the words cut deep into the stone.

Ren thought of Margaret's portrait, her look of sly amusement. He slid his hand into his pocket and felt McGinty's watch. He'd stolen it from the table on their way out of the storeroom. The metal was warm; he could feel the clock ticking against his fingers.

Colored light dappled across McGinty's yellow suit. There was a cross on the wall, hanging over Margaret's grave, but the man did not even glance at it. He simply rubbed his hand back and forth over his face, as if he were trying to wipe off the emotion that had settled there. Then he pushed Ren toward the dark end of the tomb.

'Gowan,' the man told him. 'Look.'

There was nothing in the room except for a smaller table, set against the back wall. Ren walked toward it, feeling uneasy. The slab was made of the same stone that covered Margaret, and as he drew closer he saw a name cut into the surface: Reginald Edward McGinty.

'Now.' McGinty turned to the boy. 'Let's see if yoah in theah.'

Pilot stepped into the building, along with four hat boys, all carrying long metal bars. They pushed Ren aside, fit the bars underneath the marble slab, and lifted. The scraping sound filled the room as they moved the weight. When they set the piece on the ground, a strange smell drifted from the coffin, a combination of mold and damp tea leaves.

Ren leaned forward and peered inside. There was a small bundle, wrapped in a cloth sack, the size and shape of a baby.

The bundle was covered with a soft gray powder. Spots here and there were eaten through by insects or worn away with time. Ren could see a bit of fabric underneath. It was the same thick linen that held the collar with his name. He coughed and tasted bile at the back of his throat. He knew there was no way he could be in the coffin, but still the hair on his arms began to rise.

Pilot handed over his knife and McGinty cut the bag open, stabbing through the bottom and splitting the seam. When he finished, he stood back panting, and it was only the sound of his hard laugh that made the boy gather the courage to look. The cloth was ripped through the middle, and inside it was full of stones. They were different colors and shapes, some jagged and broken, some still dusty with the earth they had been taken from, some small enough to fit in the palm of Ren's hand.

As he leaned closer, Ren saw a pair of tiny stockings. Someone had taken the time to sew the rocks into a set of baby clothes. The ends of the sleeves were gathered, the hem attached together, the neck stitched shut. There was lace on the collar, and a matching bonnet, the brim pulled closed with a ribbon. McGinty had torn through it all, the rocks spilling onto the marble. Without thinking, the boy reached forward and lifted one from the pile. The stone was unremarkable. Gray and pockmarked. No boy at Saint Anthony's would have saved it.

CHAPTER TWENTY-SIX

THAT NIGHT REN found mice in the mousetrap factory. No sooner had the lock been turned against him in the storeroom than the boy heard the animals scurry across the floor. He raised the lamp that Pilot had left and saw a mother and a set of babies feasting on a bar of chocolate. Ren pulled the stool to the opposite corner and sat down, lifting his feet out of the way.

The boy waited in the dark, his mind numb, his toes cold. Eventually he shifted the stool and began to feed bits of wood from the box of broken mousetraps into the stove. He used the lamp to light the pile and soon had a small fire going. He took off his shoes and pressed his feet against the iron door. Slowly, through the drowned boy's socks, the skin there began to warm.

After unearthing the grave, McGinty had seemed exhausted. He waved to Pilot and had Ren dragged back to the same closet as before. Now Ren looked around at the piled boxes, the sagging ceiling and the scattering of mice. It was a forgotten room. He imagined days, and then years, passing, all within the confines of these walls.

Ren took out the watch he'd stolen and opened the cover.

Margaret McGinty's portrait gazed back at him. She had a long, elegant neck, her chestnut hair pulled gently behind her ears. She wore a pearl necklace, with earrings that matched. Ren traced a finger along her perfect nose.

He set the watch down on the desk and touched his own face, feeling the shape of his ears, his nose, his mouth, trying to see if they matched hers in any way. He had never spent much time in front of a mirror. There was only one at the orphanage, in Father John's study, where Ren would glance at himself from across the room as he waited to be punished. Sometimes months would pass before he saw his reflection again. It was nearly always startling. Like greeting a stranger.

The boy dug into the pocket of his coat and pulled out the collar with the letters of his name. They appeared the same as always. The R and the E sewn with strength, the N finished at a slant. Ren felt the tiny bumps. He turned the piece over and examined the knots. Just below the tip of the last letter there was a hole, as if a needle had been pushed through, then stopped before it had the chance to thread. The N wasn't an N at all, he realized. It was the beginning of an M.

All of the years spent wondering where he'd come from or who had put him through the gate at Saint Anthony's – none of it mattered anymore. He had a name. He had a mother. And then he remembered. He also had an uncle.

The lock turned and the Top Hat and the Bowler came in, dragging a wooden rocking horse. It had glass eyes and a painted saddle and a tail made out of real hair. The men moved a few crates and boxes aside and set the horse in a corner. When Ren asked why he was being kept there, the man in the bowler looked to the Top Hat, who only laughed, and kicked some papers out of the way so that they could close the door.

The horse was for a child – a much smaller child than Ren. Crammed between the boxes, it was impossible for it to move. Still, it was a magnificent toy, with brass stirrups and a studded leather bridle, and Ren could not help but compare it more favorably to the horse carved by the chimney dwarf, with its crude markings and tiny slits for nostrils. On this animal the head was perfectly suggested and painted white, with nostrils large enough to stick a finger into.

Ren was just slipping his thumb into the horse's nose when McGinty came into the room. The man's coat was off, the sleeves of his white shirt rolled up to the elbows. A thin spray of blood stained the front. His knuckles were swollen, his collar unbuttoned and askew. He patted the horse on the rump. 'Yah like it?'

Ren eyed the blood on the man's shirt. He nodded.

'Gowan and ride it, then.'

The boy swung his body over the horse. His feet would not fit in the stirrups; his legs dragged on either side.

'I said ride it.'

Ren lifted his knees and fit the tips of his toes into the stirrups. He clutched the mane with all his might, trying to keep his balance. McGinty walked behind and gave him a shove, and the boy rocked back and forth, banging into the boxes piled nearby, until the toy horse shifted and began to slowly move across the closet floor.

'Theah,' said McGinty. 'Happy?'

The runners beat rhythmically against the wood. Ren gripped the horse with his knees.

'Good,' said McGinty. He patted his fingers against the side of his trousers, then lifted a knuckle to his mouth. He shared his sister's pointed chin. But his eyes were gray instead of blue, and his neck was short and seemed to fall down between his shoulders.

'That fellow who brought yah heah,' said McGinty. 'Yah think he evah killed anyone?'

At the mention of Benjamin Ren felt a wave of disappointment. 'I don't think so,' he mumbled.

McGinty sat on the edge of the desk, stretched his legs out, then crossed them, one over the other. 'He was probably going ta sell yah.'

'He said I wasn't worth anything.'

McGinty gave him a sharp look. 'Yah think that's true?'

'No,' said Ren.

'Yah betta believe it. My sistah did.'

Ren thought of the initials on his collar, the fine linen and indigo thread. Even though she hadn't finished, Margaret had meant the stitches to last. She had meant to name him. And if she named him that meant he was supposed to be found.

'How did she die?'

McGinty glared at him. Then he walked over to the stool, pulled it closer to the stove, and sank into the seat.

'Fevah. A few days aftah you were born.' He pressed his hands together. The fire lit him in shadow, flickering against the boxes stacked around the room. Ren took his toes out of the stirrups and set his feet on the ground.

'What was she like?'

McGinty lifted the poker and used it to open the grate on the stove. Inside, the mousetraps were burned down to ashes. 'She had a birthmahk,' he said. 'A small one. On tha sidda hah

263

face. She always wore a bonnet pulled down ta covah it. She didn't like people looking. It made hah feel different, like she'd been mahked fah something.

'Our fathah used ta call hah ugly, even though I'd heard 'im bothah hah at night. One day I came home and he was inta hah something awful. I was old enough then, and I put a stop ta it.' McGinty shoved the poker into the stove. 'Aftahwahd I found hah down by tha rivah, barefoot, hah skirt hitched up, washing tha blood off, just pressing hah hands inta tha watah. She took my clothes and washed them too, and then we dragged tha body inta tha woods.

'Theah were good days aftah that,' he said. 'Just tha two a us. I made enough from tha traps ta keep us going, and then enough ta open tha factory, and then enough ta buy hah all tha things she evah wanted. But Mahgret never took ta life in town. She'd walk fah miles inta tha forest and disappeah. I'd have ta send my men out looking fah hah.

'They brought hah home once aftah she'd been missing fah days. She told me she'd been down in tha mine. She'd found an old cave and crawled through, using a torch she made from a piece a hah dress. It was expensive, made a silk, and it killed me that she'd ruined it. All she could talk about were tha men she found theah, dead men, nothing but bones, all huddled togethah. They musta done it fah warmth, she kept saying. They musta found each othah, in tha dahk.

'Aftah that everything was different. I thought she'd finally come tah hah senses. She stahted going ta church. She stopped wandaring alone, and shopped everyday in tha mahket. On Sundays she wore a coat with ribbons, and a special hat with feathahs, and a rabbit mufflah. She looked bettah than fine.

'Then outta nowhere she tries ta drown hahself. A buncha old men carry her back, all wet and crying like it was tha end a tha world. I kept thinking a hah as a child, washing hah hands in that rivah watah.' McGinty picked up the poker again. He gripped the handle so tightly that the cuts on his knuckles opened and began to bleed again. 'She gave birth ta you a few months aftah that. She wouldn't tell me who'd done it.'

Ren held the reins of the rocking horse. His seat was numb, but he dared not move, as if any slight change would stop McGinty from talking. The fire in the stove had died. There were only a few burning embers, the room fallen into darkness again, and it stretched out between them, along with McGinty's silence, until Ren could see the man's purpose.

There was a reason why he was locked in the storeroom. There was a reason for the candy and the horse.

He got off the saddle. 'I don't know who he is.'

McGinty wiped his nose. 'You will.'

Ren held on to the horse's mane. It felt dry and coarse, as if it hadn't been attached to anything alive for years. 'What happens if you find him?'

'He'll ansah fah what he's done.'

'And if you don't?'

McGinty didn't say anything, and the boy understood that if his father wasn't found, then *he* would be the one doing the answering. All the possible ways this answering might be accomplished began to fill his mind. Ren thought of Margaret stepping into the river, feeling the current. Trying to drown them both before he was even born.

'She must have hated me.'

McGinty set the poker on the floor. He rolled down his

sleeves, put his collar straight, and slipped a button that had come loose through its hole. He was ready for business again. He took the key from his pocket.

'I wouldn't know,' he said. 'But I did.'

CHAPTER TWENTY-SEVEN

T HE FIRE BURNED down to a low flame, and then, one by one, the embers went out. The boy stuffed paper into his coat to keep warm and pulled one of the ledgers over his shoulders, the pages open to a design that involved razor wires and springs. He had spent most of the evening listening to the mice scurry across the floor and thinking of all that he had learned, set out before him like strikes of the days marked against a wall.

He had a mother – who was dead. He had an uncle – who hated him. Now that he knew the truth, all of the stories about having a family that he'd entertained over the years and held on to were gone. He was not royalty. He was not the result of a union between a nun and a priest. He was not the son of frontiersmen murdered by Indians. He was not any of the things he'd once thought he could be.

All his life he'd been waiting for this secret to reveal itself. Now here it was, and he was surprised that he didn't feel any different. It hadn't made him stronger or more courageous, or given him peace of mind. He was the same boy that he had always been, only now his chances of a different life were gone.

He wished that he could erase the steps that had brought him here, that he could walk backward down the hall, through McGinty's office, past the factory floor, and end heels first, full of possibility again, on the sidewalk.

Ren pulled the book closer. The weight of it pressed against his chest and his mind returned to his friends. He began making promises to God that he would go back and search for Dolly, that he would be nicer to the twins, that he would find Benjamin and forgive him. These thoughts pinched Ren inside, over and over, until his whole body ached. He looked out into the darkness, and he did not sleep.

After midnight Ren heard the sound of a key once more and lifted his head. The hinges creaked and a sliver of light came through. He blinked, expecting to see McGinty again, his stomach filling with dread. Instead the shadow of a figure peeked into the room, and when his eyes adjusted he saw the Harelip standing in the doorway.

She was still in her mousetrap uniform, her apron askew, her boots hastily tied. At her waist she clutched a small bundle. The girl darted inside and closed the door then stood with her back against it. She took in the piles of boxes, the candy spread across the room, the tiny rocking horse and Ren sprawled on the desk, the book on his lap.

'Living the good life?'

'What are you doing here?' Ren whispered.

'I've come to get you out.' She threw the bundle on the floor. 'Not that it matters to me.'

Ren scrambled down from the desk and opened the package she'd brought. It was a navy blue dress. A mousetrap uniform.

'I can't wear this.'

'Stay, then,' said the Harelip, 'if you're so happy here.' She went back and put her hand on the knob. But she did not turn it.

On the other side of the door came the sound of footsteps. The Harelip froze as they slowed outside. Ren and the girl stared at each other, barely breathing, and he realized how much she had risked to come to him. The footsteps stopped for a moment, then continued down the hall. The Harelip kept her hand on the knob until they were gone. Her fingers were trembling when they slipped off, but when she turned to Ren, her face was triumphant. *For a moment she was almost not ugly*, Ren thought, and he pulled the dress over his head.

The Harelip worked on the buttons. The uniform was small and nearly split across Ren's back. Together they managed to slip the bloomers over his pants. When he was dressed, she pulled the bonnet down so that it covered his face, then draped the shawl across his shoulders.

'Why are you helping me?'

The Harelip leaned against the desk, as if she were simply there killing time. She did her best to grin with her ruined mouth. 'Benjamin asked me to marry him.'

Ren doubted this.

'He did,' she said. 'We're waiting until I turn eighteen. It's only one year to go.'

'You're not even fifteen.'

The Harelip glared at him, and Ren felt his cheeks flush. *No one would ever marry her.*

The girl read the thought on his face. She grabbed his arm and turned his wrist behind his back so fast that Ren bit his tongue. A slap came next, once, twice, hard on his ear till it was ringing. Then she leaned over and kissed where she'd hit him, her lip sucking his ear, leaving a horrible, slimy wetness. Ren struggled to get away, his arm stinging, the skirt bunched around his waist. The Harelip shoved him across the room, then watched with a smirk as he frantically tried to wipe her kiss from his face.

'I'm going to open this door now,' she said.

The hallway was full of shadows and smelled of grease. They turned a corner and passed room after room filled with crates. The Top Hat leaned in one of the doorways, smoking a thin brown cigarette. He eyed them as they walked by. Ren kept his bonnet turned to the ground. The Harelip flipped hers in the direction of the Top Hat, who started to whistle and then stopped short when he saw her face.

The rows on the factory floor were lit by dim overhead lamps. The Harelip led Ren into the darkest corner and put him in place right beside her, with the rest of the girls in the line, stacking the wood and leaning the pieces into the revolving saw.

'Don't look up,' she whispered. 'No matter what happens.' A few girls glanced over, then fell to their stations. They did not acknowledge Ren, but he could tell that they knew. They kept their heads down and moved their fingers quickly and continued making their traps, as if the floor manager were standing by their shoulders and not sleeping under his coat on the other side of the room.

An hour passed like this. And then another. Ren kept his scar hidden and stayed close to the Harelip, imitating her every move, terrified all the while that he would be discovered. Grease covered his fingers, the boards screamed as they were cut, and a thin layer of sawdust fell down like a mist upon his face. His hand slipped once without his stump to steady the wood and the piece snapped, splinters spraying out across the table. The Harelip reached forward and quickly replaced it. The floor manager lifted his head for a moment, then leaned back and closed his eyes.

Ren's shoulders began to ache. But the longer he stood by the Harelip and understood what every day was like for her, the noise and the grime of the mousetrap factory, the more he felt a softening toward the girl. Ren watched how diligently she cut and stacked the pieces before her. Saving him, he realized, was how she hoped to win a way out for herself. He did not have the heart to tell her that Benjamin was already gone.

When the factory whistle sounded, the Harelip quickly tidied her area, then grabbed Ren's hand. Her palm was slick with sweat. The other workers backed away from their places and formed a circle around them. They stepped so close that Ren could smell the oil on their dresses, the sawdust in their hair, their cheap perfume and powder.

The girls moved as a group, with Ren at the center. To leave, they would have to go by the floor manager. Ren could see the man up ahead, picking his nose and counting the workers as they flowed in and out the door. The Harelip squeezed Ren's fingers, and the mousetrap girls pressed closer. Ren was sure that he would be found out in an instant. He willed himself not to run.

They were nearly in front of the floor manager when one of the girls from the boardinghouse, the one with the gap in her teeth, broke apart from the group. She stepped up to the man and engaged him in conversation, pulling open the collar of her uniform and giggling, just as Ren walked past.

The mousetrap workers stayed close together through the main door and out into the street, chattering loudly and lifting their shawls over their heads as they passed a group of hat boys milling about the entrance. Ren copied the girls' movements, pulling the heavy wool across his face. When he had finished, the Harelip gripped his hand again, and together they passed through the crowd as if riding a wave, all the while feeling the factory behind them. At last they turned the corner. The Harelip whispered, 'Now,' and broke loose, yanking Ren out of the group and into an alley.

Ren and the Harelip leaned against the wall, breathing hard. Over their heads were clotheslines, connecting one building to the next. Clean sheets and towels and long pants and underwear, resplendent as flags.

'I don't know your name,' said Ren.

'It's Jenny,' said the Harelip. She pulled her hand from Ren's fingers, but he snatched it again and brought it to his lips, his bonnet touching her wrist, his mouth warm against her open palm. Then he threw her hand away from him, embarrassed at what he had done. The girl tried to sneer, but her face crumpled instead. She closed her hand around where he had kissed her, and said, 'Don't ever come back.'

CHAPTER TWENTY-EIGHT

THE HOSPITAL LOOKED asleep, the curtains pulled tight, the building set against the night sky turning to dawn. In a few hours the doors would open, welcoming doctors and students and patients, but for now Ren stood outside, gazing through the gate at the windows. Behind one of them was Mrs Sands, and he was determined to see her before he left North Umbrage.

He did not know how much time he had before McGinty would discover that he was gone. The hat boys might already be on horseback, coming down this very road. It was a risk to be stopping, but Ren needed to say good-bye. After that, he wasn't sure. He was afraid to think of what would happen next, where he would go or how he would take care of himself. If he thought too much, he would not be able to go on. And he had to go on. Today and tomorrow. And at least one more day after that.

He found the bell for the gate, then took hold of the rope and pulled. After a few moments the basement door opened and Doctor Milton himself emerged, holding a lantern. He was still dressed in a suit. It looked rumpled but clean.

'Ah,' said the doctor. 'There you are.' As if he had been expecting Ren all along. The man took out his keys and unlocked the gate. 'Come along now,' he said. 'They're waiting. We're just about to begin.'

Ren followed the doctor across the courtyard and through the basement door. Doctor Milton slid the bolt behind them. The metal chute for the bodies ran next to Ren's feet along the stairs. The walls were covered with cobwebs. Ren could barely see and held his arms out, feeling his way as they descended. At the bottom of the stairs was a damp, cool room with a dirt floor. The cellar was lit by oil lamps and held several operating tables. Stretched across the table in the center was Tom. The twins were kneeling on either side of him, still holding his hands.

When Ren saw them he felt a flood of relief. The fear he'd been carrying fell away as the twins stood and cried out his name. Brom laughed and Ichy began to lurch toward Ren. The mud on their clothes was still there. Bruises and scratches crossed their arms, but they were the same boys from Saint Anthony's – their bad luck turned to good.

'How did you get here?' Ren asked.

'Brom stole a donkey cart.'

'The woman who owned it sent her pigs after us.'

'We threw rocks at them.'

'We looked for you.'

'But Papa said we had to get him to the hospital.'

'Then he started screaming.'

'Then he hit us.'

'Then he didn't say anything at all.'

'We were afraid he was going to die before we got here.'

'But we prayed,' said Ichy. 'And he didn't.'

Ren looked down at the schoolteacher's haggard face. His cheek was drained of color, his beard wild, full of sticks and bits of grass. Ren reached forward and plucked a burr from underneath his chin.

Tom opened his eyes. 'Where's Benji?'

The joy Ren had felt at seeing his friends drained away. He looked around the room, but all he saw were bottles of medicine and hooks and baskets and buckets of water. 'He's not with you?'

The twins shook their heads.

Tom groaned. His leg was swollen to the size of a tree trunk, the skin red, blistered, and tight. Ren was suddenly afraid that Tom might die. The twins were thinking it too. He could see it on their faces.

Doctor Milton came forward and set the lantern on the table. 'I see this is an unexpected meeting. But if you'd like to save his leg from being removed entirely, it's time to get to work.'

The doctor gave each of the boys instructions. Ichy was to clean the wound, Brom was to stand by with the bandages, and Ren was to help Doctor Milton straighten the leg. It would take all of them, acting together, to set the bone right.

The doctor moved away from them into the back of the room, unlocked a door, and soon returned with some whiskey. Brom held the bottle and Tom sucked it down, as if he were nursing. The boys quickly helped Doctor Milton make his preparations, then waited while the doctor told Tom to prepare himself. Tom was still half-delirious as they set the leather belt between his teeth. Ren's hand shook with expectation as he placed his palm on the man's ankle.

The doctor took off his coat. He rolled up his sleeves. 'Ready?'

Tom nodded.

'Now,' said Doctor Milton.

Ren took hold of the ankle, straightened it, then pulled. The leather immediately fell out of Tom's mouth, and he shrieked louder than Mrs Sands. Shrieked louder than the men beneath the streetlight. Shrieked so loud that when Doctor Milton pressed down on the break, forcing the bone back into place underneath the skin, Ren's ears popped, then closed out, leaving behind a strange, fuzzy, hollow roar.

Ichy took the soap and boiled water they'd prepared and poured it over the wound, slowly, slowly, until their hands were soaked, and Tom's clothes were wet, and water covered the floor.

Brom reached for the cotton dressing and began to bind the leg.

'Not too tight,' Doctor Milton said as he held the bone in place. When the bandages were wrapped, he started work on the splint, while Ichy wiped Tom's forehead. Brom stepped away from the table and pulled Ren aside.

'Doctor Milton wants to know where the bodies are,' he whispered.

'What did you tell him?'

'We said you had them.' He touched Ren on the shoulder. 'We were afraid he wouldn't help Papa.'

Doctor Milton finished making a sling for Tom's foot. He strung a support beneath the ankle, then bound two pieces of wood carefully to the leg, from the hip down past the end of the heel.

'With a crutch he'll be able to walk on it soon.' He slipped a blanket underneath Tom's head. 'I'll give you a salve to ease the swelling, and something for him to drink for the pain.'

Brom went back to holding Tom's hand. Ichy leaned over and began picking the weeds out of the man's beard. The doctor motioned for Ren to follow him to the back of the room, the same place he had disappeared to and returned with the whiskey. He unlocked the door and ushered Ren into his office.

The walls were covered with shelves, littered with books and paper and labeled containers. The only window had been painted over. The latch bolted shut. Doctor Milton cleared a space on a desk full of bottles and magnifying glasses and boxes of dried butterflies. He set to work right away, as if he were a cook in a kitchen, taking a powder from this shelf, a bit of herbs from another, and then grinding the whole thing together with an ancient mortar and pestle.

Ren raised the lantern. In the darkest corner of the room something glistened. There was a table, and something large stretched across it, covered by a blanket. The boy walked closer and set the lamp down. Next to the table was a basin full of water. It held a set of knives, shining beneath the surface. An image of Dolly came forward in his mind. Ren's hand began to tremble. A metallic taste filled his mouth as he reached forward and pulled the sheet back.

Stretched across the surface was a man. He was resting in a shallow tray with raised edges, floating in a sweet-smelling brown liquid. His legs had been removed, and there was a hole in his center, from his throat to his groin. Ren could see the ends of his ribs sticking out. The skin seemed as thick and tough as rubber, but inside there was nothing left. All of his organs were gone. There was only a mass of red and white and bits of purple, stripped down, wet and shimmering. The man did not seem human anymore, his face fallen in. But Ren could see that his hair had been blond, and there was a tattoo of a bluebird on the skin of his shoulder.

Milton finished grinding the powder and poured it into a jar of viscous liquid, then took his watch out from his waistcoat and checked the time. 'That needs to soak for ten minutes.' He cleared his throat and walked over to the man on the table. 'You're probably wondering why I use whiskey.' Milton dipped his finger into the pan and ran it down the skin of Ren's arm. 'Feel how quickly it evaporates? The alcohol keeps the bodies from decaying too fast. Even so, they only last a few days. I'm always looking for a better solution.'

Doctor Milton took out his pipe, but instead of lighting it, he used it to poke the body between the ribs, lifting the skin from the tray and peering underneath. 'This man probably saved ten lives today. I can't say that I've done that. Can you?'

Ren's throat was dry. The smell of soured whiskey filled his nostrils. He stepped away until his back hit the wall. He could see the knobby bones of the spine, standing out beneath a thin layer of muscle, hard and white as knuckles.

'You look faint,' said Doctor Milton. He pulled a bottle of lavender water from the shelf, poured a bit into a handkerchief, and gave it to Ren. 'It happens to everyone at first. But you grow used to it.'

The boy inhaled deeply into the cloth. His voice came out muffled. 'How?'

The doctor drummed his fingers together beneath his chin. 'How one does anything unpleasant, I suppose. Remove your senses from the process, and look beyond the task at hand. Eventually a kind of numbness takes over, and you find that you can do anything.'

Ren lowered the handkerchief and glanced at the body again. He gagged and quickly brought the cloth back over his nose.

Doctor Milton seemed disappointed. He pulled the blanket over the cadaver and picked up the bowl of knives. 'You were supposed to bring five bodies. My students are expecting them.'

Ren steadied himself against the wall. It was cool, and when he pulled his fingers away, they were wet with condensation. 'We're leaving,' he said. 'There won't be any more.'

The doctor set the bowl down again, a bit of pink water spilling over the edge. 'That is a disappointment.' He crossed the room, opened a drawer in his desk, and consulted a notebook. He touched his forehead, as if it suddenly pained him, and cleared his throat again. 'So this is the end of our time together.'

'Yes.'

'And how will you pay for the leg I've just set? And for the rest of your landlady's care?'

Ren slipped his hand into his pocket, to see if he had anything to bargain with. He felt McGinty's gold watch and reluctantly gave it over. Doctor Milton opened the cover, examined the portrait, then returned it.

'Can you read?'

'Yes,' said Ren.

'Then I have a better idea.'

Doctor Milton pulled a chair up to his desk, took out a sheet of paper, and dipped a pen in ink. As the doctor wrote, Ren looked around at the books. They were tossed every which way into the wall of shelves, piled on the floor in great towering columns, like those in Mister Jefferson's New, Used & Rare. Ren leaned a bit to the left and read the titles off a few of the spines: *Prayer and Practice. A History of Phrenology. De Humani Corporis Fabrica.*

'Here,' said Doctor Milton, handing over the pen and stepping back from the table. 'You can sign an X if you can't sign your name.'

On the paper was a brief account describing Ren as a boy aged twelve and Doctor Milton as the witness to that fact, and, with full understanding of the laws of the country, that Ren was promising his body upon death to become the property of the hospital of North Umbrage, to be used for the greater purposes of science, to further the understanding and knowledge of anatomy, for the benefit of the human race and for all of mankind.

Ren looked up from the paper.

'You don't have to give me your body *now*,' said Doctor Milton. 'It's a promise. For the future.'

The pen felt heavy, the same weight as the surgeon's knife, and Ren imagined it cutting into his skin, peeling back the muscle, spreading his sides open, down to the bone. What a job it would be. The boy felt a cramp in his side. He pressed his arm against his ribs. He was not empty, not yet, despite everything he felt missing.

Ink was dripping onto his fingers. Ren closed them around the nib and wrote his new name, the one that seemed so unfamiliar, the one he could never have imagined for himself.

CHAPTER TWENTY-NINE

UPSTAIRS IN THE private ward there was a window cracked open. Ren could feel the cool breeze on his skin as he came through the door to Mrs Sands's room. Beyond the curtain was the morning, its pink sky mixed with gray, the smell of a storm coming. The gauzy tent hanging over Mrs Sands's head and shoulders caught the dim light and seemed to glow.

Beside the bed, in a rocking chair, was Sister Agnes. She was knitting, her head bent over the needles. When Ren closed the door behind him she raised her eyes as if he had only left the room a moment before.

'How is she?' Ren asked.

'Better,' said Sister Agnes. 'God be praised.'

Ren reached forward and parted the flaps of the tent. A rivulet of steam came out, the air wet and sticky on his skin. It had been a week since he'd brought Mrs Sands to the hospital. Her face was quiet, her hair neatly plaited in two braids. She wore a clean white nightgown that buttoned up to her neck. To the side, on a table, was a kettle of hot water under a flame, the spout churning tiny white clouds that drifted and filled the space around her.

Sister Agnes looked at the boy, then down at her needles, then back up, as if she were trying to somehow match the two together. 'You've come to say good-bye.'

'Yes,' said Ren.

'Will you be returning?'

Ren thought of the body down in the basement, the bluebird etched into its skin. 'Someday.'

Sister Agnes put the knitting into a bag. She rolled back and forth in her chair, the runners sounding in rhythm against the floor, just like the rocking horse in the mousetrap factory.

'Do you think she'll forgive me for leaving her?' Ren asked.

Sister Agnes set her mouth. 'I could not say.' She stopped rocking and looked out the window. Her hand touched the edges of her habit, then fell into her lap. 'That man you brought here before. He was not from Saint Anthony's.'

'No,' said Ren. For a moment he was buoyed by the thought that Dolly had come looking for him.

'You are from Saint Anthony's, though. I believe you were raised there.'

Ren wondered how she had discovered this. But nuns and priests and brothers always seemed to know more than most.

'He is the patron saint of lost things,' said Sister Agnes. 'I always thought it was an appropriate name for the place.' She took out a folded piece of paper and handed it over. Ren opened it slowly and recognized the handwriting of Brother Joseph.

Dear Sister,

I read your letter with great interest. The boy you spoke of lived here until eight months ago, when he was claimed by a relative. I had some doubt as to the man's intentions, but it is not my place to question, and as you know our space at Saint Anthony's is limited and we must take help in whatever form God provides it.

I am thankful that the boy found his way to your door. If you should see him again, please send him our blessings. Tell him that I hope he has put his Lives of the Saints *to good use, and that I pray each night that the bad luck of threes has not followed his good fortune (he will know what I speak of).*

Yours in Christ,
Brother Joseph Wolff

'Why did you write to him?' Ren asked.

'I had to make sure you were the same child.' Sister Agnes seemed nervous and began to rock again, pressing the chair back, then pressing it forward. 'Some years ago a woman came to the hospital in the middle of the night. She said she was a Christian, God be praised. But her dress was covered with blood, and she seemed half out of her mind with fever. She told me that she had killed her baby.' Sister Agnes folded and refolded her hands. 'This is rare. But I have seen a woman driven to it in my time, once or twice. I asked her to bring me to the body so that we could give the child a proper burial. She had hidden the baby underneath a bush at the side of the road, near the gate. He was well wrapped in blankets, and when I pulled back the layers, I saw that the child was still alive, and no more than a few weeks old.' Sister Agnes covered her mouth for a moment before continuing. 'One of his hands had been cut off.'

Ren looked at Mrs Sands. He looked only at Mrs Sands. He expected her to wake up and start shouting. But she stayed completely still and quiet.

'I gathered the child in my arms and rushed back to the hospital. The doctors were able to save his life, God be praised. When the baby was out of danger, I tried to put him in the woman's arms. She held him, and wept, but refused to admit that the child was living. She removed the baby's clothes, all but the nightshirt, and filled them with stones from the yard. She kept the doll that she had made, and told me to watch over the other until she returned. She would not tell me her name, or the child's.

'After a fortnight with no sign of the mother I took the baby to Saint Anthony's. We bring all the children there who are left behind, on purpose or by the parent's death. The coach dropped me at the crossroads, and I walked to the orphanage. It had just started to rain. The baby was so quiet that I worried I had somehow smothered him in the bundle. I opened the blanket and he stared up at my face with a peculiar expression, then stuffed his blunted wrist into his mouth.

'I had been depositing children through the wooden door at Saint Anthony's for years by that time. I did not enjoy this duty, but I performed it without complaint. I was looking forward to traveling alone back to the hospital, free of my burden, with time for my own thoughts. But the way the child sucked his wrist, as if he were at his mother's breast, made it difficult for me to detach my feelings. I stood before the small door in the gate with the baby in my arms. I kept thinking of the mother weeping when she first came to the hospital, and saying, "I killed him. I killed him."

'The rain had already found its way into my habit. I made myself go cold and with one last look into the blanket, I tucked it around the child and pushed the whole package through the swinging door. But as soon as I did, I felt regret. I thought that I should have waited until morning, when someone was sure to find him. But they might suspect the baby was one of the sisters', or even my own, and it would bring dishonor and shame onto our convent. Still, I reached my hand through the tiny door, to see if I could catch hold of the blanket and take the child back. But he had already rolled away, beyond my reach. I stayed there, stretching my arm in all directions, until at last the night began to fade, and I was needed at the hospital.'

Sister Agnes looked at her hands. She threaded her fingers, then twisted them back and forth. 'It was wrong to leave you out in the rain. I've thought about it many times over the years.'

'I was fine,' said Ren. 'They found me.'

'God be praised,' said Sister Agnes. 'I'm glad to hear it.' And then she seemed herself again. She sighed. 'It will be morning soon.'

Ren saw that dawn was past. A new day was approaching. Mrs Sands's face looked younger against the pillow, as if this sleep had taken away years of worry. He reached out and took her hand. Her skin was smooth and papery, her fingers cold. Ren held them until they were warm again. Then he let them go.

'I've made an arrangement with Doctor Milton,' said Ren.

Sister Agnes sat up in her chair. 'What kind of arrangement?'

'He said it would cover the room and a nurse, until she gets well. However long it takes.'

The nun looked troubled, then sighed again. She said that she would take care of everything. Ren handed her Brother Joseph's letter, but she pushed it back. 'He sent you a blessing,' she said. 'You should take it with you.'

The steam from the kettle billowed out of the tent. It covered Ren like a fog, settling deep inside his lungs. The boy inhaled and exhaled, sensing the movement of air, and used his sleeve to wipe the damp from where it rested, underneath his nose.

A lock of hair curled against the landlady's forehead. Ren reached forward and tucked it behind her ear. He leaned close and threw his arms around her shoulders, pressing his face against her neck. Mrs Sands coughed. She lifted her hand and touched his head. Then she opened her eyes and pinched his ear until it hurt.

'TAKE ME HOME.'

'Mrs Sands!'

'YOU'RE LEAVING.'

'I have to,' said Ren. 'I'm sorry.'

'NONSENSE.' Mrs Sands tried to get out of bed, but Sister Agnes pushed her firmly and gently back under the covers. 'I'VE HAD ENOUGH LOOKING AFTER.'

'You're still too weak,' said Sister Agnes. 'You need a few more days in bed, at the very least.'

'MY BROTHER NEEDS HIS SUPPER. HE NEEDS IT OR HE'LL DIE.'

'No one's going to die,' said Sister Agnes.

'TAKE ME HOME,' Mrs Sands shouted.

'I can't,' said Ren.

The landlady fell back against the pillows. She chewed her lip in frustration. 'I MADE A PROMISE,' she said.

It had been three days since Ren had fed the dwarf. It would be even longer before Mrs Sands was able to go home. Ren imagined the small man climbing down the chimney and finding an empty kitchen, the pantry raided, no one left but the mousetrap girls.

'YOU'RE A GOOD BOY.'

'I've tried to be,' said Ren.

'I KNOW IT,' Mrs Sands said. 'AND I'VE NO RIGHT TO ASK YOU.' She grasped his shoulder and pulled him close. She tried to whisper. 'THERE'S SOME MONEY BURIED IN THE YARD, NEAR THE CHICKEN COOP. I WANT YOU TO TAKE IT TO THE MARKET. LEAVE ENOUGH FOOD FOR HIM, AND TAKE THE REST WITH YOU.'

Ren thought of the hat boys, searching the roads. McGinty, pacing the mousetrap factory. 'I can't go back.'

'PLEASE,' she said. 'I'VE LEFT HIM ALL ALONE. I TOLD HIM THAT I NEVER WOULD.' She began to cry and then to cough, her lungs struggling for air. Sister Agnes stepped forward and began to clap her hard on the back, so hard that Mrs Sands's nightcap flew off her head and onto the floor.

Ren bent down to pick it up. It was made of a simple white cotton. He pressed it to his nose and inhaled the smell of soap, fresh and good. It had been so easy for Benjamin to walk away. But Mrs Sands had not. She ran the house that belonged to her mother. She knit her brother's socks. And she still dropped to her knees every day and pressed her ear to the ground, trying to hear her husband in the earth.

Mrs Sands coughed again and grasped his hand. 'REN.'

'I will,' he said. 'I'll take care of him,' he said. 'Be quiet now,' he said.

And she was.

Chapter Thirty

IT RAINED ALL the way back to the boardinghouse. The sky above flashed with lightning, and Ren counted, holding the lead of the donkey, until the thunder rolled in behind and the animal tried to dart for the trees. In the back of the cart Brom and Ichy held blankets over Tom, his leg stretched across the boards. The storm followed them from the hospital all the way to North Umbrage. Every time Ren heard a horse approaching he pulled the wagon deep into the bushes, and they waited there, hidden under the branches, until the other travelers passed by.

With every step Ren told himself that he was not like Benjamin. Water soaked through his clothes, until they weighed heavy on his body. The rain poured down his head and into his eyes. He thought of Brother Joseph, and *The Lives of the Saints*, and all the stories he'd read late at night in the small boys' room, of Saint Sebastian, Saint Dymphna, and the martyrs, all the terrible things they had endured in order to do what was right.

Before they crossed the bridge, Ren told the twins to hide in the back with Tom, and covered them all. Then he took another blanket, wrapped it like a hood around his shoulders and across his face. He was glad for the storm. The streets were mostly empty, only the occasional widow hurrying past and looking for shelter. Ren slowly led the donkey toward the boardinghouse, keeping an eye out for hat boys and taking the side streets so that he would not have to pass the mousetrap factory. He could still see the giant building peering over the tops of houses, as if it were following his every move, the smokestack pumping black clouds that clung to the air, even through the rain.

They found the boardinghouse unlocked and disheveled. The mousetrap girls had finished off the pantry before leaving for their next shift. There were stacks of dirty dishes strewn across the table. The roof was leaking from the storm, and pots and pans and buckets had been placed on the floor here and there, catching the rain. Together the boys helped Tom inside and settled him onto the bench, the schoolteacher moaning and cursing all the way. Then the twins went to find some dry clothes and blankets, and Ren led the donkey to the stable. Once the animal was unhitched, he went into the backyard to look for Mrs Sands's money.

The chicken coop was set in the corner, covered with a pitched roof and resting on four posts in the dirt. Ren crouched down and pawed through the wet soil with his fingers. He tried digging near each of the posts, and then between the coop and the fence. Finally he slipped his hand into the dirt right before the little doorway. Just as he felt the edge of something in the earth a chicken stuck its head out of the door and pecked his hand. Ren yanked back in surprise, then blocked the hole with his arm. He could feel the hens pecking his elbow as he pulled the money from the ground.

It was sealed in a glass jar, the same kind of jar that Mrs Sands used for her preserves. Ren brushed away the grime. There was a thick roll of money inside. Plenty for the dwarf and enough to get them started on the road. They only had to wait until morning, when the market opened. Ren tucked the jar under his arm and hurried back toward the house. He found the twins huddled together, waiting for him in the doorway.

'We're going back,' Brom whispered.

'To Saint Anthony's,' said Ichy.

'We think you should come with us.'

'What about Tom?' Ren asked.

'We'll say he's dead.'

'Someone else will come.'

'Someone else will take us.'

Ren looked at his friends. Their pants were too small, their jackets worn to shreds, their prospects uncertain. If they had separated sometime in the past, while they still looked like children, they might have stood a chance. But if they went back now, they'd be sold into the army for sure. 'No one is going to adopt you.'

'What do you mean?'

'Brother Joseph said so. I should have told you before.'

The twins looked confused. Ichy tugged on his earlobe, and Brom cocked his head, suspicious. 'Why wouldn't anyone want us?'

'Because of your mother,' said Ren. 'Because she killed herself.'

Brom threw himself forward with a cry. He hit Ren's stomach and the two went falling back into the house, a jumble of legs and arms. The jar slipped and smashed on the floor. Ren landed hard, sprawled next to Mrs Sands's money, and something broke loose inside him, and he began to fight with all his strength – kicking and punching with his good hand, elbowing with the other, then felt his ankles yanked from underneath, and Ichy was on top and pummeling him, and the boy was strong, much stronger than Ren ever thought he could be.

The boys rolled into the kitchen, one on top of the other. The blows came from everywhere now, and Ren was crying out, with all kinds of furious sorrow, biting and sending his feet in every direction, trying to land a fist, and then he got hold of someone's hair, and Brom was screaming in Ren's ear and scratching Ren's arm with his nails, tearing the skin from his wrist, and still Ren would not let go.

A flood of icy water splashed over Ren's head and clogged his ears. He coughed as the water washed over them all, sending bits of uneaten food and broken plates and mugs swimming across the kitchen floor. Tom was leaning over them with a rain bucket, and he swung it now over his head and knocked Ren on the side of the face as Brom and Ichy crawled away, soaked and dripping.

'Leave them be!' Tom shouted. 'Just stay away from them!'

Ren lay on his side, catching his breath, his cheek burning. The wall in front of him was made of split wood, and it showed all the knots, all the darkened holes that seemed like faces. Bits of hair were still caught in his fingers. He had no way of telling who it belonged to.

Tom dragged himself back to the bench in front of the fireplace. 'My boys,' he said. 'Come to me.' When the twins shuffled over, he threw his arms around them both and held them to his chest, and wept, and kissed their foreheads, and wept again. In the midst of this Brom and Ichy stood frozen in a state of confusion and embarrassment. Tom rubbed his eyes and patted them on the shoulder. 'Now find me something to drink.'

The boys glared at Ren, then went to search for a bottle. As soon as they were out of hearing, Tom reached down, took hold of Ren's jacket, and pulled him close, his breath heavy and sour. 'Why didn't you tell me about their mother?'

'I didn't know it mattered to you,' said Ren.

'It matters,' said Tom. His voice was hoarse.

Ren yanked out of his grip and Tom fell forward, crumpling onto the floor. Brom came back into the room holding some wine. He saw Tom floundering, and crouched by his side.

'We need to get him upstairs.'

'He's *your* father,' said Ren.

Brom walked over and punched Ren in the leg, just hard enough to let him know that they weren't finished. Then he went back and opened the bottle for Tom to drink. He retied the splint, got the man onto his one good knee, and then, leaning, into the chair. Ichy arrived with a moth-eaten blanket and wrapped it around Tom's shoulders. The twins went to the woodbasket Mrs Sands kept near the pantry and carried in the logs that were left. Ichy crouched in the ashes and struck a light to the branches, while Brom went outside for another load and propped the wet logs around the irons. Then they took off their wet coats and Tom's, too, and hung them by the mantel to dry. The rain continued overhead, drumming on the roof and washing through the gutters. Ren sat in the corner, and rubbed his cheek, and hated them all.

Tom took another drink. 'It's time we got our bearings.' He settled his leg out before him, then pulled the blanket across his knees with a wince. 'What did that mousetrapper want with us?'

'He thinks I'm his nephew,' Ren grumbled.

Tom scratched underneath his beard. 'And are you?'

'It seems so.'

'That's a pickle.' Tom took another sip from the bottle. 'You'll have to keep out of sight. There must be somewhere you can hide.'

'Until when?'

Tom seemed surprised he would ask. 'Until Benji comes back.'

Ren touched where the bucket had hit him. He thought of the look on Benjamin's face as he said good-bye. 'He's not coming back.'

Tom waved his hand. 'He always comes back. I've been through this a dozen times.'

'They could have killed me,' said Ren, 'and he didn't care. He just gave me away. And he left you with your leg broken, wrapped up in a rug on the street. You would have died if the twins hadn't gotten you to the hospital.'

Tom took another drink and stared into the fire. The logs were blazing now, heating the room, so that steam began to rise from the man's wet shoulders, as if his spirit were slowly evaporating.

'In another hour he'll be knocking on that door.'

'He won't,' said Ren.

Tom shook his head, but Ren could tell he shook it from not knowing what else to say. He motioned for Brom and Ichy, and the twins helped him balance as he hobbled out of the kitchen and began to heave his leg up the stairs. From the doorway Ren watched them make their slow progress, Ichy pushing a rug out of the way, Brom with the man's arm across his shoulder. Tom paused on the landing, his breath uneven. 'I'm not leaving. Not until I get word.'

'If we stay in North Umbrage, McGinty will find me.' Ren was sick of arguing, sick of being the one in charge. He crossed his arms and slid down farther against the wall. 'Then what am I supposed to do?'

Overhead Tom leaned against the banister and appraised him, carefully. Then he wiped his nose in a way that blamed Ren for everything.

'You're the thief,' Tom said at last. 'You think of something.'

The storm continued, reigning over the night. Ren rummaged through the mess of the kitchen until he found a few stale pieces of bread. Then he set a blanket down into the potato basket and crawled inside. It seemed a flimsy hiding place, but at least it put something between himself and the world. All he needed was a few hours so that he could rest.

Lightning flashed against the kitchen window. Ren began counting again, tracking the distance of the storm. One, two, three – he heard the roll of thunder a few miles away. Moments later the sky flickered again. One, two – this time he could feel the walls shake. There was a crack as the lightning struck close. One – and the thunder roared. It fell down on the very top of him, as if it would split the building in two.

When it finally subsided Ren brought his elbows down from where they'd covered his head, and that's when he heard the front door. Not a knock, but a heavy, hard thumping, as if someone was trying to push the wood aside with his shoulder. Ren stayed in the basket, hoping it would stop, and when it didn't, he crawled out and took the poker from the fireplace.

They'd drawn the bolt across the front door when they arrived, and now, as he approached the entrance, he could see the boards straining against it.

Ren watched the hinges start to give. He wrapped his arms around himself. Rain was seeping in from outside, over the threshold and across the stone floor. In another moment it would touch his feet.

'Ren,' said a voice behind the wood.

The boy reached forward and pulled the bolt. The wind was strong and the door flew open, smashing into the wall, and a figure came stumbling forward from the night.

'Dolly!' Ren cried. He threw open his arms, but Dolly pushed him aside and continued walking into the kitchen, knocking against a stool and then a table before reaching the fireplace. Dolly's face held the same dark calm from when he murdered the men beneath the streetlight. He stared into the ashes of the fire, and his giant hands opened and closed, opened and closed.

'You left me,' Dolly said.

'I didn't mean to,' said Ren.

Dolly turned now and offered his backside to the hearth. Tiny droplets from his robe spattered across the stone, making a circle of water around him. He stood within this circle, the cloth plastered to his legs like a second skin.

Ren felt weak with regret. He dropped to the ground, his head against the bench. Dolly towered over the boy, as if he were a judgment. As if he were about to lift his foot and press Ren into the earth.

'It wasn't my fault,' Ren said. He told Dolly everything that had happened, from the moment Tom hit Dolly on the head with the shovel to Benjamin chasing Ren down the road. While he spoke it was as if Dolly could not hear him. The expression on the man's face was immoveable, as black and solid as the irons in the fireplace. The thunder drummed overhead, softer now. It was a mile away, and then another, the lightning only a glimmer against the window.

All the penance Ren had neglected to say for the past eight months came back to him now. 'You're right,' he said, his voice breaking. 'I left. I'm sorry.'

Dolly stepped out of the circle of water and crouched next to the boy on the floor. He took hold of Ren's head, one massive hand covering each ear as if he would crush it, and then quickly leaned in and kissed the boy on the forehead, in the space between his giant thumbs. Then he let go and turned away for a moment, mopping his nose with his sleeve. When he looked back, his countenance was ragged and soft, a mountain already toppled and fallen.

'Friends again,' he said.

CHAPTER THIRTY-ONE

REN FED THE fire. Before long it was crackling and warming the hearth. Dolly took off his boots and clothes and hung them to dry. Then he sat down on the bench in his long underwear and declared that he was hungry. Ren gave him the bits of bread that were left, then searched the kitchen and found two small apples. He handed one over and took his place next to Dolly, and together they watched the monk's robe dry.

It was in complete disrepair, the bottom torn in several places and the sleeves covered with dirt. The stitches on the shoulders were coming undone, and dried blood was splattered across the chest. It was only a costume, worn once a year for Christmas. It was never meant to last.

The ceiling still leaked, dripping rain into the buckets and pans on the floor. Ren listened to the sound of water falling into water and watched Dolly eating. The man's chin was sticky. The hair from his chest curled between the buttons of his undershirt. His forehead wrinkled as he chewed, his eyes opened a bit wider, but altogether his face seemed at peace. He ate slowly and licked his fingers. When he was done, Ren handed him the other apple, and asked how he'd made his way back.

'I followed the road,' said Dolly. 'There were tracks in the mud. And I found the wagon. And the horse.'

Ren had forgotten the mare, left half buried in the swamp – her neck broken, her eyes wide with terror. He wondered what the animal had thought as she lay there dying; if she even remembered the farmer who had loved her so well.

The bruises on Dolly's neck had healed. There were only traces of a scar where the rope had worn the skin. Ren remembered the first night they had spent together, just after they had dug Dolly out from the earth. When Benjamin unwrapped the dead man in the back of the wagon it was almost as if he had conjured him. As if Benjamin had brought Dolly to life from sheer will.

Now Dolly sneezed a great boom of a sneeze, spraying the side of Ren's face. The boy searched the kitchen until he found a rag, cleaned his cheek, then handed it to his friend. In the morning they would have to make it out of this house, Ren thought, and over the bridge, and far away from North Umbrage. With Dolly, he knew that he could make it. He looked around the destroyed kitchen. There was hardly anything salvageable. Still, he told his friend to start packing.

Dolly blew his nose. 'What about the others?'

'They'll be better off without us.' Ren waited for a moment, trying to decide if this was true. He knew that Brom and Ichy would hate him for leaving. But Tom was determined to stay, and he needed to rest his leg. And Ren knew now that the twins would take care of him. And he would take care of the twins.

Ren got up and started to gather what he could. They would have to leave early, before anyone else was awake. He pulled two blankets from the floor and rolled them and slipped them into a bag. He took a frying pan and a cup of lard. In the bottom of the potato basket he found two small neglected sprouts and packed them in too.

'Where are we going?' Dolly asked.

'I'm not sure yet,' said Ren. 'Somewhere they don't know us.'

'I've always wanted to go to Mexico.'

Ren wondered for a moment if that's where Benjamin had gone. 'We could do that.'

'Or California.'

These new territories stretched out in Ren's mind like endless deserts, the horizon as far as he could see. Hot sun and open prairies and soft red mountains that weathered to dust.

Ren helped Dolly off the ground and righted the potato basket. Then he wandered through the mess the mousetrap girls had left, wondering what else to take. There was a mountain of dirty dishes, curdled and sticky, piled on the counter, stacked on the shelves, and scattered across the floor. Broken teacups and bent forks, bowls that were cracked and plates with mold growing up along the edges.

In the pantry he found a small jar of pickles hidden behind a sack of flour torn open, and he stuffed it into the bag. He walked past the broom that Mrs Sands hit them with. And the sampler of the Lord's Prayer hanging over the mantel.

Ren chose only what he could carry. In his coat was the scrap of collar with his name, the rock that Ichy had given him back at Saint Anthony's, the fake scalps of his parents, and McGinty's gold watch. In their bag he put the stolen copy of *The Deerslayer*, the wooden horse from the dwarf, and the nightgown Mrs Sands had dressed him in the first night.

He found some ink and paper. As he sat down, he remembered the letter he had written to the twins long ago. He had wanted so much for them to think he was happy. Now all he wanted was their forgiveness. *Dear Brom and Ichy*, he began, then stopped. He turned the page over and started again:

Dear Mrs Sands,
I did not want to leave without saying good-bye. I found the money, just where you said it would be. And I promise to do what I promised.
There are two boys here. Their names are Brom and Ichy. I hope that you will take care of them the same way you took care of me. They are clean and honest, even though they are twins.

Yours sincerely,
Ren
PS I'm sorry about the dishes.

Ren folded the paper twice, then sat there, not knowing what to do next. In the end he climbed the stairs and left it on Mrs Sands's bed. As he went back down, he passed his old room. He could hear Tom shift in his sleep and the whisper of Ichy's nose as he breathed in and out. From Brom there came nothing, even as Ren waited on the steps, hoping for something to remember.

In the kitchen Dolly was back in his monk's robe. 'It's dry,' he said. 'Feel it.'

Ren touched the coarse brown fabric. 'We need to get you some nicer clothes.'

The fire had burned out. Ren spread a blanket on the floor. He stuffed dishrags into his boots, wrapped a quilt over his shoulders, and curled up in a ball, just as Benjamin had done long ago, making their bed in the farmer's barn. Dolly sat beside Ren, his feet in the ashes. The evening closed around them and the hearth began to cool.

'I've decided,' said Dolly. 'I'm not going to kill him.'

'Who?'

'The man I was hired for.'

Ren could feel his own breath against the blanket. Everything he'd ever done seem to rest on this moment. 'Why?'

'Because you asked me not to.'

The words made their way through the dark, until Ren shuffled closer and leaned against Dolly's leg. Together the man and the boy listened to the rain slow, then stop, the pots and pans around them on the floor go quiet.

As the hours passed Ren drifted in and out of sleep, then woke with a start to Dolly's snoring. For a long time he watched the window, thinking over all that had happened and feeling the warmth of his friend beside him. Outside the sky began to change from black to blue. The birds began to sing. And the night was over.

Ren lifted his head. His first thought was that a mouse had been caught and was scratching its nails against the door of a trap. But the squeaks were too loud, and they were coming from the hall.

'What is it?' Dolly asked.

'I don't know.' Ren threw off the quilt and went into the hall. He could hear shuffling now, as well as the tinny sound of metal, coming from the back entrance. Ren stared at the doorknob.

There was a clink, and a small blacksmith's file fell out from the keyhole and clattered to the flagstone just inside.

The boy dashed back to the kitchen, closed the door behind him, and then stayed there, leaning against it. Dolly was standing by the fireplace, his hands ready.

'The window!' Ren whispered. He grabbed their bag. He climbed onto the counter and pressed against the cold pane of glass. He could see the hat boys, huddled just outside the back door, and now they were opening the door and now they were moving into the boardinghouse.

Ren frantically searched for the latches – two small metal turns – and tore at them with his fingers. He threw his weight against the pane, and then there was air, beautiful cold air covering his hand and his face.

Someone grabbed Ren's legs and yanked him back inside. He kicked, but the Top Hat held fast. There were three other hat boys taking on Dolly. They had ropes around his arms and neck, and were trying to wrestle him to the floor. He had one by the throat, and the other two were beating him with a stick, throwing all their weight against him. Then Pilot walked through the door.

He clapped his hands together, as if applauding a performance, and Dolly and Ren were surprised enough that they stopped fighting. The man still looked like a scarecrow, his arms twice the length of his legs, and he swept one across the kitchen table, sending all of the plates and garbage and bowls of half-eaten food to the floor. 'Set him up.'

The Top Hat came forward and threw Ren onto the table.

Pilot leaned over the boy. 'You've disappointed your uncle. And after all the things he gave you.'

'I didn't want any of them,' said Ren.

Pilot produced a burlap bag from his coat, just like the ones Benjamin and Tom had used in the graveyard. 'Either way, he's not through with you yet.'

He passed the bag to the Bowler, who began to stuff Ren's legs inside. Ren struggled against the men until his arms were twisted and numb. The burlap was up to his waist now. The Bowler and the Top Hat gripped him by the shoulders. They shoved the rest of him in and pulled the bag up over his head.

And then a huge thundering came from across the room, as if the entire house had been lifted from the cellar to the attic and was being rocked from side to side. The kitchen table banged, then slanted, teetering for a moment on two legs before crashing to the ground, and Ren was falling too, onto a pile of clothes – or was it a body? He could hear someone cursing – it *was* a body – he could smell the man's breath. Someone was holding on to the bag, and Ren used his fingers – he could still feel his fingers – to rip free.

Dolly pulled him up from the floor. In a moment he had the boy out of the burlap. Ren could see Pilot blocking the doorway, his mouth full of blood, his right arm dangling at the shoulder, his left struggling to pull a gun from his coat. The Straw Hat was dead. The Bowler and Watchman lay twisted on the ground. Dolly threw the empty bag at the last man standing – the Top Hat, now holding a chair over his head – then pushed Ren toward the fireplace.

'Get up,' he said. 'Get out.'

The Top Hat launched the chair. It broke across Dolly's back as he turned to protect Ren with his body. 'Now,' Dolly said, giving the boy another push, and then he took hold of the poker and bashed it across the face of the Top Hat until blood broke over his hands.

Ren propped a foot against the wall of the fireplace. He glanced over his shoulder, and saw Pilot with the gun in his hand. The boy knew he had to move, but he couldn't get a hold inside and his feet were sliding against the bricks. And then Dolly was right underneath him, and Dolly had him in his arms, and he was shoving Ren up the chimney, pushing with all his might, the ashes falling down upon them both. Dolly had Ren's foot, and he was holding Ren up by that foot, and the boy found a ledge to grip and he heaved himself, one inch, and then another, until his weight left Dolly's hand.

The bricks surrounding him were still warm, the dust stinging his eyes. The space was so tight he could barely look down. But he managed to turn his chin, just enough to see his friend at the bottom, looking up at him through the gloom.

And then there was an explosion. The walls vibrated with the sound of it. And then there was another. And another. And another. Ren felt his breath go out and away from him, up into the night like smoke, and then, just as quickly, it came back with a push of cold air that numbed his fingers and chilled his bones and made his body remember that it was just a body, and that it could die many ways, and the first of these was falling down the chimney, and the second of these was being shot.

He braced his feet against the crumbling sides and held on. His palm was sweating and slipping. Ren scrambled, fell, scrambled again. And then a rope was lowered down from above, and he was holding on to it, and pushing against the walls with his legs, and his body was being lifted through the chimney, soot and sand falling into his face. He wrapped his fingers against a knot and then he was through; he could feel the wind on his face, and the dwarf was grabbing his shoulders and turning him out onto the roof.

Ren spun around and grabbed the chimney. He peered down into the gaping hole. 'Dolly!' he shouted. 'Dolly!' He waited for a response. But the only sound that came back to him was the wind, which made a hollow low note as it passed over the top of the flue.

'He's on the roof!' one of the hat boys called from below. Ren drew away, and the dwarf stepped beside him. The small man's hair was wild, the buttons on his tiny coat undone.

'They'll be up here in a minute.' The dwarf ran to the edge of the roof, climbed onto the raised molding, then leapt. Ren cried out and hurried over. When he reached the molding he saw that the man had landed on the roof of the neighboring building, some ten feet below. The dwarf tilted his head and waved. 'Come on.'

Ren could hear the hat boys behind him. They had found a ladder; it was scraping against the side of the boardinghouse. He closed his eyes. And he jumped.

The next few buildings were row houses, with only raised stone dividers between the roofs. The dwarf barreled over them and Ren came behind. Several men were following them on the street, and two more had made it to the top of the boarding-house. The small man dodged behind chimneys and skylights and climbed over gables. The boy had trouble keeping up with him, the wind whipping around corners, the roof tiles slick from the rain. Ren lost his footing and slid to his knees. He grabbed hold of a pipe, just in time to keep himself from falling over.

The next roof was some fifteen feet away, the drop between three stories. The dwarf reached underneath a piece of canvas and took out a wide plank of wood. He settled the plank between the buildings and then scampered quickly across. On the other side he steadied the board. 'Hurry.'

Ren put one foot out and then the other, sliding carefully with his arms reaching for balance, trying not to look down. He could hear the men coming over the roof behind him and shouting up from below. The dwarf cursed him. 'They're coming!' Ren's legs began to shake and he crouched, gripping the board with his hand. And then there was a gunshot from the street, and the plank toppled, bits of wood cracking into the air. The dwarf threw out his arm and Ren took hold of it, and there he was, dangling for a moment above the street, and then he was over and the dwarf pulled the board away, just as the men tried to get on from the other side.

One man lost his footing and nearly tumbled over the edge. The other held him back, and they took their guns out. Pieces of glass and metal showered over Ren and the dwarf. A weather vane was hit and went spinning. Up ahead there was another group of hat boys. They had moved down the street to cut them off, climbed onto the roof from an outside window, and were coming toward them now, waving to the others to stop firing.

'Inside,' said the dwarf. 'Quickly.' He dodged a pile of shingles and ran for a chimney. In a moment he was scaling the brick and made it over the top. He took one last look back at Ren, beckoned him on, and disappeared into the flue.

The boy hurried after him. He had one leg at the edge of the chimney, then another, searching for a foothold inside. The men were closing in. He could see arms coming toward him, and he pushed himself down, the stone scraping his sides.

He was half a foot into the darkness when the tunnel narrowed. He could not fit past it. 'Help me!' he cried. He felt the small man grab hold of his boots and pull. He wiggled and tried to force himself farther with his elbows. He was stuck. Halfway in, halfway out, and then one of the hat boys reached down and seized a chunk of his hair and another took hold of his jacket and he was dragged back into the early morning, his shoes left behind with the dwarf.

CHAPTER THIRTY-TWO

REN WAITED FOR McGinty in the office overlooking the mousetrap factory. He had been there since dawn, and now he watched as the front doors creaked open and a new shift of girls came forward to their stations. They moved quickly, their shawls over their heads. When they reached their places, the shawls came down and wrapped around their waists. The foreman strolled the aisle, poking one girl in the back, smacking another on the behind. In the corner Ren could see the Harelip at her saw, stacking and cutting pieces of wood. She did not look up at him, but he knew that she had seen him up against the glass.

The machines sent a small vibration through the floor. Ren stood without his shoes, feeling it through his socks. He touched the window, and the glass shuddered against his fingers. Behind him, the paintings of fox hunts shook against the wall.

The office door opened. McGinty came in, followed by two hat boys, who took their places on either side of the entryway. One of them was the Bowler. His nose was broken, his neck covered in welts. The other wore the top hat, with the same dark stain on the brim. But the face underneath was different again,

308

as if the hat had grown a new body, straight up from the ground.

McGinty did not say a word, just shoved the boy hard against the factory window and began tearing through his pockets, throwing all that he found – the collar and the scalps and the rock – to the floor before finding the watch. Once he had it in his hand he pushed Ren away. He opened the cover to check the portrait, staring at Margaret's face with relief, and started cleaning it with his handkerchief. When he was finished, he closed the watch and began to wind it, squinting first at Ren and then at the timepiece; setting the hands in place.

'Yahra thief,' said McGinty.

'I guess so,' said Ren.

'Not a very smaht one,' said McGinty. 'I've caught yah. Twice.' He tucked the watch inside his waistcoat. He sat behind the desk. Then he took Pilot's knife out of his pocket, the same one that had cut the bartender's hand, and set it down in front of Ren.

'I undastand theah was a man with yah.'

'Is he all right?'

'He killed Pilot, and three moah besides.'

'He's my friend.'

'Some friend.' McGinty rubbed the end of the blade with his finger. 'He came heah ta kill me about a month ago. I sent two a my boys ta get rid a him. But I guess he got rid a them instead.' McGinty picked up the knife. 'Maybe he's tha man I've been looking foah. Maybe he's ready ta do some ansahring.'

'He's not my father.'

'Then tell me who.'

'I told you I don't know.'

Ren waited for the man to strike him, but instead McGinty

309

jammed the knife into the desk. 'I'm goanna make yah remembah.'

He opened a drawer and removed a silk bag, embroidered with black thread. The tassels that tied it together were black too, and it took McGinty a few moments to untangle them. Then the bag was open, and McGinty revealed a small, square cube of glass. He set it on the table. There was something inside, suspended like a fracture breaking out in five different directions. It was a tiny, tiny hand.

McGinty pressed his lips together. 'Look familiah?'

Ren stared at the hand on the table. Behind the glass the fingernails were translucent as pearls. The skin still pink. But there were wrinkles. Hundreds of tiny wrinkles that made the hand look as though it belonged to someone very old. Someone who had already lived a thousand lives.

'I saved it,' said McGinty. 'A souveneah.' He bent over and whispered the rest in Ren's ear: 'All she had ta do was give me tha fathah's name. And she wouldn't do it. Even when I had yah on tha table. Even when tha knife was going in, she wouldn't say a word.'

Ren pushed him away. He made a dash for the door, but before he could get his hand on the knob the Top Hat and the Bowler had him. After a nod from McGinty they lifted him onto the desk. The boy fought back, but the men easily mastered him and soon had his arms straight out on either side and jammed tightly against the wood.

'I tried ta bahgain with yah. I tried being nice.' McGinty pulled Pilot's knife from where it was stuck in the desk. He took hold of Ren's left arm. He examined the scar. Then he gave the boy a look and moved to the other side of the table.

Ren could feel the blood leaving his right arm, the fingers on his hand going numb. McGinty leaned in, close enough for Ren to feel his breath. He took the edge of the knife and ran it gently across the boy's wrist, right at the base of the thumb. It was a thin break of the skin, just enough to make a clear red line. 'I like ta have a mahk,' McGinty said. 'A place ta aim fah.'

A bit of blood trickled down Ren's arm. McGinty set the blade against the boy's wrist, against the cut he had already made. In the reflection of the metal Ren saw himself, handless – nothing but two empty ends of arms – and he screamed and he screamed and he screamed.

'I want his name,' said McGinty. 'I wanna know everything about 'im.'

The air around Ren was suddenly different – heavy and tasting of metal, like a storm about to come. He could feel the thunder building up in the room, the air charging with electricity. All he needed was a crack to release it. A glittering vein set against the dark.

Underneath him was a floor. A floor his mother had walked on. The chair was a chair she had sat in, this very desk a place she had leaned her elbows. The same hum from the machines had come through the window. The same small tremor tickling her feet. This room had once held her. And now it held Ren. When she was in this place, she had loved him. And that love was still there, in the walls. He could feel it. He opened his mouth, and the words came out.

'My father was from the West,' Ren said. 'He was an Indian hunter, even though he'd been raised by a tribe himself. No one knew who his mother or his father was. Some said that he'd been stolen by some Gypsies from a wagon train and passed on to the Indians for beads and a rifle – but he was white for sure and he even learned English from a schoolteacher passing through who took a shine to him and to the Indian life and stayed on and married a squaw named Happy Feather.'

McGinty slowly lifted the knife from Ren's wrist. He gave the Top Hat and the Bowler a nod. The hat boys relaxed their grip and Ren continued talking, straight to the ceiling, his heart beating in his chest.

'When he was still young, my father began to track down scalps. He did this for a fee, paid by the relatives of the dead. He'd look at the body of the victim, and he'd be able to tell by the way the hair was taken which tribe was involved, what kind of knife was used, and sometimes even the warrior who'd done it. Then he'd get on his horse and be gone for weeks, sometimes months, and a few times even a year. But he'd always come back, and in his saddlebag he'd have the scalps of braids or curls, and the people would dig up the graves and open the coffins and put the missing pieces inside so the dead could be at peace.

'After a few years he grew restless on the plains and traveled east. He sold his horse and went to sea. He sailed around the world on a merchant ship, to Africa, to India, to Europe, and the Orient. Places where people live high on mountain peaks that no one can reach, in glass boxes suspended under lake water, and in giant castles made of ivory and gold, with so many thousands of rooms that you could live in one for a day and just leave it behind you.

'From there he joined a whaling ship and spent years chasing down monsters in the sea. He battled pirates and discovered faraway islands with nothing on them but volcanoes and monkeys. He became a famous wrestler of strange creatures, diving into the waters to battle with giant squids and sea serpents, with his shipmates watching from the rail and making bets.

'And then one night there was a terrible storm, and it broke the boat into pieces and then into flames, scattering the men in all directions. My father was the only survivor. He decided to swim home. And he did, thousands of miles across the ocean, battling jellyfish and sharks and turtles and anything else that tried to take a bite out of him along the way. When he finally washed up on shore he was nothing but skin and bones and half-mad from being in the water so long.

'He was found by a fisherman, who fed him until he was healthy and then sold him into the army to cover a gambling debt. His commander was an angry dwarf, who barked orders and ate as much as ten men, but who also looked splendid on his small white pony and inspired great courage among his soldiers. After five years the dwarf gave my father a leave of absence so that he could visit his Indian family. But instead my father set out for the countryside, and he stumbled upon an entrance to an old mine, and it was in that mine that he met my mother.'

McGinty was leaning back in his seat, his face expectant. He had the glass square, and he was spinning it now, round and round against his palm. Ren watched the tiny hand turning, like a gear in a clock, and the rest of the story came forward.

'My mother told him about the workers trapped under the earth. She led him through the tunnels, to the places where the bodies lay huddled together for warmth. When death came, she said, all that mattered was this: to be next to one another. My mother was wearing a silk dress, and as she pressed her fingers into his, all of my father's adventures and hard living melted away. He knew that he had met the woman that he would love until he couldn't love anymore. She made him forget what it was like to be bitten by sharks and chased by wild natives. He opened his arms, and she stepped inside.

'After his troop moved west, he wrote my mother everyday, and nearly lost his senses over worry and fear and desire for her. Finally a letter came in return. She was going to have his child. She asked him to come back to her, to take her away from North Umbrage, to give her and the baby his name. That very night he deserted. He left his army post and became a wanted man. He traveled after dark and hid in the forest during the day, calling on tricks he'd learned over the years to stay alive. But even with all those lessons it wasn't enough, and the soldiers caught him. They starved him and beat him until he became not a man anymore, but a living skeleton – a hollow shell of what he'd once been, until months passed and he forgot who he was and where he came from, until the only thing he could remember was my mother's face and he didn't even know who it belonged to.

'They put a killer in the next cell, a man with giant hands, who used them to crush throats and bend open bars. And when he used those giant hands to escape, my father went with him. But by the time my father's mind returned and he had made his way to North Umbrage, it was too late. My mother had died, and my father turned his back on the world. He began to drink. And it was there, in cheap taverns and the bottoms of mugs, that he fell into the deepest and darkest place of his life.

'Years and years went by. He associated with the lowest of people, kept himself going with the lowest of pleasures, and performed the lowest of tasks to pay for the next round. But he also began to hear rumors that I was alive. And he remembered that part of himself that used to wrestle sea creatures and climb volcanoes and swim oceans, and he knew that surely he could uncover that strength again and use it to find his only son. He drew on all of his hunting skills from long ago, the navigation he'd been taught on the seas, the discipline he'd learned in the army. Every night he looked up into the immense darkness of the sky and told me he was coming. He told me not to be afraid. He said that soon I would never be alone and that, even then, he was searching for me with his heart.

'And then one day he found me. He looked over a group of a thousand children and picked me out in an instant. And I knew him at once, because he'd visited me in my dreams. So I wasn't afraid. He wasn't a stranger. We held on to each other and we were together and we knew we'd never be parted again.'

McGinty slammed his fist onto the desk. 'That's enough,' he said. 'I don't wanna heah anymore. I want his name. I want his real name.'

'His name,' said Ren, 'is Benjamin Nab.'

Chapter Thirty-three

EVERYTHING THAT HAPPENED next happened quickly. McGinty was screaming at the Top Hat and Bowler, who called down the hall as more hat boys came bursting through the door and falling into the room, one after another. 'Bring him,' McGinty shouted. His breath was short and wheezing. 'Bring him now.'

Ren rushed to the window. He watched the hat boys running through the mousetrap factory. The girls stopped working and stared from their stations as the men rushed past. Only the Harelip stayed in place and continued to stack and cut, stack and cut.

McGinty sprang from his seat and paced back and forth in front of his paintings. He paused at the window, looking out at the factory, his face contorted with glee. He slapped Ren on the shoulder, then squeezed it, as if some kind of deal had been made between them. 'Yah did it fah me, boy!'

The door opened and in came Benjamin Nab.

He was supported on either side by the Bowler and the Top Hat. Around his head was tied a bit of blue cloth with blood soaking through. Benjamin's face was pale and bruised, the black eye he'd taken from the accident settled in a dark line beside his nose. One of the sleeves of his jacket had been torn off. It looked as if one of his arms was broken. But he was there. He was alive.

'Mistah Nab,' said McGinty. 'My money was on yah, right from tha staht.'

Benjamin lifted his head. When he saw Ren, he smiled. But it was not the bright and beaming smile that Ren remembered. His front teeth had been broken and his lip was split and bleeding. The hat boys dumped him on the floor. He held out his hand, and Ren took it.

'I heard you told them quite a tale,' said Benjamin. 'I hope I had a good part.'

'I thought you were gone,' said Ren. 'I thought you'd left us.'

'Wouldn't dream of it.' Benjamin winced, then shifted so that his arm was cradled in his lap. He looked the boy in the eye. 'If you remember how to pray, this might be a good time to do it.'

'Yoah fatha's been my guest,' said McGinty. 'In a special room I got in tha basement. I try out all my traps theah. I had a feeling he was tha one, as soon as I saw yah. Nobody but a fathah wouldha picked a cripple outta that orphanage.'

'I was lying,' Ren said. 'I was making it up.'

McGinty walked behind the desk. He opened a drawer, took out a pistol, and set it on the table. It was the same gun as before, with the inscription on the barrel. He took out the box of bullets and began sliding them, one by one, into the chamber. When it was full his face fell; he almost seemed disappointed.

'Margaret,' Benjamin began.

'Don't say hah name.'

'I didn't know about the baby. Not until after she died.'

'Yahra liar.'

Benjamin squeezed Ren's hand, and the boy understood that he had already claimed him as a son, long before Ren had claimed him as a father. All the time Ren had been locked in the closet, even when he was laid out on the table, McGinty had already known what he was going to say.

The room began to stink of sweat. McGinty nodded and the hat boys stepped forward. The Top Hat pushed Ren out of the way, and the Bowler wrapped a thin cord around Benjamin's neck. It happened so quickly that Benjamin didn't even take a breath. His hands went up to the cord and clawed at it; his face turned desperate. His legs kicked out, banging against the giant desk.

'Enough,' said McGinty.

The Bowler slipped the cord off and Benjamin fell to his knees. He pressed his face against the rug, coughing and sputtering for air. In his right hand he held the blue bandage that had been around his forehead. McGinty watched it all from across the desk.

'That's fah wasting my time.'

Benjamin shuffled to his feet. Around his neck was a thin red line. He opened his mouth and his voice came croaking out. 'I want to write a will.'

'Yah got something ta leave?'

'My body,' said Benjamin. 'The boy can sell it.'

McGinty thought this over for a few moments. He pulled some paper from one of the drawers and slid the gold pen across the desk.

Benjamin leaned on the table, resting his injured arm. With

his left he opened the inkwell and dipped the point of the pen. Then he started to write. He put the words down quickly, as if he had been thinking of them a long time, memorized how they should be phrased and in what order of consequence. When he was finished he dipped the pen once more and handed it to McGinty. 'It needs to be witnessed.'

McGinty snatched the paper and quickly wrote his signature at the bottom. Then he threw the pen on the floor. 'Done,' he said.

'Done,' said Benjamin. He sat back down on the ground and ran the blue bandage through his fingers.

McGinty took up the gun. 'Now we'll have some ansahring.'

Ren held on to the edge of the desk. The desk that took up a room. The wood had recently been oiled, and the oil came off now, on his fingertips, leaving his prints behind on the finish. At his feet lay the scrap of collar with his name. It had been tossed when the boy's pockets were rifled, and now the three letters stared up at him like a sign. Ren reached forward and picked the cloth up, staining the material with the oil, right below the N that was an M.

McGinty glared as the boy pushed the tattered collar at him. Then something changed in his face and McGinty came closer and felt the linen with his thumb and forefinger. He traced each letter. He traced them again. 'Wheah'd yah get this?'

'It was left with me at the orphanage.'

'This doesn't prove a thing.'

'It proves she loved us. It proves she meant to take his name.'

McGinty put the collar down. He ran his tongue across his teeth. 'All it proves is that she was a lousy sewah.' He picked up the collar again. He opened a desk drawer and threw it inside.

Ren watched his name disappear. Now there was nothing left. It was over.

A strange look came over McGinty's face. He reached into the drawer again and removed a small glass jar. He lifted it up to the light, curious, and put it down on the table. 'What tha hell is this?' It was filled with a strikingly yellow liquid. Ren stared at the jar, puzzled, until he realized. It was Ichy's pee.

The Bowler and the Top Hat looked frightened. If there was ever a time to play innocent, Ren knew that it was now. Meanwhile Benjamin had crawled over to the factory window and was holding the blue bandage in the air like a flag, as if he was trying to signal to someone below.

McGinty unscrewed the lid and sniffed the contents of the jar. As he inhaled, his face began to shift, from red to a darker shade of crimson, and he turned it directly toward Ren. He lunged for the boy's jacket, then dragged him across the table; papers and pens went flying off the edge. The lamp got knocked over and smashed as McGinty pressed his full weight down.

'Yah filthy little bastad.'

'It wasn't me!'

'Nobody else was in heah. Nobody else had tha chance!'

McGinty grabbed for the revolver and shoved it underneath the boy's chin, leaning hard, until Ren gasped for breath. Ren swung his arm, trying to find something to hold on to. His fingertips touched the edge of the jar. And then he had it in his hand. And he threw the contents into McGinty's face.

The man let go of Ren, sputtering. He backed against the window overlooking the factory. The front of his suit was soaked. Yellow on yellow. The smell of urine filled the air. The hat boys came forward and pulled Ren from the table. And there was Benjamin on his knees, wildly waving the blue bandage over his head, like it was going to save their very lives.

A huge boom sounded and the glass shattered, splinters spraying in every direction. The Bowler and the Top Hat fell to the floor, covering their faces. Ren rolled under the desk. There was grit on his skin and as he moved his arm he felt a hundred little cuts and scratches. He peered out into the room, now covered in dust and shards, a gaping hole letting in a sudden breeze.

McGinty stood before the broken window. He swayed on his feet. He sighed, and then he coughed, and across his chest there came a blooming of red.

The Bowler crawled across the room, grabbed hold of McGinty and helped him to the floor. The Top Hat rushed to the window, drawing his gun. He pointed the pistol at the factory floor, swept it back and forth across the mousetrap girls. The Top Hat screamed, 'Who fired?'

Down below, the girls stood at their stations, their hands at their work, the machines humming around them. None of them looked up. The glue girls slapped the glue in place. The spring girls fed the wires. The saw girls held on to the wood before them and placed and cut, placed and cut. And there, standing at her station, her cheeks flushed, was the Harelip, her head bent over her trap.

McGinty tried to turn himself. The glass stuck to his body, like a broken layer of skin. The Bowler held him still. He told him to wait. They'd get a doctor. McGinty shook his head.

'Get tha boy,' he said. The Top Hat and the Bowler looked at each other, then dragged Ren out from underneath the desk. The hole in McGinty's chest was ragged and deep. Each breath he took sent another wave of blood over his yellow suit. He stared at Ren as if he expected something from him. Then he shut his eyes. 'Mahgret,' he mumbled. 'Open tha door.' And then he was dead.

Chapter Thirty-four

THE STREETS WERE wet from the rain that had come and gone. The air smelled fresh, the stink and soot of the town temporarily washed from the sky. Ren stumbled outside in his socks, his face covered with tiny cuts, his heart pounding and Benjamin clutching his hand.

They'd slipped away as the room tumbled into confusion. Shouts and screams echoed in the factory as the hat boys gathered around McGinty's body. Some immediately began to rummage through the desk for money, while others started to roll up the rugs or grabbed paintings off the walls. Soon the men were all scrambling to take what they could, hurrying through the hallways. Benjamin held on to Ren and maneuvered down the stairs, wove in and out of the mousetrap girls on the factory floor, passed through the side door that the Harelip held open – her face anxious and smiling – then sauntered by the group of soldiers on the corner, who turned and looked at them curiously as they made their way down the street. Now they turned toward the boardinghouse, toward home, and started to run.

There were puddles on the sidewalk, and Ren's socks grew

wet and slippery. He glanced up at Benjamin. The man's face was still swollen, but the bandage on his head had been tossed away. His arm no longer seemed broken. He stumbled a bit now and then but his legs matched Ren's stride for stride.

'You're not hurt.'

'I am,' said Benjamin. 'Just not as bad as they thought.'

'But your teeth.'

His hand went to cover his mouth. 'I'll have to make a visit to Mister Bowers.'

Behind them, the bell at the mousetrap factory began to ring. Not once or twice as it did calling the girls to work, but over and over, until the vagrants lying in the street lifted their heads, and the doors and shutters of houses opened, and the widows leaned out, and the old men fishing by the river frowned and pulled in their lines.

At O'Sullivan's bar, the patrons stumbled out the door to see what the clamoring was about. Two soldiers, their uniforms askew, watched Ren and Benjamin rush past. Then they heard the calls of their captain and began strapping on their guns. Benjamin pulled the boy into an alley crossed with clotheslines, the same place Ren had stood with the Harelip, and they both waited there, pressed against a garbage bin, catching their breath as the soldiers went by.

'I thought he let you go,' Ren said.

Benjamin shook his head. 'He knew who I was. Right from the start.' He leaned against the bin, holding his fingers to his side. 'I think he just wanted to hear you say it.'

'That you were my father?'

'Yes.'

Ren waited for this truth to fall away like the others. But it didn't. It stayed in the air between them. As real as the clothes hanging from the line over their heads. Ren felt like he was in a fairy tale. As if all he had to do to make something happen was to say it out loud.

'Take this.' Benjamin reached into the pocket of his coat and pulled out the paper McGinty had witnessed. 'Give it to Tom. Don't let anyone else touch it.'

The paper was fine between Ren's fingers, the edges straight enough to cut. 'Are you leaving?'

'They're looking for me already. I'm going to have to disappear for a time.'

'But you didn't kill him.' Ren could not stop his voice from cracking.

Benjamin patted him on the back. 'Come on now, little man.'

It was too late. Ren was crying. He wiped at his nose, ashamed. 'Can't you take me with you?'

'I'm trying to do what's right,' said Benjamin. 'Don't make it any harder.' He reached over their heads and plucked a shirt, some overalls and a jacket from the line. Then he removed his own torn coat and put on the new clothes, hopping for a moment back and forth in his long johns. When he was finished he looked like a different man. A man with worries. A father.

'Why didn't you tell me before?' Ren asked.

Benjamin looked serious for a moment, then poked the boy hard in the shoulder. 'I didn't think you'd believe me.'

Ren tried to laugh, but he was shivering. The wind was rushing through the alley, as if it wanted to send them on their way. Dust blew into the street and the sheets snapped over their heads.

Benjamin took a sweater from the clothesline. He pulled

it over Ren's face, fit his arms one by one into the sleeves. The sweater was so long it hung to Ren's kneecaps. But it was thick and it was warm, and the cold didn't seem so bitter as before.

'Hold still,' said Benjamin. He reached forward and picked a piece of glass out of the boy's cheek. Then he held it there, shining, on the tip of his finger, as if he were waiting for Ren to make a wish.

'What's the thing you want most in the world?'

The boy closed his eyes and Benjamin slipped something into his hand. He could feel the square shape, the tiny indentations where the baby fingers were spread. A frozen greeting. The glass warmed in his palm, as if the tips were bending into his own. As if his hand had been simply waiting until they were together again, to close back into a fist.

The bell was still ringing when Ren stepped out of the alley. He could hear it tolling, like a call to prayer, marking each street as he ran down it. Five, then four, then three, then two. All of the words he'd given up came flooding back like an old way of breathing. *Thy kingdom come. Thy will be done. Forgive us our trespasses. Pray for us sinners, now. Now. Now. And at the hour.* He stopped himself. He started again.

He passed a few mousetrap girls clutching their shawls and prostitutes, still in their dresses from the night before, peering at the factory from the street. Behind them the boardinghouse looked abandoned and lifeless. There was no smoke from the chimney. The shutters were closed. The doors were locked. Ren banged against the wood and shouted at the windows.

He could hear furniture being pulled away, a bolt being

drawn back. The door opened and the twins stood in the entryway. Ren threw his arms around them both.

'Are you all right?' Brom asked.

Ren nodded. Ichy took hold of his elbow and brought him inside. The boarding house was worse than ever – holes in the walls, the furniture in pieces.

'We heard the fighting,' Ichy said.

'We woke Papa.'

'And he got his gun.'

'By the time we could get him downstairs, you were gone.'

'And the kitchen was full of dead men.'

'We dragged them out to the stable.'

'We thought they'd taken you away to be murdered.' The boys tried to look brave, but Ren could tell they had been undone by the thought.

'Papa made us barricade the door.'

'He was afraid they were coming back to kill us.'

As they talked, Ren looked at the blood. It covered the rugs in great swirls, streaked over the wood and trailed in spots, leading out to the backyard.

'Where's Dolly?'

The twins exchanged a look.

'They shot him,' Ichy said at last. 'They shot him so many times he couldn't get up.'

Dolly was in the same stall where they had kept the farmer's horse. The smell of manure was slightly faded, replaced by dust and gunpowder. A quilt was thrown over him, and a pillow Ren recognized from Mrs Sands's parlor was propped underneath his head. There was a bandage on Dolly's neck and another across his shoulder. His arms, legs, and chest were plugged and oozing, his monk's robe wet with blood. Underneath it all, the ground was turning red.

Outside the stall was a pile of carefully arranged blankets, hiding the bodies of Pilot and the hat boys. Beside this pile the donkey was slowly chewing through a mound of hay. Tom sat grimly on a stool, watching the animal eat, his leg stretched out before him, his gun cradled in his lap. When he saw Ren in the doorway, his face softened. 'Our fellow,' he said.

Ren stepped forward and touched the wrapping on Dolly's neck. His fingers came away stained, the color of wine.

'He said he put you up the chimney.'

'He did.'

Tom lifted his eyebrows, then shifted his foot. 'I thought he'd lost it.'

Ren put his head to Dolly's chest.

'He's gone,' said Tom.

Ren kept listening.

The schoolteacher stuffed the gun into his coat. He sat and watched the boy for a while. He shook his head. 'Why don't you come inside?'

'No,' said Ren.

Tom tugged at his beard and sighed. Then he balanced, stood, shifted the splint, and dragged his leg out of the stable. Ren heard him cross the yard to the boardinghouse and then shut the door behind him.

The afternoon passed into evening. As Ren waited, he told his friend all that had happened. He talked until he could think of nothing to say, and then he talked some more. He could hear the donkey eating on the other side of the stable. Occasionally the animal stuck its long, gray nose over the railing as if it were wondering what Ren would say next. When the stars came out, Ichy and Brom brought a candle and another quilt. Ren wrapped the blanket around his shoulders. But he did not want to leave the stable. Not yet.

At dawn he opened a window so Dolly could hear the birds. Their songs went on and on without stopping. His own throat was dry, but he felt that if he could talk to Dolly for just a little longer, his voice would reach him. That the right words could make anything happen. He thought of the statue of Saint Anthony, and all the empty prayers he had said before it, wishing for things that had never been lost.

Ren spoke to Dolly about the orphanage, and then about Saint Anthony himself – how he preached to the fishes, and reattached Leonardo's foot, and raised a little boy from the dead. 'At the end of his life,' said Ren, 'Saint Anthony moved into a walnut tree. He didn't want to touch the ground anymore. He wanted to get as close to heaven as he could.'

Now the boy took Dolly's giant hand in his own. It was cold, the fingers stiff and unyielding. Outside, the morning birds chattered and sent out their calls. There was a flutter, and a swallow's nest high in the stable rafters began to peep with life. A bird cried out, its mate answered; its babies opened their mouths to be fed. Ren leaned against Dolly's pillow. He watched for signs and he kept talking, about a saint leaving the world of men, and climbing up into the leaves to spend the rest of his days, and how, when he did, Christ had come to him, and miracles had happened in the branches.

CHAPTER THIRTY-FIVE

T HEY BROKE UP what was left of the furniture; threw boards and pieces of chairs into the fireplace. They took the odds and ends wedged in front of the door, and pulled the stuffing from the sofa in the parlor to use as kindling. Before long a fire was built up. And Tom and Ren and the twins drew around it.

The kitchen was destroyed. The table was in pieces, pots and pans bent out of shape, food splashed on the ceiling, the bench splintered. Black soot and ashes spread across the hearth.

Ren found the bag he had packed to run away with underneath a broken chamber pot. The jars of pickles had smashed, the cup of lard smeared over the cloth. Ren found a knife and used it to peel the last few potatoes. Brom fetched some water and they put it in a pot over the fire and added the lard, and the sprouting potatoes, and a bit of dried parsley still hanging from the ceiling.

There was nowhere for them to sit, so they crouched on the floor. A kind of sadness began to sink in as they ate. All four stared at the fire and told their stories as best they could, while picking glass from the sour pickles on their plates.

'Benjamin's got nine lives,' Tom said after Ren had finished. 'Will he come back?'

Tom took a bite of potato with his fork. It was still raw, and he made a face as he returned it to the pot, then dried his mouth on the back of his sleeve. He shook his head.

'What about us?' Ren asked.

'I'll return you to the orphanage.'

The boys were silenced by this. It didn't seem possible.

Tom put his plate down. 'I can't feed and clothe three boys. I can't provide for myself even.'

'I'm not going,' said Ren.

'You want to live on the streets? Become a thief? Or a beggar?'

Ren sat in silence. He was already both those things.

'Look at your friend,' said Tom. 'Look what happened to him.'

'He was protecting me,' Ren said.

'He was a killer. He was made to die that way. But you weren't.'

In the fire was a set of kitchen chairs, a piece of the bench, and the top of Mrs Sands's chest. It was burning, the hinges glowing red. Ren glanced around the room. The boardinghouse seemed ready to collapse upon them, the heavy beams overhead bending low. They were sitting in a pile of wreckage. A sinking ship.

'It'll be the one good thing I've ever done,' said Tom.

Ren pulled his sweater close. It was hard to believe that after all that had happened he would be going back to where he started. Ren wiped his cheek and a spot of red came away on his fingers. The glass was gone, but it had left a mark. He reached into his pocket and felt the paper Benjamin had given him. He unfolded the page and handed it to Tom.

The schoolteacher squinted his eyes and began to look it over. He read it through. He read it again. He read it once more. Then he burst out laughing, shaking the paper in the air before giving it back to Ren. Brom and Ichy leaned over their friend's shoulder, and together they studied the words.

Being sound of mind and memory, I do constitute and appoint this my last will and testament revoking all former wills by me made. Imprimis, after payment of just debts and funeral charges, I will and bequeath all of my estate both real and personal in manner upon my death, to my nephew, Reginald Edward McGinty.

At the bottom was a signature, hurried and slanted, and it read: *Silas McGinty*.

'What does it mean?' Ren asked.

'It means you get the factory,' said Tom.

Ren dropped the letter in his lap, confused. 'What am I going to do with a mousetrap factory?'

'Make mousetraps?' said Ichy.

Tom started scratching underneath his beard, first with one hand, and then with both, rubbing back and forth until the hair on his chin began to rise from the static. 'He must have planned it,' Tom said with a grin. 'He must have planned it from the very beginning.'

Ren thought of Benjamin's broken teeth. His busted arm. How he'd made himself look so defeated. How he'd written the will, as if he'd been dreaming the words for years. How he'd held it out to be witnessed. Benjamin had known that McGinty

332

would not read the paper before signing. He knew the same way he'd understood that Ren had been beaten by Father John, that the farmer would not chase them after they stole his horse.

'I'll bet that factory's worth a lot,' said Tom.

'But he's gone,' Ren said. 'He won't get anything.'

'He didn't do it for the money.' Tom took the will back from Ren and examined it again. 'He did it for you. His own little monster.'

The front door rattled, as if it was listening in.

Tom and the boys looked at one another. The schoolteacher drew his pistol from his jacket. Brom reached for the poker, and Ichy grabbed a piece of wood from the fire. Ren looked about for some kind of weapon, picked up a dented frying pan, and held it over his head. Slowly they moved to the entrance, Tom dragging his leg behind. He nodded, and Ren and the twins moved what remained of the broken furniture piled there and slid the bolt. Then they stepped back into the shadows and Ren said to the other side, 'Come in.'

The clinking stopped. The latch turned. And there stood Mrs Sands. She was wearing her old brown dress and pinafore, a heavy blanket across her shoulders and a white cap pinned to her hair.

'LOCKED FROM MY OWN HOUSE! WHO'D BELIEVE IT? AND HERE'S THE DROWNED BOY, COME TO WELCOME ME.'

Ren lowered the frying pan. She seemed thin. She seemed pale. But she was taller, somehow, and stronger in the bones, as if something inside was lifting her up. Her eyes were sparkling and her face had a glow. And when she opened her arms Ren ran forward and buried his face in her skirts.

She smelled just the same – of rising yeast and warm water. She bent down and Ren felt himself being lifted until she was cradling him, just as she had when he first came into her home. 'NO,' she said. 'NO MORE DROWNED BOY. MY BOY. MY BOY.' Mrs Sands was smiling with her crooked teeth and rocking him back and forth. After some time she put the boy down and turned her face away and wiped it with her skirt, until it was wet from her own tears as well as Ren's.

'I COULDN'T STAND BEING IN THAT PLACE ANY LONGER.'

The twins stood by, confused by all the shouting. Finally Brom put down the poker, and Ichy tossed the wood back into the fire. Tom slipped the pistol into his belt, hopped over and took her hand. Mrs Sands allowed him this, but it was hard to say if she was annoyed or amused as he brought it to his lips. She looked the group over and shook her head.

'WHAT HAVE YOU DONE TO YOURSELVES?'

Ren looked down at his clothes, streaked with filth and blood, and then at Tom, his leg tied up in bandages, his beard arranged in every direction, and then the twins, their feet bare and filthy, their faces drawn and half-starved.

'We've been lost,' said Ren.

'THAT'S WHAT THE SISTER TOLD ME. AND SHE TOLD ME ALL THE REST. ABOUT MY BOY THAT NO ONE WANTED. AND WHAT HE DONE FOR ME. AND I COULD THINK OF NO ONE ELSE WHO'D DO THE SAME. NO ONE ELSE WHO CARED. AND NOW WE'VE FOUND EACH OTHER, HAVEN'T WE? WE'VE FOUND EACH OTHER FOR ALL TIMES.'

She brought her skirt to her nose again as she cried. Ren led her into the kitchen and brought her to the fire, and then realized that there was no place left for her to sit down.

Mrs Sands lowered her skirt and looked around the room. She eyed the shredded sofa, the ruined rugs, the smashed mirrors. The torn books, the broken vases and dismembered pillows. She saw the busted windowpanes, the blood and soot strewn across the floor, the pile of busted furniture. She put her hand against the wall, and it came away smeared with dirt. She kicked aside a pile of potato peelings. She lifted the needlepoint sampler of the Lord's Prayer, and put a finger through the cloth where it had been sliced in two.

'WHAT HAVE YOU DONE TO MY HOUSE?' She broke away from Ren, suddenly full of force, and ran around the kitchen, tripping over pots and pans and spoiled food, pushing aside the remains of chairs and tables, and stood before the open, empty pantry door. She screamed. And then the broom came out, the one article still in the same place she had left it, hanging on a nail by a small, worn piece of rawhide, and she began to hit them all – Tom and Brom and Ichy and Ren. 'WHAT HAVE YOU DONE TO MY HOUSE?' They scattered in every direction, but she managed to thrash each and every one of them, until Ren got down on his knees, the bristles battering his shoulders, and promised to stay and make everything right again.

Epilogue

THE FUNERAL TOOK place in the oldest part of the cemetery, where markers were made of slate and trees had taken root, some growing straight out of the graves. Ren stared at one ancient elm tree, its trunk settled in the middle of a plot and the bark grown up thickly around the headstone. It was only a matter of time before the tree consumed the grave completely.

Ren reached for Mrs Sands's elbow. She had dressed in her finest – the pale gray silk with a cameo fastened at her throat. 'OUR FAMILY'S GOT ALL THIS CORNER,' she said. 'I'LL BE THERE.' She pointed to an untouched piece of land between a holly bush and a maple tree. 'AND MY BROTHER WILL BE THERE, AND YOU'LL JOIN US WHEN YOU'RE READY.'

The boy thought of the paper he'd signed for Doctor Milton. Mrs Sands had burned it in the fireplace, after marching to the hospital with Ren and paying off the doctor with the money from the backyard. He had seemed disappointed as he returned the envelope, but Sister Agnes had closed the hospital gates behind them with a tiny smile hidden underneath her habit.

The minister cleared his throat and opened his book. He was

young. Very young. Fresh and full of spirit and ready to do good in the world. When he read the Lord's Prayer, everyone began to recite it too. Ren and Brom and Ichy stopped at 'Deliver us from evil,' while the rest, not being Catholics, went on, 'For Thine is the kingdom, and the power, and the glory, for ever and ever. Amen.'

Tom removed his hat. In the past few days he had surprised them all by organizing Ren's legal papers, spending hours at the kitchen table with a pen and ink, then dragging his broken leg to the factory and going through McGinty's business records. He talked to the foreman about getting the factory up and running again, and accounted for all that had been stolen by the hat boys – who had stripped what they could before leaving town. It was enough to earn Mrs Sands's forgiveness, as well as a room for Brom and Ichy, for he had promised not to return the twins to the orphanage. Once Tom had made the promise it seemed easier to live up to, and it was possible now, at times, when he was sober and working, to see in him the kind of man he must have once been.

Behind Tom and the twins was the rest of the mousetrap factory – the Harelip, the girl with the gap in her teeth, and all the rest – a whole crowd of ugly girls in their church dresses, their bonnets pulled down over their faces against the sun, and several heavy baskets of food held between them. On the other side of the church wall Ren could hear the widows calling to each other and opening their stores for market.

The minister finished his blessing and motioned for Ren to come forward. The boy glanced into the hole. It was a long way down. Dolly's coffin was settled at the bottom, and Ren took a handful of dirt and threw it on top. Then he watched as the gravediggers filled in the rest. He thought about the men buried in the mine, who had died so many years before. Some of them could be under this very churchyard, only a few more feet beneath this grave.

He was glad that Dolly might not be alone underneath the earth. He thought of the abandoned tunnels, the lost men huddled together in the darkness. The boy hoped these men would be comforted by his friend's company. At the very least he hoped they would not be afraid of him.

'WELL,' said Mrs Sands. 'THAT'S FINISHED.'

The mousetrap girls spread out their blankets, and Mrs Sands began distributing the food – roasted chicken and fresh bread and corn and potatoes and apple pies and cream. Tom leaned on his crutch, lined up a row of glasses and poured out the cider. Ichy shyly offered the girls napkins. Brom walked among the crowd and spooned out the cream, a cloth over his arm.

It was the first true summer day. The grass was green and there was a breeze coming off the river. The mousetrap girls finished all of the food, coming back for seconds and thirds until the sun was high and the headstones cast no shadows. The girls leaned against the markers as they ate, pressing their necks to the granite and cool white marble. Tom sat among them licking his fingers. When he finished, he released a soft belch and began to recite poetry – a talent that surprised everyone but interested only a few.

Mrs Sands busied herself making up a plate of leftovers for the dwarf. Ren knew he must be watching them from one of the roofs nearby. The first night he crawled out from the fireplace and saw Mrs Sands, he hid his face, and would not let her come to him until he had composed himself. Then he began to complain loudly of all that had happened while she was gone – that he was starved, and abandoned, and that he was driven half mad by mousetrap girls and murderers crawling over his roof. Mrs Sands shouted in return that he was a glutton and a sneak besides, and she was sure that if she took the ladder to the roof, she would find more than half her preserves hidden underneath his bed. The dwarf gave Ren a look of betrayal, and Mrs Sands began to laugh until it turned into a cough, and she had to sit, and the boy and the dwarf stood by anxiously until she was well again.

'YOU'LL MAKE YOUR OWN DINNER NOW,' she said. But as she grew stronger she began to cook for her brother again, setting aside part of their meal each night. In the months to come, the kitchen would slowly be set right and cleaned, the table rebuilt and the preserves restocked in the pantry. And if she made a cake, it would be divided, with pieces set aside for Tom and the twins, and the biggest slices going to Ren and the dwarf.

When the group had finished their picnic, a game of tag was started among the graves. The girl with the gap in her teeth chased Brom up and down the rows. He easily outran her, dodging in and out and around the memorials and crosses. The other mousetrap girls began to join in, and then Ichy, and soon there was a chorus, shouting and shrieking as the boy continued to elude them.

The Harelip had taken off her heavy shawl and draped it over a headstone. The grave was tilted and covered with moss, the name worn away by the weather. The person underneath had been forgotten and was no longer mourned by the world. But for a moment, Ren thought, the small black slate looked warmed, and grateful for being chosen. The Harelip stood nearby, her eyes scanning the edges of the graveyard. Ren watched her for a few moments before realizing that she was looking for Benjamin. Her face was animated and full of hope.

He considered whether Benjamin was hiding there in the trees. But after a few moments other places seemed to hold more possibility – behind the wall, or around the corner of the church – until he realized that he would always be looking for him. Ren lifted his hand, blocking the sun. He could see past the gates and over the common, all the way to the river. Even from this distance, he could feel the pull of the current. The promise of deep water.

Brom was outrunning the mousetrap girls, dodging left and right and leaping over the graves. He ran past Ren, the wind coming off his back. Ichy rushed after him and the girls came next, one after the other, the colors of their dresses blurring. Ren fell in and joined the game. He was right behind them now. His fingers reaching out, closing in, then missing, missing, missing, missing.

ABOUT THE AUTHOR

HANNAH TINTI GREW up in Salem, Massachusetts. Her work has appeared in magazines and anthologies, including *The Best American Mystery Stories 2003*. Her short-story collection, *Animal Crackers*, has been sold in sixteen countries, and was a runner-up for the PEN/Hemingway Award. She is co-founder and editor-in-chief of *One Story* magazine.